THICKER THAN WATER

A TONY FLANER MYSTERY
BOOK 2

JOHNNY WORTHEN

Rough Edges Press
An Imprint of Wolfpack Publishing
9850 S. Maryland Parkway, Suite A-5 #323
Las Vegas, Nevada 89183

roughedgespress.com

Paperback ISBN 978-1-68549-321-9
eBook ISBN 978-1-68549-320-2

For my family

THICKER THAN WATER

PROLOGUE

THE SCRATCHING HAD to be an animal trying to get under the house. Any creature without a burrow by now would be panicked. The desert gets cold. For Thick's sake, she'll let it be if it manages to nest, at least until spring when she'll chase it away with a broom and a garden hose. Even a skunk? Even a skunk, she decides. Especially if it's a skunk.

The creaking door is imperceptible to anyone who doesn't know to listen for it. Hardly a squeak. But the house is small, and Vicky knows every sound in it. Downstairs and across the hall, the opening door sends a draft up the stairs to stir Vicky's curtains and confirms her friend is back.

The scratching had been a misguided key. The light must be out again. Sophia is home early.

Vicky rolls to the other side of the bed, feeling the cool sheets draw heat from her old body and warm them. It isn't much, but Sophia will appreciate it. She hates cold sheets as much as Vicky loves them.

She listens to the soft, considerate footsteps below and imagines Sophia taking off her coat, hanging up her purse, and putting away the perishables. In the morning, together, they'll unload the rest of the groceries.

It takes time, and Vicky falls back to half-sleep.

The crash wakes her with a start.

"Sophia?" she calls, throwing off the duvet and fumbling for a light. She slides into her slippers. "Sophia? Are you alright? Say something, dear."

She listens for an answer but hears nothing.

"My god, Sophia!" she cries. "What's happened?"

Real panic enters her thinking. She has lost so much in her life. Would fate take Sophia too? Their seventy-two-year-old bodies are so frail, and the stairs are so steep. Could she have fallen down them? Could this cursed place have taken Sophia from her as well? It is too horrible to conceive of and too early to believe, but there has always been that part of Vicky that expects clouds on a sunny day.

At the bottom of the stairs she flips on a light. There is no lifeless body sprawled on the floor. No old woman. No Sophia.

"Sophia?" Vicky calls. "Sophia, are you there, dear?"

Her friend does not appear from the kitchen. By the dim light of the hall, Vicky can see into the living room. There is no one there, but on her coffee table she sees the red-brown shards of a shattered decorative pot.

"What's all this then?" she says in her best Monty Python and waits for Sophia's giggle. It doesn't come. Vicky steps forward.

To her left is the washroom, the door ajar, the space dark in shadow.

She feels a spike in her side. The point careens off bone and finds a valley between two ribs. It slides into her like a needle through suede. It takes her breath.

She feels the needle withdraw, and blood fill the cavity in her chest and then spills down her side in a steady trickle. Her pulse skips with the familiar pain of a heart attack. She'd had one before and survived it but doubts she'll make it through this one.

She collapses to the floor. She hasn't screamed; she hasn't fought. She lies there, glad it hadn't been Sophia. Sophia is safe.

She looks up then at her attacker, blinks, and draws breath.

"You?" she says hoarsely.

She forces her chest to fill, her one lung obeying, her head spinning, her life ending. She raises her hand weakly.

"You…" She extends her middle finger. "You asshole!"

THE BULLET KILLED HER INSTANTLY. All he could do was hold her limp body upright on the dance floor. The earlier din of wild Calypso music and yapping dog receded to near calm—slow dance music and yapping dog.

It was a shot in the back meant for him. He'd caught sight of the gun between the red and yellow technicolor curtains just in time to turn the redhead in the blue dress between the killer and himself. The killer was too slow, too aggressive, too mean, and the bullet entered between his fingers and penetrated her cold, evil heart.

And the frenzied dog yapped in the kitchen.

The waiting black-clad thugs saw the shocking mistake; their leader, the beautiful femme fatale who only hours before had slept with this man, was now dead in his arms. They fled to tell Number Two. The dog barked like it had been set on fire. I cranked it up. The music was calmer, but the dog more frantic. Even at maximum volume, the baying couldn't be ignored. I tried anyway.

He maneuvered her dead body to a table beside the dance floor and plopped her in a chair.

"You mind if my friend sits this one out? She's just dead."

The never-ending *papier-mâché parade* marched up and down the streets of Nassau, and the doorbell chimed.

The barking turned to feral madness. A cacophony of deranged howls, yips, and yelps suddenly cut off when the lunging canine met the end of its leash.

Things were going bad for Largo's team. Their siren temptress was dead at the Kiss Kiss Club, and Bond was loose on the island. I paused the movie, and the room fell silent but for the doggy tantrum in the kitchen.

At the door was Policeman Petersen. I knew his name because it was on a shiny metal plate over his pocket. He knew mine because he'd been here before.

"It's the noise, Tony," he said before I could say hello.

He scanned my fashionable ensemble. A white terrycloth robe I'd stolen from the Rio in Las Vegas, appropriately embroidered. Shame it was a size too small when I stole it. Two sizes now. I tried to keep it closed over my pair of vintage *My Little Pony* boxer shorts, but it wasn't easy. I trusted the pattern to conceal any stains. My socks covered my ankles, preserving Victorian sensibilities, but my bare, hairy, unwashed chest was his to behold.

"It's daytime," I said, squinting in the late autumn afternoon light. "And it's Bond Week. Show some respect."

"The complaint came in last night. And this morning. I'm just getting around to it now."

"What complaint?"

"Dog barking," he said. "It's a valid complaint."

"What proof do you have?" I shouted over the barking dog behind me.

He looked into the house. I moved to block his line of sight. I didn't have anything to hide, but it was annoying, and so I had to do it.

"It's a guard dog," I shouted. "It's supposed to bark." It was, in fact, barking then. It had, in fact, barked all morning. It had barked all night. It had barked all fucking week.

I could sympathize with my neighbors. The night before, I had nearly called the cops myself, thinking maybe I could get a good night's sleep in jail. Instead, I'd stayed up late watching *The Thing* with headphones on and still hadn't been able to shut out the noise. When I'd finally dozed off, I dreamed of shooting the dog from a helicopter while it fled across a frozen wasteland. Its name was Precious.

"Your neighbor said you made the dog defecate on her lawn."

"You can't make this dog poop any more than you can make it not poop. You're thinking of a well-trained dog. What I have here is baby Cujo."

"She said you tied the dog to a lawn chair, sat and read for an hour until the dog did its business on her property."

"The sidewalk is a public conveyance. I had every right to sit there. Besides, she wasn't home then. How does she know that?"

"The Jenkins across the street told her."

The Jenkins were a young DINK couple—double-income-no-kids—who'd moved into the nice Sugarhouse neighborhood the previous spring. Their hobbies were paying other people to do their yard work daily and throwing wine-tasting parties. I'd been invited to one. It was peopled with stick-figured women who made Popeye's Olive Oyl look voluptuous and men who shaped their hair with plastic molds purchased from the back pages of *GQ*. I devoured the cheese plate, drank a whole bottle of wine myself, and listened to each conversation dissolve into silence when I approached. They'd called the County on me in August because I hadn't mowed my grass in four weeks. I had a few dead spots and figured the best thing to do was to let the rest of it go to seed and solve the problem as nature intended. That's when I learned about the county's "unsightly neighborhood" ordinances.

Today I got to learn about "noise ordinances."

"Those Jenkins don't like me," I said. "They've had it in for me ever since I called them 'stuck up social climbing hipster-pricks.'"

"Why'd you do that?"

"It was a Tuesday."

"Yeah, well, that might have done it."

Precious howled from the kitchen. I could hear her talons tearing at the floor. I'd tied her to the sink and hoped that the excitement of having a policeman at the door wouldn't cost me a faucet. I could hear pipes bending as she fought to sniff Petersen's ass.

"Listen," I said. "I have the dog for only a couple more days. It's not mine. It's a job."

"Your house looks like shit," Policeman Petersen said.

It did, but who wants to hear about that from an uninvited guest with a gun? Now that's pressure.

"My maid was deported for visiting the Grand Canyon, Arizona side. I'm looking for a replacement."

"You look like shit too, Tony."

"You say the sweetest things." My robe fell open. I left it.

"Have you been drinking?"

"Drinking? I just got up."

"It's one in the afternoon, Tony."

"Oh, then sure. You want one?"

"This is serious, Tony," he said in police command voice number four™.

"Listen, if you're going to get all authoritarian on me, you need to start calling me Mr. Flaner, or perhaps, Mr. Taxpayer which would naturally evolve into Boss, or Sir and then Your Highness. Anyway, this isn't serious. Wasn't there a gang shooting out west yesterday? Isn't there a howler monkey still loose from the zoo? Aren't there thousands of tons of drugs being transported across our beloved Utah highways right now? And you're here hassling me about a spoiled blonde cocker spaniel? This is not serious. It can't be serious. I refuse to take it seriously. My neighbors need to mellow out and pick up their filthy lawns. Look at them; there's dog shit everywhere."

"They're taxpayers too."

"They're lonely and bored," I said.

"At least they bathe."

"Ouch."

"Tony..." he began but stopped. He withered under my piercing squint and rephrased his remark. "Mister Flaner. Animal control will get a report of this. If they get two more, there will be a fine and other sanctions."

"Like an arms embargo?"

"Like they'll take the dog away."

Precious was the closest thing to a job I had. I was getting paid to keep the dog safe for a rich couple while they visited friends in the Cayman Islands. I suspected their friends were bankers, but if they wanted to pay me five hundred dollars a day to dog-sit Precious, I didn't care what kind of scum they hung out with. Well, I did care a little bit. I tried to imagine them meeting with drug traffickers, arms dealers, and bio-terrorists rather than bankers. Bankers are so sleazy.

"Okay, so I've got one strike," I said. "I'll be good."

"Maybe you should talk to your neighbors. Get to know them better."

"I tried," I said. "We were all chums once. Then they got all bent out of shape when someone shot at my house. Like I had anything to do with that."

"You were on a case then?"

"So you know about me?" I said. "Yeah, I was on a case."

"Didn't someone firebomb your house too?"

"No, just the dumpster. But it spread when the plastic caught fire. It was put out before it reached anything valuable. Besides, I wasn't even home then."

"You've reported six burglaries yourself," he said.

Petersen had done his homework.

"Only four were real," I said. "The others were friends."

"And you got the spotlight handled?"

I'd installed the spotlight to discourage burglaries. I'd picked up a 10,000-lumen "prey spotter" off the internet that could track planes and charge solar-powered satellites at night if shone upward. I'd aimed it down the side of my house where most of the break-ins had entered. It happened to be on the same side as my neighbor's bedroom, so there was a week of complaints and peeling paint before I put it on a motion control switch. Then I got a heated call from my other neighbor, a lesbian couple with a cat named Rosebud. They claimed Rosebud had permanent retinal damage due to the prey spotter. I finally took it down and replaced it with a yellow bug light that made the side of my house look like a urinal. I'd slowed down on the detective thing, so I wasn't as worried about break-ins anymore. Plus, I saved a hundred-thirty dollars a month on my electric bill by taking the prey spotter offline.

"Yeah, that's all over with," I said. "No more searchlight."

"Okay, Tony, I'll leave you alone. But you need to get yourself together."

"Thanks, Dr. Phil. I'll get right on that."

I watched him walk to his car, taking in my brown grass and bullet-ridden mailbox and waved as he drove off. Precious barked like bees were attacking her.

She'd pulled the spigot from the counter. The plumbing had held, but the calk hadn't. Just another piece of home repair to ignore. She'd also left me a puddle of appreciation on the tile. How sweet. I dumped a pile of dog biscuits out on the floor and poured myself a coffee.

Precious gulped down milk bones while I crammed pizza boxes, coffee grounds, and empty bourbon bottles into a half-full black plastic bag before realizing that Precious had made a secret escape hatch at the other end of it.

I try to keep my kitchen clean. Nothing says "dirty house" like an untidy kitchen. Forget that I hadn't dusted since May or vacuumed since July. Forget the knee-high pile of mail in the entryway or the smell of unwashed socks perfuming the air, a house is tidy enough if the kitchen is clean. Looking objectively at the mop of dog snarfing cookies off the floor and the half-chewed pizza box, coffee grounds, and glass shards pooling around my feet, I had to consider that maybe, just maybe, my house was a mess.

I went into the bathroom.

I faced the mirror like a firing squad. I admired the week's worth of beard shadow that made me look like an insane hermit having problems passing puberty. I needed a haircut, and the ten pounds I'd put on since I last cared made me feel like a drowned Michelin man.

It had been a rough summer. When it began, I was still taking cases, solving crimes, and finding lost treasures, but mostly stalking unfaithful lovers. It wasn't fun, and I didn't need the money.

I'd had a nice settlement with Nancy, my ex-wife, the year before. My hobbies sucked away many shekels, but she'd planned on my immaturity and set up a trust that paid me monthly so I couldn't blow it all overnight. I was not in danger of starving. Ask my pizza guy. What I was in danger of was dying of boredom.

I'd made a splash in Utah by solving a fraud/murder case, and that had led to a short career as a paid private investigator. It was a dream job, right out of Mickey Spillane and Agatha Christie. I was living as Marlowe, Rawlins, Rockford, and Spade. But it didn't last.

The dream job quickly turned into spouse stalking. At first I took the cases thinking they'd lead to stolen jewels and international intrigue, but they all just started seedy and ended sleazy. It's hard to compare yourself to the Hardy Boys when you follow someone to a motel and snap pictures through parted curtains with an eleven-foot lens like porno paparazzi. The cases are emotional. Feelings ran high, and people often get all violent and shooty. Some of the culprits—more than you'd imagine—thought if they could get the film from my house, everything would go away. Thus the many break-ins. Most just spit in my face like I'd somehow betrayed them. Some hit me. Some tried to stab me. Everyone cursed me. It was always an ugly mess. Family detective work was nasty, but I took it thinking that something cool would come along if I just hung in long enough.

Finally I stopped taking the jobs and just waited for a worthy case to fall into my lap, a case worthy of my energies. I got the idea from Sherlock Holmes. I should have started a heroin habit like the great detective, but I hate needles. Like the noir greats, I went for bourbon instead, but this did nothing to bolster my ambition.

Then I lost my girlfriend, Delores.

We'd gotten along really well, but I stupidly ran background checks on her while researching an unfaithful shoelace heiress. She was furious when she found out I'd been snooping around her past.

"I'm a detective," I said.

"You had no right," said she. "We agreed not to talk about old flames."

"Yeah, but don't you think this was a little different? This is more family than friend. You could have mentioned you're divorced. It might've come up."

"I haven't seen him in years," she said.

"I know." I knew this because I'd found out her ex-husband, Benjamin James Ulrich, was doing a nickel at the state prison for assault and battery against a Mr. Peter Sommers. It was a long sentence because he'd broken parole for a previous assault and battery on a Mr. George Beck.

Just for giggles, I contacted Peter and George for a little background. Both were recovering nicely. George said he really liked his new physical therapist but had no interest in ever dating Delores again. Neither did Peter.

"How could you?" she yelled. "We promised not to talk about old lovers."

"I talked to them, not about them," I said. "And I didn't know they were your old lovers."

"I am so mad at you right now," she'd said.

It had been a warm June day. We were in my living room. It was clean and nice then, and I was ten pounds lighter.

"Delores," I said. "I think we need to talk about this. Benjamin James is being released soon."

"He is?" She looked genuinely surprised. Score one for her. "Oh, shit."

"What does this mean?"

"It means I'm breaking up with you right now." She bolted into the bedroom.

I followed her.

She fumbled down a suitcase and filled it with clothes, some of them hers.

"I'm not sure I understand," I said. "Are you breaking up with me because I broke a trust and found out about this, or because your husband is a dangerous felon?"

"Yes," she said. "He's my ex-husband. Have a good life."

She stormed out of the house, and I watched her drive across the lawn. Two days later, she burgled my home to recover the few things she'd forgotten. I'd called the cops before I realized who it was. That didn't help our chances at getting back together. We haven't spoken since we talked that night through the grating of a police car window.

After Delores left, I had no one to impress with my detective work, so I became a bum for the summer. I'd been a detective for a long time, longer than most jobs I'd done. Its spark was gone, washed away like saccharine perfume under a barbecue wet nap. I still wanted to be a detective, I just didn't want to be a peeping Tom, and that was all the work I was getting.

My life has always been defined by what I call the push/pull phenomenon because I'm not very creative. I have a wanderlust and a short attention span. Suddenly I don't like what I'm doing or otherwise get pushed out of it. It isn't always my fault. My divorce, for example. Okay, maybe I had been involved in that, but it's a cyclical thing. As one thing pushes me away, suddenly, like a cocker spaniel to unguarded lasagna, I'm pulled toward a new thing. Thus destiny plays me.

As fall came on, I got the familiar childlike urge to begin something new and masochistic. It's a leftover from school days and I doubt there's a public school graduate that doesn't feel a stirring for new faces, schedules and creamed corn every fall. It's Pavlovian. So I wasn't surprised when I was offered a dog.

I agreed to babysit Precious for Ronald and Rosalyn-Janet Levis. They said they'd received several threats about their dog being kidnapped. The fiends had demanded big money to let the dog alone. Nothing more had come of it, but they wanted an armed guard for their poop machine while they laundered money in the Caribbean. They offered me five hundred a day, easy money, and I could feel useful again.

Watching a high-maintenance mop didn't do much to fire the detective juices, though. I figured I'd use the money for a radio spot next week and gum up my shoes looking for crime. I did my best to ignore the dog, which only made it bark more. Thinking of Petersen's visit, I saw that Precious, the dog-mop, barked because it was lonely and bored. Just like me. Just like my stay-at-home neighbors. It missed its family, and I was a poor excuse for a companion. Drowning in irony, I showered and shaved.

"Precious," I said, "Let's go to the park."

The dog yapped and spun like a top, either recognizing its name, park, or was just happy to be noticed.

I untied the leash from the faucet and took her into the living room and even brushed her with the special thousand-dollar grooming kit Mrs. Levis had left for me. When I had a bushel of hair ready for the baling wire, the phone rang.

"I'm looking for Tony Flaner," said a woman. "Is this the right number?"

"Uhm. Maybe. Who's this?"

"Tony? It's me, Allie. Allison Braise. From Moab? Do you remember me?"

I did. Memories fell in on me like the roof of a collapsing tunnel. My breath caught in my throat, and my tongue dried to a piece of windswept jerky.

"How're you doing, Allie?" I mumbled.

"I'm fine," she said. "But your aunt Vicky, Tony. Your aunt Vicky is dead."

2

WHEN I WAS LITTLE, my father got fed up working for "The Man" and started his own business. He took all our savings, mortgaged the house, took out loans, sacrificed a goat, played banjo at a crossroads, and then opened up Flaner's Flapjacks. He specialized in hearty breakfasts of exotic pancakes like blueberry, chocolate chip, and brie. A miscalculation of the traffic and tastes in the area made him pack up his eight-page menu in short order. In desperation, the store became "Flaner's Café," and out went the pancakes and in came specialty burgers, like the Hawaiian with pineapple or the Parisian with brie. Again he saw his business slip, and by the time "Flaner's Pizzeria" took out its only ad in the phonebook, specializing in "brie cheese two pounders," it was all but over. A grease fire took the kitchen and added 'insurance company investigation insult' to 'smoke inhalation injury.' The business closed.

My father wasn't a proud man. If he could have escaped paying his bills, he would have. He filed for bankruptcy, grew a mustache, and began calling himself "Javier." He talked about the wonders of Tijuana and the great schools they have in Mexico. My mother was more sensible and put us on a budget.

According to Mom's figures, things had to change. We were living too extravagantly. Certain things had to go, like cars and electricity. We were in that deep. My father found work in Wyoming on an oil rig and made payments to his creditors with tar-stained Oilman's Credit Union money orders. My mother stayed in Salt Lake City and slept on her friend Mindy's couch while working two jobs. Our house was sold to a real estate investment group who painted a wall, put in new carpet and flipped it in a month for twice what we got.

I was sent to stay with Aunt Vicky.

It was scary to be sent away from home, but I was so sick of brie, by that time I'd have agreed to anything to get away from it. That year, ten-year-old me was treated to an extended vacation with Aunt Vicky and cousin Rick down in Moab, Utah.

Aunt Vicky Victoria Racine, was my mother's sister and only living relative. She lived in Moab, which bears a striking resemblance to Mars and is nearly as close. Vicky's husband, Lance, was an adventurer who was last seen heading to South America to search for sapphires in the Andes.

Being as brave as my Mom, I didn't complain. My parents assured me everything would be fine. Aunt Vicky was nice, and Rick was about my age. They were family. I'd be welcomed. And they never ate snotty cheese.

I boarded a Greyhound for parts south with nary a tear. Nary.

Mom was right, as Rick was friendly and robust but dumb as a rock. His nickname was 'Thick Rick,' but most people just called him Thick for short. Someone told him it was due to his big size. But it was obviously a cruel joke. Rick liked the name, though, and used it himself, so it stuck.

It could have been a very bad time for all of us, but my Mom's plan was effective and direct, and neither Aunt Vicky nor Rick would let me get homesick.

"Oh my god, Allie," I said. "How's Rick taking it?"

"You don't know?"

"Know what?"

"Thick died last year," she said. "I thought you knew."

"No," I said. Things were spinning. "We've been out of touch. What happened?"

"Thick died in Atlanta," she said. "Vicky died in her home. A random thing. I'll tell you later. Sophia says you should come down."

"Who's Sophia?"

"A friend of Vicky's."

"I can't get away until Friday," I said. "I could be there around five, maybe."

"That's great," she said. "I'll meet you at Vicky's at five."

We hung up and I sat down. Precious tugged at the leash.

I hadn't seen Aunt Vicky in forever, not since that Autumn, which meant she had to be old, really old, in her seventies at least. I imagined she fell. Her house had steep stairs. She probably broke a hip and had complications. Old people die from broken hips all the time. They claim more lives each year than smoking and daytime television combined. I didn't relish a funeral, but I liked the idea of seeing Allie again. Plus, there was something in her voice that troubled me, and something in the back of my head that made me ashamed.

Precious barked and squatted for the sofa. I pulled her before she could finish redecorating. We went to the park.

Public parks always make me think of quaint Twain-infested, turn-of-the-19th-century, brass band, bustle-wearing, Fourth of July picnic sack races—which I truly think they were originally designed for. That was when people went outside. Now they're cheap gyms. For every picnicker at a public park, you will see forty-six joggers, twenty-three dog walkers, and eight bums looking for aluminum cans in wasp-swarmed garbage cans, unless it's the Fourth of July when you meet hoards of drunks with sparklers.

Sugarhouse Park never had any turn-of-the-century brass bands and parasol-covered bustles. It's a new park in an old part of town. Up until 1951, it was the prison—a huge rock castle of a prison that was first the territorial prison and then the state prison. A prison. It was a prison.

Land developers finally forced it farther south because new homeowners complained about the sound of firing squads during breakfast. Either as a deterrent or a PR campaign, the prison used to sell tickets to the executions. Still, it didn't do much for property values and they moved it to Point of the Mountain, where Delores' ex-husband was being released this week. The area of the prison that didn't become a park was turned into a high school, so it didn't change that much.

There's a pond in the middle of the now mostly convict-free park where ducks paddle around, and dogs lunge after them. Kids dig in mud and duck dung to find broken glass and 1974 Coors pull tabs. The pond is all of sixteen inches deep in the middle. There are mature trees, a hill that invites sledders in the wintertime, several gazebos and a stream that feeds the pond from a hole under an asphalted street. I like to think it's a river, but it might just be a broken water main. Naturally, there are infinite jogging paths that wind through parking lots and lawns like Möbius strips. All are mined with a hundred breeds of dog shit. There's a lot of shit in Sugarhouse Park. I brought Precious there to do her bit.

My mind was all over the place getting Precious into the car. I wanted to think about Moab, but there was a repressed rebellion there and instead I contemplated the park and my yipping charge. I was slow to open the doors, so the dog jumped through a window.

Precious didn't soil my seat as we drove the few blocks to the park for some exercise. We could have walked, but what would that have proved? She sat in the cargo space of my little Prius, licked the window, and yelped at passing cars, trees, gnats, and the pollen that startled her.

"Precious is a purebred American cocker spaniel," Mrs. Levis had boasted.

Precious was a high-strung disease. Mrs. Levis told me that she was pampered. Based on the number of pharmaceuticals I had to sneak into her food each meal, I quickly concluded that she was a pampered, inbred, sickly, bark-o-matic. I'm sure the papers Mrs. Levis spoke of would back me up on this.

I don't know much about dogs, but I know plenty about hobbies. This dog was a hobby. Between the vitamins, grooming and epileptic seizures, she had a continual eye illness, regular urinary tract infections, ear mites and knots in her hair that only stoned gremlins could make in the wee hours of the night. Precious' inexplicable sleep-barking and kicking proved the existence of these invisible gremlins weaving Gordian Knots into her fur. I was under strict orders, under no circumstances to ever cut them out. I had to comb her long blonde dog hair twice a day. To be fair, I'd combed the dog as often as I combed my own hair. Today was the first time in a week for both of us.

Supposedly, Precious had been trained by the best trainer in the state and would obey my every command, provided they were "stay," "come," and "lick my face until it bleeds." Mrs. Levis bragged about how well-behaved the dog was. Mr. Levis bragged about how much the training had cost.

When Mrs. Levis said goodbye to Precious on my doorstep, she and the dog shared a long, drawn-out tongue kiss that could have launched a Rule 34 website. Mr. Levis showed me how to use the eye drops and the best way to knead the ground beef into bite-size pieces. Gravy was optional. He brought a cooler full of Grade-A organic ground beef from Whole Foods that probably cost as much as their tickets to Grand Cayman. They also left me a shoebox full of drugs and a six-page bound instruction manual on how and when to administer each pill, drop, salve, and combing regiment, complete with diagrams.

Before he left, Mr. Levis asked to see my gun. I opened the kitchen drawer where it happened to be, and he was satisfied. If he'd have asked to see the bullets, he'd have been disappointed. I don't remember where I put them. Besides, I'd never pulled the trigger in anger on anything more dangerous than a frisbee. Still, Mr. Levis was pleased to think I'd kill anyone who tried to harm his hobby.

At the park, Precious didn't wait for me to open the hatch or stop the car before exiting. She climbed over the seats and licked the windshield into an antibacterial froth and then out the window she went.

"Come here, you little shit," I said. She stopped and wagged her tail. She liked the nickname. I doubt I was the first to use it.

Cocker spaniels are not big animals. They're not threatening and not particularly useful as far as I can see except for dusting the floor and watering ferns. Precious was groomed into a pyramid shape. Her back was practically stubble, but the length increased as you went down the dog until her feet were lost in a broom of hair that swept the ground as she trotted. The fur on her head was thin, but her ears hung lush and bushy like unbraided ponytails. She always looked to be smiling, but it was a sad smile because her eye infections had stained the fur on her face and she always looked to be crying; a sad clown.

I gathered the leash. She pulled at it and sniffed around the cars and peed on anything that didn't have sense enough to move. We strolled along the jogging path and Precious greeted each jogger with a bark, a tail wag, and a lunge for the crotch. Charming.

Sugarhouse Park officials didn't like all the poop that dogs made, and there were signs posted every five or six paces reminding dog owners to clean up after their "friends." The threatened two hundred dollar fine made civic-minded most of the hipsters that haunted the greens, but not all. This being a progressive liberal Sugarhouse, there were biodegradable plastic dog poop bag dispensers every forty feet. The green and white plastic bags flapped in trees all over the park like snared birds. Kids without kites learned to make parachutes out of them. I made use of one about ten minutes into our walk, and like the conscientious citizen I was, deposited it into an overflowing trash bin beside a stripped bicycle frame chained to a lamppost.

I wasn't watching my James Bond, but I was getting five hundred dollars a day to pick up dog shit.

One thing Bond Week has over strolls in the park is the power of distraction. Without over-the-top villains and sassy supermodels stripping in letterbox, it was hard not to think.

I was ashamed of myself. I'd completely lost touch with my family in Moab. They'd been the center of my life and then poof—they were out of my thoughts completely, replaced by new schools, new friends, new affordable house, and then life. I'd packed them away and forgotten them like my Star Wars cards which would be worth more than my house today if I hadn't thrown them out after high school to prove how grown up I was. I felt I'd let them down by forgetting them. My family, not the cards. I felt I'd let them down by being the kind of flighty guy who'd let them down.

I'm a lazy man, I concluded. This was no revelation. Nancy compared me to flotsam just floating haphazardly on the sea. I'd countered that I was more like jetsam. Score one for Tony. I wasn't lost; I just didn't know where I was going. I was keeping my options open and picking up dog shit for money.

We were on the far side of the park. The walk, slow and easy as it was, had tired my American frame, and Precious and I sat at a steel picnic table to watch joggers pass us for the fourth time. Coming up the walkway on my right was a pack of half a dozen dogs attempting to pull a young man's arms out of their sockets. He paused to introduce his dogs to mine, as was dog walker etiquette. Precious yipped and trotted over to smell some dog butts and have hers smelled in turn. What fun.

"Hey, buddy," the man said. "Can you hold on to these for a second while I get that?" He jerked his head over to a newly fertilized patch of grass.

"Sure," I said.

The leashes were all connected to a single big steel D-ring fastener that in a previous life might have secured an M1 Abrams battle tank to the belly of a plane during a hurricane.

The dogs all sniffed and peed on the table in turn. I pulled my legs up. Several dogs decided the lawn wasn't green enough and did their business there. I waited for the young man to return and clear me a path.

The dogs froze and Precious bolted.

The unexpected burst of speed and my awkward positioning pulled me over, and I went headlong onto the newly moistened and fertilized grass. Precious' leash slipped my grasp.

The other dogs all barked and watched Precious race up the hill. They tried to follow but got wound in all the leashes. I held the ring tightly and was only dragged a few hundred yards before the young man saved me.

"Shit, mister, you okay?"

My coat and the front of my shirt, which I admit wasn't clean to begin with, was worse now thanks to the dogs. Much worse.

"Help me get my dog back, will you? Something spooked it."

Barking and cursing, we all ran up the hill to the road.

"Precious," I called. "You stupid stuck-up rug ornament, let's go home and shower."

At the top of the hill, twenty yards down the road, I caught just a glimpse of the auburn-haired animal being pulled into a black sedan before it sped away.

"Shit," I said.

3

THE DOG WALKER'S name was Blaine Nelson. I wrote down his information from his driver's license. He said he'd help me fill out a police report.

"That's just lame," he said. "I hear about this kind of thing once in a while, but I never thought I'd actually see it."

"See what exactly?"

"A dognapping."

"They nap all the time," I said. "You're not very observant."

"No, I mean like a kidnapping, but with a dog."

"Why would anyone do that?"

"Same reason anyone snatches anything, I suppose. Money usually."

"You mean a ransom?"

"Yeah, sometimes. Or it's such a valuable breed that they sell it on the black market."

I imagined a seedy, dimly lit cellar where people traded dogs for briefcases full of cash under the gaze of cigar-smoking underworld kingpins. The image morphed into a picture of dogs playing poker. The two at the bottom were cheating. This was bad.

"That really happens?" I asked Blaine.

"Yeah, I heard about it from a friend up in the cove. A schnauzer was taken. The owners had to pay, like, ten thousand dollars or something to get it back."

"Can't you just buy a new dog? Don't they sell them?"

"Of course, but people grow attached to their pets, man. They're family."

I knew what Blaine was saying. The Levis themselves had given me an overview of the fiends who stole pets from rich people, but I hadn't taken them seriously. I seldom take people like the Levises seriously. Besides, paranoia seems to be a side-effect of wealth, and I figured I was just a placebo babysitter, there to make them feel better for not taking their dog to the Caribbean.

"How much is an inbred American cocker spaniel worth?" I asked Blaine.

"Not that valuable. They're nice dogs but prone to health problems. A couple of hundred bucks."

I wondered if the Levises would notice the switch if I bought a replacement. It worked when my son Randy's goldfish bellied up three days after Christmas and then again a week after New Year's. Eight days before Valentine's Day, Randy saw it first, so we told him that Flippy had had a good long life and it was time to give him a noble aquatic burial. We scrubbed the toilet until it gleamed, and with a fistful of fish food to see him off, flushed him to the waters from whence he came. Somehow I didn't think the Levises would buy such a stunt. Still it was my first thought, and it took a while to shake.

I left Blaine to his arm stretching and went back to my car. I jettisoned my shirt halfway. My pants would have gone too if I had been wearing underwear. The 'My Little Ponies' were on the bathroom floor.

I left the car in the driveway, doors open, and stripped in the garage. Naturally, Mrs. Jenkins chose that moment to come out of her house and do whatever it is Mrs. Jenkins does on her front lawn in the afternoon. By the time I noticed her, her hand was over her face and she was running back into the house.

A shower later, I was on the phone. I'd made a few connections with the Salt Lake constabulary as a private eye, but none of them were available. I steered through a labyrinth of telephone menus until I finally got a human being who said, "May I put you on hold?" Before I could answer, I was cut off and listening to a dial tone.

Animal Control was more helpful. The clamor in the background made me imagine the woman on the phone in a safari outfit and pith helmet, and Jane Goodall gray hair thrown in to complete the illusion. She probably had an elephant gun and bottle of gin too. Safari basics.

"So I think it's a dognapping," I said.

"That does happen, I'm afraid."

"What's to be done?"

"Well," she said, "it's a theft and the police would need to be contacted."

"I tried that. Could you give me a name of someone who might care?"

"I've heard about people hiring private detectives to help. Maybe you can try that."

Ouch.

"I don't think the police will help," I said.

"No, they don't usually. The police don't have the manpower to do anything about it. A lot of times it turns out that the dog just ran away. In the rare cases that a ransom demand actually appears, it can be a felony and all kinds of resources have to be committed to it. The FBI even. But that doesn't happen. You can buy dogs, you know. The cops just won't deal with it usually. The dognappers know this and so get away."

"Great."

"Yeah...the best thing to do is to buy another dog. Dogs die every day. They get lost, get put down, or find new homes with better kibble."

"That would be the smart thing, but I don't think the people I'm dealing with are that smart."

"They usually aren't. There's an emotional attachment. The nappers play on that. It's sad but true. People feel obliged to do all they can to help their family, even if it isn't the same species."

"Do you know where I can get an inbred American cocker spaniel for cheap?" I hadn't shaken the Flippy plan yet.

"You mean purebred?"

"Not really."

"Check the phone book. Dog breeders are everywhere."

A couple of calls later, I found the most expensive cocker in the valley. It would cost me a grand. It came with papers, which would be useful since it wasn't housebroken yet.

I could afford a grand. Hell, I could sell Precious' unused prescriptions on the street and raise that and more. I'd had worse defeats as a detective. I'd been shot, beaten, chased, poisoned several times and fired. Losing a dog didn't even make the first page of a list of bad things that'd happened to me.

I just had to be calm when Mrs. Levis called that evening to talk to Precious. She did it every night. The dog would hear her voice and bark and wag its tail and sometimes lose control of its bladder or collapse in an epileptic fit. It was heartwarming. Afterward, I'd hold the slobbery phone far from my face and go over bowel movements and snack consumption. She'd hang up and I'd go through half a can of wet-naps before replacing the receiver.

It was getting late. I made a single serving ramen in five minutes and ate it over the sink in six. Back in my comfy chair, I pulled out my detective notebook and made some quick notes to clear my head.

I wrote: Let ramen cool before eating. Dog nappers. Money? Dog not worth a grand. Breed? Common. Levises are rich. Won't take this well. How'd they know where I'd be? What the hell happened? Was it targeted at Precious or just any dog? Was Blaine involved? Isn't Blaine that guy in the box in Times Square? Will Manhattan survive global warming? How high will the water rise? Can buildings be made to float? Need to lose weight.

What's on TV? Stay on target. Han shot first. Focus. Focus. Find Precious. Defeat Sauron. Give it up. Move on. Remember the ramen thing.

The phone rang. I checked my watch. Too early for the Levises' call.

It was Standard Flox—yes, that's his real name. He's one of my friends from the Comedy Cellar where we test our amateur comedy against a half-drunk crowd every open mic night. He said, "Perry got a gig at an Indian Casino in Arizona. He's headlining for two months."

Perry Whitehouse is one of the gang. He's nuttier than squirrel vomit but funnier than most of the stand-ups I've ever seen. If any of us will ever go pro, it'll be Perry. In fact, Perry has been working pretty steadily at stand-up for over a year. He's a great guy, but if he doesn't take his antipsychotics, he becomes unpredictable. Even so, he's paranoid, sees conspiracies everywhere and is probably right.

"A big room?" I asked.

"Not the biggest one, but a good one. He's second on the marquee. Only Styx or Perry Como or someone like that will get bigger letters. He had to audition against Wayne Matticks and shut him down like a, like a..."

"Like an Alabama drive-thru abortion clinic?"

"Had to go blue, didn't you?"

"Well good on him," I said.

"Yeah, but the best part is he gets free rooms."

"I'd expect that."

"No, Tony. I said rooms. Plural. He can get us up there anytime. We're thinking of all going up over Thanksgiving, if not sooner. I could do with a turkey buffet and no family this year. Whatcha say? Are you in?"

"Who's we exactly?"

"Well, you, me, Perry, Garret, and Dara. Dara might have a date and you can bring someone if you want."

"I'll have to check my calendar—okay, I'm in. Just let me know."

Working for yourself, even when you suck at what you do and lose stupid yellow-haired, slobbery mops, does give you a certain amount of freedom. In fact, the more you suck at what you do when you work for yourself, the more free time you have. Maybe there's a connection.

"Great," Standard said. He liked to be called Stan, but I call him Standard because that's his name, and it bugs him. That's us.

"I see an epic road trip. We gotta get the right car," he said.

"Kesey's bus might be available."

"Yeah, you check on that."

"Great news about Perry. Looks like he's going places."

"And we get comped at a casino."

The days of being jealous over each other's success will one day be behind us. But we're all wannabe comedians, which means we're all pretty self-absorbed, shallow people to begin with, and even when it's one of our own who's succeeding, there's the caveman part of us that wants to grab a rock and pound on something.

Still, Perry was one of us and if Standard was telling me about the free stay at the casino, he had to have heard it from Perry. Perry was the exception to the rule. He wasn't selfish like the rest of us and he was the most successful. Maybe there's a connection.

The phone rang again. Still too early for the Levises. It was Nancy, the ex.

"Don't forget about Randy's concert tomorrow," she said.

Randy, our fifteen-year-old only child, was forced to take a music class this year. He chose drums much to Nancy's annoyance.

"Yeah, I'll be there. What's the theme? Music for the hearing impaired?" I asked.

"End of quarter progress concert."

"Oh, yes. How festive."

"A big guy came by looking for you earlier," she said.

"How big?"

"Big. He had a tattoo on his arm."

"Colorful?"

"No. Blue."

"Fuck."

"Who is it?" she asked.

"He didn't say?"

"No. He left when I said you didn't live here anymore."

"I have no idea, but blue tattoos are bad."

"Why?"

"Bad Feng Shui," I said. "Probably done in prison. Never a good sign."

"Be careful."

Nancy meant it. We were divorced but still friends, which is not an easy thing to do by all accounts and observations from a marital strife expert like myself.

"Did Ms. Braise get a hold of you? From Moab?"

"Yeah. I gotta go down there for a funeral. Aunt Vicky died."

"Sorry to hear that," she said. "You still have that dog?"

"No, it's gone."

"Thought you had it until Friday morning?"

"Nope."

"Okay, don't forget about the concert. We should be there to show support. Bring a date if you want to."

There it was. A carefully laid but unmistakable ex-wife trap. We promised to stay out of each other's lives beyond our son, but we still peeked at each other as much as we could. She wanted to know if I'd recovered from Delores dumping me. I knew she'd go unaccompanied even if she was engaged. She wouldn't give me the satisfaction of knowing more than she did.

"See you there," I said.

My life was confusion and chaos. It was a familiar feeling and I settled into it like a spider down a drain. I just knew that the Levises would blame me for losing their dog. True, they had warned me, paid me, and entrusted me with their most valued possession, and I'd lost it, but who were they to throw the first stone? Any minute now I knew they'd be calling for the nightly check-in.

"Hello," I said.

"Is Precious there?" It was Mrs. Levis.

"How's your trip going?" I said. "The island phones are particularly bad today. I can hardly hear you."

"We're in Miami now," she said. "I can hear you perfectly."

"Oh, well, that explains it."

"Explains what?"

"Exactly," I said. "So you guys on your way back?"

"No, we'll still be in Friday morning. Have Precious ready by eleven am. We'll be there by noon. Now put her on. I want to talk to her." The last sentence was spoken in the inane baby talk only pet owners and cartoon mothers use.

She wanted me to put the phone up against Precious' head so she could coo to the dog, make it yap and slobber. I considered barking into the phone, but I don't do impressions.

"I can't," I said, forming an elaborate string of intricate lies only true panic can create.

"Why not?"

I was about to go with "yoga class" when I decided to get it over with.

"There was an incident today," I said. "I'm afraid Precious was stolen."

There was a long pause during which I heard the sound of a collapsing sixty-six-year-old woman, the breaking of something ceramic, the sound of rushing footfalls, rubber skidding on tile, something in Spanish, the sound of Mr. Levis demanding to know what was happening, something muffled, a fart, a splash of liquid, the tumbling of ice cubes across a tile floor and someone commanding "to giver air." After the radio show, Mr. Levis picked up the phone.

"Who is this?" he said.

"It's Tony Flaner, Mr. Levis," I said. "I'm afraid Precious was stolen today."

"What happened?" he asked.

Encouraged by his calm, sensible question, I detailed the entire incident down to the black sedan and the reaction of the police. I apologized several times and promised to buy him a new cocker pup and have it waiting for him when he landed back in Salt Lake.

"I'll destroy you," he said as calmly as if he were ordering a Sprite with his taco.

"It wasn't my fault," I said.

"Of course it was. You have not heard the last of this, Mr. Flaner."

"I'll do whatever I can to—" My phone beeped. Another call was coming through. I don't think I'd had more than a single call a day for a week and that was Mrs. Levis and Precious trading spit across fiber optics. Today I ran a switchboard.

"Hold on Mr. Levis, let me see who this is." Before he could threaten me again, I changed calls.

"Hello," I said.

"I'm going to get you."

"I'm sorry. I thought I put you on hold." I pushed the phone exchange again.

"Hello?"

"When I get through with you…" It was Ronald Levis. I switched back.

"Who is this?" I said.

"Your worse nightmare," said a voice I didn't recognize. "You better watch your back, because I'm coming for you."

"Oh, that's a relief. I thought my phone was messed up. Hold on, I'm putting you on conference."

"You fetchin' A-hole!" The dialect was classic 'Mormon-non-swear.' Ronald Levis was back on the line.

"Ronald Levis, I have Mr. Nightmare here with us."

"Don't fuck with me, I'm serious," said Worse Nightmare.

"What's going on? I'm not used to this kind of barbaric language," demanded Levis.

"You should get out more," I suggested.

"You call me barbaric? I'll show you barbaric," said Nightmare.

"You better hand over my dog when I see you Friday, or it's going to be bad for you."

"What the fuck are you talking about?"

"I want my Precious!"

"The hell?" said Nightmare. "I'll beat you bloody."

"I'd take him seriously if I were you, Ronald. He sounds serious," I said. "Are you serious?"

"Hell yes."

"There you have it, Ronald, I can call you Ronald, right? I think threats should be made on a first-name basis. To be fair, I should call Mr. Nightmare 'Worse.'"

"Who is worse?"

"Good question," I said.

"I called for Tony Flaner. Who's this?"

"Oh I'm here," I said. "And Ronald is here too, Worse. He's calling long-distance so be concise."

"I'm going to fuck you up!" said Worse.

"What did I do to you?" said Ronald.

"Not you, Flaner," said Worse.

"Well I'm glad it's not me," I said. "You sound confused."

"Fuck this," said Worse and hung up.

"You haven't heard the last of this, Mr. Flaner," said Ronald.

"Call me Tony," I said and hung up.

4

I KNEW why Ronald Levis was pissed, but why Worse Nightmare was after me was anyone's guess. There are many people who don't like me, most recently divorced. I assumed it was the same tattooed gentleman who'd visited Nancy. I suspected Delores' ex-husband, but I wasn't sure. I'd figure it out sooner or later. I was after all, a detective, and the day's events had rekindled my gumshoe paranoia. Suddenly I didn't know who to trust.

I heard a voice across the room say. "I don't know who to trust."

It was Wilford Brimley. He was speaking to Kurt Russell in Antarctica, 1982.

"Trust's a hard thing to come by," Kurt told Brimley before locking him in the tool shed for having destroyed all means of escape from that doomed outpost. Mayhem ensued.

Curled up on the couch under a thick blanket, I'd muted my phone and watched my copy of John Carpenter's *The Thing* for the third time that week. Bond Week would continue tomorrow with *For Your Eyes Only*.

The next day, Thursday morning, I had twenty-eight messages. Most were "non-swearing" curses. I fast-forwarded through Mr. Levis' threats and Mrs. Levis' cries of anguish and fainting spells and found a hang-up or two. Killers most likely, or possibly worse—telemarketers.

I felt for the Levises, but they were assholes. Mr. Levis was all threats and accusations. Mrs. Levis was all emotional torpor and babbling. "Don't you have any thoughts for our feelings?" "How could you lose my baby?" "When we get back from Disney World, this better be over." At least all this hadn't upset their plans to visit the Magic Kingdom.

Using my secret detective data archive, which I call "the internet," I researched the Levises in more detail. Mr. Ronald Levis and Rosalyn-Janet

Levis had one son named Mark. They owned *Family Saving/Family Values*, a free periodical that litters every supermarket in the city in chrome wire stands next to real estate catalogs by the cart returns. There's a monthly personal editorial on the wonders of family love and conservative politics, and a fluff column or two on the miracle of nitrogen fertilizer on indoor tomatoes or the perils of recycling. These two pages of content are hidden amid forty-six pages of coupons for everything from Tide detergent to cut-rate tattoos and escort services. It made them money. They were hardcore fringe radical conservative Mormons, the kind that rise up every so often to embarrass everyone in the state with polygamy, end-of-the-world prophecies, and multi-level marketing schemes.

Reading the issue of *Family Saving/Family Values* Ronald had left me, I ran across this little padded gem:

"Our family has a new addition! We have a precious new love puppy called Precious because she is so precious to us all as a family. We've only had her a day and already she has won the hearts of all of us with her precious love. Owning a pet that gives love makes us all love each other the more."

This was last month's editorial. They'd had the dog for what? At most, five weeks?

I had a hard time taking them seriously, so I didn't.

I thought of the call from Allie about Aunt Vicky. I looked for a mention of the death in every online place I could think of and found nothing.

I had a churning in my stomach that all great detectives identify as a hunch, but normal people pass off as hunger or gas. Over a piece of toast on the toilet, I thought about calling the Moab police. I hesitated, remembering how little police like private investigators. "Open cases are off limits," I'd been told more times than, "Have a nice day." Many, many more times. Cops and PIs don't get along. I'm not sure if anyone knows why exactly, but it's a custom, like Christmas and planting evidence, so it continues to this day by faith and habit.

I knew I had to go to Moab. My life was sliding into familiar patterns. I smiled as I felt the familiar push and pull. The Levises and Worse Nightmare were clearly pushing me out of town with threats of beatings. Allie and my gas were clearing, pulling me south with promises of...dunno.

I wanted to leave immediately, but I couldn't. First, there would be another beating.

I called Randy's drum concerts "beatings" because they were. I'd promised to go that night. Nancy had bought eight tickets and given me four to share with my friends. The friends I'd taken to his last recital were adamantly opposed to going again. Ever. So I invited Dara Sutter who'd skipped last time and didn't have anything better to do. She couldn't believe the stories the others had told about the experience, and she had a self-abusive curiosity that leads one to accept invitations to school concerts. Darwin would sort her type out soon enough.

Dara is a comedian. She devastates audiences with her innocent looks and unbearably offensive language. The disconnect of her elfin size, pigtails and vibrator jokes can induce tremors in Hells Angels and 4chan readers.

"Thanks for going with me Dara," I said when I picked her up.

"You know this isn't a fucking date, right?" she said.

"I know. Just company."

"Fucking right. So where are you taking me to dinner?"

Since Salt Lake didn't have a seaport, I was hard-pressed to think of someplace we'd blend in. I settled on a bar we knew and had sandwiches and beers while Dara told me how she hadn't seen her last boyfriend since he ran out of her house crying, "for no apparent fucking reason."

"I still have his stuff if you want it," she offered.

"How long has he been gone?"

"Two months."

"Have you tried to call him?"

"Once. He changed his number. Changed his fucking email and deleted his fucking Facebook too. Someone said he was in goddamned Canada now. Asshole."

"Does he owe you money?"

"Just the opposite actually," she said.

"You better hang on to his stuff."

"Whatever."

Randy's high school was having a food drive for the less fortunate. This was announced in a hundred handmade posters that smelled of 'required art assignment' and looked like preschool graffiti. They covered the halls leading into the auditorium.

"Help the homeless," "feed a fellow," read Dara as we passed through the thin crowd. I was impressed she could read it. I couldn't make out the words in the glittery finger paint. Must be a girl thing.

In front of the auditorium was a nook, the kind of place a school displayed its treasures and trophies. In support of the food drive, it contained piles of canned goods now. There were probably a hundred cans in it divided equally between creamed corn, green beans, and pickled beets. I spotted a single can of tuna, badly dented, and one big food-storage can of freeze-dried prunes from 1948. The Civil Defense label was faded but still eye-catching. Other than those two, it was all corn, beans, and beets.

"At least there are as many cans as signs encouraging people to bring shit," said Dara.

"So that's what happens to canned beets," I said. "I never knew."

"Insult to injury. Like life doesn't suck enough for the homeless, we have to give them beets."

This was the second concert recital for Mr. Tamm's Sophomore orchestra.

As we wandered into the auditorium, I accurately figured that there was about a third as many people here as there were for the first concert. Small knots of folks with worried expressions crowded to fill the seats farthest from the stage.

This was Mr. Tamm's first year teaching. He was fresh out of college, scarcely older than the kids he taught, and he'd come to the job with a very liberal sensibility. In a letter he sent home, he proclaimed that he wanted "to foster each child's creativity" and let each choose whatever instrument they wanted. Just bring it, and he'd teach it and have regular concerts.

It turned out that Mitchell's Music was having a blow-out sale on drums the week the kids had to declare their instrument, and Mr. Tamm ended up with eighteen drummers in his class of twenty-two students. It was a hell of a deal. Full drum sets can cost a fortune. Mitchell's had them for under a hundred bucks, so Mr. Tamm had nearly a score of identical Chinese drum kits, one violin, two bass guitars, and a trumpet for each concert.

I caught sight of Nancy sitting alone. She nodded but didn't wave me over. She gave Dara an assessing glance, then recognizing her, and turned back to the stage where Mr. Tamm was just getting up.

"Welcome all," he said in a strained voice over an ear-piercing microphone. "I think we've waited long enough for any stragglers. Anyone who's late will just have to come late."

I glanced at my watch. He'd waited fifteen minutes. This was it. It was coming. People were already edging off their seats to make a dash for the exit when the lights went down. Foolishly, I'd sat in the middle of a row. I'd be noticed leaving.

I love my son Randy. I like supporting him in all he does, but his orchestra is really awful; horrible really. No one knows how to play a note. Sophomore orchestra fulfills a graduation requirement and it's torture for everyone involved.

It's not often I pity Nancy for anything but thinking of Randy pounding away on a snare drum at home for thirty minutes a day made my heart bleed for her. Sure she could find excuses to be out most times—she'd had a huge increase in open houses lately I'd noticed, unusual for this time of year, but she couldn't escape it all, and she looked nearly as frazzled and scared as did Mr. Tamm.

He swung his baton from the podium. The curtains parted, revealing eighteen identical complete drum kits crowding every square inch of stage. There were no xylophones, no bongos, and no big thunderous orchestra drums. Each kit was pulled right out of a rock video and put in front of an eager young hormonally-imbalanced adolescent, who had bet their classmates they could break more drumsticks that night than anyone else.

On either side of the stage, nearly pushed into the wings, was a bass guitarist. Both were girls and the difference in their relative sizes made one think that you were looking at some kind of perspective illusion. The one on the left couldn't reach the farthest frets. The one on the right could play professional basketball. The violin was in the center and the bugler beside him. Broken strands of bow string hung off the fiddle like Spanish moss, and I wondered if there were enough left to actually work the thing.

I waved at Randy in the third row. He didn't see me. He put on a pair of ballistic quality hearing guards I remember buying for the leaf blower. With a start, I wondered why I hadn't thought of that.

Mr. Tamm touched the podium, and everyone lifted their drumsticks. There was a pause, the silence before the storm, the timer counting down before the bomb exploded, the moment you realize you had no business being there, that you cut the wrong wire, but it was all too late. You're in for it now. It was coming and you're doomed.

Even though we all saw it coming, sitting in paralyzed anticipation, we all jumped out of our seats when the crash hit. A dozen drumsticks snapped like pretzels and pitched shards and splinters into the air. Nine drums were torn wide open, punctured and otherwise made useless in the first volley. The trumpet, clear and loud as any reveille, played by someone who'd actually studied the instrument, was completely lost in the din of what I think was "Go Tell Aunt Rody."

With each note, Mr. Tamm was visibly affected, buffeted by deafening sound waves. Several students improvised and any semblance of melody vanished as small children cried and exit doors swung open.

Dara's hands were to her ears and her jaw hung open in a scream. It might have been a pantomime or a real one. I couldn't hear anything. Ragnarök was upon us.

I glanced down at Nancy and saw her face aglow in the light of her phone. Electric earbuds stretched from the device into her ears.

"Cheat!" I yelled at the top of my lungs, but the sound was forced back down my throat as if by a black-powder ramrod. I shrunk back in my chair and cupped my hands over my ears. After a while, the thundering stopped, and the ringing began. Mr. Tamm turned around and took a bow.

He acknowledged the silent applause. All I could hear was the unmistakable bells in my head, fearing the permanent loss of half a dozen frequencies.

Dara was in my face pushing something into my hand. Unable to hear, I read her lips:

"Cats color pimento eels!"

She wasn't making any sense, then I looked in my hand and saw a clump of pink Kleenex. Dara pointed to her head. She had stuffed a wad of the tissue into each of her ears.

"Apple juice is best when from Brazil!" she mouthed to me.

I was beginning to question my lip-reading skills but gathered her meaning and stuffed Kleenex in my own ears.

I felt more than heard for the rest of the concert. In between each song, Mr. Tamm would shout about what this or that song was about, how hard the kids had worked to learn it and how great it was for all of us to come support them.

"The support of family is at the root of all excellence," he screamed over the PA.

He spoke for maybe five minutes between each two-minute song, just enough for us to catch our breath before the next beating began.

By the third song, the violinist could only clap his hands because his bow was totally spent. The trumpeter had walked off stage a song earlier during a recognizable Queen' *We Will Rock You* that loosened my fillings. He did not return.

When the lights finally came up, my skin tingled and my ears buzzed. I applauded and waved at Randy who waved back.

Dara, twitching and blinking, stood up, put an arm around me and leaned in close. "What the fuck was that bullshit?" she screamed into my face.

If anyone had heard her, it would have been a scandal, but of course, no one could.

5

DARA WAS quiet on the way home, or at least I think she was quiet. She might have been screaming or sounding her rape whistle for all I knew. My hearing hadn't returned, and based on the scathing glares she shot me whenever I looked over, hers wasn't working either.

"Did you enjoy the beating?" I yelled as she got out.

"You did fucking warn me," she screamed, popping out her jaw in a vain attempt to hear again. She staggered to her door and went in.

The percussive battery had taken my mind off things for a while. When I got home, I threw Precious' food bowl in the dishwasher and thought of Moab.

I hadn't been much of a nephew to Aunt Vicky nor a good cousin to Rick. Since I hadn't been much of a son to my own mother, this wasn't surprising, but I wasn't above the shame and guilt of lost opportunities.

My mother died while I was in college. My father followed not long afterward. They were always competitive. After my mother died, I regretted not apologizing enough for removing the light bulb in her bathroom and pouring honey on her toilet seat. Though she never said anything, I suspect she knew it was me who sent the male stripper to her office on St. Patrick's Day. How was I to know there'd be such a dramatic and spectacularly well-documented wardrobe malfunction? Her next job was better anyway.

Pangs of guilt and sirens of damaged hearing sent me off to sleep that night.

The next morning, I checked my pillow for pools of dried blood that might have leaked out during the night and was happy to find none. I was less happy to find myself unable to remember the last time I'd washed my sheets. The thought haunted me in the shower when I remembered buying them two months before. I remembered putting them on, but not taking them off. I scrubbed extra hard and weighed the ecological and economical implications of just burning the old sheets and buying new ones. How much were the mattresses?

The phone was ringing when I got out. I answered it before thinking who it might be.

"Mr. Flaner, this is Ronald Levis. Rosalyn-Janet is still very upset about all this and frankly, so am I."

"Yes, it's affected me in ways I can't begin to think of."

It's a Small World played in the background.

"What are you doing to recover our baby?" he asked.

"Well, I've made a police report, included a witness, and I left the porch light on."

"Is that it?"

"Pretty much," I said.

"Aren't you taking this seriously?"

"Not really. There's been a death in my family. That takes priority."

"So someone's dead. Big deal. You can't do anything about that. Someone in my family has been kidnapped. That should be your priority."

"Precious is a six-week-old cocker spaniel with epilepsy and more infections than the World Health Organization mail order catalog. I'll tell you what. Keep the money you owe me, take the money you were going to pay me, and buy a kennel full of cocker spaniels. Name them all Precious. Teach them to read and take them on Oprah."

"Mr. Flaner. You are a heartless Philistine! You have not heard the end of this. You've ruined our world."

"It's a world of laughter, a world of tears," I sang along.

"Are you mocking me?"

"Sure am," I said. "I'll leave your dog stuff on the porch. I'll be gone for a while. Enjoy the ride."

I didn't pick up when he called back.

I surveyed my clothing options for a trip to Moab and found myself again faced with cleaning versus buying. I made the mature decision and collected as much as I could carry, and using race memory, I found my way to the laundry room.

The door creaked on unused hinges and I carefully and reverently approached the white enamel altars of Maytag. I couldn't see any use in sorting whites from colors since nothing was white anymore. I threw it all in, added a handful of detergent, pushed the magic buttons and watched water flood into it.

I'd had nothing to do, no one to clean up for, no one to impress, and no need for more than the most basic hygiene. I'd let the house go to hell, and a spoiled cocker spaniel hadn't helped the tidiness one little bit.

Feeling a need for a change, I cleaned my house. I tracked down the vacuum and a yellow can of pine-scented insect repellent masquerading as wood polish and went domestic on the rooms. While the clothes were in the dryer, I collected Precious' possessions in a box and took them to the porch. I didn't plan on being here when the Levises came. I had places to go and people I didn't want to see. The Levises could pick up their kibble, frozen hamburger and canine pharmacy from my porch if they wanted them.

I folded my clothes and stuffed them into a duffel bag, wondering why I'd bothered folding them. I dusted off my best dark suit and hoped Moab had a dry cleaner. I didn't know the details, but I knew I was going to a funeral. I packed up and hit the road dreading the arrival more than the distance.

Like most people, I try to avoid discomfort, and funerals are unpleasant. I think it's because they remind us of death. It's just a working theory I have. I'd distracted and deafened myself for a day, as long as I could. I'd tried to ignore the whole unpleasant business of death, funerals, and guilt, like the overstuffed garbage can under my sink.

I stopped the car, ran back into the house and took the trash out from under the sink. Then I began the drive again.

Moab is four or five hours from Salt Lake City depending on the weight of your right foot and the size of your bladder. I'd been so unusually productive that I regretted giving Allie such a late time to arrive. How was I to know acoustic damage can cure lethargy? It was a nice day, so I drove leisurely, not overtaxing my little half-electric car.

There is a terrible rite of passage every American faces. It's that moment when their youthful exuberance for driving disappears and operating a motor vehicle becomes, at best, a chore. Sometimes it's after a cracked windshield or while scraping thirteen inches of snow off your hood for the fourth time that week that something inside snaps, and we curse the day the eternal infernal internal combustion engine conquered the world. The love affair is over, and on a daily basis, time spent driving is time lost. It blanks our memory, giving aliens the opportunity to abduct and probe us at will, because we are on wasted-time autopilot. Of course, like love affairs, there are moments when the old spark can be rekindled for a brief flame. Autumn drives and long road trips through beautiful country can do this, especially if it's unfamiliar and lit by John Ford.

Such was the drive I took to Moab that Friday. I hadn't left the valley for a year. Everything I'd needed was confined in the nice smog-catching bowl which is the Salt Lake valley. As I drove south past the prison and gravel pits which marked the end of civilization and peered down into ultra-conservative Utah County, I felt like a pioneer getting forty-eight miles to the gallon. Past the steel mill and rendering plants, I rolled down my window and let the fall air blow hair into my eyes until I was nearly blind and every scrap of paper I'd tossed on my passenger side floor was whirling around me in a tornado, jumping out of open windows like bats fleeing hell. When I could no longer feel my nose for the cold, and my car was tidy and bare, I rolled up the windows, put on some nice music and cranked up the heater.

Moab is situated in the middle of freakin' nowhere in a state known for having a lot of nowhere. It's not far from the Colorado border and though there are roads that go through Moab, no one does. It's either a destination or you're lost.

From Salt Lake City, you take Interstate 15 south. I-15 is a real freeway, the fourth largest in the entire friggin' universe—I looked it up. It runs from Canada to Mexico and is a pillar of American greatness. Never a day since it was finished has it not been under repair. Utah gets its official state flower, the Orange Traffic Pylon, from I-15. But of course, I-15 does not go to Moab. No no no.

Unless you want to add a hundred miles at speed, you leave I-15 just as the Wendy's signs thin out. You then snake through the state along back-roads and highways made famous by 1970s slasher films. Small towns and scenic mountains enchant and frighten as you drive through forestry land, farmland, mining land, and no-man's land.

Eventually you meet up with another freeway, the great I-70, just a few miles from where it dies an ignoble death in the center of the state. Your time here is short because you quickly leave it for a more quaint single-lane slow winding road that eventually brings you into red canyons and interesting rocks.

Moab began as a place to dry off after crossing the Colorado River on the Old Spanish Trail. It was the only place the river could be forded for a hundred miles that offered more than a fifty percent chance of survival. It was a custom for the first travelers after drying off, to look for the bodies of their unlucky comrades before moving on. This custom ended when the Mormons settled in Utah.

Brigham Young started a program of colonization in the hopes of creating the huge state of Deseret. He sent missions out all over the territory to start new Mormon towns, claim land and discourage the less Mormon from sticking around. One such mission was sent to Moab.

A settlement on the Old Spanish Trail would really help the cause, so a bunch of guys went down to try. Since Moab was in the middle of nowhere, it took them a while to get there. The town wasn't called Moab then. They called it the Elk Mountain Mission. The missionaries made friends with the gullible Indians and tricked them into trading their wild horses, worth easily twenty dollars each, for stupid meaningless guns and ammunition, which retailed for, like, at most, five bucks.

A couple of months later, chased by well-armed Indians, the last Mormons fled on foot across the same bleak wilderness I drove across that day, and I imagined some serious explaining when they got home. Where were the horses you bought? After that, the Mormons decided that Moab was just too remote to bother with and gave it up.

Twenty years later, more white people got together and finally settled in the area now called Moab.

There are two theories as to why the city is called Moab. The first is that it's biblical. This makes sense because Bibles played a big role in the early settlement of the West. Without the added weight of family bibles, stories like the Donner party and Custer's last stand might not have happened. Moab, in the Bible, sits on the east bank of the river Jordan. Moab sits on the east side of the river Green. Close enough. However, Moab is not a nice place in the Bible. It's loathed. In fact, it runs a close third to Sodom and Gomorrah in focus group hate testing. I didn't read the bible. I couldn't beget into it, so I'll have to go on faith about why Moab was disliked.

The other theory about the name is that it comes from the Paiute Indian word 'moapa,' which the white folks, unwilling to give the Indians any more syllables than necessary, shortened to Moab. Moapa means "land of mosquito bites." Remembering my time along the river in my youth, I tend to believe the second theory.

For most of its existence, Moab didn't do much. The locals revived the tradition of fishing bodies out of the water until someone thought to build a ferry and the mortician had to lay off staff. Later, much, much, much later, they built a bridge, and Moab was finally a place you could get to by car. Then, instead of staying away by the hundreds, visitors could stay away from Moab by the thousands.

Word spread about how wonderful and beautiful the area around Moab was, but tourism wasn't a big thing until relatively recently and it was still bloody hard to get to. Even when you got there, all Moab could offer you was a place to park your car. The real fun happened later when you dragged your sorry thirsty butt up Slickrock trails that mules shied away from to see a hole in a rock. Moab had to survive on ranching, limited mining, farming, Indian fights and mosquito repellant until the Russians had an A-Bomb.

Uranium was found around Moab, and it became a boomtown in the fifties. Millionaires were made overnight and the town literally glowed with the newfound wealth of gamma radiation. Then the government had enough uranium, made mining any more of it illegal, and things went to shit again.

They improved the bridge and at the height of American prosperity, the 1970s, people began to explore, and Moab finally became a destination.

Beyond having happy American family units in silver streamline campers and roads that didn't threaten to kill you every mile, there were two key pieces of publicity that brought folks to Moab. One was Hollywood which filmed plenty of westerns there thanks to the Moab Film Board. The Marlboro man developed his life-ending cancer, riding the scenic paths of Canyonlands. The tobacco industry would point to the huge radioactive tailing piles around the city as the cause of his cancer, and they might be right, but he smoked a lot too. I saw it on television when I was a kid.

The other thing that shot Moab into fame was the work of one of the twentieth century's greatest ironic writers, Edward Abbey. His exquisite essays extolled a love of nature and the outdoors that moved every reader to an inner yearning. His close ties with the spiritual effects of natural beauty and stunning landscapes were shaped in Canyonlands and Arches National Parks—Moab's backyard. His bestselling book Desert Solitaire is still a bible for many environmentalists.

The irony comes from the fact that *Desert Solitaire* became a bestseller. Abbey's lonesome, beautiful vistas drew pilgrims by the thousands, hundreds of thousands, then millions. Driving jeeps, riding bikes, or walking the trails—the nature lovers Abbey had inspired—removed the solitaire from the desert and gave Moab a thriving economy in tee shirts, maps, towing services and Edward Abbey reprints. Abbey spins in his grave.

With good roads, a solid bridge and a seasonal society of tourists, Moab survives today.

These thoughts bounced in my mind as I drove through the last valleys along the mesa, past the road leading to Canyonlands.

The red cliffs thrilled me with visions of spiritual isolation, peace, and spray-painted graffiti. I slowed down to savor the feeling and was passed by a blue jeep from Montana with balloon tires and five fog lights. The driver flipped me the bird as he sped by.

It was like coming home.

6

RICK WAS a cheerful boy who might have been dropped on his head or was just blessed with an impenetrable naive stupidity. The one photograph I have of my cousin Rick and myself was taken the day I arrived in Moab. Aunt Vicky took it to send to my mother to show her how quickly Rick and I had become friends. Rick was immediately friendly, make no mistake. As I got off the bus, he ran over, hugged me, threw me over his shoulder like a grain sack and carried me to the car.

"Thick, don't show off," Vicky said. "We all know you're strong."

"Tony, don't," he said.

"I do now," I said to his back.

He plopped me down next to the dusty Dodge.

"You can ride in the back with me," he said.

On the short drive to Aunt Vicky's house, he pointed out every gas station and cottonwood tree along the way. He pointed to people he knew and people he didn't know. Some he said he wanted to know, others looked like jerks and he wouldn't care to meet them. Most were tourists, while one was a schoolmate, and another a drunk. Off Main Street, the vacationers evaporated, and Vicky drove me past the school I'd be going to.

"Just for a while," she said, "until things get sorted out."

At Vicky's house, she had Rick and I stand together on the porch. Rick put his arm around me like we were the oldest chums. We'd just met a half hour before, but he was sure we'd be pals forever.

"We're family, you know."

Vicky snapped the picture. I looked a little bewildered, and Rick looked elated. His right arm was wrapped around my neck like reunited war buddies and his left hand, thrust squarely in front of him, flipped a middle finger into the camera.

I hadn't noticed the bird at the time, but when I later saw the photograph, I was not surprised to see it. That was Rick's thing. He thought it was hilarious. Every photo ever taken of him when he had power to realize he was being photographed, included his signature middle finger obscenity. I remember the pictures of him on the mantel—fishing at the river and receiving his Webelos badge all offending the viewer. I've since seen his high school yearbooks. His was the only picture airbrushed in his sophomore one. In his junior year, he stealthily snuck it in by leaning on his fist in a pensive pose of contemplative wisdom. His senior picture was cropped so tightly that his ears didn't make it in.

There was nothing mean-spirited about it. It was just his silly act of rebellion. If he offended anyone, he didn't care. After the first time, I don't think anyone thought it was funny, if they ever did. I know that, for a while, there was a challenge at his school to take a picture of Thick Racine without his finger. He heard about it and walked the halls with it extended at all times.

The Montana jeep that passed me didn't know that he was welcoming me to Moab in the only fitting way possible. He didn't mean it that way, but I was nonetheless pleased and repaid the gesture in the spirit in which it was given.

The mesa drops down after the Canyonlands turn-off and runs through a gorge past the entrance to Arches. It then goes over the life-saving bridge, now with multiple lanes. On the west bank of the river is a nuclear tailing dump that no one likes to think about. Bulldozers load dump trucks with innocent looking sand and cart it away. None dare say "Nuclear Superfund Site." It's bad for tourism.

I knew that Moab would be different than I remembered, but I was still blown away. The season was ending, and it wasn't half as crowded as I imagined it got, but still, Main Street was thick with out-of-town cars loaded down with bike racks and rubber rafts. I knew none of the stores, but quickly found several places where I could get a latte or a stone-baked pizza. If I ever ran low on souvenirs, I had only to fall down and I'd be in a shop pushing tee shirts, polished rocks, plastic arch snow globes and collector spoons. If I wanted some high art, something for a wall or garden or the lobby of my new high-rise, there were plenty of galleries offering wine tastings on the weekends to fill my needs. I saw Industrial sized wind chimes and hand-woven Indian blankets. I saw signs for guided tours, heard hip-hop competing with country from dueling car radios and smelled cannabis in the air. There were hotels and motels, bike repair shops, jeep rental garages, used bookstores, restaurants and a brewery. The McDonald's drive-thru had a line around the block. The McRib was back.

Once I got off Main Street, the place became familiar again. Moab is a small town for all its activity, and like Vegas off the strip, life slows down a hundred yards from the neon, or in Moab's case, the burning sage bundles.

I found Aunt Vicky's house without trouble. It's a great old house, one of the few brick two-story houses in the city, if not the county. It was built in the late 1950s when the family had money. They had some land and leased it to a mining company who pulled potash out of it while looking for uranium. The lease money was enough to import top-notch red bricks from the closest top-notch red brick factory, probably Vermont. It was a cool design with some of the bricks sticking out as blocks at the corners of the house. They're called quoins and I've always loved them. Had it not been for them, Rick and I wouldn't have been able to climb out our window at night and meet Allison.

There's a reason you never hear about potash millionaires, and it's not just because no one knows what potash is and it also takes a long time to explain. It's because it's not that valuable. The money the family received from their lease built a nice but small house. By modern Utah standards, it's tiny. In Utah, five thousand square foot McMansions are packed together like Tetris blocks. But at the time, it was stately and still looks cool today. It's colonial and boxy. It has five street-facing windows on the front, one on each side of an arched front doorway, two above those in bedrooms, and a small one above the door where I remember the bathroom being. White shutters that actually close frame all the windows, and the slanting roof is broken by a triangular pinnacle above in the center. A little wooden pole is stuck on it. I don't know why.

Behind the house was a garage. It was built much later than the house, probably in the seventies. It doesn't match the architecture with its aluminum siding and a manual door. A charming, white, knee-high picket fence ran around the property, and rose bushes struggled to get enough light and water under a towering cottonwood tree in the front yard. Rick told me that the town used to hang bandits from that tree in olden times. There'd been a tire swing hanging from it when I was there. Nothing hung from it now.

There were several cars in the driveway. I parked in front of the house, got out, stretched, and walked to the door.

It opened before I could knock. Allison Braise stood there, a broad smile across her face.

"Tony! It's good to see you," she said.

"It's good to see you too," I said. Smooth.

Allison Braise was my first kiss and I have never, must never, will never forget it. Since that autumn night so many years ago, she'd been a fixture in my imagination and dreams, whether I knew it was her or not.

"You look great," I said.

"No, I don't."

She had sun-faded brown hair four inches below her shoulder and straight as pencils. She wore no makeup but had a natural tan that had etched a few wrinkles into her face and made her look vibrant and active. She looked healthy and rough, a no-nonsense kind of air I remembered from years ago, and beauty only first love can describe.

"Who's at the door, Allie? Is it that idiot Danny again?"

Allie moved aside and gestured me to come in.

The house hadn't changed much in the many years since I'd been there. New carpet, new couch, new television, but most of the original wooden furniture, heirlooms when I'd first seen them, were still there like gems in an antique show.

An old woman I didn't recognize sat on the sofa in front of an old coffee table and squinted at me suspiciously.

"Who are you, young man?"

I glanced behind me to make sure I wasn't being followed. Realizing she meant me, I said. "I'm Tony Flaner. Aunt Vicky's nephew."

"If she was your aunt, I guess you'd be her nephew. No surprise there."

"This is Sophia Curtis," Allie said. "She lived here with Vicky."

"I still live here," she said. "Unless you have a mind to chuck me out."

"What's she talking about?" I asked Allie.

"Sophia says you're Vicky's only relative."

"Only living relative," she said. "There is a difference, you know."

"I'm not following," I said.

"Don't you know the difference between living and not living?" she snapped.

"Of course I do. Non-living crave brains, and the living hold up in barricaded shopping malls. I watch TV."

She smiled. "You planning on selling the house?"

"What about the house?" I said. "Are you saying it's mine?"

"Not necessarily," said a voice from the doorway.

Standing in the frame was a uniformed policeman. His jaw stuck out like it was chiseled. His nose was straight and Roman, and his blue eyes were piercing and transfixed me. His blond hair was perfectly cared for and framed his face like a golden halo. His clothes were tailored and showed a natural athletic physique worshipped in classical times and still lust-worthy today. I recognized Danny Hinds and instantly hated him all the more.

"Danny, you remember Tony," said Allie as way of introduction.

"Thick's cousin Tony? Yeah, I remember you. I heard you got in some legal problems up north. Shouldn't you be in jail?"

"That's just like you to read only the first sentence of a story," I said. "I got out of that little fix and did it with style. Maybe I can find you a Cliffs-Notes of the whole thing and you can read the back of it on the way to the test."

"Ha ha," he said.

He was always ready with a witty comeback.

"What are you doing here?" snapped Sophia at Danny with a scorn only true familiarity can produce.

"Seems Victoria Racine left a will," he said smugly. "Tony might not be in it. I'd be surprised if he was. I don't think she even remembered she had a nephew."

"She remembered just fine," said Sophia. "She could outthink the likes of you stoned on Anasazi Red Rope, face down in a trough, gin in her veins."

Happy but confused, I looked at Allie.

"She means marijuana," she told me. "The local name for some potent stuff."

"I didn't mean any offense, Sophia," said Danny in a suddenly calm and soothing voice. He overly enunciated and gestured like he was on a stage. "I just meant that Tony hasn't been around much." He stuck out his chest in a sincere imitation of a Superman comic cover.

"What the hell are you doing?" I said.

"What?" His eyes widened and his posture returned to human.

"I hope you're not the only law around here."

"He's not," assured Allie.

"I'm a sergeant and acting detective."

"Acting is right," I said.

"What are your plans, Tony?" Allie said, stepping between Danny and me. Not for the first time in my life, I measured myself against Danny Hinds. This time I outweighed him by at least twenty pounds, but even without his gun, nightstick, club, taser, and handcuffs he could beat me to death with his chin alone.

"The only plans I have so far is to find a bathroom quickly or step outside for a minute. I don't want to scare any children—or Danny here, so if you don't mind…"

Sophia pointed down the hall.

When I came back, Allie was sitting next to Sophia, but Danny, still framed in the doorway, held his post. The light shone around him like an aura and he cast a shadow across the room. He'd found a comfortable position for his arms on his waist and his chest again stuck out too far.

I walked straight at him with purpose and he shrank back perceptibly as I approached. Still, he kept his heroic pose even if his eyes betrayed uncertainty. Just before walking into him, I veered to the left, reached around and pulled the door closed behind him.

"If you leave the door open, all kinds of pests can get in," I said.

I left Danny for a vintage beige easy chair and sat down in time to see Allie force a smirk off her face.

Sophia didn't bother removing hers.

"You said something about the house and a will?" I said to Danny.

"I did?"

"Well, what you said was 'not necessarily,' and unless that's your new catchphrase, I assumed it had something to do with the private conversation you were eavesdropping on. Do you know something about the house and a will?"

"Oh, that," he stammered. "You see, I was just coming up the walk, and the door was open. I saw you drive by the—"

"What about a will, you idiot?" interrupted Sophia. "Do you know anything, or were you just being melodramatic?"

His hands dropped from his hips. He squinted his eyes and exhaled deeply, a cleansing exercise popularized by method-acting gurus. He took another deep breath, returned to his Captain Arrogant pose and said with authority, "It will be read after the funeral," and then he turned three-quarters profile to admire the curtains.

"Isn't that usually when they read wills?" I said.

"Is it?" he said. "Well, not everyone knows that. I just wanted to make sure everyone knew about it. Everyone should be getting a letter from Archie Rumbold about it tomorrow."

"Thanks for the heads up," I said. "When's the funeral?"

"Sunday," said Allie.

"Where can I get a good room?" I asked Allie. "I'll stay in town for a while."

To my hormonal delight, her face brightened, and she began to speak, but before she made a sound, Sophia interrupted.

"Are you trying to be insulting?"

"Usually, but not now. I just thought that—"

"Bull. You didn't think at all. It's a contagious condition, Tony Flaner, one that Vicky said you had some immunity to. You'll stay here of course. Vicky thought you were smart. Don't go proving a good woman wrong. She'll haunt you and give you scabies."

Not knowing what scabies were but definitely not wanting any, I agreed to stay with Sophia in Vicky's old house.

7

SERGEANT DANNY HINDS EXCUSED himself to get back to work, which I took to mean manning a speed trap.

With Danny gone and Allie committed to my long-term memory, I finally focused on Sophia. She was in her seventies, if not eighties. Her hands were gnarled as ginger and as spotted as a blueberry muffin. Her gray hair was bobbed short and she'd long since given up trying to hide her wrinkles. Her lipstick was straight, and her mascara hadn't run. When she stood to start dinner, she didn't hunch, but there was frailty in her step. She was healthy and headstrong. Her eyes were as quick as her tongue and maybe as sharp, but I could see in them a pain that she struggled to bear. Then again, it might have been the beginning of cataracts.

I collected my things and found my room. The bedrooms were all upstairs, all accessible from a single upstairs landing. I remember Vicky's room in the front corner and Rick's on the diagonal. The room next to Vicky's was a sewing room in my time. The door was closed, and I assumed it was Sophia's. The next was Rick's. It still had his name on the door carved in pine from a school wood project before I met him. The last was the guest room. I got the guest room. There was one bathroom accessible from the landing and all had to share it. Its window overlooked the front door as I remembered.

When I first came to Moab, Rick and I had shared a room. I was sad but hid it behind a sullen melancholic veneer only a blind cabbage couldn't have seen through. Sharing a room with Rick was the perfect cure. He was so excited to have me there that I swear his tail wagged. Even the first night, he talked and kidded so much that I forgot about my mom and dad and fell asleep from exhaustion mid-sentence.

That was how the summer nights went. We'd stay up all night talking about anything and everything. He was fascinated with the movies I'd seen, the books I'd read, and how smart I was for being so young. He was full of local color and tales of daring-do he had done, or others before him. He couldn't wait to show me where Indians had massacred whites up the canyon "Just like Custer." He knew where the best fishing was and had M80 fireworks to prove it. He loved playing catch with anything from baseballs to frisbees to tree roots, and I had to be on constant guard on my fold-away cot lest he choose that moment to start a game with a pillow or a lamp.

When school started, Aunt Vicky separated us so we wouldn't stay up all night. "It was fine in the summer, but now it's time to be responsible," she'd told us, and I got the guest room.

I knew where it was, finding it by nostalgia. I put my duffel on the bed and remembered something peculiar downstairs that had been repeated here. All the photographs and pictures were covered in cloth. I peeked under one on my wall and saw a Western scene of a mountain man fleeing two Indians down a steep hillside. Underneath another cloth teepee on the end table was a picture of my mother as a young girl, Vicky beside her in front of a car as big and round as a submarine.

I went downstairs.

"Why are all the pictures covered up?"

Sophia was in the kitchen cooking.

Allie answered me from the sofa. "Sophia said she saw it in a movie once. She's a real movie buff."

"I still don't get it."

"Superstition," called Sophia from the kitchen. "You keep them covered until after the funeral."

"Why? What's the effect?" I called back.

"Hell if I know," she said. "Probably something with spirits. Don't you dare take them down or I'll mash you."

Mashing was a threat unique to my family. Outside of cookbooks, I never heard the word in any other context than when I was rousing wrath by bad behavior. I never knew what mashing actually entailed. I never got mashed. The threat was enough. It was probably like scabies but hearing Sophia use the term made me recall Aunt Vicky getting ready to mash Rick and I for not taking our muddy shoes off.

"I wouldn't think of taking them down," I called back. To Allie, I said, "It makes the house look like it's in mourning. It's fitting."

We sat for a moment listening to pots rattle and knives chop.

"Let's catch up," Allie said. "What have you been up to?"

"I change jobs about every seven months," I said. "I'm currently coming off a long stint as a private detective, and I got divorced. I have a son, fifteen, who would rather have a new computer monitor than a car and I've kinda let myself go."

"I heard about you being a detective," she said. "Sophia told me."

"How'd she know?"

"Vicky told me," Sophia shouted from the kitchen. It was a small house.

"What about you?" I said to Allie. I remember Allie had a small house on a lot of land, with many outbuildings. It was the remains of a much larger farm that had failed and been sold off in pieces.

"Well, I never married. I'll work odd jobs as I find them; river guide, waitress. Never one to be lazy. I turned the old place into an animal shelter. Really. I look after pets for travelers and have a few horses I'll rent out for rides in the canyons. It makes ends meet. Mostly I train animals, break horses and nurse wounded birds. I'm not a vet, but I have a reputation."

"I don't know if it's good for me to be seen talking to a girl with a reputation," I said. "What would the neighbors think?"

"They'd think Allison Braise has gone insane talking to a tourist," she said with a smile that made my mouth dry up. "Are you staying long?"

I cleared my throat. "I really haven't thought about it. You called at the right time. I wanted to get out of Salt Lake, and this was just the thing."

"We're all pleased that Vicky's death was so convenient for your emotional needs." It was Sophia in the kitchen. Allie bit her lip, half smiling, half horrified.

"She was always thoughtful," I said. "Not sure about her taste in friends though."

Allie's expression turned wholly horrified.

"I chided her about that all the time," Sophia retorted without a pause. "Come and get it."

We met Sophia in the dining room, which was practically part of the kitchen, and sat down. Sophia placed a blue china plate of cheese ravioli in the center. She put a glass bowl of tossed green salad and a tureen of marinara sauce beside it.

"What would you like to drink?" she asked me.

"Water's fine."

"Really? You look more like a beer guy."

"Okay, a beer."

"All out. I'll get you some water."

"Wine?" asked Allie.

"Sure, dearie."

"I'll have some too," I said. "Please."

She returned with a bottle of burgundy and three glasses.

"Have to let this breath," she said, sitting down.

"Why?" I asked, dishing out some salad.

"Hell if I know. I saw it in a movie."

The wine was tasty and local. The red-brown label had a black stylized Kokopelli figure, but instead of blowing a flute, the ancient icon was sucking on a bottle of hooch. It was chic and trendy and bordered on—if not danced across—bad taste. *Ashe Winery, Moab Utah,* I read.

We dug into the chow. Though she came off as abrasive as twenty-grain toilet paper, I liked Sophia. Allie, of course, I loved. Puppy love. A longtime crush from my childhood that made me feel giddy and nervous at the same time.

"So you still a detective?" Sophia asked. "Or were you just posturing to get into Allie's pants?"

For being as tan as she was, Allie could still blush.

"I am," I said.

Allie coughed on a mouthful of pasta and turned from the table.

"I mean, I am a detective still," I stammered. "The pants thing—that's something else."

Allie turned back to us, her eyes bright. She shook her head at me, but was grinning, so I grinned back.

"You any good?" asked Sophia.

"Sure," I said. "But the job's been dreary lately. I've done a lot of bullshit cases and it's lost some of its charm."

"You mean you've failed and you're giving up?" she said. Blunt as a board.

"Have we met before?"

She shook her head and stuffed some pasta in her mouth.

"Well, actually, that is usually how I work," I admitted. "When things get hard or boring, I've been known to lose interest. But this is different."

"How?"

"Well this time it's..." I was about to say "hard," but I stopped myself in time and shrugged. "It's boring," I said.

"Go on," she insisted in the "don't cross me" tone my mother used to use on me.

"It got seedy," I said after a sip of wine. "It's not like in the movies. Mostly private detectives follow unfaithful wives and husbands. I had a rule not to take any more of those, but I did anyway and now I'm sick of the whole career. There are other crummy detective jobs too, like watching a stupid dog for a weekend, or tracking down old school friends for people who haven't figured out Facebook yet. And I don't get paid half the time."

"Boring isn't a bad reason to leave a job," Allie offered. "If you're not challenged, you should find something else."

"Vicky said you were quick-witted," Sophia said. "She showed me all the newspaper stuff about you and that case you busted open. And I read them all the way through, unlike Sergeant Ass."

"Hinds," corrected Allie.

Sophia and I both looked at her.

Allie blushed.

My heart fell a little bit. I sensed a rival.

"You said it was some kind of good thing for you to be called down here now?" Sophia said.

"I didn't mean any disrespect."

"Shut up," she said. "I don't believe in coincidence. You felt a need to come down here, and I felt a need to have you."

"You did?"

"I did," she said. "And I don't need no quitting detective. I need a real detective. A good detective. A smart detective. Victoria didn't die in her sleep. She didn't die in an accident. Someone killed her. The police have already written the case off. They've got to ticket litterers and keep a little thing like murder quiet lest some Michiganers go to Yellowstone instead of Arches."

I looked at Allie. She nodded.

"Danny told me," Allie said. "It's already under the carpet. There will be an obituary in the paper, but no mention of the crime at all. They're not doing anything."

"To tell you the truth, Allie," I said, "I had a WWMD moment when you called."

"I know some good pills for that," said Sophia.

"It stands for 'What Would Marlowe Do.' Marlowe, Phillip Marlowe, is a great fictional detective."

"Robert Mitchum played him in the movies," Sophia explained to Allie as way of identification.

"And what would he do?" Allie asked.

"He'd find out why you were worried," I said to her. "I could hear it in your voice."

Allie leaned back, appraising me, not wholly without appreciation.

"At first, I believed the police when they said it was a random break-in," said Allie. "There was a big group of bikers—gang bikers—in town that night. They all left the day after and can't be tracked. The police think it had to be one of them. A sad, random act, but all over now; nothing to see here."

"Why don't you believe that?"

"Because she listens to what I have to say more than acting detective sergeant Hindmost and the others," said Sophia. "Things don't add up. We need help and I knew if I got you down here, you'd have to repay the debt."

"What debt?"

"The debt of kinship," she said. "You owe it to your family—your own blood to help, so Vicky can rest easy. No murdered spirits ever rest easy unless their killer is found and brought to justice. I saw it in a movie." The fork in her hand and the tone of her voice told me she was deadly serious. "This is how you repay the debt."

"Okay. I'm on it," I said, not following the train but arriving at the station. "So, tell me what happened."

"After pie," Sophia said proudly.

She served us peach pie and ice cream.

"This is great," I said. "How'd you make it?"

"I opened the box, took out the pie, and put in the oven for as long as it suggested. The ice cream was nearly as hard. I needed to find a scoop."

"The red sauce?" I asked.

"From a jar," Sophia said.

"The pasta?"

"That's homemade."

"Really?" I brightened.

"Hell no," she said.

After dessert, we carried our plates into the kitchen and tidied up.

"You want some coffee?"

"Sure," I said.

"None for me," Sophia said and sat down on the couch. "But Allie might want some. Go make it Tony. You'll need to know your way around the kitchen. Hell if I'm going to cook for you all the time."

I searched the pantry for coffee supplies while the women whispered together in the living room. I figured this was a test to measure my detective skills, and they wanted to talk about me behind my back. Great detectives notice things like that. I rose to the challenge and like Colombo, I opened the cupboards and peered in with one eye. Like Sherlock Holmes I located the coffee maker on the counter, and like Hercule Poirot I measured the ingredients. I pushed the button like Jim Rockford and tidied up afterward like Adrian Monk.

In a drawer beside the spoons, I found the police report. It had been stuck in there like so many elastic bands, odd nails, and measuring tapes. The junk drawer. I read it while the coffeemaker burped. It was a summary of the police findings, and it didn't say much. There was a diagram of the "victim" where someone had indicated where the fatal wound had entered. The note read:

> Single wound, left side behind breast, under arm, puncture to the heart from possible
> ice pick, knitting needle, or some other spiked weapon.

Vicky's case was being run by amateurs. Unless the killer used military-grade titanium reinforced uranium enriched steel craft supplies, there was no way to get a knitting needle through a ribcage without a pneumatic hammer.

I joined the others and sat down in the easy chair. My appearance brought on an awkward silence.

"Coffee will be ready soon," I said.

"Good," they agreed.

I let a moment pass which gave Allie's blush time to clear.

I leaned forward and said, "So let's have it."

8

"IT WAS Monday night when I was in Price," Sophia said. "Vicky was alone in the house. Someone forced open the back door early in the morning and crept inside. Police speculate that she heard something, came downstairs and was clobbered. Then the burglar ran away and left town, and that's it."

Sophia spoke clearly and deliberately but there was a hitch in her voice when she mentioned Aunt Vicky that told me that she was holding back tears.

"I found her the next day. She lay right there in the hall at the bottom of the steps. There was blood everywhere from her left side, under her arm, behind her..." She stopped and closed her eyes. She'd been quoting the police report, trying to be precise, but it was too much. Allie offered her the nearest box of tissue this one on the end table. Aunt Vicky had always kept boxes of tissue on every flat surface.

I stared down the hallway where my aunt had died. I could make out a spot on the carpet just in front of the bathroom/laundry room that had been recently scrubbed. I'd walked right over it and not noticed. Even Watson would be ashamed of me.

The stairs turned ninety degrees at the bottom and blocked any vision into the first-floor hallway until you were in it. The stairs were steep. I'd slipped down them the first week I'd been here. I'd bloodied my nose and bled right on that very spot.

"Oh, don't feel bad about slipping down the stairs," Rick had said to me. "I fall down them at least once a week, sometimes on purpose."

And with that, he ran to the top of the stairs and threw himself down. He didn't bloody his nose. Instead, he'd opened a gash in his cheek that required a stitch. He laughed and said it was nothing. I felt sorry for him and ashamed I'd made a big deal of a bloody nose. Rick hadn't complained once and joked on the way to the clinic where all the nurses knew him by name.

"I bet you won't do that again," I said as we left.

"How much? I'll do it right now." He sprinted up the road toward the house.

"No," I yelled after him. I knew with grave certainty that he was on his way to throw himself headlong down the stairs again. "Let's play outside," I said.

"Okay."

And we did.

Aunt Vicky didn't even ask about the bandage when she came home that night, she just kissed it gently when she said good night to her son. I got a kiss too.

"Give me one of those tissues," I said to Allie. "I got a coffee ground in my eye."

"That can happen," said Sophia.

I steered the conversation away from blood on the floor.

"Why were you in Price?" I asked.

"I go once every other week," she said. "I'm a better driver than Vicky, and I'd go up there and do some shopping. I stay overnight if I'm tired, which I usually am, and drive home the next day."

"Twice a month?" I said. "So it was just blind luck the burglar came when you weren't here."

"No," said Sophia. "I don't think so."

The coffee maker beeped with the promise of a caffeine-fueled sleep-deprived night, like I needed more to keep me awake. I ignored it and waited for Sophia to go on.

"It happened before," said Allie. "The last time Sophia went to Price, someone broke into the house then too."

Sophia nodded. "When I got back that first time, Vicky asked me if I'd gone in the backyard the day before. I hadn't. She said she'd swept up sand from the back garden that morning and asked me to be more careful wiping my feet when I came inside. But I hadn't been out. And I knew better than to track dirt in the house."

"So what did you do?"

"Nothing. We shared a cross word and then forgot about it. We finally figured the wind blew it through the cracks. It was no matter. Nothing was stolen. Nothing was broken. Nothing weird except sand on the floor."

"Vicky didn't hear anything?"

"She didn't say she had."

"Was there sand Monday?" I asked.

"Yes," said Allie. "It looked like the burglar stole in through the back door and then came into the living room here. He knocked over a vase, breaking it. That must have woken up Aunt Vicky. The cops think he hid in the bathroom and was cornered there."

"He broke a vase?"

"The mate to the one by the door." Sophia pointed to a majestic red clay hand-thrown pot decorated with glazed petroglyphs. I hadn't seen it when I came in. I felt like I should hand in my detective license. The pot was common, and I remembered seeing one in every house in Moab. This one was bigger than most. It stood knee-high on the floor and sprouted dried sunflowers. There was an empty space on the other side of the door. I nodded and pretended I'd noticed the missing mate all along.

"He knocked it over?"

"More likely he dropped it," said Allie. "It broke on the coffee table."

Sophia pointed to a dent in the wood concealed under a doily. What is it with doilies? I leaned over and touched the spot. I knocked on the wood. It made a loud thud that carried through the house like a drum. The house was small, and the wood seasoned and melodic.

"That would wake somebody up alright," I said. "Did they find a weapon?"

"No."

"Neighbors didn't hear anything?"

"Nothing," said Sophia.

"And nothing was taken? Was anything else broken?"

"Just the door," said Sophia, pointing.

I stood up and went to the back door. I switched on the porch light, and it didn't come on.

"Your light is burned out," I said.

"Vicky just changed it."

I stepped outside and removed the glass cover. A half twist later the light was on.

"Was the dead bolt set?"

"It usually was, but the police said it hadn't been that night."

The back door had a nice thick dead bolt over a keyed doorknob. Though the house was sturdy, the doorframe looked weak. I doubted it would have withstood a solid kick even with the deadbolt. There was no sign of the lock having been picked, but I did see some scratches around the doorknob. I pulled the door shut and using a credit card I opened the door easily. It had been harder in the old days when it took Rick and me three tries to open it with the butter knife we hid under the back porch.

I came back inside.

"Fingerprints?"

"They didn't look," said Sophia in disgust.

I knew the way of cops. The CSI team didn't spring into action unless there was a camera on them, if there's a CSI team at all.

"Anything else?"

"I think I heard someone sneaking around the house," said Sophia. "I thought I heard someone a couple of times last month. But then it stopped."

"Is there anything valuable here? Are those vases valuable?"

"Hell no," said Sophia. "Vicky was as poor as a church mouse. She couldn't pay the taxes on what she had. After Thick died, she took in boarders to keep food on the table. If there was anything of value, she sold it long ago."

"No," corrected Allie. "She wouldn't sell her land. That's all she had left from her family. She said it would stay in the family as long as she breathed."

"Is there a mortgage on the house?" I asked.

"Several," said Sophia. "I think she owes more than it's worth."

"I loaned her money sometimes," said Allie. "And I know the guy who makes those vases. They were a gift. He sells them at the Duncan gallery for fifty apiece. They're practically mass-produced in his barn."

"What else wouldn't the police hear?"

"That she'd been acting suspicious lately," said Sophia. "She went to town and met people and kept the whole thing secret. She said it was a surprise. She said it would be a surprise I'd probably never see."

"I'm going to look like the complete shit I am," I said, "but how old was Aunt Vicky?"

"You mean you're a shit for not knowing this yourself?" said Sophia.

I nodded.

"Her birthday was a week after mine and I'm seventy-two."

"Was she well?"

"Her eyes were worse than mine, but once she got well, she could move better than I could."

"Got well?"

"After Thick died, she fell to pieces," said Sophia. "She had financial problems, and her health, which was already failing, got worse. I got back in touch on a whim when my husband finally died. I took one look at her, came right down here, emptied the house of strangers and nursed her back to life with bacon and tea. She turned around in a couple of weeks, all the color coming back, or in her case, leaving. She looked like a lemon when I got here."

"Okay, another stupid question," I said, carefully choosing my words so as not to upset anyone. "Exactly who the hell are you?" I said to Sophia.

She smiled. "I'm Sophia Curtis. I was born in a house not half a mile from this one. I went to school with Vicky. We were best friends. Then I went off to college and she married Thick's father, Lance."

"So why are you here now?" My tact and subtlety were a work of art.

"We kept in touch a little bit. For fifty years we exchanged Christmas cards and crisis letters. Like when Lance left, Merrill got cancer, and when Thick died. We'd always talked about getting back together but didn't until last year. Merrill died a few months after Thick, and Vicky was taking in boarders to make ends meet. I can pay rent as well as a stranger. We figured to spend our last days together here."

"Allie?" I said, turning my charm to my old school mate, "what's your role in all this?"

"It's a small town," she said. "I liked Vicky. When I was flat on my back last fall, she let me stay here for free while I rented out my ranch to a film crew. We grew close."

"Are you and Danny dating?"

Okay, I wasn't sure what this had to do with my nascent investigation or even how the words managed to escape my mouth, but once they had, all I could was put on an earnest investigatory face and wait for a reply.

"What?" she said, as shocked as I was.

"You heard the question," I said, doubling down with my earnest face.

"No. We did for a while. Small town. I dumped him."

"Allie hasn't had a lot of luck with men," Sophia said. "I think she should stop trying."

"Danny still thinks he can patch things up between us," Allie said. "I don't think he accepts that I'm not interested. I don't think his mind can register when he's unpopular."

Sounded like the Danny Hinds I knew.

"Okay," I said. "I'm beginning to get a feel for the situation."

"Uh-huh," said Sophia.

"The cops think a tourist did this?"

"Bikers, they said."

"Bikers? Like a gang? Were there any here two weeks ago when the first break-in supposedly happened?"

"Supposedly?" spat Sophia. "Are you saying you don't believe me?"

"No, the bikers weren't in town," said Allie, always the peacemaker.

"Sand in the house is not great proof in Moab. There's lots of sand in Moab. Hills of it. Streets of it. Gardens of it. Nostrils and undershorts full of it."

"Not in this house," said Sophia.

"When did Rick die?"

"Last year," said Allie. "Thick was out of the Army and had a janitorial job in Atlanta. There was an accident."

"What did he do in the Army?"

"Base maintenance technician," said Sophia.

"He was a janitor," said Allie.

"He got decorated while in Iraq."

"For what?"

"Three purple hearts," said Sophia.

"As a janitor?"

"In the Green Zone."

"Nothing suspicious about his death in Atlanta?"

"Vicky said he had a bad fall, and it was an accident. There was a small insurance payout from the company he worked for, but it didn't last long. She really depended on the money Thick sent home."

"So she took in boarders after Rick died?"

"Before," said Sophia. "Thick had a hard time keeping jobs. The money he sent home was sporadic."

"The boarders were tourists mostly," said Allie. "Weekenders. She couldn't charge much since everyone had to share a bathroom, but she opened up three rooms, made pancakes and coffee each morning and fed herself with the extra."

"Can I get a list of the tourists who stayed here?"

"I'll check the databanks," said Sophia. She put a finger to her temple and pinched her eyes tight. "Nope, they've been wiped."

"A guest book?"

She shook her head.

"I stayed for nearly three weeks. Roy Stirps stayed a long time. He was the last to go. He might remember some of them."

"Who's Roy Stirps?"

"He's a park ranger and a local historian. He's pretty bright."

"Nice guy?" I said instead of "are you dating him?"

"He's alright."

"Single?" I said through my crumbling detective mask.

"Allie's not dating anyone, Tony," said Sophia. "Are you?"

"That's neither here nor there," I said, caught in the act. "But for the record, I'm currently unattached."

"There, then you two can go on a date. See a movie. I'll come if you need a chaperone. Can we get back to Vicky now?"

"I wasn't—" I stammered.

"We weren't—" began Allie.

"Vicky!" said Sophia.

"Yes, uhm," I said. "Was the back door all carved up the first time you thought you heard anyone, or is that new?"

"All new. Just the sand in the house before. I didn't notice any alien footprints or DNA."

"Heat signature scans? Bioplasma readings?" I asked.

"Inconclusive," said Sophia.

I was falling in love with two women.

"The police don't want to make a big deal of this because this town is driven by tourists, and death, accidental or otherwise, doesn't exactly fill the Ramada. So they've kept it out of the news."

"Are they really not investigating it?"

"Danny said no," said Allie. "There's nowhere to look. No clues. If something comes up, they'll check it out, he said, but they don't have a trail to follow."

"Or anyone to look for one. Who's in charge of the case," I said. "Tell me it's not Danny?"

"It's Danny," Allie said. "Acting Detective while the real one, who isn't much better, is working his off-season job in Farmington."

"What does he do there?"

"Short order cook."

"Times are hard," said Sophia.

"It's the off-season. The city lays off half the cops in the fall. No need for them. Only locals after Labor Day. Some latecomers in through Halloween, but it's dead here until Spring," Allie blushed again. "Sorry, poor choice of words."

"Halloween is next week," I said. "Why the early exodus?"

"Poor revenues this season. Bad economy. Fewer tourists. Lower budgets."

"Police chief?"

"Left the day before the murder."

"Who's in charge then? Tell me it's not Danny."

"No, Lieutenant Levis is in charge," said Allie.

"Any relation to Ronald and Rosalyn-Janet Levis?" I asked.

"Cousins," said Allie. "Do you know them?"

"Ah fuck," I said. "Is Lt. Levis a nice guy? Level-headed?"

"Not really," said Allie.

"He wants to know if you dated him," Sophia said.

"Actually, not this time," I said. "It's something else. But did you?"

"No. He's married."

"So what now Sherlock?" said Sophia.

"She was making a surprise for you, acting suspiciously, and now we find out there's a will."

"Everyone has a will," said Sophia.

"What do we know about Archie Rumbold, the lawyer?"

"New in town. Only been here about ten years," said Allie. "I don't know him well."

"Ten years is new?"

"Small town."

"You thinking the will is what got Vicky killed?" said Sophia.

"According to Agatha Christie, it's the number one cause of death among old people who drink tea."

"That's true," said Sophia. "I saw it in a movie."

"That's enough for today," I said. "Tomorrow I'd like to go through her papers, bills, letters, scrapbooks, internet history, computer files and such."

"No computer here," she said.

It shouldn't have surprised me that Aunt Vicky didn't have one, but it did. If there is a clearer sign of generational difference than not possessing a computer, I couldn't think of it. I'd been plugged in since high school. My son was practically a 'Neuromancer,' born with an input jack at the base of the skull.

"Is there a phone?"

"The house was built in the 1950s, not the 1850s. It was remodeled in the '70s to connect to city water and sewer. You can flush and everything. New stove sometime in the '90s by the looks of it. The fridge might even be from this century," said Sophia.

"It's a great house," I said. "I should be able to flip it in a week."

Sophia glared at me. She hadn't totally thrown off the belief that I was a no-account carpet-bag relative come to pick the bones.

"Real estate isn't what it used to be," said Allie. "And there're the mortgages."

"Yeah right."

"Yeah right," repeated Sophia.

"I should go," said Allie. "It's getting late. I have to feed the animals."

I walked Allie to the door and waved goodbye like a tongue-tied schoolboy. I should have at least gone for a handshake.

"Lock the door," called Sophia from the hallway. "Lock them all tight."

I did.

I cleaned up the coffee and set the kitchen back as I remembered Vicky liking it.

When I went upstairs a few minutes later, I heard Sophia crying softly in Vicky's bedroom. I tiptoed to my own room and quietly pulled the door shut. I sat a while on the bed in the dark, listening to the quiet sobs from a woman I'd only just met. Her crying broke my heart nonetheless.

9

THE NEXT MORNING, Sophia was up when I came downstairs. She gave me a disapproving look and glanced at the clock. It said ten-fifteen.

"Breakfast ready?" I asked.

"Three hours ago."

I found a pot of cold coffee, but I knew I'd need to go shopping soon if I was to survive. There wasn't a single Hot Pocket or frozen pizza in the place. I made toast and read *The Moab Picayune*, a weekly newspaper serving the entire county. It was twelve pages in total, including classifieds.

After breakfast Sophia took me upstairs to go through Vicky's papers. She led me to the room beside the master's which used to be the sewing room and I'd assumed was now Sophia's. Inside was a vintage sewing machine, a table strewn with dried flowers and fabric swatches, a roll-top desk, an antique oak chair carted across the plains in the back of a buckboard, and a gray steel file cabinet. The room was dusty except for the roll-top which had a stack of recently handled papers.

"I'll leave you to it," Sophia said and left.

I sat down at the desk and pulled out my detective notebook. It was really just a school notebook, but that doesn't sound as cool. I turned to a new page when I saw the words "ramen" and "Precious," both of which brought up painful memories.

The paper tower was nearly a foot high and chronologically arranged, the older at the bottom like layers of sediment. These were papers waiting to be filed. There were the usual power bills, phone bills, sewer bills and such —marked "paid" with a check number in Aunt Vicky's elegant, rounded handwriting.

I kept the order and dug through the pile moving backward in time like an archaeologist. I found a form letter from a real estate agent seeking to represent her if she wanted to sell her house. There was a letter from a Hopi Indian calling himself "Tiponi" demanding that Vicky's land be returned to "The Nation." Tiponi's return address was a Pack & Ship franchise in town.

I found three identical business cards for Archie Rumbold, Attorney at Law, specializing in "Property Claims and Land Rights." Each had a date and time written on the back. The first was just after Rick's death, the last just over a week ago.

There was a receipt from the County Recorder stating that all taxes on her parcel and home were up to date.

A letter from a Mr. T. S. Crew, of Crew Development, offered to buy her land parcel and requested an immediate appointment to make a "generous" offer. It referenced the taxes owed on the property and a "win-win scenario" for everyone.

Before that, the bank wrote to tell Vicky that foreclosure proceedings had been terminated and she was up to date on her mortgage payments.

An engraved card invited Vicky and a guest to a wine tasting at Ashe Winery to celebrate their new Phoenix Wine Label. Locals only. The invitation was bent and stained, suggesting it had been used.

Moving farther back in time, I found a third and final notice of imminent foreclosure on the house if the payments weren't brought current immediately. "We appreciate your payment, but you are not making progress toward the note as a whole. You remain consistently one year behind and Green River Savings and Loan must foreclose if the situation is not remedied immediately. Have a nice day." It was signed 'Owen Weaks.'

"Cash for Houses" made a personal appeal to "Mr. Victor Racine" to save him from impending foreclosure. I'd seen the scam in Salt Lake. Volvo driving leeches take your house and your equity and you become a renter until they can flip it. It was the real estate cousin to payday loan stores and back-alley tire-iron muggings.

There were more letters about foreclosure and tax notices for both the house and one hundred acres listed only by a parcel number.

I found more letters from T. S. Crew wanting to talk about buying the parcel.

Bank notices listed the mortgage and amount due to bring it current: over $13,000. Each was marked in Vicky's hand, "paid $1,058." This was the normal mortgage payment required but did nothing for the year or so that she was behind.

There was an expired page of pizza coupons with one clipped out and a free tire rotation with any brake job at Sam's Garage. Sam's Garage was a landmark in Moab, specializing in flat tires and broken axles since 1941. They repaired them too.

A federal tax notice stated that Vicky was years behind on property taxes and the parcel would be subject to seizure and auction to pay back taxes if not remedied.

The deeper I went, the bleaker the papers became. But I'd read the ending first and knew it all worked out in the end. Well, except for the murder.

I turned to the filing cabinet. More bills, better organized.

One drawer was personal. There was a file called "Thick's Letters" which contained missives my cousin had sent his mother over the years. There were some from Atlanta, some from Iraq, some from Texas, some from Denver, and some from summer camp when he was eight. It wasn't a big file, but I bet it was complete.

There was a folder containing miscellaneous documents about Rick. There was a letter of condolences from an Atlanta janitorial company after "Thick's tragic accident." The army had sent three letters of condolence about Specialist Rick Racine's injuries and congratulations for his Purple Hearts. Rick's letter of acceptance to Southern Utah State College was still in its original envelope. I found report cards for his entire school career from high school back to kindergarten, with a few notable absences. He maintained a solid low C average because he had hours of extra credit helping the janitor.

I caught my breath at a collection of letters from my mother. I left them alone. I didn't have the emotional strength to delve into those just yet.

A suspicious file marked "Sophia" was empty but dog-eared.

Vicky had a pre-paid funeral insurance policy. It wasn't much, and she'd had it for twenty years. It was for two people; her and her husband Lance I assumed. It included public funeral service, internment and a headstone.

My name was on a file containing newspaper clippings, good and bad, about miscreant Tony Flaner. Every Christmas card Nancy had sent while we were married was accounted for in that file. I didn't even remember signing them. Vicky had kept the single report card I got while staying with her. I'd done surprising well that quarter. The unsatisfactory citizenship grade I received in gym was due to Danny Hinds.

The rest of the space was devoted to craft supplies. There was a deep drawer of sewing patterns. Most had never been opened and some were older than me.

I took notes of names and dates and of course the land parcel number, but I left the sewing patterns and my mother's letters for another time.

Aunt Vicky kept sentimental papers, but except for the missing letters from Sophia which I figured had disappeared that morning, there was one other blatant omission. Where were the letters from Lance, her husband?

Lance had left the family for South America the year before I visited. He'd never returned and had since been declared dead. Rick talked about his father all the time. He adored him. Vicky didn't speak much about him and would steer the conversation away from his father if she could hear it, to keep me from getting homesick, she said. In private, Rick would weave yarns about his father finding the "Lost Inca Dungeon of Sapphires." He'd brag about how manly his father was, how he fought in the war and taught him to shoot and gave him his first gun and took him fishing and climbing and camping. He showed me the gun, a .22 rifle his mother kept locked in a closet.

"I once used it to scare away a robber," he boasted.

Rick had shown me pictures of his father. Lance was big like Rick, tall and muscular. They stood together on a dock holding up a five-pound trout. Lance beaming in pride, Rick flipping off the camera but looking every bit as proud. But there was no trace of him in Vicky's files.

I brainstormed a few notes. The threatening tone of the Indian and the insistent tone from the developer gave me my first suspects.

The earlier break-in was very suspicious. No marks of forced entry had been left that time. Why then the second? Why carry a big junk vase from the front door to the living room? Did it slip? Did it contain Sapphire's from Lance's Incan dungeon? The sand was the only giveaway for the first break-in, and any normal Moabite would have ignored it. Only the fastidious habits of two spinsters would have noticed it in this desert. Two separate burglars? Mistaken witnesses? Vicky and Sophia were old but nothing in Sophia's demeanor suggested she was diminished mentally in any respect. Two break-ins. Why?

It was thin. There wasn't enough to interest the police, but police don't like cases they don't have a good chance to solve. In a town like Moab, which is so vulnerable to bad publicity damaging its tourist trade, there'd be even less motivation to go digging. What if they found something for heaven's sake? Why prolong a grisly crime into another news cycle?

That pissed me off. Even if it wasn't my blood relation, I'd be righteously indignant about this. Someone had been killed and the police weren't doing anything about it. If it was a biker from out of town, that didn't excuse it. Someone needed to pay for this. It was only right. Vicky was a nice person.

I thought about Danny and the see-no-evil tourist bureau ignoring this and my face burned red. I turned the page in my book and composed a spoon that would stir the pot.

When I came down, Sophia was in the backyard dead-heading roses. I could see she'd been crying. I decided to pretend not to notice.

"Have you been crying?" I said instantly.

"Old people are allowed to cry."

My mouth and brain are only neighbors. Sometimes they communicate, but mostly they keep the blinds drawn. I rocked on my heels and studied the bushes.

"Did you find anything useful?" she said.

"Maybe. Do you know anything about a parcel of land Aunt Vicky owned?"

"The last of the ranch," she said. "Used to be a potash mine."

"She still had that? Why didn't she sell it?"

"It was the last of the ranch," she repeated and sniffed.

I had more questions, but another time would be better.

"I'm going to go into town for some Pop-Tarts. You want anything?"

She shook her head.

I grabbed my suit and headed to town.

It was the off-season. Yesterday's tourist flight was the last bustling this place would see until next year. I felt like *Omega Man* driving down Main Street. I pulled into a dry cleaner drive-up and waited for Mathias and the family to jump me. The sun was up but behind a cloud. A perky brunette appeared instead. No sunglasses.

"Can you do a rush on this suit?" I asked. "I don't think I need it cleaned, just dusted and pressed."

She took the suit and smelled it.

"You should clean it."

"I need it by tomorrow. Can you do it?"

"We're not open on Sunday," she said.

"How about later today then?"

"Cost you extra," she said. "You want me to do anything about this gravy stain?"

"Yeah, do your best."

"And this mustard here? You want me to try and clean that too?"

"No, I like the mustard stain," I said.

She nodded.

"On second thought. Yeah, try and clean the mustard too."

She gave me a ticket and told me to come back at six.

It took me a while to find the newspaper office. It was a small building off retail Main Street but within walking distance to the town hall and courthouse. A stenciled sign on the door was all there was to indicate its existence. A felt sign with plastic letters listed operating hours behind a glass window. They were closed weekends. I knocked anyway, seeing a car in the editor's parking space.

No answer. I knocked harder. Then I pounded. Then I went around the building and found a back door and knocked and pounded on it. I was about to go for a rock when the door opened.

"Stop the damn pounding already. We're closed." The man before me was most likely in his fifties. He had an ample waist like me, but I had more hair. He spoke without taking the cigarette out of his mouth and it bobbed up and down with his bushy eyebrows.

"I want to place an ad," I said.

He brightened immediately.

"We're now open," he said. "I'm Clem Tucker, owner and editor of *The Moab Picayune*."

"I'm Tony Flaner, about to be very unpopular in Moab."

The building smelled of chemicals and cigarettes. The back room contained a computerized high-tech printing press, rolls of paper, and shelves of ink.

"My office is just over here." Clem led the way.

Clem's office was a miasma of cigarette smoke. A pie tin sat on the desk next to a computer and served as an overflowing ashtray. The side of the computer monitor was stained amber from smoke.

"Why are you going to be unpopular?" he asked, flopping down in a thick leather chair. The rush of air sent the pie tin ashes whirling around like a menthol-flavored genie.

"Do you know Victoria Racine?"

"Yep, just typeset the obituary today. Shame it didn't get in in time for the funeral."

"Does the obit say she was murdered?"

"Nope," he said, showing no surprise at the word.

"Did you run a story about the murder?"

"Nope."

"Why?"

"City asked me not to. Might interfere with the investigation, they said."

"And you bought that?"

"Nope."

"But you did it anyway?"

"If I had a dollar for every tourist scaring story I didn't run, I'd be rich. *The Moab Picayune* is a good-news newspaper, tourist stuff, and local happiness. Nothing scary unless it absolutely can't be avoided."

"And this was avoidable?"

"Meth-head biker breaks into a house and kills an old lady by mistake. Making the locals scared of the tourists is worse than the other way around. I'm a businessman."

"Then I'd like to take out an ad. And pay you to run it."

His eyebrows and cigarette bobbed up. Ash fell into his keyboard, not for the first time.

"Let me see it."

I handed him a piece of paper at the top of which was a crudely drawn spoon. I had to read part of it to him. My handwriting sucks.

Clem stared at me skeptically. He lit another cigarette from the tip of the last one.

"You'll get lots of ink from this," I said. "Reaction, follow-up, stranger run out of town stuff. It'll sell some papers here in the off-season."

I understood. "Off-season" is a dirty word in tourist communities, like salmonella at a buffet—inevitable but despised.

He puffed and thought. I fought back an urge to cough up my lungs, lower intestines and ankles. My eyes burned from the smoke, but I kept my steely gaze on the newspaperman as tears ran down my cheeks.

"Even if you're not a journalist," I said, really needing to blink. "You're still a businessman. Take my money."

He took a check, and I shook his hand. I showed myself out and fell to my knees gasping for air once I had passed beyond the door.

10

TOURIST TOWNS HIBERNATE during the off-season, but they're not above venturing out for an easy kill. My dry-cleaning bill was slightly less than a semester at Yale. Luckily, my plastic had room. I'd just have to buy that yacht next month.

I spent the rest of the day familiarizing myself again with Moab. It had changed a lot since Rick and I rode bikes down the red dirt roads or walked to school in the frost, but not as much as it might have. The tourist areas were built up and new. I could get a double, no-foam, decaf eggnog latte from no fewer than six main street vendors within shouting distance of each other. There were some new condos and houses that were obviously time-shares watched over by a myriad of property management firms with local twenty-four-hour hotlines. Still, the older part of the town, where the locals lived and grew up, where their ancestors had huddled together before the jeeps, bikes, and runners invaded the red rocks, were mostly unchanged. Some of the great cottonwood trees I remembered had died. Others had grown to princely heights from which to shed leaves like avalanches in the fall and seeds like fog in the summer.

It had been over a quarter century. Most of the scenes of those days I'd forgotten. Maybe it's a guy thing or an age thing or a cerebrally challenged thing, but that time had become more feeling than image for me. Seeing the old places, changed as they were, brought back forgotten times like a spilled filing cabinet: "Scout's Incredible Journey," an essay by Tony Flaner for Mrs. Shaw 5th period English. I got an A on that one.

There was one summer day in August that Rick and I snuck into the movies. We waited until a show was over and people used the parking lot exit. As casually as we could, we bolted through the door and ducked into the seats.

"Get down," Rick said. "The usher."

I was in the second row, Rick in the third. We both dropped to our bellies on the floor.

The theater was raked downward and a week's worth of spilled soda, popcorn shells, milk duds and ice cream twists coated the floor like a roach trap.

"Thick, get up off that sticky damn floor and show some sense," said an usher in the aisle.

I heard Rick get up. It sounded like Velcro ripping as the floor reluctantly released him.

Scared out of my adolescent mind, I held still.

"Your feet were sticking right out in the aisle," said the usher.

"Really?"

"Really, Thick. Don't go looking for trouble. You ain't smart enough for it."

"Yeah, okay," he said, brushing off the insult and candy debris. "Can I use the bathroom to wash my hands?"

"Sure, okay." The usher escorted Rick out through the lobby.

I lay there alone and stuck to the floor for ten minutes until the lights went out and the previews started. I carefully got up. My shirt ripped open where it had been glued to the floor with a Sprite and bubblegum cement NASA should investigate for its heat tiles. I'd made the mistake of putting my cheek against the floor and now carefully removed popcorn shards and M&M's from my face.

I sat down and glanced over my shoulder. There were maybe six people in the theater. It was a weekday matinee.

When the MPAA rating appeared on the screen, I walked out the door to the parking lot.

"What are you doing here?" said Rick running to me. He'd been sitting against the wall outside the door. "Is the movie over already? Did you get caught?"

"No, I didn't get caught." I wanted to tell him how rude I thought the usher was for insulting him.

"Yeah, did you see how I pulled the usher away from you?"

"You did?"

"Hell yeah. No need for both of us to miss the movie. Why'd you leave? I'da waited for you."

And he would have. Bored and without complaint, alone in a hundred-degree desert parking lot, soda syrup sticking his fingers together, Rick would have waited so I could see a movie.

I can't believe I ever let that moment leave my mind.

"It was probably a dumb movie," I said. "I'd rather play with you."

"Okay. Cool," he said. "You have a Twizzler on your neck."

The theater is still there. The parking lot where Rick waited for me is still there. I hope the usher is still there being outsmarted by kids like Thick Rick. But most of all, I hope someone has cleaned that floor. Seriously, it was disgusting.

———

It was after nine at night when I returned to the house with a clean suit, a new familiarity of the city, Pop-Tarts and a bucket of chicken.

"Do anything useful today?" Sophia asked, helping herself to some of Kentucky's finest. She pulled the skin off. This woman had a discipline I could only admire.

"Can I have that?" I asked.

"If you want a heart attack."

"Works for me." I gulped down the Colonel's secret spices, fat, and infused fryer grease like the heaven it was.

"Yeah, I was productive," I said and left it at that.

"Funeral's at ten tomorrow morning," Sophia told me. "I'll be getting you up at eight. Turn off the lights when you come up. I've already locked the doors."

After "dinner" I blinked through TV channels from the sofa. Directly above me was the master bedroom. Vicky's room. I heard the door close and Sophia's footsteps. Sound carried in the house, so as soon as it was quiet upstairs, I turned off the TV. There was nothing on but mind-crushing reality shows anyway. Five minutes in front of one of those, and I could feel my head melt like a Nazi with a Lost Ark. I checked the locks, turned off the lights as directed, and went to bed.

The next morning, I freed my newly laundered suit out of its hermetically sealed, child-suffocating plastic shell. The mustard was mostly gone. Mostly. I don't think they even bothered with the gravy stain. It looked like an acorn cufflink halfway up my arm. If I kept my arm straight at my side, I could hide it. And if I could find a carnation, I could hide the mustard stain on the lapel. The carnation would be on the wrong side and three inches too low, but it would work. Nobody would be looking at me anyway.

The shirt had more starch in it than a potato bar. It felt like corrugated cardboard. I was afraid to bend my arms for fear of breaking it. I wanted a hammer to thread the buttons through the buttonholes. The shirt was bright and clean and might stop a bullet. A little hot water at the elbows and I could shape the sleeves into a more natural pose.

Sophia wore a hat with a black veil and a thick brown cloth coat that went to her knees. I escorted her to my car after coffee and strawberry toaster pastries. She didn't eat much.

The funeral was at a Shady Grove Mortuary. The cemetery was right behind it.

I picked up the funeral brochure. I'd been meaning to ask who'd put the funeral arrangements together but figured it out pretty quick. After a selection of "appropriate hymns," a "usual benediction" would follow. Thereafter there'd be time for "family speaker number 1," then "family speaker number 2—a close friend or colleague" and a "possible video montage" with "appropriate music." It promised to wrap up with a "denominationally specific prayer" and then "instructions and announcements."

It was a pauper's funeral.

The cover said: "Victoria Racine, beloved mother and friend," but that was as personal as it got. There were folks in the seats, but it wasn't overflowing. You'd think that all the locals would have come. Vicky had lived here her entire life.

Sophia took a front seat, and I sought out Allie. I found her talking to a hunched skeleton in a black suit behind a wreath.

"Seriously? This is the best you could do?" she said.

"We weren't supplied with any information," the skeleton said in a low, slow whisper. "It'll be fine. I'll knock ten percent off the printing costs."

"Hey Bones," I said, stepping up. "Are you in charge?"

He looked at me suspiciously. "Yes, I'm the director."

"What's with this lawsuit-inducing program here?"

"I was given limited information and a more limited budget."

"Vicky had a small funeral insurance policy," said Allie.

"Prices have gone up," explained the specter.

"The policy was purchased from your company and guarantees a decent burial."

"There's nothing indecent going on."

"I'd like to ask a jury about that and show them your little homage here. I figure six figures easy."

His eyes widened a little and shifted from me to Allie and back again.

"Alright, I'll deduct the cost of the printing and apply it to what is owed on the plot."

"If I see a bill—any message from you but a condolence card, I'll take it to my brother-in-law Tyler Bodin, Senior Analyst, Utah Insurance Fraud Division. I'll show him my aunt's policy, your bill and this little insult." I waved the pamphlet. "He'll see if your licenses are in order and if a class action lawsuit hasn't already been started."

His eyes narrowed.

"I understand," he said. "I still have some things to see to."

"See to them," I said. "I'll send someone by tomorrow with the text for the stone: I'm thinking single monument, morning rose granite, twenty-four inches, thirty-inch base, deep letters and double polish. Include a flower vase. That'd be nice."

I used to carve tombstones and knew what they cost. My request wouldn't be cheap. It was not at all covered by Vicky's burial policy. But if he came through with the marker, I'd not come back later with Buffy for revenge.

He smiled with his bloodless lips but not his eyes and retreated behind a curtain.

"It's okay," I said. "At least all her friends are here."

"Those aren't her friends," Allie said. "They want to meet you. She had no friends."

"Why?"

"She was a hermit. After Lance left, she was sullen. Then she became a shut-in. It's a small town, and rumors fly. It's a conservative and suspicious place, so she just kept to herself."

"Rumors?" I said. "What rumors?"

"Later," she said. "Will you speak?"

"Am I family speaker number one or two?"

"Both. You're the only family here."

"Okay."

"Do you really have a brother-in-law with the Insurance Fraud Division?"

"There really is an Insurance Fraud Division? That was lucky."

She smiled.

"Did you say these people want to talk to me?"

"I think so. Everyone's asking about you."

"Who are they? What do they want?"

"Later," she said. "Say something nice about Vicky."

An appropriate hymn came over the PA, and I sat down next to Sophia and Allie in the front row.

I've done stand-up on a semi-professional level for years. Semi-professional means "rank amateur nobody," but it looks better on a business card. I knew how to work a crowd, but as I sat down and frantically tried to pull together a routine, I realized how little material I had to work with. I didn't know Aunt Vicky. I hadn't spoken to her in decades. I didn't know of any rumors. I didn't know what she'd been like in the last quarter century. I was a lousy nephew.

"You're on, Tony." Allie elbowed me in the ribs.

"And don't fuck it up," whispered Sophia.

I took the podium and looked over the crowd. There were a dozen people there. I recognized only three—Allie, Sophia, and Danny Hinds. There was a sunburned blonde, his long hair braided down his back. In the middle sat a pair of twins wearing dazzling Italian suits that made me remember I'd forgotten the mustard stain carnation. There were several young professionals huddled together who seemed sorely out of place. There was a cluster of police around Danny, and with a fright, I thought I was looking at a younger Ronald Levis wearing a gun belt.

I then noticed Clem Tucker from *The Moab Picayune* stealthily keeping to the back and taking pictures with a wallet-size digital camera. A young fellow in a green ranger outfit I pegged for Roy Strips, the boarder Allie had told me about, looked genuinely sad, which was more than I could say about a big fellow in a polo shirt who sat straddling two chairs with his arms wide like he was hogging a bus seat. His crew cut didn't cover up the fact that he'd been wearing a hat recently, a hat which hadn't done much to shade him. His face was tan as the gravy stain on my sleeve.

Remembering that, I dropped my arm straight to my side.

"Hello everyone, I'm Tony Flaner. How are you doing tonight?"

It was my usual stand-up opening. It usually played better. Like at night.

"I mean morning," I said.

Tough audience.

"Victoria Racine, Aunt Vicky to me, was a great woman," I began. "She took me in when times were hard and taught me the meaning of ovine and diurnal. I didn't know those words before Vicky taught them to me. Ovine means having to do with sheep and diurnal means every other day. Or was it twice a day? I'll have to look it up."

Blank stares.

"Aunt Vicky began her career as a mother shortly after she gave birth to her only child, Rick Racine. You all knew him as Thick because none of you thought he was smart, and he wasn't, but he was a good kid, a fine friend and stellar cousin, traits he learned from his doting mother Vicky."

Polite stares.

"Vicky didn't have it easy. When her husband Lance was lost searching for sapphires in central America, she had to go it alone." Several faces rolled their eyes at this, and it threw me.

"She raised her son as best as she could and loved him, even when he lit the shed on fire with a homemade flamethrower. Hairspray companies have since altered some of their products thanks to Vicky Racine's letter-writing campaign. She nursed me back to health after Thanksgiving and never chided me about eating that third pie even when it was running down my chin into the toilet. She took me in and treated me like her own son and loved me. We were family, and though we fell out of touch, that love, and the connection, endures."

I turned to leave the lectern and noticed Sophia's nod of approval when an urge returned me to the microphone.

"And no one fucks with my family and gets away with it," I said.

The hall fell to funeral silence; shocked faces stared up at me. They were outraged at the threat, or the bad word, or my mustard stain—I didn't know, but they were shocked, nonetheless.

"Remember to tip your waitress," I said and sat down.

Tough crowd.

11

"APPROPRIATE MUSIC" played and Skeletor made a heart-felt denominationally ambiguous prayer, I think from The Egyptian Book of the Dead, The Bhagavad Gita or The English Patient. I'm not a hundred percent sure. It was nice enough. Allie announced that she would be hosting a small reception at her house after the services. There were no pallbearers listed, but people answered the call to carry the casket a few yards out the back of the building to where a hole in the red earth had been dug by a tidy backhoe.

The casket was placed on the straps crossing over the grave where it hung like truth suspended over the yawning abyss. After a short inspiration reading from Twilight I think, people walked away. Soon it was just Sophia and me by the grave. Allie apologized that she had to go home to get things ready. She didn't expect anyone other than Sophia and I would come, but still, she wanted to make it nice.

Beside the hole, half covered under a green AstroTurf carpet, I found a flat headstone for "Thick Rick Racine, Beloved Son and Soldier."

Sophia had held up well during the service, but it hadn't exactly been a moving eulogy. Now, however, sitting on a folding metal chair under a tarp canopy staring at the casket over the open grave, tears started to flow. Soon my bawling affected Sophia, and she cried a little too.

Funeral tears are about loss and inevitability, fear of the day you'll be in a cut-rate brass casket. I hadn't let the reality of Aunt Vicky's death touch me until that moment. Without Aunt Vicky to help me remember, all of my mother was gone. Her generation had died out. I was the only survivor of the next. I understood a little better the importance of my son Randy in the universe. I wondered if he'd ever know the terrible burden he carried. The debt to our ancestors.

I could see the red sandstone mesas surrounding Moab, the desolate cliffs walling it all in and wondered why Vicky had stayed here. My sadness turned to indignation. Where were her friends now? Why hadn't there been a parade for one of their own? What is wrong with this town?

"What kept everyone away from the funeral?" I said out loud. My mouth often parrots my thinking without permission. I think just for exercise.

"The rumors," said Sophia, staring into the distance.

"What rumors?"

She took a deep breath and blew her nose. Nothing dainty about the honk she made, but it did the job. Her voice was firm and clear.

"People around here thought she was a lesbian," she said.

"What?"

"And they think that's why she killed her husband."

My mouth hung open so long that a paper wasp began building on a molar. Sophia stood up uncertainly, and I moved to catch her if she fell. She let me put my arm around her and together we walked back to the car and drove to Allie's in silence.

———

Allison Braise had inherited a small homestead on the east side of the city. Most of the land had been sold over the years, but she could trace her family's ownership of what she had left back a century.

A stately white house surrounded by a covered porch stood just inside the wooden gate that proclaimed the "Double B" ranch, named after Allie's great, great-grandfather Berachiah Braise who lived at a time when names like Berechiah were as common as opium-enriched soft drinks and brass spittoons. There was a large wooden barn, a more modern stable, and a wire-fenced kennel. A handful of dogs leaped up on the wires and sounded the frantic alarm of welcome. Stuck in among the dogs was a thin pale gorilla. It was a huge white beast that when it stood on its hinds to get a better look at me, looked out over the top of the six-foot fence. Its muzzle and slobbery tongue suggested dog. Its size suggested clandestine scientific experimentation with gamma radiation, steroids, growth hormones, and a diet of Alice's "Eat Me" cookies. From fifty feet away, its bark made me jump.

The dirt driveway was filled with cars. Overflow had chosen the lawn instead of the street which was lame. Lawns are precious in Moab. Green is precious in the desert. I sorely wanted to drag a key across the silver Mercedes as Sophia and I walked past it.

The house was crowded with people. Everyone held a paper cup and a plate. Most had crumbs on them, while others still had cookies. There was little talking. Mostly just standing around. Everyone turned to look at me when we walked through the door. Boredom morphed into insincere grief-tinged friendliness. Allie was nowhere to be seen. I heard a bottle being uncorked from where I remembered the kitchen was.

"Hello, Mr. Flaner," said the gravy-tanned, hat-wearing, spread-out guy from the funeral.

"Is that your Mercedes on the lawn?" I said.

Something else was about to come out of his mouth, but it stopped, swirled, and reshaped into, "Yes, that's mine."

"You shouldn't park on the lawn," I said and escorted Sophia deeper into the house.

"Mr. Flaner," said a park ranger. "Allie told me about you. I am so sorry for your loss."

"You're Roy Stirps, right?"

"Yes. I knew Vicky very well. She'll be missed."

"Yes, we'll all miss her," said 'gravy man' edging beside me. "You must be pretty shaken up."

The blond I'd seen at the funeral with the peeling sunburn and long braid appeared. His arms were folded high on his chest. His eyes were the lightest aquamarine I'd ever seen, like pools of ice water seeping down a Norwegian glacier to a distant fjord.

"Victoria's spirit soars now with the eagles," he said.

For effect, he waved his hand in an arching gesture from shoulder to shoulder, encompassing the whole sky before folding again on his chest. Everyone stared at him.

"Would anyone care for some wine?" said the twin in the Italian suit. "Allison has run out of punch, but Phil and I had some wine in the car." He walked up to me and put a glass in my hand.

"Roy, would you care for some? It's in the kitchen. How about you, Tiponi?"

The blond shook his head from side to side solemnly.

"Tiponi doesn't touch firewater," said the other twin emerging from a hall.

So this Scandinavian tool was Tiponi?

After refusing the wine, he held still as a cigar store statue. When my attention could finally leave those blue eyes, I realized he was dressed more casually than the others. He wore jeans with a big silver belt buckle with turquoise accents. His shirt was plaid and held together at the neck with a black leather bolo tie fastened with an arrowhead clasp.

"Is this the good stuff, Bill, or did Phil make this batch," joked 'gravy man' pushing his way into the kitchen.

"I'm Bill Ashe," introduced the first twin. "My mirror over there is Phil. We own the Ashe Winery. We were friends of your Aunt Victoria."

They'd dressed alike, and they looked alike, but it was easy to tell them apart. Bill wore his suit like he was born into it. He could walk a Venice runway to applause. Phil's suit was wrinkled in places suits don't usually get wrinkles, like the calves, lapels, and shoulders. His tie was crooked, and a shirt button was undone. His eyes were bloodshot, and his wide perma-grin confirmed the underlying smell of cannabis lurking beneath half a can of air freshener that had followed him out of the bathroom.

"My friends call me Phil," he said.

"That's convenient."

"Yep, keeps us straight."

"Apparently not too much," I said.

Bill's eyes bulged and Phil began laughing uncontrollably for a whole minute before he caught his breath.

"What do you think of the wine?" said Bill.

I took a sip, sloshed it around my mouth like I knew what I was doing, then tilted my head back, gargled a little, swallowed, smelled the glass, and swallowed the rest with my nose pinched.

"Fabulous. Better than the Marquis de Sade, 1865," I said.

Phil lost it again and excused himself to the bathroom.

Bill smirked and shook his head. "It's not our best, I admit," he said. "But it's surely better than torture."

"And I said as much. But not just ordinary torture, if you get my meaning."

Bill smiled. "I see. High praise indeed."

He filled my glass again, and I recognized the Kokopelli figure on the bottle from my first night here.

The gravy man returned from the kitchen, a paper cup filled to the brim with red wine.

Before he could say anything, I turned to Sophia.

"You all remember Sophia Curtis," I said. My righteous fury was rising at the offense that no one had acknowledged Vicky's closest friend standing right in front of them.

The others' faces all blanched and each quickly said hello, offered their condolences and best wishes. After a moment, the house was quiet as a tomb again. The only sound was the barking from the kennel. Allie came out to see what all the silence was about.

"I'm making some Rice Krispies treats," she said. "Shouldn't be a minute. I didn't expect so many people."

In fact, more people were still arriving. The dogs had announced the fuzz. Danny Hinds appeared and held the door open for Lieutenant Levis. I would know who he was even without the name tag. He wore the face I'd left Salt Lake City to get away from. He smiled at me, and I braced for a tazing.

"Mr. Flaner, sorry I missed you at the funeral," Levis said. "I want you to know that I have been in touch with the city fathers, and they all wish to extend their condolences for the terrible random tragedy that has befallen your family. The culprit behind this heinous act will be brought to justice." As he spoke, his eyes rolled back in his head occasionally. It happened when he paused to remember his lines. I don't know how much he'd rehearsed his speech, but it wasn't enough.

"Do you have any leads?" I asked.

"We've passed all available information to state officials and they're on it," he said. "Don't worry."

"What, me worry?"

"That's the spirit," he said. "Have a nice day."

With that, he turned on his heels and marched out of the house. Danny hadn't even closed the door yet. Levis was a busy man. Danny followed after him.

"Glad they came," I said. "Gladder they left."

"What was that about?" asked Roy.

"Politics," said a new voice. "Herbert Levis wants to be mayor."

I turned to see one of the fresh-faced, out-of-place people I'd seen huddled together in the back of the funeral parlor. A smile wider than his head showed unnaturally white square teeth.

"I'm Guy Skingle," he said, handing me a card instead of a handshake. "If you're selling real estate, I'm your *Guy!*"

The tagline was on his card beneath a full-color photo of his unholy smile.

"Hello Guy," I said. "I'm—"

"You're Tony Flaner, Victoria Racine's only surviving relative. You live in Salt Lake City now and don't really want to be bothered with a little place like Moab. I'm ready to help you sell the house so you can put this whole terrible experience behind you. Cut the old ties. Start again."

"Now let's not get ahead of ourselves," said Mr. Gravy, grabbing my hand and shaking it like a rat in a dog's maw.

"I'm Thomas S. Crew," he said, not releasing my hand from his thick spongy fingers. "Your aunt Victoria and I were in negotiations over the purchase of her hundred acres of worthless desert shrub before her death. We don't need no middleman to complete that."

I extricated my hand and took his card.

"You can call me T. S., or T. S. Crew, if you like."

"What do your friends call you?" I asked.

That stumped him. His face went blank as his mind reached into deep cavities of unknown possibilities for a suitable answer.

"I'm not interested in the land, Mr. Flaner. I specialize in houses," said Skingle. "Condo conversions for the elite. I have a buyer right now from California who'll pay you top dollar—cash, for that old place of yours."

"Maybe now's not the time," said Roy.

Behind him, I saw Sophia crying quietly at the table, alone and deserted.

"Now is definitely not the time," I said.

"The Hopi have a claim on the red land," said Tiponi.

"Later," I said. It was something in my voice, an unconcealed expression of burning vitriolic rage about to flip out on them like a deranged orangutan with a basket of grapefruits, that got my point across, and I was given space.

Phil came back from the bathroom, his eyes whiter than Skingle's teeth, a teardrop of Visine on his forehead. "What did I miss?"

"Two cops and an attempted land grab," I said.

"The hundred acres? Yeah, we'd like to talk to you about that too."

"He said later," inserted T. S. Crew. "That means not now. And stand in line." The last little bit was said under his breath.

Allie appeared with a tray of snacks and put them on the table in front of Sophia.

"Are you staying in Moab long, Mr. Flaner," asked Roy.

"Call me Tony."

"Are you staying long, Tony," asked Skingle.

"You may call me Mr. Flaner." The rebuke weakened his grin but only for an instant.

"Yeah, I guess so," I said. "I have a few things to do."

"Then I'm your *guy*," said Skingle.

"We'll talk later, Mr. Flaner," said T. S. Crew. "Again, sorry about your loss." He finished his drink and went out to his grass-killing car.

With the big crew cut cutting out, the rest of the party began saying their goodbyes. They were careful to include Sophia and Allie in their farewells and sympathy.

Soon it was just Sophia, Allie and me with some red wine and a plate of untouched Rice-Crispy treats. I touched a few.

Sophia went to the bathroom to freshen up. She was upset.

"You see what's going on?" said Allie. "Vultures and creeps."

"I don't blame Sophia for being angry. Did anyone even talk about Vicky or the Racine family or anything? It was insulting."

"Sophia is scared. She has no place to go. No family. Little money," Allie said softly. "She's scared to death you'll sell the house, and she'll be on the street. This onslaught had to be terrifying for her."

"She doesn't think I'd do that, does she?"

Allie shrugged. "She doesn't know you."

I was about to ask Allie if she thought I was that kind of person but remembered that we were more out of touch than Rick and I had been.

"Give me some credit."

"I do," she said.

My heart melted.

"Sophia is a great gal. So was Vicky. She knew you'd be hounded by those thieves, but still she demanded you come down."

"To find Vicky's killer?"

"That and you're family. You had to be here even if it sped up her eviction."

I recalled the faces at the funeral when I'd dropped the F-bomb on the sycophants. The detective in me couldn't help wondering if I had been addressing my quarry.

"Sophia said there were rumors that Vicky killed her husband. Is there any truth to that?"

"Hell no," Allie said. "She loved Lance. Thick looked up to him like he walked on water. Absolutely no way. That's just shit they say because..." She dropped off.

"Because they thought she was a lesbian?" I asked.

"That's the rumor," said Allie.

Sophia appeared at my side. I hadn't heard her come back. Eighty-five-pound old women can move like ninjas. Must be the frail hips that absorb the sound.

"She had a husband and son," Sophia said. "She loved them like nothing else. How does that make her a lesbian?"

She sat down and poured some wine. There's a reason wine isn't usually served in paper cups. I'd refilled mine so many times, I was getting pulp in my teeth.

"So where did these rumors come from?" I asked.

"Does it matter?" said Allie.

"I don't know," I said. "Probably not, but the more information I have, the better. You want me to do my private eye thing, right? I work better when I'm informed. That's kind of what a PI does, collect information. It was in the course description."

Allie didn't say anything.

I looked at Sophia.

"Rumors don't matter," she said. "They used to, back when we were young and cared what others thought, but not anymore."

"When did it matter exactly?" I asked.

"When we were in high school, it mattered to some people then. That kind of thing could cause a family shame. Get a girl sent out of state for college."

"Now, not so much," I said.

"Nobody's business now. No family to shame."

Now I knew why Sophia didn't have a room of her own. I can be really slow sometimes.

"Could anyone care about those old rumors enough now to do something terrible about them?"

Sophia looked at me with defiant eyes. Allie's grew large as she contemplated the suggestion.

"Small town," Allie said. "I can't think of anyone as mean as that. Maybe a cold shoulder, a terse hello—an empty funeral parlor, but nothing so bad as murder. I can't imagine it."

"An outsider might have heard the rumor," said Sophia. "Small town, small minds, big mouths."

"Maybe," I said. "I frankly hadn't considered that until now."

"So what have you been considering?"

"Tell me more about the hundred acres."

12

WHEN I WAS A KID, Rick had demanded that Vicky take me to "the ranch." It wasn't easy, neither convincing her to go nor getting there. It was hell and gone out of Moab. We drove paved roads for an hour and then dirt ones into the afternoon. Eventually, Vicky maneuvered her Ford Fire Hazard through narrow, sandy, stone canyons and washed-out sandy creek beds that turned into sandy flash flood corridors once or twice a year killing everything in the sandy canyon and feeding the remains into the sandy Colorado River.

Rick called it a ranch, but Vicky would sometimes call it "the farm." Neither name made much sense. Beyond the cliffs, there were plains and plateaus that might have supported a crop or fed a sheep or two, but those days were long gone by the time Vicky drove Rick and I up there.

There are lots of wonderful and beautiful places around Moab, places to excite your imagination and make you drive all day just to glimpse it at sunset.

The Racine Ranch was not one of those. The Racines may have tried farming, maybe even ranching, but unless they were raising Pet Rocks, the land offered little for agriculture. Underground, however, there were minerals, which in essence were just more pet rocks, but with a fancy name and so some imagined value.

We picnicked in front of the crumbling remains of a potash mine entrance, and Rick explained how once all the mesa was theirs.

"Now don't go exaggerating, Thick," Vicky had warned him.

She wrapped me in her blanket while we watched my cousin run up the hills to point at distant mountains that he claimed marked the end of the once great Racine empire. Rick slipped trying to free-climb a slick rock wall and tumbled through cactus. He brushed himself off, smiling, and sat down with us to eat a sandwich. Vicky casually plucked thorns out of his neck as he ate.

"Truth is, Lance's family had a thousand acres once," Aunt Vicky told me. "It's been sold off over the years until this is all that's left. Like us."

"Are you going to sell this?"

"Not planning on it," she said.

We had our picnic peppered with blowing sage and sand, packed up, and left.

I told Sophia about my recollection of the ranch.

"Vicky didn't want to sell it. Every so often folks would offer to buy it; lots of them lately. And every other so often the tax man would demand his due, which we never had."

"But the taxes were all paid up, like last month," I said.

"I don't know nothing about that," said Sophia. "Vicky didn't like talking about money, good or bad."

We helped Allie clean up after the reception, and then I led Sophia to the car. I wanted to stay with Allie, meet the gorilla, go back into the barn, and just be with her, but the day had beaten all of us. I drove home, and we had an early night.

———

Sophia didn't wake me the next morning, but I smelled coffee waiting for me when I got up. I put on my last clean shirt and skipped down those slick stairs into the kitchen. Beside the coffee was a pile of opened mail and a note. "Gone to store. Don't waste the day. BE PRODUCTIVE!"

And I thought she didn't know me.

I noticed an official letter from the law offices of Archie Rumbold. The envelope had been opened and lay within easy reach after I dug through all the other mail. It was a letter of condolence and an invitation to the reading of Victoria Racine's will on Thursday.

She'd saved me some Pop-Tarts, all of them actually. I enjoyed a couple with my coffee and turned my phone on for the first time since Friday morning.

I had missed a few calls, fifty-two to be precise. I listened to messages and in summation, gathered that the Levises were concerned about my efforts in recovering their dog. They questioned my ancestry in the strongest possible words that wouldn't jeopardize their place in heaven. "Total Jerk," "Son of a beep." Yes, he actually said "beep" in self-censorship. The Levises' lawyer had called and wanted to know with whom I was insured. Nancy wanted to know if the Levises had reached me and how I was holding up in Moab. Randy called me by accident and hung up before saying anything. He did that twice. Worse Nightmare explained that he knew how to string up a man by his own intestines—an interesting skill, I thought; eclectic and rare.

He was an obvious hipster. Standard said the gang was getting together for the Wednesday open mic at the Comedy Cellar and wanted to know if he should put me down for a spot. Dara had a new routine, something about child rearing's adverse effect on long-term hearing. At least our evening together at Randy's recital hadn't been a complete loss for her.

I texted Standard,

> Get me a spot. B-ing detective.

He texted back.

> Sure thing, Sherlock.

With Perry away, our group's usual headliner was missing. That meant that any of us other regulars could assume the prime position and try for glory and attention at the Comedy Cellar. I had been working on four new bits all summer and with them I stood a good chance at the main spot. I'd have to convince the owner and beat down the others, but here was an opportunity for a big moment of short-lived unpaid fame in front of drunk date-nighters and the mythical talent scout that only shows up when you're not performing. If I didn't go, he'd be there and someone else would get that sitcom instead of me. If only to keep my fellow comedians away from success, I had to go.

Having heard Rosalyn-Janet Levis faint twice more on my messages, I felt a little guilty about ignoring them in their terrible canine tragedy. Something in Ronald Levis' messages, maybe the threats of horrible physical violence without a curse word, or his promise of financial ruin under God's direction, made me think that I should do something more than hide from them. Maybe I could give them a call and see how they were doing, offer to help in any way they needed. Or I could ignore them some more. It wasn't a tough choice.

Sophia had taken all the cloths off the pictures. All the towels and hand-kerchiefs were in a basket in the washroom. I considered doing a load of laundry, but I was afraid my gesture would be lost in the damage I was liable to do.

There was a picture of Rick on the mantel under Delicate Arch, a big grin on his face, both middle fingers extended. He must have been really happy that day. There was an army picture of Lance, Rick's father, in front of a flag. Beside it was a picture of Rick in uniform. He looked hard and brave. He held a salute over his right brow, the middle finger slightly higher than the others. Not a regulation salute, but it made me happy.

Hanging on a wire in a wooden frame, was a small family picture in fading Kodachrome colors. The ink and bell-bottoms placed it squarely in the time before good fashion and stable pigment. In it I saw my mother,

Aunt Vicky, Uncle Lance and my father. They stood with grandparents I never knew. They were all in front of another arch, one that didn't merit its own state license plate. My mother held me in her arms like a trophy. Vicky held her son by the hand and even though Rick couldn't have been three years old yet, I wondered if it was to conceal the finger. Both his legs were covered in Band-Aids and his bangs were cut at an angle only a kid not yet three years-old could have made. I'd never seen the picture before. I'd never felt closer to my relatives than I did at that moment. There was an eerie sense of responsibility as I realized among all those bright happy summer faces, mine was the only one still alive.

The doorbell rang. It probably meant there was someone there, and they wanted to get in. I was a detective; I had a sense for these things.

Standing on the step was Tiponi. He wore a different plaid shirt than yesterday, but the same bolo tie. His hair was still in a tight braid down his back. His eyes made me think of North Sea raiding parties and Valkyries.

He held his arms crossed high over his chest, and his face was turned upward slightly as if he'd been following an interesting contrail from a passing aircraft and hadn't changed position to greet me. His face peeled in flakes under a terrible sunburn like a shedding snake.

"Tony Flaner," he said. "I Tiponi."

"I remember," I said. "You're some kind of Indian? Is that it?"

"I Hopi."

"The Hopi don't believe in verbs?"

No answer.

"You don't look like an Indian," I said. "You look like a surfer or Greenland raider."

"I have some white blood in my veins."

"Some?"

"Most," he admitted. "But I, Tiponi, from Hopi nation."

"Not big on articles either, eh? Do I detect an English accent?"

"I spent a semester at Oxford, and it slips out sometimes."

"And that? Was that like New York?"

"New Jersey. I grew up outside Trenton."

"But you're an Indian?"

"I, Hopi."

"I, don't believe you."

His burned and peeling face pinched in frustration.

"I chose to identify with my Indian roots. Okay?" he finally said. "Can I come in?"

I stood aside, and he entered. He went straight to the living room like he knew the way. He walked through the tiny house as though he had a destination in mind. He sat down on the sofa. I took a chair. It's always awkward for two guys to sit side by side on the sofa unless there was a chance for some hanky-panky. I hardly knew this guy and decided to play hard to get.

"You've been here before?" I said.

"Yes, I talk Victoria about land."

"Really? Dropping prepositions now? You're going back to that?"

He put on a proud stony face which meant either he had no idea what I was talking about, or he'd just glimpsed a Gorgon through the window. I gave up.

"What about the land?" I said.

"It is sacred land for Hopi." He produced a photograph from his breast pocket and placed it in front of me.

It was a folded three-by-five, printed from an inkjet running low on cyan. It showed a blocky stick figure scratched into the face of a pink sandstone cliff. The figure had a rectangular body, stubby arms and legs and what were either horns or Pippi Longstocking braids. The figure was among other scratches which extended beyond the photograph. I could see part of a palm print above it. The picture was from a petroglyph gallery. There were hundreds of them around Moab, some more impressive than others, some older, some younger; all are kind of creepy and indecipherable.

"This is a Hopi medicine man," he said.

"How can you tell?" I looked at the square figure. "The horns? Are those what he uses to gouge ancestral insurance carriers with unnecessary chants and exorcisms?"

"Trust me, it is," he said. "This proves Hopi ownership."

"Where was this taken?"

"On the Racine ranch, of course."

"I don't remember seeing any galleries when I was there."

"That's because you don't know secret ways of Indians," he said.

"Yeah that was probably it."

"It's in a small overhang high on cliff in one of the canyons. There are many secret canyons there. It is sacred place."

I wasn't surprised I hadn't seen the glyphs. The Ranch was all canyons and crags, at least what was left of it, and I hadn't explored beyond the picnic area.

"I'm beginning to see," I said. "You approached Aunt Vicky with this picture, and she laughed at you. Just like I am." I paused to laugh, then went on. "So now that Vicky is dead you thought to steal it from me on the cheap before I recovered from the funeral and your moisturizer kicked in."

"No, I'm not here to buy. I expect you to surrender land. Give it back."

"Oh, then that's different," I said.

I sat up in my chair, cleared my throat, found a middle C, then fell on the floor laughing. For emphasis, I rolled on my back and kicked my legs like I was being tickled by Muppets. This went on for five minutes or so. Wiping tears from my eyes, I sat down in the chair again.

"I know an agent," I said. "He could get you five minutes on the late show with that kind of material."

"I'm serious," he said.

I fought back the urge to return to the floor, but I think he suspected I was being ironic.

"There were people lining up at Allie's house to buy the ranch. Why on earth would I give it to you?"

"It Indian land. Hopi land before white devils steal."

He was sliding back into thick stereotype. I tried to keep up.

"You not Indian," I said. "You heap full of shit. You go now. No land. No firewater. No blankets."

"Land must be returned to Hopi or Great Spirit be very angry and we sue your ass in federal court under the Indian Heritage Rights Act of 1976."

"Whoa there, Squanto," I said. "Them's fightin' words."

"Indians great fighters."

"Indians ARE great fighters. Man, you're annoying."

He folded his arms in stony defiance.

I leaned back and studied him. He wore a wallet-sized turquoise ring on his right index finger. On his left wrist sat a two-tone silver watch band similarly adorned with blue pebbles. The watch was a new Citizen Eco-Drive. It was a pricey piece of technology. I'd had my eye on one myself. Above the watch, where his sleeve had been pulled back, white skin glowed as pale as half and half on a linen napkin.

"You got some nerve," I said.

"The law not on your side."

"It seldom is. I'm not sure I know what's going on. No, wait, strike that. I am sure I don't know what's going on. If you treated my Aunt Vicky half as pleasantly as you're treating me here today, you are officially on my shit-list, which shouldn't be a surprise to you because you're so full of it and I feel like reaching over there and twisting that Nordic nose of yours to see if it flushes you."

I reached across the space between our chairs, and he pulled back in horror.

"Mrs. Racine had no right to that land. It's sacred Hopi land."

"I feel for you, my Aryan friend, but it's time for you to leave and for me to fumigate the couch."

"You haven't heard the last of this or seen the last of me," he said. "I will not be moved. This is Hopi Rosa Parks moment. I will not leave."

"Pick a dialect and stick with it," I said. "Those were actually complete sentences."

He folded his arms tighter and scanned the ceiling for contrails.

I took him by his Walmart collar and waistband and flung him through the door as I'd seen John Wayne do it. Tiponi would have staggered out but caught his feet just in time for another quick comeback had the door been open. Since it wasn't, his head crashed into the frame and his nose started bleeding immediately.

Without missing a beat his hand reached into a back pocket and produced a blood-stained handkerchief which went immediately to his face like it knew the way by rote. Some of the stains were fresh, others rust-colored memories.

"Sorry," I said. "I thought the door was open."

"Yeah, I can see that you were going for dramatic effect there," he said.

"You want some ice on that?"

"No thanks." He pinched his nose. "Flaner, I didn't disrespect your aunt. I don't want you thinking I did."

"Just me then?" I said.

"Yes, just you." I could see his face change as he slipped back into Indian. "Tiponi honorable and brave and apologizes for disrespect," he said. "He deserve bloody nose. You mourning. Me have no right now. Me come back later."

"Flaner short-tempered, acts out, sorry too," I said.

"I go now."

"That'll work."

He opened the door and left.

I watched him walk down the path pinching the bridge of his nose. He got into a rusty Chevy pickup, with an Arizona license plate. No tailgate.

I went back to the table and put the photo he'd left in my pocket.

13

RICK WAS an easy target for bullies, kids and grown-ups alike. No kid tormented him more than Danny Hinds and no grown-up tormented him more than Haddy Miller, or "Haggy" Miller as most people called her. Rick raised a litter of six wild kittens secretly in the garage once. One day he showed them to Haggy Miller's twin daughters who begged to take them home to play house with them. Rick was a nice guy so he let the twins take them as long as they were careful.

Rick was always gentle with the kittens, giving them milk and stolen food scraps from the table, but the girls were rougher. They tried to dress them in doll clothes and give them tea. Of course there are no wild kittens in Moab. There are, however, wild skunks. Haggy Miller never forgave Rick for ruining her carpet, drapes, couch and wardrobe, while traumatizing the girls. To this day I doubt her daughters can come within ten feet of any creature smaller than a horse without crying. They'd be in their thirties by now.

Haggy Miller went out of her way to call Rick stupid, and she'd watch out her window whenever he played and report everything he did that didn't seem right. She was kept busy. The day we searched the front lawn for water with a wire-hanger divining rod, she came out and abused both of us.

"If you two aren't the dumbest pair of boys I've ever seen, I don't know what," she'd said.

"Well, why don't you figure it out and get back to us," said I.

Rick's eyes bulged with admiration. Even before I'd met her, I'd heard about Haggy. When I saw for myself the bullying Rick suffered at her hands, I snapped. She fumed. If we'd have been closer, I have no doubt that she'd have cuffed me for my insolence.

"You're Thick's cousin, aren't you? You're no better bred than this retard with the hanger. Your mother didn't teach you manners. Don't you know to show respect to your betters?"

"When I'm in the company of one, I will."

Haggy Miller called the police on us for abusive language. We were given a stern talking-to and weren't allowed to say anything in our defense. When Vicky got home, we were grounded for getting the police called on us.

After Tiponi left, I went for a stroll and passed Haggy Miller's house in the crisp Autumn desert air. She didn't own it anymore. "Casa Pinion" was on the mailbox. It had been renovated and painted and was now a rental. No one was there now.

The night we were grounded, Rick and I snuck out of our rooms through my window down the quoins on the outside of the house. The quoins stuck out three inches from the house, making for an easy climb. He took me behind the barn with a flashlight and showed me where the skunks lived. It'd been years since the twins incident, but he'd kept up an association with the creatures and regularly dropped food behind the barn for them to scavenge. They came up to him like tamed pets to a beloved owner.

He shined a flashlight on one and I turned around to run.

"Hold up, cousin," he said. "This one is Betty Boop. Get it? She's in black and white."

The animal curled up its tail and grinned a mouth of white daggers lantern-fish would fear.

Rick lowered the flashlight and walked right up to it, cooing kisses. Like some kind of skunk-whisperer, he purred, "Hi Betty Boop, can you do me a favor?"

He picked it up and stroked it like a cat. He gave it half a Mars bar. The animals smelled like a skunk just in case there was any doubt of its breed but it wasn't overwhelming which I knew meant it hadn't sprayed recently.

Under cover of darkness, we skipped across the block to Haggy Miller's house.

"Lift up the garage door," Rick said.

I lifted it just enough for him to let Betty go in.

A couple seconds later, we heard a huge crash as a garbage can fell over inside. Then there was a barking from a small dog and then a high-pitched yelp from the same dog and the sound of paws on tiles and lamps being overturned, precious family heirlooms crashing to the ground, and upholstery being ripped open.

Rick lifted up the door a few inches and Betty Boop ran out and into the darkness. We ran back to our house and scaled the bricks back to my room.

"That was pretty great," I whispered. "But we took a big chance. Grounded ain't so bad. Was it because she called you dumb?"

"Heck no," Rick said, watching lights flash on in Haggy's house, listening to the panicked and biohazarded dog crash through rooms. "I'm used to it, but she insulted you and your mother. I had to do something about that."

Even at ten, I was a smart-ass and thought I got my licks in pretty good, but Rick had risen to more brilliant heights to defend the family honor.

He winked and snuck back into his room before Vicky came up to check on us.

The next morning, Rick smelled like skunk at breakfast, but everyone pretended not to notice anything. Aunt Vicky opened a window halfway through the meal and sprayed Lysol over the table, but she never said a word.

The police came by later that afternoon while Rick and I were playing checkers and asked if we'd seen a skunk recently. No one had.

———

I wandered the old roads toward town. Once on Main Street, I followed the trendy sidewalks. The light was stark as only autumn skies can make it. It glistened off recycled tuna-lid wind chimes and made the hand-thrown pots look particularly hand thrown. On a weekday many stores were flat-out closed for the off-season. Maybe they'd open up later in the week if tourists returned. Maybe not. In the meantime, I'd just have to buy my polished rocks and jackalope busts online.

My earlier drive had shown me where everything was—Main Street— but I'd known this town by foot with Rick, so a walk did much to reorient me. I wandered with only a vague idea of destination. As I passed the fifteenth blown glass art gallery on my right, I marveled at how Moab had already changed me. I'd chosen to walk instead of drive. That wasn't like me. Back in Salt Lake, I'd fallen into a lazy routine that bordered on crippling. I'd toyed with the idea of tying Precious to my car's bumper for our walks, but Chevy Chase's cautionary tale had warned me off that. Then it hit me like a fresh breeze. Allie. I was doing it for her. This walk would remove the extra weight from my belly and strengthen me into a male-model Adonis. Yep, this little walk was all I needed. Well, this little walk and three thousand just like it. Uphill. Carrying a boat anchor. In each hand. While eating wheat germ sprouts for every meal. And liposuction.

Across the street, I saw an official building made from local red sandstone and plenty of exposed pine logs. The sign in front read: *National Forest and Moab information Center*. I went in seeking a map.

"Tony," said a cheerful voice when I entered. "What brings you out?"

"Three drinks and *Dancing Queen* by Abba usually does the trick," I said.

It was Roy Stirps behind the counter. He wore a sharp, creased, green uniform with the gold badge on his breast, and a big Smokey Bear hat.

"You a cop?" I asked.

"No. Not really. Well, kind of. Rangers are Homeland Security affiliates. We can make arrests and carry guns."

"What fun," I said. "Do you get extra pay for posse duty?"

"Time and a half. The town fathers don't like me to show a gun in the information building though. Gives the wrong impression."

"'Visit the jackbooted, militarized, scenic wonders of Moab! Bring your sunscreen and Kevlar,'" I said. "Yeah, I see how that's a turn-off."

"But in the field, I get to carry one because terrorists might try to blow up an arch. It's great. Telling people to pick up their trash is a lot more interesting when you're packing a Glock."

"I'd think Colt Peacemakers would be standard issue. To keep with the aesthetic. I prefer revolvers anyway—less chance of forgetting how they work."

"You a cop?"

"No. I'm a private investigator." I showed him my identification and badge. Really, all I have is a permit, but I'd had Randy put together an impressive laminated ID in Photoshop and I'd custom-ordered a badge from Mexico that came with a tailored wallet.

"Pretty impressive," he said. "What kind of gun do you have?"

"It's silver."

"Silver?"

"Yeah, and black on the holdy part, behind the pully thing."

"You don't shoot much?"

"No, not much. My arches have fallen. No need to blow them up."

He smiled.

"I didn't know Vicky had any relatives left," he said. "Will you be staying long?"

"I don't know yet. You stayed with Vicky for a while, didn't you?"

"Yes, for a few months. We grew close."

"She never mentioned me?"

"Never. Not once. Sorry," he said.

"Don't be. We weren't that close."

Roy must have seen some self-pity leak out.

"Don't take it too hard," he said. "It was a bad time for her. She'd lost her son shortly after I moved in."

Yeah, reminding me that I hadn't even known about my cousin's death did wonders to make me feel better. "Did you know Rick?" I asked.

"Who?"

"Rick, Vicky's son. Everyone called him Thick."

"Oh, Thick. I didn't know him. I'd seen him in town once, and talked to him a little when he visited his mother, but that was all. He was..." He paused. "Good-hearted."

"And soft-minded?"

"Well, during that one visit when I met him, he got hit by a car crossing

Main Street and then later was hospitalized when he opened a can of beans with a blow torch. He was accident prone."

"Why'd he open a can of beans with a blowtorch?"

"Rumor was he couldn't find a can-opener. The beans exploded. That was a bad one. But the Illinois tourists were cool about the dent in their car. They even sent flowers."

"How long did you stay with Vicky?"

"I moved in shortly before Thick died and moved out when Sophia came. I have a house on Mesa Road. I was remodeling it. It's easier when you don't live there. Luckily, it was done just in time. I think she liked having company. Her health was failing and then her son died. She withered away before my eyes. She was a good woman though. I'll miss her."

"Yeah." I suddenly felt horrible. Well, more horrible. The guilt of losing touch so thoroughly beat on me like a meth-head woodpecker.

"Did you come looking for something?" Roy asked before I started bawling.

"Is this a ranger station? I thought it was a tourist kiosk."

"It's both. Shared costs and all that. I'm lucky. They lay off most of the staff in October, but not me."

"How'd you get this gig? Kill a man in arena-style unarmed combat?"

"What? No, just seniority. And I work cheap. I'm usually stationed in town. I have joint problems so can't do the long hikes."

The survival guide to a bad economy: lower your expectations and get on disability.

"I need a map," I said. "Moab's changed from when I was here last, and even then I never knew the street names."

"Most of the maps I have are of the parks. Highways and tourist stuff," he said, looking through a display of pamphlets. There were brochures for river trips, timeshares, hang-gliding courses, Indian adventures, horseback riding tours, pizza delivery, and real full-body Moab mud baths at the Arches Day Spa "just like the pioneers enjoyed," while they were drowning in the reeds, I thought.

"Here's a decent map," he said. "Oh, no it's not. It just shows how to get to the LARP meet-up. Shows some of the back streets but only if you're going that way."

"LARP?"

"Live Action Role Playing. It's kind of like a renaissance fair, but geekier."

"That's saying something," I said.

"Yeah. There's a meet-up next week. The Knights of the Southern Kingdom are questing for the Goblin Trove, but rumor is that the elves won't commit to the cause."

"I don't do politics," I said. "How about a map?"

"Canyonlands or Arches?"

"Do you know where I can find Archie Rumbold's office?"

"Oh yeah," said Roy. "This map will work for that."

He traced a route from where we stood, down a side street, and then made some pencil marks to complete the map to an out-of-the-way office on a distant side of town. It wasn't far from Allie's place.

"He works out of a room in his house," he said.

"Information is what I came for," I said. "You were the right guy to ask."

"Thanks."

"Hey, Allie said you're something of an historian."

"I'm just an amateur," he said. "I got started tracing famous outlaws and just picked up local history as I went along. Did you know Butch Cassidy hid out in Canyonlands? I think Moab should have been called "Hideout" for all the bank robbers, rustlers, and renegade Indians who've hidden out around here."

"Now it brings in tourists and the thieves are in the stores," I said.

"Something to be said about that. Did you know Moab once boasted more millionaires per capita than anywhere else in the country?"

"Who says?"

"McCalls magazine 1956 named Moab the richest town in the U.S."

I stared at him blankly. Did I care about this?

"That's cool," I said and then had a thought. "Take a look at this."

I pulled out the picture Tiponi had left on my table before I accidentally beat him up. "What do you make of this?" I showed it to Roy.

"No idea. Looks like Indian art."

"I thought you were a historian and a local one at that?"

"Only after the whites arrived. My father was a builder and told me stories about this place. He said it was the most interesting place he'd ever been. That's what got me interested."

"How long you been here?"

"Nearly five years. Moved from Greeley, Colorado. I'm a local now."

To Allie, Rumbold was a "newcomer" after accruing ten years, that made Roy a tourist as far as the locals were concerned. I didn't tell him.

"So who might have an idea what this is?"

"There's that Tiponi fellow. He claims to be an expert."

"Anyone else?"

"I can't think of anyone."

"And so the information ends."

"Sorry. Would you like to know about rafting adventures or where the best restaurants are?"

"Thanks, no. I'll just go see Archie."

"His office is accessed around the back. Follow the gravel road past the gate."

"Thanks for the information."

"It's what I do, detective," Roy said and saluted.

"One more thing," I said at the door in my best Columbo false exit. "Do you know of anyone who'd want to kill Vicky?"

"It was a burglar," he said. "Wasn't it?"

"That's one theory. Do you have any others?"

"Hadn't thought of it," he said. "I will though. If I think of something, I'll let you know."

"You know where to find me." I handed him my card.

14

I HADN'T HANDED out a card in months. Mine now read "Tony Flaner, Private Investigator to the stars, supernovas and black holes." It listed my cell phone number and a post office box where I like my subpoenas to end up. Giving my home address just leads to break-ins, shootings, and poison on my lawn. It was harder to get a bag of burning dog shit in a post office box than a mail slot.

A block from the tourist information center, I regretted not having my car. My muscles had cooled down, and they worked again only after great hesitation and complaint.

I found a bench and scratched out some notes on the back of a business card. I'd left my detectivizing notebook at the house. If I'd brought a car, I might have brought that too.

I wrote down a game plan. My mind was still muddled with thoughts of doting Aunt Vicky suffering under the loss of her only son while I was on my fictional yacht, eating caviar surrounded by bikini-clad French supermodels.

I wrote, 1. Lawyer. 2. 100 acres? Land office? 3. 2 Twins, 1 TS Crew, 0 Tiponi. That was all I could fit on the card. I had to write really small to get that on it and Tiponi was written in the margin after an arrow. I'd have to transcribe my little opus to my detective notebook for later reference. Or not.

The lawyer's office was at least half a mile away. The land office might be in the courthouse which was only three blocks. Change in plans.

I moseyed up the sidewalk which is the only fitting way to walk through a western town. I crossed the street past a frozen yogurt shop that had abbreviated hours of operation: *Closed for the season*, to be precise.

I'd just put my foot on the other curb when I heard a burp and a whoop.

I turned to see a police car roll up behind me, Danny Hinds at the wheel. He parked the car against a red curb, the lights flashing on top. He got out, straightened his black Batman utility belt, ran his fingers through his conditioned hair, and walked toward me—cleft chin first like Achilles approaching Troy.

"Jaywalking is against the law," he said. "I'm going to have to write you up for that."

"Hi Danny," I said. "I always knew you'd find a way to be an even bigger prick when you grew up."

"The law's the law." He pulled a thick notebook from a pocket.

"You're not seriously going to give me a ticket are you? What would the city fathers think? I represent a sizable chunk of the out-of-town tourist trade right now. If you alienate me, it might have dire consequences on the local economy."

He paused and pondered. It was a long pause.

"How long are you staying in Moab?"

"You running me outta town, Sheriff?" I asked. "Isn't it normal to give me until sundown?"

He paused and pondered.

"How long?" he said.

"I don't know. When I do, you'll be the first person I won't tell," I said. "Your number still 1-800-Fucktard?"

He paused and pondered.

"You're a smart-ass," he said.

"Guilty as charged. Is that ticket worse than the jaywalking? Will I do real time?"

"You're getting close," he said. "These are serious matters. You've got to show more respect."

"I respect the uniform. It's very nice. Good color, tailor fit, lots of intimidating black pockets for cuffs, keys, and anti-shark spray, but the creep within it has to earn my respect, and he's already in a pretty deep hole from past experience."

"You still holding a grudge against me?"

"You mean for all the bullying and fights?"

"What fights?"

"How about the one where you got the shit beat out of you?"

His face went red.

It was late October, not unlike today, that it happened. Vicky had enrolled me in school with Rick. He was a year older but had been held back a grade so we were together in every class. The school held all grades from first through twelfth, and the grades often intermingled in the halls.

Danny was a year or two ahead of us and even then he was drop-dead gorgeous and athletic. He was on every sports team Moab had to offer. He'd have been a star on the football team if Moab had had enough boys to make a roster.

Like most of the kids in the school, he picked on Rick. In the small town, Rick's reputation for doing stupid things was an easy target. He wore the name Thick with pride and that just made things worse. He was good-natured and took everyone's ribbing as if it were all a good-hearted joke. Sometimes it was, other times it was just mean.

Danny was one of the mean ones. I don't know how he was before I got there, but when I was there, he was a real asshole. Rick's grades improved with my help, and he finally had somebody to eat lunch with. I was a wise-cracker even then, extroverted by nature, and I made friends and enemies quickly. Only a week after school began, our lunch table was the one to sit at. I'd crack jokes and tell stories, and Rick would tell some of the things he'd done, and give us cautionary tales of how not to gather wild honey—a plastic bag over your head will keep the bees out of your eyes but posed other risks, he explained.

Danny's table emptied and he grew surlier by the day. In thinking back, it might have been when Allie joined our table that he cracked.

The first attack on me was easily thwarted. I'd spilled some sloppy joe on my shirt. They were sloppy after all. Danny saw it in the hall and said, "You know you're supposed to eat that, not wear it." Two bully friends stood behind him and laughed at his wittiness.

"Wow, that's funny," I said. "You should go on television." I walked away while he paused and pondered.

He continued his weak torments for a week. He kept trying to get the better of me verbally, and every time I parried and cut him deep. The bigger the crowd, the deeper the wound. He offered to play me one-on-one in basketball.

"How about chess or Scrabble?" I said. "Spelling bee? Name that tune?"

I'd made a point in my putdowns to target the jock's mentality. It was an easy target, full of tradition and stereotype. Danny wasn't that dumb, but he carried himself like he owned the world because he was handsome and strong, and he'd neglected reading for his hair too many times. I'd even slipped in the word "dumb" a couple of times, "stupid" and "ignoramus" popped up as well, usually when I was asked to explain what I meant by a previous insult. Word of advice: if someone calls you stupid and you didn't get the insult, it's not a good idea to ask to have it explained to you.

His harassment toward Rick grew to blatant bullying. It wasn't winning him many friends, but he kept at it. Maybe because it was the only way he could get at me.

That October day in gym class, we had a dodgeball game. A throwback to caveman days when wars were won and lost with rocks. Danny grunted trash talk at me and my cousin.

When he'd knocked Rick out for a third time that game, he taunted him.

"You've got to be the dumbest thing I've ever seen. Did anyone else see him try to catch my ball with his face?"

Rick had been hit in the head. It should have been a foul, and should have sent Danny out of the game, but the officials were having a cigarette outside. Rick took it in stride, though the hit had reddened his cheek a deep crimson.

"You throw too hard, Danny," I said. "Take that troglodyte shit and stick it."

Saying the S-word would get me suspended, but there it was. Danny seized on it and began a soliloquy.

"It's your stupid cousin's shit-for-brains that's the problem. He is shit-for-brains," said Danny. "A useless piece of shit with shit-for-brains."

In all calmness, I walked across the line toward Danny. The game stopped. Everyone watched us. The gym teachers were still gone making cancer out of lung cells. I walked up to Danny, looked up at that handsome face and said, "That's my cousin, you fucker."

The F-bomb. I'd gone nuclear. No turning back now. I swung at him.

I hit him with a glancing blow on his shoulder. I didn't know how to fight. I still don't. Seeing his chance in an arena he had some mastery of, he unloaded on me. He hit me in the gut so hard I still haven't recovered. He swung a foot at my ankle, and I was on my back. He jumped on top of me and landed punches to my face and neck at will. I was going to die.

Suddenly he was off me. A dark shape flashed past like a hypersonic lynx and Danny was on his back wrestling with my cousin. I could only roll over and watch as Rick went crazy on Danny. I had a colorful vision of a leopard on catnip with its tail on fire cornering a bunny. His arms and legs lashed out, smashing against the floor and Danny alike. Danny screamed through a broken and bloody mouth. He flailed and tried to fight back, crawl away. He screamed for help, but finally could only ball up and wait for it to end. Thick didn't let up. Silently but furiously, he pounded on Danny. After bloodying the face, he moved to work the belly. It was then that Danny moved, or rather his bowels did.

Smelling the S-word, Rick stopped and got off him. He came over to me and helped me up. Rick's attacks weren't particularly effective. He'd scared Danny more than anything and the bully lay whimpering on the gym floor, his face scratched and bruised, his nose bloody and his pants unspeakably foul.

The gym teachers finally came back and Danny was sent to the showers. Rick and I were sent home.

Rick had asked me to call him by his nickname and I'd tried it out a couple of times, but not after that. That was the day I stopped calling my cousin Thick forever.

The teachers weren't as dumb as I thought. They'd seen the coming confrontation, and being sensible, small-town family values kind of folks they were, they gave everyone two days' suspension and the whole thing was chalked up to experience. Danny left us alone after that. It was too easy to burn him down with a "poopy pants" comeback and he knew it. He quietly seethed at me until the day I left. To his credit, Danny seemed to have overcome that humiliation and was now writing me a ticket for jaywalking.

"I don't like you, Flaner," he said. "I didn't like your cousin, but we got along a lot better with you gone. You're a troublemaker."

"Well, that ticket should fix me right up then."

"And what's with you and Allison?" he said. "You stay away from her."

"Wow. Really? You're freaked out because I might connect with a girl you've been unable to impress in forty years? That's sad. Why don't you do your job?"

"I am doing my job," he said, handing me the ticket.

I looked at it. The fine was fifty dollars and I had a court date in mid-December if I didn't pay up.

"I think I'll stay and fight this," I said. "That means I'm here through December, at least. I'll argue harassment and recount in stomach-churning graphic detail, the gym incident and your lust for revenge."

He paused and pondered.

"And as far as doing your job, I'm sure this ticket fits well under the "optional tax collection" scheme of any tourist town, but I think tomorrow your job will be a lot more interesting."

"What do you mean?"

"When have I ever explained anything to you?" I said. "Look it up."

More pondering, more pausing.

"Where's the land office, acting detective sergeant Danny Hinds?"

He pointed to the courthouse.

"You've been very helpful," I said.

Gears turned, levers moved. "Hey, hold up there," Danny called.

"Yes, ossifer?" I said.

"Forget about the ticket," he said, taking it out of my hand. "For old time's sake."

"Gee, thanks. That's swell," I said and jaywalked to the courthouse—twice, since I was already on the right side of the road when Danny had stopped me.

————

The court building was deserted. Most of the staff was on furlough until the criminal elements returned in the spring. Then justice would be dealt, fines collected, and permits issued. I found an open office with a round woman behind a counter slowly mouthing the words as she read a paperback copy of *The Brand Demand*.

"Hi," I said.

She finished the page and then the next. Using my lip-reading skills I made out, "The aardvark lusted for the chimney bacon to electrify Polansky the Sith." I've never understood modern poetry, nor did I know Johnny Worthen wrote any even though he is my favorite writer. Live and learn.

Finally she put down the book and acknowledged me.

"How can I help you?"

"I'd like to research some land."

"Down the hall, to the right. Ring the bell."

I walked down the hall to the right. I accomplished this by taking longer steps with my left leg than my right until I was scraping against the right wall. No one was there to witness my brilliant slapstick, so I went into the Recorder's Office unapplauded.

I looked through a vacant single window with a "Take a Number" snail-dispenser on the side. My number was 2. I was alone in the office, but the red LED sign said they were Now Serving Number 33. I had a long wait. I saw a domed silver bell on the counter and rang it.

I waited a minute and then rang it again. Twice more. That would show them I was serious.

Two more minutes, nothing.

I was about to go for another ringing, a morse code barrage of dings and maybe some yelling, when a shape appeared through a back door.

The same woman I'd met in the hall previously appeared and slowly climbed aboard a stool behind the counter and then looked at me.

"Can I help you?"

"Finish your book?" I asked.

She sneered.

"I'm looking for information regarding the Racine family holdings. A hundred acres of desert and a house in the city. I'd like to look at those."

"Do you have a parcel number?"

Shit, I did, but I'd left it in my real detective notebook. I was unarmed and helpless.

"Eh, no, not with me," I said, hoping she wouldn't tell me to come back.

"I'll have to look it up then." She heaved herself off the stool to a book-shelf behind her.

"Racine you say? Is that with an 'R?'"

"Usually."

She thumbed through a book and scribbled down some numbers on a slip of paper. She handed me the paper. "Here you go."

I looked at the paper, then up at her.

"I have the parcel numbers now," I said and handed the paper back to her.

She took it and disappeared into a back room.

I pondered job security in the public sector until she reappeared.

"Sorry it took so long," she said.

It hadn't taken more than fifteen minutes. I figured that was a speed record around here.

"I couldn't find them on the shelf," she explained. "They were on the cart to be re-filed."

"What does that mean?"

"Means I couldn't find them right away."

"Why might they be on the cart?" I pressed.

"It means they were looked at recently and nobody bothered to put them back."

"Who puts them back?" I asked before thinking.

"Me," she said matter-of-factly.

"Do you know who looked at them last?"

"No," she said. "I've been off for a while. Must have happened then."

"When was this?"

"Why?"

"I'm conducting a survey," I said.

"I've been gone two weeks. Must have happened then. I went to Ogden to visit my sister Pamela. Pamela just got a new litter of rabbits and needed help naming them before sending them off to the furrier."

"Noble work," I said. "Let me see those records."

"Sign here," she said and passed over a log book. She'd written down the parcel number and book identification for me in clear cursive handwriting that hadn't been taught in schools since the Eisenhower administration.

I signed and glanced over the sheet. I noted the same book having been checked out before. Several times, six or seven on that page alone. Actually it was the only book listed. There were several signatures, all messy and illegible and made by several hands. I tried to make them out anyway but when I looked too hard at the page, she pulled the log away and snapped it closed.

"That's internal bookkeeping," she said, putting the log under the counter. "There you go." She gave me the land book.

I'd done land research before and knew where to look. Mostly it's done on computer or if they've really suffered budget deficits, or lack of energy, they're still on ancient microfiche. Moab was still on paper. It was, however, complete in one volume.

I traced the land back to the original settlements in the late 1890s and then the slow sell off the original thousand acres to the last hundred now. Each time the land was sold, the mineral rights were retained. Good intuition, but poor location. In the '50s, the Racine's leased the mineral rights to a potash mining company. The lease was for "any and all salts, water, and minerals—precious and otherwise," and included underground rights to the original thousand acres. Mining companies were allowed to tunnel, drill, and make arrangements with the top-side owners for open mining should they find anything. They hadn't. A survey report that had no business being in the official records explained how there was no useful potash left on the land, and sadly, after many test drillings, they'd found no oil, gas, or uranium. Nothing had been done with the lease for nearly half a century. It expired this year with all rights returning to the Racines, who were all dead now.

The survey report I found was dated nearly fifty years earlier, but it was a recent copy of a copy of a copy of an original one-page typewritten letter. It was folded in threes as if it had been in an envelope and stuck in the book as a bookmark and forgotten. I took it.

The neighbors were more interesting. To the north was the Ashe Winery. They'd acquired part of the mesa where things could grow and had made it work. They had three hundred acres of useful land in a patchwork of acquisitions. The remaining Racine parcel stuck into it like a thumb in a pie. It didn't look neat on a map, but on the ground, who could tell?

I was expecting to see T. S. Crew listed as another neighbor, but he wasn't. The land was bordered by the Bureau of Land Management on one side and several small landowners on the others. None of the private landholders seemed to be doing anything with their parcels. A cattle company owned one. Dune Buggy Burial Ground, LLC owned another.

Though the Racines were out of the picture, the old ranch lands they'd once owned had traded hands often and profitably throughout the '50s to speculators and mining companies. Then in the '60s, 70s and 80s, banks owned it all and sold it off in short-sales and repossession auctions. That's how Ashe Winery got most of their land.

The Racines still had three hundred acres during the uranium boom. Before he disappeared, Lance sold two hundred for a fraction of what it would be worth even today, which isn't much. Though potash had been discovered on the land, the big uranium deposits were found south and west of Moab. The Racine Ranch was north and east of it. Bad luck.

When a bell summoned my hostess back to the other desk, I helped myself to a stack of papers behind the counter and wrote down some notes. She'd taken the logbook with her or hidden it better than I expected. Jerk.

I went to the front desk again where the woman sold US Geological Survey topographic maps for ten bucks and I paid cash for a couple. Big spender me. I went back to my book and penciled in the borders between the properties as best I could figure.

Finally, bleary-eyed from reading small print, I left the courthouse as the sun set.

15

DESERTS ARE TERRIBLE PLACES. It's only been in the last weird century of safe vacationing that they've become more than imminent death traps. Really, they're full of snakes, rocks, water that's easier to plow than drink, mind-boiling heat in the day and scrotum-clinching cold at night. Soft-core backpackers coming off the desert with their sippy-bladders nearly spent and the batteries on their pocket GPS reading a scary thirty percent, often remark how cold the desert nights are. They congratulate themselves on their survival sense in purchasing the five-hundred-dollar goose-down sleeping bag instead of the lame four hundred dollar one and recount harrowing tales of bats, ants, Chupacabra, and nearly freezing to death in a desert of all places. Lame as it sounds, they're right. The temperature differential is startling. In the winter months, the days are as cold as the summer nights and the winter nights will send an Eskimo to the mall for a blubber-powered space heater.

With the sun sliding behind a mesa, Moab was in shadow when I left the courthouse. Not for the first time, I regretted not bringing my car on my little day trip. My nylon windbreaker-reinforced T-shirt might not be up for the walk home. And I was hungry.

Acting as nonchalant as I could, pretending not to be the blatant idiot tourist I was, I walked the sidewalks looking for an open restaurant with central heating, a period coal stove, or candles on the tables. Several people passed me going the opposite direction dressed in heavy parkas, thick gloves, and mufflers, nodding polite warm hellos. Their alpine clothing may have been incongruous in the warm, desert-themed town but I smiled back through chattering teeth and envied them.

"Tony."

A Blazer pulled up next to me. Allie leaned across the seat and spoke through the passenger window.

"Where are you going?" she asked.

I could feel the warm air from the cab and reflexively took a step closer.

"J-j-just looking for a place to eat," I said.

She was dressed as a waitress. She smelled of bacon and coffee and looked tired.

"You coming from w-w-work?" I forced my teeth to be still.

"Just covering for a friend."

"You hungry? Want to g-g-get something?"

"Yeah, okay," she said, brightening. "Get in."

"Oh, if you ins-s-s-sist," I said, but had already closed the door, rolled up the window and was adjusting the heater controls to high.

She laughed.

"I used to live here," I said. "I should know better. I guess I lost track of the time."

"People forgot how quickly the temperature changes. I do it myself all the time."

"No you don't."

"No, I don't," she said.

"This is the warmest thing I brought with me," I said. I didn't mention it was also my last clean shirt.

"I know a warm place," she said.

I turned my phone on to call Sophia and saw I had accumulated another dozen messages. Recognizing numbers I didn't want to talk to and Worse Nightmare's "blocked" extension, I ignored them all and called Sophia.

"Hi Sophia," I said. "Is it alright that Allie and I go out to dinner tonight?"

"Is your homework done?" she asked.

"It's not due yet. Are you okay at home?"

"Can you talk me through how to open the fridge again in case I've forgotten?"

"There's a manual in the drawer," I said. "With pictures."

"That'll do," she said. "Have fun. Be careful. Use protection."

I hoped Allie hadn't heard that.

"Thanks for the call, though," Sophia said. "You don't have a key so be home by ten."

"Home?"

"Home," she said.

We hung up.

"Sophia reminds me a lot of Vicky," I said. "The way she accepts me reminds me of her."

"She's nice," agreed Allie.

We parked on the street in front of the Cataract Canyon Brew-Pub. This place hadn't existed when I was here last. It was like one of those trendy restaurants with odd and interesting shit hanging on the walls; moose heads, pictures of the Beatles, old street signs and model trains. This one had a definite theme though: white-water adventure. Kayaks hung like chandeliers from the ceiling, and rubber rafts like bloated piñatas. Oars and paddles were the accessories of choice for picture frames, and the soothing colors of driftwood-brown and life-vest orange brought the whole restaurant into tragic tranquility. They could seat half of UCLA, but most tables were empty. Allie asked for seating by the fire and the hostess led us to an eight-foot wok filled with burning juniper. A black iron chimney stretched to the ceiling between shattered pieces of a broken canoe.

"Cozy."

"They have good beer here," she said.

"Good beer and white-water canoeing. I think I understand all the debris now."

The restaurant was named after the famous, or infamous, Cataract Canyon, a forty-six-mile canyon that contains what is considered to be some of the most challenging—read dangerous—stretches of rapids in the country. The Colorado River, not being dangerous enough, is joined by the Green River there and together they drown people all the way to Lake Powell at the bottom of the state. What fun.

We ordered nachos and a pitcher of Broken Paddle Pale Ale. It was either that or Bloated Drowned Body Lager.

"I saw Danny today," I said, marveling at how comfortable I felt with Allie.

"Was he nice?"

"Is he ever?"

"Sometimes he's tolerable. He's pretty insecure."

"Fits the profile of a bully," I said. "I'm not surprised he became a cop."

"He was pretty rough in school." Allie munched on a chip. "But after you left, after the gym thing, he mellowed a lot."

"Tell me he left Rick alone?" Since I'd arrived in Moab, I'd walked the fine line of guilt and calm and I felt myself teetering.

"It's so weird to hear you call him that. No one else did. Not even Vicky."

I shrugged. "My own special pet-name," I said. "Did Danny lay off?"

"Yeah, he did. Everyone else did too. No one knew he had a tipping point before that day. He'd laugh and smile and joke along with whatever cruel taunts were thrown at him. That day, when he literally beat the crap out of the school big shot, he garnered respect."

I didn't tell her that it wasn't the personal taunts that had fired him off, but family loyalty.

"Everyone just kidded with him," Allie continued. "He became something of a mascot, everyone's silly little brother. A special needs kid."

I grimaced.

"But not in a bad way. People looked out for Thick. Like when he caught his leg in the basketball net. No one blamed him. We all helped get him down before the teacher caught him."

"How did he—?"

"Don't ask," she said. "It was before school. I think he'd been hanging there an hour before we found him. Superficial rope burns, a turned ankle and a headache that lasted two days, but he joked about it."

"So why did the town rally around Rick and not Vicky?"

She sipped her beer, fidgeting.

"It's a close-minded town," she said after a while. "It's one thing to be born *impaired*, it's another thing to choose to be different."

I joined her in the beer. The alcohol and the fire were thawing me out nicely.

"And Vicky didn't make things easier," Allie said. "They were just rumors in the old days, but she never denied any of them. I know it drove Sophia out of town. I think her family made denials, but Vicky told everyone to go to hell and mind their own business. Lack of contrition sealed it. She never confirmed anything mind you, but she never blinked in the face of it either. When she was asked to leave the library board, she said some harsh things. That didn't get her any friends. But things are better now. New blood, new thinking."

"Getting married and having a son didn't help?"

"No. It just made life hard on Lance. He finally left Moab to get rich so he could take Vicky and Thick out of here."

"This was before Vicky supposedly killed him, right?"

"Yeah, before."

"Is there any truth to that rumor? The one about Lance?"

"You already asked me that."

"No, Sophia here now."

"No difference," she said. "No. No. No. No truth. Of course not."

"What do you know?"

She took another drink.

I had to swallow when she licked the foam off her lip. I mentally measured how long it had been since I'd seen a woman naked without a mouse cursor over her body.

"I was pretty young when all this supposedly happened," she said. "It was before that summer you visited. Most of it came from Haggy Miller spreading lies."

Our entrees arrived. Allie had a Caesar salad. I had a bottle of A-1 Sauce with a side of steak.

"So why did she stay? Aunt Vicky? Why didn't she just move?"

"Pride, I think. She was stubborn. She wouldn't give them the satisfaction. Also, her parents are buried here. She was the last Racine in the town. I always thought she was waiting for Lance or Thick to take her away."

"What did she do? Seems like she was lonely."

I must have sounded as sullen as I felt because Allie was quick and put her hand on mine. At first a flash of electricity, primitive sexual energy, shot up my arm, but it was brief and I felt only an old friend comforting a lazy man.

"She liked being alone," she said. "Seriously. Don't kick yourself. She was smart and determined. If she needed company, she'd have gotten it."

"Is my guilt that clear?"

"I see it," she said. "I don't know if others would."

My heart skipped.

"Really, Tony, I have never in my life seen a happier hermit, never seen anyone as comfortable in her own skin as your Aunt Vicky. She could teach gurus about contentment."

I looked into her eyes, sympathetic and honest. I felt better.

"How is it, after all these years, I feel as close to you as any person I ever knew?"

"We met at a crucial time in our lives," she said. "It imprinted on us."

"I feel equally ashamed for not contacting you."

"Now you're just being silly. I recovered fine after our little make-out session," she said nonchalantly but then added, "But I also never forgot it."

It had been my first kiss. I don't know if it had been hers, but it might have been. Allie was a tomboy in school, still is. She met up with Rick and me one afternoon at the river while we were hunting frogs in the reeds, and we became a trio by the end of summer and into the school year. She helped me talk Rick out of making a reed boat to float down the river, probably saving his life that day.

We all had curfews and loved to break them. The quoins on the side of Rick's house made escape exciting and easy. Vicky was a deep sleeper, but I think there were times when she heard us creeping in or out and just let it alone, recognizing how magical stolen summer nights could be.

And we had some wonderful stolen summer nights. The three of us would sneak into the Hot Lizard Motel swimming pool when everyone was asleep and play until the guests complained and had the management chase us off. We toilet-papered houses, friends of Allie's who wouldn't call the police. Danny's once. Maybe twice. We walked the dark paths along the river, told stories, and made up games of cowboys and Indians, pretending to be Indian scouts pinned behind a boulder by bench-sitting tourists until one of us circled around to get them in a crossfire. We freaked out a few people with our war whoops and midnight stalking. They were great times.

Then there was that last night in the Braise hayloft. The night before I was to return to Salt Lake and my finally financially afloat family, Allie invited Rick and me to meet her in the barn. It was a cold late November night. Vicky had kept us up talking, as though she didn't want our time together to end. It was past one in the morning when we snuck down the wall.

Allie wasn't in the barn. I tossed pebbles at her window until I broke the glass. She met us downstairs and took us to the barn. It was warm in there, comparatively speaking. We played in the loft under the hay and talked for hours, saying our goodbyes and making promises I didn't keep. Rick had a sudden urge to go for a ride. He dropped to the ground and started to saddle the milking cow in a stall. That left Allie and me alone together in the loft, watching him with flashlights.

"I want to kiss you," she whispered. "Do you want to kiss me?"

Hormones raging, emotions afire, I looked deep into her eyes and said, "Bluh mugga smuuuu abocki."

Charmed by my expert oration, she leaned over and kissed me.

Is there anything as sweet as the first kiss? The second was as nice, as was the third. I ran my fingers through her hair, and she held me around the shoulders. It was a moment out of time. I don't know how long it lasted but not long enough. Never long enough. It was only the sound of Rick being trampled by the cow that pulled us apart in the pre-dawn light.

"How did you ever explain the window?" I asked Allie.

"I showed it to my dad the next morning without explanation. He thought a bat had flown into it and that became the story. My mother wondered about the smell of alfalfa in my hair, but I shrugged that off over a pancake."

"So never been married?"

"No. I came close a couple of times. Then my folks died right after each other and I had to focus on the ranch. Not much time for dating. Too much work."

"Judging from Danny Hinds' behavior, I don't think it would've been hard to find a date."

First-degree felony date foul: displaying jealousy toward other suitors. Lose fifteen points of esteem, demonstrate childish insecurity and lose any chance of further progress in the foreseeable future. Recalling the laws, I braced myself for the ruling.

She raised an eyebrow.

"It's just that he warned me off seeing you today," I said, trying to make it look like this was an anecdote. I put on my poker face and chewed. It worked. I'd gotten away with it. Thank god for no instant replay.

Allie said, "I told you. We dated for a while, but it didn't work out."

"Oh," I said. Not pressing my luck, but then pressing it before the order could be received by my mouth.

"How long ago? How serious was it exactly?" Poker face.

She had a definite look of disapproval this time.

I cut a big piece of steak and crammed it in my mouth so I couldn't fit my foot in there again. That bought me some time. If I tried to talk again, I'd choke to death on Black Angus. Death would be quick and less embarrassing than pouring out my heart in a nostalgic love-struck sex-deprived lonely jealous fit for a girl I dreamed of but hadn't even called. With steak fries.

I chewed slowly, and found something interesting on the wall to the right —oh look, a plaque memorializing all those who died on the rivers this season next to last year's.

"Are you the jealous type?" she finally asked.

The beef wasn't enough to stop my neck, and I nodded in quick assent before burying my face in my hands.

"I'm probably the only girl in Moab who wouldn't marry him if he asked. I saw him as an arrogant jerk in school, and my opinion hasn't changed. But, to be fair, I gave him a chance to change my mind. Small town, you know."

Chew slowly, nod and smile. Realize too late how much you need dental floss.

"We tried it for a month, and then I'd had enough. I'm over it," she said to my sinew-packed incisors.

"But he isn't," I said.

Why had I swallowed?

"That's his problem."

"Sorry." I stabbed the rest of my steak and made ready to cram it into my date-wrecking maw.

"It's okay," she said. "He doesn't understand why he doesn't get everything he wants. He's insecure."

If I opened my mouth for the steak, words might come out. I clenched my jaw so tightly that my ears hurt.

"You were married?" she asked.

I nodded. She waited for a better explanation. She could wait me out.

Breaking the lockjaw, I said, "It fell apart early, but we stayed together for Randy, my son. She had this thing about putting up a front for his psychological development. He saw through it as soon as his eyes focused. We finally made it official last year."

"Still have feelings for her?" she asked.

Tit for tat.

"We're friends," I said. "That's all we've been for a long time."

"Benefits?" She suddenly clenched her own jaw shut.

"Not lately."

I didn't have to put on a face. It was true, and I think she recognized it.

She chewed for a minute, but I don't remember her putting anything in her mouth.

"And now you're a detective," she said after a while.

"I've been many things."

"But always Tony," she said.

"Yeah."

We caught up on college and goals, life-changing near misses, and friends' fatal flaws. We talked easily and warmly as only reunited old friends can. We ignored our food and laughed at stories and some of my stand-up routine.

"How are you keeping the ranch?" I asked.

"Any way I can. I have a knack for training animals. Or rather, I have the patience. What I do everyone could do ten years ago, just no one wants to put the time into it now. I've got a reputation, so I can charge top dollar to train dogs to heel, horses not to buck, and cats to walk across a mantle on demand."

"Really?"

"Yeah, there was this movie where in one scene a cat had to walk across the mantle. They paid me ten thousand dollars to train that cat."

"Ten grand? Why so much?"

"It took two years," she said. "Cats are hard to train. They ended up cutting the scene. But that led to training a horse for Cameron Diaz and another, bigger, paycheck. She kept the horse. It all works out. Always does."

"You amaze me," I said with a drunken sultriness I hadn't consciously intended.

She smiled; her cheeks were bright from alcohol. Our eyes met. Hers were melted chocolate-brown, mine were surely blood-shot-strawberry cheesecakes. My groin quivered, and I blushed. I pulled away to read a framed newspaper headline hanging on a wall:

Ten Feared Dead in Rafting Mishap

"If I owned a rafting service in this town, I'd sue this restaurant," I said.

"It's their best advertisement. The owners run a big river guide service. Danger sells, but it's actually very safe."

"How safe?"

"Only eight fatalities last year," she said. "Six the year before."

I blinked.

"Twelve died from air accidents, parachuting and hang gliders. Ten from snakes. Fifteen from outdoor mishap, including dehydration and sunstroke."

"Best odds in the casino," I said.

"Some people need danger to feel alive."

"Chlorine in the gene pool."

My groin under control, I met her eyes again. That was short-lived. I crossed my legs and ordered dessert.

"So, Detective," Allie said. "Any progress on the Racine case?"

"Gathering pieces, but I think tomorrow I'll get some help."

"Why?"

"Because a town like this is all about image," I said. "News of dead boaters may bring more boaters, but I doubt dead residents will fill any restaurants."

"I don't know," she said. "Have you been to the buffet?"

16

ALLIE DROVE me home because I didn't have a car. Or warm clothes. Or the musculature for long tipsy frozen desert trekking. Or a sense of direction. I tried to correct her when she turned left instead of right. I'd have taken us to Colorado if I'd been in charge.

She'd had only one beer but I worried about Utah's inane alcohol laws, mis-calibrated breathalyzers, and her petite frame. What were the chances of seeing a cop on the short drive back to Vicky's place? About one hundred percent, as it happened. Moab did not teach its cops how to conduct unobserved surveillance. The acting detective was as subtle as a burning parade float.

"Danny's following us," I said.

"Ass," said Allie.

"Will he pull us over, play cop again?"

"I doubt it. Sounds like you burned him pretty good today. He wouldn't want that to happen in front of a witness."

He didn't pull us over.

At the house there was no easy way to steal a kiss, so I waved her goodbye from the sidewalk and off she went. I waved to Danny too, just with not as many fingers.

Sophia was asleep in front of the television. I woke her, locked up, and went to bed.

———

I was up early the next day. Nine o'clock. Practically a working man.

"You're not down here to socialize," Sophia chided me. She was eating a

Pop-Tart. "You're here to work. Remember the femme fatale in Spillane's *Kiss me Deadly*?"

"Book or movie?"

"There's a book?"

"I worked all day yesterday," I said. "Hey, wait a minute. Are you saying you suspect Allison?"

"No. I just couldn't think of another example. I don't want you to forget your Aunt Vicky."

I could see then that she'd had a hard time this morning. Her eyes were swollen.

"I'm on it," I said. "I'll show you."

I grabbed my keys and drove to the supermarket. I bought a box of donuts and *The Moab Picayune*. I read it while waiting in line and was pleased.

———

The kitchen had been put away by the time I got back. Sophia was sweeping the floor.

"Look at this," I said.

"Donuts? You ever hear of protein?"

I handed her the paper.

"The local fish wrapper?" she said. "What about it?"

I opened to my full-page ad. Sophia stared at it, took it from me and read it out loud.

Home Invasion Murder— Killer Still at Large. Police Cover-Up?

Your neighbor, Victoria Racine, lifelong resident of Moab Utah was brutally murdered in her home. Person or persons unknown broke into her Cottonwood Lane home and murdered her when she came downstairs to investigate a noise.

Moab police state—without proof—that the killer has fled the city. They have chosen not to investigate this crime further even though there is compelling evidence that the crime was committed by someone with intricate local knowledge. It could be your neighbor!

This is being swept under the rug. Your safety is being sacrificed for tourism.

There may be a killer among us. Keep your homes locked, your guns loaded, and don't count on the police to help.

Beneath my message was Clem's legal shield:

This is a privately placed advertisement, not a news report. The opinions and suggestions contained herein do not necessarily represent the views of The Moab Picayune or its editors and is printed as an extension of the First Amendment of the Constitution of the United States. God Bless America.

The font was huge, black, and imposing. It could not be missed. If someone had the paper turned out at a sidewalk café, a passing motorist could read it driving past at thirty miles per hour. The last part Clem had added to cover his ass. I didn't mind. He better not charge me for the extra words, though.

"Why is there a little spoon at the end?" asked Sophia.

"He put that in there? I guess it's my signature. I'm stirring the pot, see? Spoon. Stirring the pot. It's symbolic and cryptic all at once."

"A spoon?"

"Yep."

"What will this do?" Sophia asked.

"Well, the killer, if local, will see this and panic. Maybe turn himself in or make a mistake." If I had any suspects, I could watch them and see if they trip up, but I didn't, so this was a premature and idle boast.

"Mostly, it's to stir the pot," I said, pantomiming a stirring spoon. "If we're lucky, someone will come forward with evidence, a witness maybe. But it'll surely scare people, piss off the cops, and put pressure on them to do something."

"So you're being lazy and want the police to figure it out?"

"Ouch," I said. "It's what they do. I'm one guy, and I can only do so much. I've just hired me a bunch of deputies."

"They're going to be so angry with you," she said.

"I'm used to that. It's how I work."

She read the ad again, and tilted her head from side to side, appraising it from different angles. A smirk pulled up the corner of her mouth, and she nodded.

"Okay, Tony," she said. "Be careful. Contrary to the popular saying, there is such a thing as bad publicity and the town fathers won't be happy."

"Is there actually a group of people calling themselves 'town fathers' or is it just a hive mind of business owners?"

"I think the latter," she said. "Though the mayor always talks about it. He's in Texas for a month."

"Of course."

"Let's get to carving pumpkins," Sophia said. "We'll have little ones by five."

It was Halloween. As the last truly pagan holiday on the calendar, I try to make it count. I hadn't even noticed this one coming.

Sophia pointed to three big pumpkins on the floor my detective senses had overlooked. We laid out the *Picayune*, ad and all, across the table to catch the carvings. I'd have saved the ad, but the paper was so thin, it wouldn't cover the little table without it. I'd pick up more later.

Sophia put on a record of scary music, doors opening and closing, wind in the trees, and far-off hysterical laughter. The crackle of actual vinyl added to the mood. I was ten again.

I was into my second pumpkin, a funny one this time, probably with a tongue out or maybe barfing pumpkin seeds, I hadn't decided, when the doorbell rang. Elbow deep in squash guts, Sophia answered it. I heard Danny's voice, and to my horror, heard Sophia invite him in. I gripped my knife.

"Tony, you gotta get out of town," he said.

"Why hello to you too, constable." I could see he was worried. Years of fading and reassembled memories made me hate that face. Not that I needed much of that. Natural jealousy of his fit body and sculpted features would have put him on my shit-list without knowing who he was. Guys can be catty too.

He sat down at the table.

"Everyone knows it was you who put that ad in the paper. Levis will go nuts when he sees it."

"I figured everyone would go nuts."

I didn't deny anything.

"I understand why you did it. I really do. I agree we need to work the case. I want to. But it's too hot for you. Let it cool down for your own safety."

Under normal circumstances with someone I didn't have a pre-pubescent past with, I'd have been convinced he was trying to help me. Unfortunately, I'd conditioned myself with thirty years of imaginings to deny any possibility that Danny Hinds could mean me anything but harm.

I scooped up a stringy glop of pumpkin innards and weighed it in my hands, aimed at his bright blue eyes and surprisingly, plopped it back on the table. I am growing up.

"Danny, Danny, Danny," I said. "As much as I'd like to think you're looking out for me, I can't. I am impressed that you thought you could use this to get me away from Allie, but really it's pretty amateurish. Don't pretend being a cop has anything to do with this."

He ran his hand through his hair, and it fell into place with shampoo commercial precision. He looked hurt. His eyes were sad, emotive, and dreamy. The cleft in his chin was embarrassed. I waited for a comeback. It didn't come.

He got up and walked out of the house.

An hour later I was arranging pumpkins on the front porch when three police cars rolled up. Danny was driving one. Two other Moab police exited the second. The third had Chief stenciled on the door. Out of it came Lieutenant Levis, Cousin to the Gollums of the lost Precious.

Levis marched up the walk, an alligator smile under his one eyebrow.

"Mr. Flaner," he said. "Do you know that it is illegal and immoral to meddle in an ongoing criminal investigation? Do you know that it's illegal and immoral to cause a public panic? Do you know I could have your license for what you've done?"

I pulled out my wallet, removed my five-year-old fishing license and handed it to him. It was a phase. For half a year I collected poles, flies and lures and sat on the edge of muddy lakes catching beer cans. I still had the license. It was expired, but if I wanted it that badly, what could I do?

He took the paper and read it slowly, or multiple times, understanding coming in waves like water-skeeters into an eddy. Now *those* are hard to catch.

Eventually, he smiled an even broader alligator smile and then socked me square in the gut.

I doubled over, and collapsed to my knees. I hadn't seen it coming. If I had, I'd have *so* kung-fu blocked it. I'd have thrown him over my shoulder onto the porch and ground my pinky finger into his fifth rib for the Shaolin pincer-poke-of-death. But he'd caught me off guard. The sucker-punch blurred my eyes, bruised my ribs and sent all my oxygen into the street.

"Cousin Ronald told me about you," he said. He leaned in close and screamed in my ear. "I don't like you!"

"You hide it well," I gasped.

"I understand your aunt was a lesbo," he said. "They die all the time, don't they? Aids and such. Just another dead drain on society. Good for us."

"Glad you got something out of that sensitivity training," I said, half rising to my feet. "Hate to think it was wasted. Taxpayer money and all that."

He kicked my feet out from under me, and I was down on my side. I kept my oxygen, but my elbow smashed into the vampire pumpkin, crushing it. It was really a good one.

"Who do you think you are?" I said to buy time.

"I'm a redneck policeman who has no time for out-of-town city trouble-makers like you."

"So do I call you Lieutenant Cliché or Officer Cliché?"

He went for the other leg and I was back on the ground. I missed the pumpkins this time, but not the flowerpot. I hoped the breaking sound was only the pottery and not my arm.

"Acting police chief," he said.

"From the Steven Seagal school of acting, apparently."

Lucky for me he didn't get the reference, or he might have squinted.

"So where can I send you a Christmas card, Acting Police Chief Redneck Cliché?"

Yeah, I had to press my luck. The next kick moved my spleen next to my shoulder blade and caused me to contemplate a new line of conversation.

"Lieutenant Levis—Lieutenant Herbert Levis, Moab Police." He was still smiling his malicious grin. At least one of us was having a good time.

"Of course it is," I mouthed.

"Ronald and Rosalyn-Janet say hello," he smiled. "But this little meeting is for the mayor. He says hello, too."

"He's in Texas," I said. "Tell him from me, 'Yippee-ki-yay, motherfucker.'"

That got my supporting arm kicked out.

"I think your little vacation is over, Flaner," he said. "It's the off-season, didn't anyone tell you?"

He turned around and marched back to the patrol car. The other cops stared bug-eyed and cast glances back and forth.

Levis gunned his engine and spat up a tail of gravel as he sped off. Gravel spitting peel-outs were required drivers' education training in redneck police schools.

When he was gone, Danny came up to the porch.

"Get him up," he said to the other officers.

They helped me up.

"Anything broken?" Danny asked.

"That jack-o-lantern was a masterpiece," I spat. "I'll sue."

"Tony, I want you to know I had nothing to do with this," Danny said, his deep blue eyes glistening in the afternoon light.

Mad as I was, his eyes made me question my sexual orientation, but my elbow brought me back around.

"What is your job exactly in regard to the public citizenry?"

"I didn't hit you."

"You didn't stop it either. I believe that makes you an accomplice," I said. "Do you know that word, Acting Detective? Accomplice? I know it's a big one, but if you have access to a dictionary and someone who can read, I think you'll find it interesting."

"Tony, I tried to warn you."

"He tore up my fishing license? Now how will I troll?"

"It's too hot, Tony. Go home."

I glared at him and rubbed pumpkin off my clothes.

"I'm sorry," Danny said and turned away.

"But not too sorry," I said.

"No, not too sorry."

Sophia had watched the whole thing through the window and rushed out when the last cop left.

"Thanks for the backup," I said, gathering up terra-cotta shards. My elbow ached with a familiar pain of cracked bones.

"I just saw the end of it," she said. "I ran to the phone but didn't know who to call."

"Good point," I said.

"It was like *L. A. Confidential*. Didn't cops beat up people in that one?"

"That one and all the others too," I said.

I noticed then several neighbors standing on their porches, all their faces horror-struck.

"Keep your homes locked, your guns loaded, and don't count on the police," I yelled. It wasn't as catchy as "Freedom" or "Into the Breach," but it'd have to do. With any luck, word of this little police visit would permeate through the small town before dinner, and make a fine punctuation mark to my ad. My physical sacrifice would not be in vain.

I went inside for a drink of water and an ice pack for my elbow. It was my left elbow. I'm right-handed so my love life wouldn't be affected. Small miracles.

My phone had more messages. I played the most recent from the Levises.

"Flaner, where are you, you fetching a-hole?" Ronald yelled. At least I was a fetching a-hole. "No thanks to you, we got our Precious back. I should warn you that the article I mentioned will run in tomorrow's *Family Saving/Family Values.* I warned you."

That didn't sound good.

Delores, my new ex, had left a message too. It was buried deep in the hang-ups and ignored Levis' non-profanities.

"Tony, we gotta talk," she said. "I'll meet you at the Comedy Cellar Wednesday before the show."

Could an ex-girlfriend leave a more ominous message than that?

"Sophia," I said. "I think I gotta go back to Salt Lake for a while. I have things to do."

"And it's dangerous for you down here," she said. "They've run you out of town. Yes, I understand. I saw it in a movie."

"I'll come back," I said.

"I know you will," she said. "I saw that part too."

17

I HADN'T MISJUDGED the town's reaction. If the younger set had had a say in it, they might have found a way to capitalize on the murder publicity, like the rock climbing body count or Roy's stories of outlaws. But the "town fathers" and vacationing mayor saw only mud kicked in their face and so had sent someone to repay the favor, less the mud.

My Halloween was wasted. I spent the rest of the day in my car driving north through cold snowy passes. I eyed my fellow travelers, sizing them up for possible future meals á la Donner Party. If you fail to plan, you plan to fail.

The passes were plowed, and I only had a few flurries before dropping down on the other side of the mountains and then up to the city just before dark when the trick-or-treaters were first coming out.

In my usual paranoid fashion, I kicked the door open and did a somersault into the kitchen. I flung open the drawer containing my gun and showered the floor with plastic utensils, tape, screws, coupons, putty knives, tile samples, glue bottles, paperclips, and a revolver. Naturally, I'd rolled on my hurt elbow and the pain made my arm shake. My gut wasn't thanking me much for the exercise either. I flicked on the light and waved my empty handgun around like Dirty Harry dying of Anthrax.

I checked each room in turn, doing my best SWAT impersonation until I was sure the house was clear. Whenever I left the house for more than a day, I always did this routine. I'd never actually caught anyone, but it was the only regular cardio I got. I made a mental note to find my bullets.

The doorbell rang and I jumped. Peeking out the blinds, I saw a Wookie, an orc and a princess waiting to be bribed to leave me alone. Shit. Halloween.

I ran to the kitchen and grabbed my usual.

"Trick or Treat!"

I passed out packs of Pop-Tarts.

"Thanks!" they said.

I quickly turned off every light in the house and hid in the back. I needed my pastries for the morning.

I started a load of laundry in the dark and called the Levises.

"Hi, this is Tony Flaner," I said. "I'm just calling to check in. How is everything?"

After saying that, I put the phone down on the table and collected my mail. By the time I got back, Ronald was nearly done faux-cursing me out. I waited for him to catch his breath.

"That's fine," I said. "I've been out of town. A death in the family."

"We paid ten thousand dollars for our Precious, Mr. Flaner. You will be receiving a bill."

"That's nice," I said. "What did the police say?"

"We didn't call the police. The kidnapper said he'd kill her if we did."

"When were you first contacted?"

"The day you left."

"While you were on vacation?"

"Call came in during a layover in Chicago," he said. "They used a voice scrambler. Rosalyn-Janet fainted, it was so scary."

"Rosalyn-Janet would faint at the thought of a blackhead," I said. "They called you on your cell phone?"

"Yes. What do you mean about Rosalyn—"

I cut him off. "How many people have your cell phone number?"

"Not many. Family, some people at work, and of course you, Mr. Flaner."

I'm sure if I'd listened to all of his earlier tirade or any of the messages he'd left I'd have seen he suspected me as the dognapping mastermind. But I didn't, so I was disappointed that my charming tactic of ignoring his every plea and insult had failed to show me as the champion of justice I was. Who'd have thought?

"I didn't get any messages down in Moab," I said. "Bad reception."

"I've been down there, and I never had any reception problems."

"You actually paid ten grand for that dog?" I turned the conversation away from my detected lie.

"Of course we did. We'd have paid twice that for our lovely Precious."

"Well then it was a bargain," I said. "Glad everything worked out."

I hung up. At least that was over.

I fell asleep in the laundry room, pretending I didn't hear the doorbell all night.

———

The next morning, someone had placed a stack of *Family Saving/Family Values* issues on my front porch in the exact spot I'd left Precious' pharmacy and chew toys. I guess this was the trick for not paying the pagan extortion. Harsh.

I was on the cover.

Local Celebrity Private Eye Can't Even Watch a Dog.

The picture was my last mugshot. I had a collection. An amateur Photo-Shopper had turned my eyebrows in and shrunk my eyes to give me a crazy Manson makeover.

I'd merited an entire page, over half the editorial content of Levis' coupon rag. The dognapping was sensationalized to include a suggestion that I was either high on drugs—probably paint thinner, or complicit with the kidnappers. Probably both.

They made a big deal of my disappearing during the family's time of crisis. They thought it was crass, unprofessional, and highly suspicious. The article was the best piece of libel I'd ever read. It was meticulous and suggested a bad lawyer had edited it. The word "alleged" appeared more times than "untrustworthy," "unscrupulous," "villainous" and "uncaring," combined, each of which appeared two or three times.

The article ended with a plea for all dog owners to be careful and not to trust their precious family members to the care of "such unscrupulous, alleged detectives, such as Tony Flaner. Alleged." They included my home address for reference.

"Oh shit," I said aloud. I'd been doxed.

I searched my bathroom for bullets and finally decided to just buy some. The ones I had were old and probably past their freshness date anyway. I hastily paid bills, stuffed the stamped envelopes into my suitcase for later posting and tossed it all in the car. I remembered a warm coat.

I started the car, pushed the garage door opener and slid back into my driveway. I'd just pushed the button to lower the door when the first sack of dog shit splattered against my car's rear window. Then a stick skidded across the roof. Cries of "dognapper" erupted from a cluster of dog-walking yuppies. Another green and white "biodegradable dog dirt disposal bag" splattered on my driver's side window. An enraged dog lover released a Doberman who ran into my door like he had a chance to break through it.

I reversed into the street too slowly to catch anyone under my bumper. The Doberman mounted the hood and peered in at me through the wind-shield with dazed but aggressive eyes. It bared its teeth, slobbered foamy spit over on the glass and barked like Cerberus after Red Riding Hood.

A quick J turn and I sped away. The dog slid off the hood, tumbled, rolled, and then got back up and was after me. How did Aragorn defeat the

Wargs? I couldn't remember my Tolkien, so I floored it. Halfway to Rivendell, the Doberman gave up. I was safe, for now.

Never had the employees at Coopers Complete Car Wash and Detail better earned their money than when they de-crapped my Toyota. I ordered the full-service and drove into the Tunnel of Suds. While starving students in hazmat-suits scrubbed my car from behind lead-lined walls, I doodled in my detective notebook.

The three ingredients to a murder conviction I knew were motive, means, and opportunity. When the police couldn't figure a motive, they were done. I faced much the same problem. I couldn't figure why anyone would want to kill my aunt Vicky. If someone in the town was so offended by her rumored alternate lifestyle, they had plenty of chances to do something about it before now. Or not. She'd been married and then a widow for years. Sophia had been a "roommate" for nearly a year. If some kind of Moral Majority Mob finally cracked, why now?

Then there was the land—the only valuable thing Vicky possessed. At least three people wanted it. How badly was up in the air? How could killing Vicky get it for them? Was it a hit? A wannabe Jason Bourne hired from Craigslist to off a nice old lady and make it look like a botched burglary?

Miss Marple, one of my heroes and sleuthing teachers, once said, "Yes, thanks. Tea would be delightful." But she also said that the most obvious conclusion is usually the right one. Or something like that. She was always going on about tea. Was I looking for bogeymen because I felt guilty for losing touch with the Racines? Could Sophia, who reminded me of Vicky, my mother, myself, and Helen Hayes, have been too quick to dismiss the official story of a random killing as a way of coping with her loss? Was she a victim of her own psychosis?

I wrote "Allie" on my pad and dotted the "i" with a heart. I thickened the lines and circled it with another heart. At least my motivation was coming into focus.

I tipped the traumatized car washers and drove to a library. The invitation to Vicky's will reading hadn't come in the mail yet. It was tomorrow, but I couldn't remember what time. I was dreading it. What the hell was I going to do with a hundred acres of sandstone gullies?

At the library I got a computer, since I'd left mine at home. I dug up T. S. Crew's business card and did some Googling. My hacking skills amaze even me. At the prompt, I "Felt Lucky" and was directed to T. S. Crew Home Builders and Development company's home page first try. I'm surprised the CIA hasn't recruited me.

I quickly deduced T. S. Crew Home Builders and Development was not in the mayonnaise business as I'd imagined, but were building "affordable luxury homes in scenic Utah." They'd moved from road construction, the most lucrative business in the State as far as I was concerned, to more risky home building at the height of the bubble. They had a huge project south of Moab toward the far entrance of Canyonlands that would consist of "86 condos, pool, clubhouse, and nightclub inside a gated community" so none of the trashy jackrabbits could threaten the luxury condo owners. The mixed language name of the place was "Moab Pueblos." In the prospectus I read that it was supposed to have been completed several years before but had instead gone into phased construction. They were nearly done with Phase 1. Any day now. Yep, any day, it promised.

The Ashe Winery was a bigger deal. They were a rags-to-riches story, the Ben and Jerry of red desert wine production. So said their biography. They'd moved to Moab during their "impressionable youth" and never left. Having received the coveted Red Bottle Award two years running, Ashe Winery is "the taste of the desert," which I imagined meant their wine tasted like wind-blow abrasive grit and dehydration cottonmouth. Whatever sells.

I searched a little deeper. I used some of my little-known detective pages that, for a nominal monthly fee I'd never taken off my credit card, search yearbooks and police records. I discovered that the Ashe brothers grew up in Southern California and Phil had several misdemeanor indiscretions involving getting high behind a "Chongs," which was either a Chinese food take-out joint or a head-shop. Even money. The report was unclear.

Tiponi was impossible to find. I discovered that there is indeed a tribe called the "Hopi," though, so that part of his story checked out. I couldn't find any contacts for the tribe in New Jersey however, so I wrote "full of shit" under his name in my notebook. I'd already written it twice. I'd need to move to tally-marks soon.

Danny Hinds didn't have much of an internet footprint. Personally, he had a Facebook page with more pictures of six packs than a Budweiser marketing brochure. I thought I'd stumbled onto a gay porn site, but it was just Danny in the mirror holding a flashing camera over his shoulder.

Not surprisingly, he was the Moab police poster child. He, and his chiseled face, perfect hair, and healthy-skin smile was the centerpiece on the official Moab Police website. "Employed by the Community, Serving the Visitor." Even their police force was tourism based. Gotta love the single-mindedness of the Moab town fathers.

Having only deduced my motives, I left the library for the Comedy Cellar. With a thrill, I read my name on the marquee. It is always cool to see your name in lights, or rather black taped-together plastic letters against a dirty, backlit sign that had once announced the opening of Birth of a Nation. Barry, the bar owner, had bought it from a pawn shop. I was so proud.

My friends were at our usual table. It was too early for comedy, just six o'clock, lubrication time.

Standard, Dara, Critter and Garrett were in the midst of a heated argument. They paused as I sat down.

"Well if it isn't the Lassie Lex Luthor himself, Tony Flaner," said Critter, a googly-eyed, fanged muppet which was Garrett's comedy act and alter-ego. "Come out of your lair to hunt poodles for your nefarious schemes?"

My friends read *Family Saving/Family Values.* Who knew?

"Got all I need," I said. "Looking for muppets to cross breed."

Critter shot me a dirty look, which was something for a muppet.

"Hi, Dara," I said.

"HELLO TONY!" she yelled at the top of her lungs. The entire bar went still.

"THANKS FOR THE OTHER NIGHT!" she screamed. "DOCTOR SAYS MY FUCKING HEARING SHOULD COME BACK BY SPRING!"

Some patrons went back to drinking. Others pointed to me and mouthed the word "dog." For once I hoped my lip-reading skills were off, but the hard looks and sinister stares told me I didn't have many fans in the room.

Standard said, "We haven't decided on the order yet."

"Yes, we have," said Dara. "I'm going last."

"Garrett and I will take clean up, Dara," said the puppet. "We don't want to leave the room traumatized. There might be children."

"Your routines are stale and stolen as a Jean Valjean muffin," said Standard.

"Wow," said Garret. "That there takes you out of the running for headliner."

"No, it doesn't. I'm going last. Tony can go first. Get all the hate out of the room and any vegetables that might have been smuggled in."

"That's not happening again, is it?" I asked.

Dara pointed to a group of conservative housewives, the very kind of people who don't visit comedy night clubs. They were drinking soft drinks and stealing glances back at me. All had ominous grocery sacks at their feet.

"Does Barry know about this?" I asked.

"Doubt it," said Dara. "He doesn't clip coupons."

"You got some free publicity," said Garret.

Critter kept his gaze at the value shoppers, staring them down as only non-blinking felt could. "If he knows, Barry's pleased. It's bringing people in."

"No such thing as bad publicity," said Standard.

"So Tony gets to headline? Because he lost a fucking dog? How's that fair? Hell no," said Dara.

"I don't think I'll go on tonight," I said, watching more tables fill up with Humane Society Volunteers, value shoppers, and vegetable vendors. "I've got a long drive ahead of me. Have to get back to Moab."

"So that settles it. I'm clean-up," said Dara, daring anyone to argue with her.

Standard, one of the bravest men I know, was readying an argument, when Delores walked up.

"Tony. I'm glad you're here," she said. "Can we talk?"

My friends, sensing a private and personal moment, slid over and gave her room to sit at our table so they could all hear it.

"In private," she said.

Dara patted the seat next to her, winked, and gestured a key locking her lips.

Delores looked at me for help.

I looked at the growing crowd and caught sight of Milk Bones being passed under the table like ammo magazines before a raid.

"This will do," I said. "They'll all just ask me about it afterward."

Everyone nodded. She shrugged and sat down.

Before she could say anything, I blurted out, "It's your choice. Either way, I'll support your decision."

Dara's eyes went big.

Critter slowly turned and looked at me and then back to Delores.

"You think I'm pregnant?"

"Aren't you?"

"You know I'm not," she said.

She was right. She told me she couldn't have kids. Several times. I felt stupid. So I was in my element. I leaned back and drank Critter's beer. He seldom finished his anyway.

"Oh, yeah," I said, a little relieved, a little disappointed, a little alarmed at my fading memory.

"My ex-husband thinks we had sex," she said.

"You did," said Critter. "In the kitchen that once. And the hot tub. Some of the Best Tony ever had, he said."

Everyone nodded. I have a big mouth.

"Really? Well he thinks he's honor-bound to beat you to a pulp for it."

"How long have you been divorced?" asked Dara.

"Twelve years."

"That's loyalty," said Garrett.

"No, that's crazy. Whenever he's in jail, he gets through the time by imagining how he'll beat up whoever touched me while he was in."

"How do you know that?"

"Before the restraining order, he told me."

"Oh, okay. How long have you had the restraining order?" Standard asked.

"Eleven and three-quarter years."

"Ah."

"And he knows about us?" I said. "Does he know we're broken up?"

"It doesn't matter."

"Complicated fellow," said Garrett.

"I called the police but there's not much they can do. If they catch him in the act of beating you to a pulp, they'll violate his parole and bring new charges, but until then, he's on the loose."

"He's done this before?" asked Standard.

"Every time," she said.

"How long was he out the last time?"

"Sixteen hours."

"I'm ahead of the curve," I said. "Don't worry. I'm out of town. He'll cool off."

"I don't think so," she said. "He likes prison. He wants to go back. You're his 'honor ticket.'"

"Honor ticket?"

"Family honor," she said. "He says I'm all he has."

"How long were you married, exactly?" asked Standard.

"Five months, three days, six hours. I was a kid."

A middle-age guy at the bar wearing a poorly thought out "I love cockers," T-shirt started barking at our table. Growls erupted from the door and were picked up by other tables who added yips and yaps.

"Does your ex-husband have blue prison tattoos?" asked Critter.

"Yeah, a snake through a skull on one arm and a rainbow unicorn on the other," said Delores.

"Silver belt buckle with a silver dollar on it?"

"Yes," she said slowly.

Garret was the first to look, but we all followed Critter's gaze across the bar to the large blue armed, prison-iron ripped ex-husband. His eyes were narrowed on the table trying to figure out which one of us to kill.

Delores stood up. "Fifty feet, Benjamin!" she yelled.

His eyes widened in shock, and he took several steps backward, counting the paces.

"So you two going to make up?" asked Garrett.

We looked at him, then at each other.

"I'm kinda liking the single thing," Delores said apologetically. "Maybe later."

"Yeah, okay," I said, sliding out of the seat toward the door. "Sounds good. I think I'll go now."

A flash mob of conservative couponers followed me through the back door. Three steps behind them marched Delores' ex-husband, my Worse Nightmare.

18

ONCE AT THE DOOR, I sprinted into the parking lot. Benjamin James Ulrich, Delores' tattooed ex, was confused by the pensioners and soccer moms that followed to my car, but he came on nonetheless.

He wore a short sleeve shirt to show off his scary muscles and tattoos. Below the waist, were Randal Flagg cowboy boots and black light-absorbing Levis. He had a silver belt buckle the size of my car's side mirror with an Eisenhower dollar looking off to the right.

"Tony Flaner," he said, seizing the initiative. "I'm going to mess you up."

The crowd applauded and stepped closer.

I backed toward my car, but it was still too far.

"We're going to make you pay for how you treated that bitch," someone said.

Benjamin whirled around. "What did you say?" he demanded.

One lady wrapped a leather dog leash around her knuckles while another woman with engorged lips and multicolored fingernails got ready to throw a fistful of dog biscuits.

"Who said that? Who said she was a bitch?" demanded Benjamin.

"I did. It was a bitch. The article said so." It was a silver-haired man, about sixty. He wore a golf shirt in November and had very little sense of modern American linguistics. He was in good physical shape. I figured him for a beagle and a good golf handicap.

"What the hell are you talking about?"

"The article," the man stammered. "It told how Flaner mistreated that bitch—that dog—that was with him."

Benjamin lunged at the man and drove his head into the side of a Buick, shattering the side window.

The golfer screamed, a high-pitched, manly, golfer scream. Benjamin pushed him back and staggered forward out of the window.

The ex-con took his shirt off, showing a glorious canvas of ballpoint pen prison tattoos. Cartoon characters intermixed with the logos of rock bands. I thought I caught a glimpse of a Care Bear sliding down the Pink Floyd prism. He flexed, spat, and balled his fists.

A handful of corn-filler dog biscuits hit him in the face. Then a chew toy, which bounced off with a mousy squeak. Enraged, he spun around. He peered into the dim parking lot scanning for targets.

Edging toward my car, I backed into someone and froze.

"Mr. Flaner," said a voice behind me.

I ducked and rolled between two cars, catching my bruised and probably broken elbow on a bumper.

"Ow!" I yelled.

The figure leaned between the cars, a silhouette against the cheap orange streetlight.

"Get back," I yelled. "I have a raging case of herpes." I didn't, but that sometimes made attackers pause.

"I'm not going to hurt you," he said. "I want to talk to you."

I stood up and looked back at the fight.

"Who threw the dog cookies!" Ulrich demanded to know.

The golfer blindsided him across the right ear with a golf club, spinning him but not knocking him down.

Benjamin may have had prison-iron dense forearms and forty pounds on the old man, but the gray-haired golfer had forty years and a putter. It could go either way.

More kibble flew, but Benjamin ignored it.

The dog lovers spread out in a circle as the two fighters faced off.

"We can talk in my car." I opened my locks by remote control and bolted inside. I slammed it into gear as hard as you can slam a hybrid into gear, which just means I pushed a button really hard. The stranger got in. We skidded forward, out of the lot, and into traffic.

Three blocks away, we passed two police cars racing in the other direction.

"Garret and Critter should headline," I thought randomly out loud. "They're really the crowd favorite."

"What?"

"Oh yeah," I said, remembering my passenger. "You're here. Who are you?"

"I'm Mark Levis. You can call me Mark."

The light turned red, so I stopped to avoid attracting undue attention by getting killed.

"You're Ronald and Rosalyn-Janet's son?"

"Yes."

"And you say you're not going to hurt me?"

He was maybe twenty-two years old. He was gaunt, had dyed, jet-black hair and wore black eyeliner that trailed across his temples like an Egyptian mummy. It was a style started by Depeche Mode and carried forward by goth/emo/lost/sad/fashion-challenged kids ever since.

"Are you really that pale or is it makeup? Because if it's real, I think we should find you a blood bank right now."

"It's some of both."

"Don't die in my car. That might piss your parents off."

"I won't."

"Let me guess, you're in a band," I said.

"How did you know?"

"I'm a detective."

"We call ourselves the Entitled Offspring. I play drums, just got a killer Yabuchi X98-Z Alpha electronic drum kit with amps and woofers and a box of engraved sticks. It's great. As soon as Paul gets his new guitar, we're going to start looking for paying gigs." His sudden enthusiasm was a complete reversal from the sad, undead demeanor of a moment earlier. I suspected he could have talked about underground music for an hour if I let him. I could give him tips about agents and the difficulties of making it in entertainment, but his family had just made my life a living dog-shit-hurling hell and I didn't feel charitable.

"What do you want?" I said.

"You mind if I light up?" he asked. "This isn't easy."

He produced a thin joint and lit it with a snap of a Zippo. The car filled with the scent of marijuana and sage, an earthy, arrest-worthy perfume. I rolled down all the windows and maxed the heater.

"I want you not to sue my family," Mark said.

"I hadn't thought about it," I said, cruising south on instinct. The heater kicked into life, cooking my legs while my head froze from the autumn air. "But now that you bring it up, it's a damn fine idea. How much are they worth?"

"Really, Mr. Flaner. They're just weird. We know it wasn't your fault losing that dog. They were warned and everything worked out. They got Precious back and now they're just being pricks. They're tight-wads and hate parting with money for anything, but really, don't be too hard on them."

"Did they send you?"

"No," he said. "If they knew I was here, they'd be pissed. They really hate you. They promised to destroy you, to use every tool they had to make your life miserable and see you suffer for the evil you brought upon them. They cursed your name in a rite of their own devising. They summoned the leaders of the church to—"

"That's enough," I said. "You're not helping your case, kid. Beyond these other Hallmark sentiments, they've already harmed me. Did you see that mob back there? They weren't after my autograph."

"Dog people can be hardcore. They can't see how stupid all this is."

"Stupid is as stupid does," I said.

"Mr. Flaner, I know they're wrong about you. If this gets legal, they'll lose. I have family down in Moab and I know you were down there for all of this. I checked."

"Yeah, I was there since the day after the dog was taken. Lots of people saw me. I spoke at a funeral, had dinner, got beat up by your cousin. Yep, lots of witnesses. But that's only useful if this goes to a real court, not a coupon-clipping libel rag."

"There won't be a court case," Mark said.

"Unless I bring one."

I glanced over and tried to read his face in the glow of red brake lights. He looked like the devil, but in those lighting conditions the Pope would look like the devil. Okay, poor example, but I couldn't read him.

"Where can I drop you?" I said. "I've got a five hour drive, it's 7:00 PM, it's dark, and I'm not wearing sunglasses."

"It's dark. Why would you need sunglasses?"

"Where can I drop you?" I said.

"My car's back at the club."

"I was afraid of that." I swung the car around. "I'll get you close, but that's all."

"Okay. It's good I saved you from that mob though, isn't it? I mean, you didn't get hurt or anything. It's all good."

"Listen, Mark, I appreciate your family loyalty, but honestly, I have other issues on my mind right now. I have no idea what I'm going to do about this stupid dog thing or your stupid parents, but whatever it is, it'll probably be stupid."

"Is that good or bad?"

"Now you're catching on," I said.

We could see squad cars encircling the front of the Comedy Cellar. A line of people sat on the curb, their hands bound in plastic handcuffs looking like neat, little twist-tied biodegradable poop sacks. Two blocks away, I let Mark out.

"So what do you think, Mr. Flaner?"

"I think therefore I'm not your parents."

"I think that's good."

I saw Benjamin James leap over a fence across the street and disappear into the night.

"This isn't over," I thought out loud.

Mark looked pained. I let him stay that way.

Barry, the owner of the Comedy Cellar had a love/hate relationship with me. I'd brought people into his club but usually for all the wrong reasons. I hope the dog-lover mob had paid their minimums. I was grateful the fight was in the parking lot instead of the stage like when an angry husband who I caught sleeping with a TV weatherwoman, leaped up and took me to the floor. The bouncers were on him before I could unleash my fury. Lucky for him. I recovered and ad-libbed a bit about my keen catlike reflexes which explained the catlike screechings I'd made.

The push and pull were back. I pointed my car south and didn't stop for a cup of day-old coffee you could use to pave a driveway until I was an hour on my way.

I called Sophia and said that I was on my way and not to wait up.

"There's a key under the white rose bush in back by the garage," she said. "Vicky put it there for Thick, and it's still there. Look for a broken flowerpot."

"Will do," I said.

That rose bush was new when I visited at ten. It had become quite a big bush now. I remember seeing the last white petals in the backyard and thought they were snow. Vicky loved roses. The front of her house was always a contender for a magazine cover and discouraged young boys playing there due to thorns. Except for that one white bush, Vicky had left the backyard clear of brambles for laundry and horseplay.

Anyone who likes night-driving has a death wish. I know there are many people, death-wishing people, who drive at night as a career. They're scary and shouldn't be allowed to breed. Either they're vampires with a gasoline fetish or hardcore boredom junkies immune to hypnotism. After the first hour, I pulled into every truck stop on the way, first to stretch and buy coffee, then to stretch, buy coffee, and pee. After I left the main freeway, the parallel lines in my headlights became a lonely roller coaster to the Outer Limits. I rolled down my windows, sang show tunes, spilled coffee on my crotch and screamed.

Then I hit the zone. The road took the car, and I was a passenger. I was wired and awake and the wheel was an extension of my bladder, and suddenly I didn't need to know what was more than fifty feet in front of me. There was no moon and little ice and my mind went into power-saving mode.

The unbroken solitude of the drive let me concentrate. Though I'd done some digging, I'd done little thinking. The night road and the coffee that wasn't in my pants, conspired to spark my synapses. Maybe I was mistaken about nighttime drivers.

The police report had suggested a spike, a knitting needle, or an ice pick for the murder weapon. Ice picks were used by Mafia hitmen back in the day, but their use declined with the invention of the modern refrigerator. Knitting needles were made of wood or aluminum and were as sharp as the cop who'd made the suggestion that one could have been used to kill Vicky.

A spike is a general term for something pokey and the writer of the report was just covering his bases.

The damage done on the back door wasn't done by a knife. There were dots where a "spike" had caught the wood, splintered it, and pried at it. A regular knife would have been better for the work. Hell, you didn't even need to chip the wood. If the bolt was undone, a credit card would have opened the door.

There was nothing to discount what the police thought had happened. I was working off a hunch. My theory of a local villain was supported but not proved by circumstantial evidence of a possible earlier break-in. Even there, I was going on faith that Sophia had sussed out events correctly.

I shouldn't discount Sophia. No one else knew that Vicky would be alone unless they were watching the house for a long time. I didn't like how suspecting Sophia made me feel, so like the objective professional I am, and against Phillip Marlowe's ardent dissent, I crossed her off the list of suspects on a hunch and the fact that she'd hired me in the first place.

As far as we could tell, only three things were touched in the fatal break-in; the door which was crudely stabbed open, the vase, and Vicky herself.

The vase was the giveaway. It was as far from the back entry as any burglar would go—at the front entry. The burglar had to cross the entire house and pick it up with both hands, since it was so big. Then, they had to carry the cheap trinket, not outside, but to the living room, right underneath Vicky's bedroom, and drop it on the coffee table.

Unless Vicky was already dead, that woke her. If the house wasn't so secluded behind rose bushes and hanging trees, it might have woken the neighbors. Then, instead of fleeing the scene having just played the *1812 Overture* crescendo with pottery, the killer hides in the laundry room where they can ambush Vicky at the bottom of the stairs. Then they run.

I'd like to think that if there'd been something obvious to gain by her death, the police would have taken a more serious look at the case. If Vicky wasn't a hermit, an outcast haunted by rumors and suspicion, then maybe they'd have done more too. And I doubt it helped that Vicky's son had literally beaten the shit out of the acting detective.

Bats flew through my headlights. I imagined drunk lizards in golf shoes on a cresting wave in Vegas. Can't stop here. This is bat country.

When that had passed, I joined up with I-70.

I was glad to put Salt Lake behind me. I'd have to figure something out about the Levises' libel in the paper, but first I'd have to survive the poison pen I'd left in Moab. Live by the paper, die by the paper. I'd kicked over an anthill before I left, and I knew I was driving into a storm of enraged badge-wearing, pepper-spraying, tourist-centric ants more concerned with appearances and punishing me than solving Vicky's murder. But at least that was now on their list of things to do.

Moab was aglow in neon, but there was nothing happening. In the summer, the streets would be populated 24/7, but now, tumbleweeds couldn't be bothered to show up.

My car pulled silently up the driveway in electric mode and I got out. I left my bag of stuff and grabbed a flashlight to look under the white rose bush.

There it was, beside the carport. The only bush in the yard. I thought of Vicky planting that bush specifically for Rick so he wouldn't get locked out. He told me that it had happened to him several times. That's how he'd learned to climb the quoins on the side of the house.

The key was in a broken music box, under a piece of broken terracotta pot shard. I took it to the back door, turned the key in the bolt and then the knob and was in. I ran the key back before grabbing my suitcase and lugging it in.

It was past two in the morning and I was more wired than a T1. I drank a beer in the front room to soften the drive's caffeine and perused a photo album I found on the shelf.

For an hour in that album I witnessed the Racines come to Moab, build a house, grow old and die. There were pictures of a pioneer family in front of a cabin beside a blurred cow. Rick's face was just a hint in his great-grand-mother's eyes. A picture of the house being built showed Lance Racine as a small boy in his father's arms, his mother beside them in an apron. Behind them stood the hired help posing before an unfinished wall I recognized as the corner quoins below Vicky's window. Though black and white, it was bright and hopeful, and dusty enough to make my tired eyes water. I dabbed at them with a handy tissue.

There were wedding pictures of Lance and Vicky, and newborn pictures of Rick. There was a postcard from Costa Rica and pictures of Rick's middle finger throughout his life. There were a few pictures of Rick in the army, holding a gun, lying in a hospital bed, eating in the barracks, and lying in another hospital bed. There was a final picture of Rick atop a skyscraper overlooking a city, smiling and pointing far into the distance with his left hand, his right in a traditional salute.

An entire family history contained in one small book. It was like the story began with the crossing of the Green River and ended with Rick on that skyscraper. Rick was my cousin, son of my mother's sister. I was a Racine by marriage, but Rick and Vicky were blood, and all of them were my people. The book grounded me in my frazzled beer-soothed mind, and I felt my feet sink through the floor and into the red dirt beneath the old house before I fell asleep in the chair.

19

SOPHIA WOKE me from my chair before six. She was dressed and bright-eyed. I groaned and dragged myself up to bed, collapsed, and got in two more hours before my bladder sent me in search of porcelain. I showered and chanted the magical mantra "a shower's worth an hour of sleep" I'd learned in college. I turned off the water and still felt like shit. I dried off, hung up my towel and got back in the shower. One more hour should do it.

I was downstairs again at ten.

"What time's this will thing?" I asked.

"Eleven," she said. "You should probably get ready."

"I am ready," I said.

Her eyebrows disagreed. I went back upstairs.

My suit was getting a workout in Moab. To accompany the gravy stain and mustard patch I now had wrinkles and a dirty shirt. Still the tie was neat and passed Sophia's critical inspection, if only on pity points.

"Do you know where it is?" she asked. "The address is on the letter, but I don't recognize the name. They changed so many over the years."

"Well, actually, I have a map," I said. I dug out the LARP brochure and map I'd gotten from Roy at the kiosk. "Take us ten minutes, tops."

On the way to Rumbold's office we passed some actual traffic which was something of a novelty in Moab that time of year. We followed a white Ford Explorer with "Goblin War Chief" written in large green dripping letters on its side. The family of white decals in the back window depicted two large goblins, two little goblins and a goblin in a dress. They also had a cat. They drove slowly, studying a map like I had. We turned off and let them find a lair on their own.

Archie Rumbold's office was indeed a house. There was nothing to indicate an attorney's office and the only sign was "A. Rumbold" on the side of his mailbox. The house was from the '50s, and the yard from the last millennium, before cultivation and irrigation were fashionable. One tree hugged the property line where I imagined its roots mined for water under the neighbor's lush lawn. It bent a little that way as if seeking asylum.

The front door was accessible from the street along a sage and cactus-bordered sandy path that made you check your water bottle before starting. There was also a gravel road that led around the back. We followed that.

Behind the house was an unattached garage like Vicky had. An old wire clothes tree I recognized from history books and civil defense films stood in the backyard, a callback to a less civilized time before electricity made wind so yesterday. Instead of clothes however, the tree was garlanded with wind chimes. There had to be a hundred different ones hanging from it. I'm sure each one was a soothing chorus of natural music, but when a hundred all chimed together it was a glass waterfall on tin rocks. I figured Archie Rumbold had problems with vermin—skunks, bears, Jehovah's Witnesses—and this was an audio deterrent, like those ultrasonic mouse gizmos guaranteed to piss off rodents from fifty feet.

"Ever been here before?" I asked Sophia.

"No. I always thought this place was abandoned."

On the back door we finally saw a sign advertising: "Archie Rumbold, Attorney at Law, Semi-retired, by appointment only. Specializing in land disputes and estate planning."

I checked my watch. We were five minutes early. Even with the goblins, it hadn't taken us ten minutes to get here.

"Hey ho!" came a shout through the concussive wind chimes.

We looked down the lane and saw a mountain bike barreling toward us. It skidded to a stop behind my car, spitting gravel onto its roof.

"You guys here for Ms. Racine's will?" he asked.

We nodded. The man was in his thirties, but younger than me and as fit as a survival show host. When he took off his helmet, black curly locks tumbled over a dust-covered face. He had dark, but bloodshot eyes. The right side of his head had been shaved and a line of stitches three inches long extended over his ear. His left knee and shin were bleeding from fresh road rash. As he reached out to shake hands, I noted his little finger bent thirty degrees askew from his others.

"I'm Archie Rumbold," he said. "Sorry I wasn't here to meet you. I had a little crash on the trail." He pointed to his leg and the blood pooling in his shoes.

"I tried Big Rock Trampoline," he said, producing a key and opening the door. "I nearly made it."

He gestured for us to go into his office while he sat down and peeled a scab-cemented sock off his foot and put his finger straight with a disturbing pop.

This part of the house was separated from the rest of the building by a door at the end of a short hallway. On this side of the door, there was a mudroom for shoes, coats and bandages, a small office with books, chairs and crutches, and a bathroom with an industrial sized first aid kit mounted on the wall instead of a mirror. The hall was a photo gallery of Archie's daring exploits. There were pictures of him hanging from cliffs, kayaking down waterfalls, bungee jumping from a tree fort, and being airlifted by a search and rescue helicopter from the side of a red cliff. There was a picture of him in a body cast throwing a thumbs-up from a hospital bed in Hawaii. The flower Lei gave it away. There was one of him on crutches giving the thumbs up while being wheeled out of a Mexican hospital. He held a little flag in that one. There was a telephoto picture of him hanging upside down from a tangled parachute off a bridge, again thumbs up, or rather down that time. His face was red and full of blood. He looked like a zit about to pop. In a wider angle, you could see emergency firemen looking over the edge at the tangled cord. One held a chainsaw.

"Big Rock Trampoline is a gnarly jump," Rumbold said, coming into the office. "I've never done it, but it has been done, so I will do it eventually."

There was a sofa, a steel office chair, and a scattering of folding chairs crowding the room before a wooden desk. Sophia sat in a steel chair. I stood behind her.

Archie smiled.

"Who are you?" he asked me pleasantly.

"I'm Tony Flaner."

He stared.

"Here for the reading of Victoria Racine's will," I offered. The head injury was recent, so I gave him the benefit of the doubt.

"I'm Sophia Curtis," said Sophia.

"I'm Archibald Rumbold, but you can call me Archie." He smiled at her and glanced at me.

"You're together?" he said. "Okay. Have a seat. The others should be here soon. I'm just going to wash up. Have a juice from the fridge."

He skipped to the bathroom and closed the door.

If I wasn't already anxious that he didn't remember me, or perhaps didn't even know my name, the addition of "others" gave me a start.

I helped myself to bottled water from a miniature fridge behind the desk, though the Ultra-Max Energy Jam Slam with Pecans looked good too.

I read his framed UCLA diploma and Bar Association credentials hanging on the wall while sipping the Italian tap water.

Archie came back toweling his hair dry. He'd changed into clean shorts and a buttoned shirt. I felt stupid in my suit. "They're late," he said, glancing at the clock.

"This is the reading of Vicky's will, right?" I asked.

"Mrs. Victoria Racine, yes," he said. "She left specific instructions on who should be here. She wanted to make things easier. You'll see." He turned to Sophia. "Hey, I'm sorry I missed the funeral. I was up in Washington, free climbing before the ice took total hold. That's where I got these stitches."

Sophia didn't answer.

Sensing problems, I said, "You do know I'm Vicky's only living relative, don't you? Tony Flaner? A Nephew?"

He raised an eyebrow, but there was a knock at the door. He excused himself to answer it.

I wanted to ask Sophia what this meant, but I saw her slipping into personal melancholy. I'd have to work through my selfish insecurity myself. If only there was someone I could lash out at.

God answers prayers.

"Danny Hinds," I said. "To protect and serve. Accomplice to assault and battery, police cover-up, dereliction of duty, brutality, and chronic halitosis."

Danny stopped in the doorway and held his hand up to his face and breathed out. It was cinnamon fresh. I could smell it across the room, but it was fun to see him check.

"You disobeyed a lawful order," he mumbled.

"Is that what your acting detective senses tell you, or are you cheating off someone else's paper again?"

Before he could answer, in walked T. S. Crew. He stepped carefully around Danny and plopped down on the sofa, his pastel pink polo shirt tight around his chest. He spread out to take up the whole thing. The Ashe brothers followed him in, casual as a picnic. Phil had on a tie-dye; Bill business casual, no coat. Both waved at me and found chairs.

After them, Tiponi walked in like he was balancing a book on his head and a chip on each shoulder. His sunburn had healed a little and was now a blotchy tan and red tapestry of confused origins. Last, a suited man taking little mousy steps shuffled in. He had a pinched face and a briefcase. His tie was too wide and, besides me in my condiment coat, he was the only man formally dressed. Sophia looked nice, but not courtroom nice.

"Hi everyone," I said. I had to be careful. I had to skillfully and subtly broach the question eating at me.

"What the hell are you all doing here?" I said.

"We got a letter from Rumbold," said Phil waving a piece of paper.

"Me too," said T. S. Crew, shifting on the couch so he was slightly more sitting than lying.

"Tiponi receive letter," said the Aryan. He remained standing, arms crossed.

The mouse man with a briefcase bobbled his head in agreement from a folding chair as far from the desk as possible. I think he wanted to move into the hall. I'd have helped him.

It was an Agatha Christie moment, and I seized it. I didn't grind through all those dreadful Miss Marple stories not to know to take advantage of such a gathering. The detective in me spoke.

"Tiponi," I said.

He swayed a little and I knew he'd locked his knees. Blood was pooling in his legs and he'd fall over like a severed sycamore any second. He realized it too just in time, caught himself and took the last folding chair.

"Tiponi, had you ever been to Vicky's house before the other day?"

Everyone glared at him, accusation and suspicion clear on their faces. T. S. Crew's ears glowed pink.

"Yes, I visit many times. I tell you this already. Me talk Miss Racine about Indian lands," he said.

"T. S. Crew," I said. "You ever visit Vicky at home?"

"Yes, a few times," he said. "I thought we agreed on a moratorium to let the family grieve?" He looked at Tiponi and the Ashes in turn.

The brothers looked at Tiponi who stared into the middle distance over the desk as if sensing a herd of buffalo spirits.

"Why'd you visit her?" I asked Crew.

"I dropped by to talk business. She wouldn't come to my office, so I thought I'd make things easier for everyone and visit her at home. She was a lovely hostess, charming lady, a wonderful woman. A real loss to the community."

Sophia rolled her eyes.

"And you Ashe boys. How about you. You guys ever visit Vicky?"

"A few times," Bill said. "Just visiting."

"No business talk?"

"Yes, some," said Bill. "We talked about being neighbors."

"About the land? The one hundred acres?"

"We just wanted to know her intentions with it," said Phil. "Just curious."

"She wasn't interested in selling it," said Bill. "So that was that."

"We gave her some wine," said Phil.

"We drank some," I said.

"How'd you like it?"

"Change the label."

Phil looked hurt.

Archie spoke. "Sorry guys. I should have told you to come to the back door in the letter. Can't hear the bell from this side." He'd gauzed up his leg wound but a red stain spread over it like spilled juice in a Brawny commercial.

He sidled through the group and took his chair behind the desk. The little office was packed. If I'd been claustrophobic, I'd be nervous. I am, so I was.

"Usually these kinds of things are invitation only," he said. "But since Mrs. Racine was the victim of a violent death, the Moab Police Department asked to have a representative be present today. If anyone is opposed to Officer Hinds being here, I can have him leave. I will however need to reveal some, if not all, of the will's contents to the police later. Does anyone object?"

My hand went up.

Danny narrowed his eyes, his long luscious lashes would be the envy of Maybelline.

"I have a question," I said.

"Yes? Mr. Flaner, is it?"

That worried me.

"Is Allison Braise invited?"

Danny scowled all the more.

"No, just the six of you," he said.

"Seven," I said, "unless you're counting the Ashes as one person."

"Six. The names listed to be here are Sophia Curtis, Tiponi the Indian guy, Bill and Phil Ashe, T. S. Crew and a representative from Green River Savings and Loan." He gestured to the mouse sitting in the hall.

"And Tony Flaner," I coaxed.

"Afraid not."

No one cared. Everyone stared at me. I wasn't the only one surprised by this news, but I was the only one to have his feelings hurt by it. I felt my lower lip quiver and hoped no one noticed.

On cue, Bill offered me a handkerchief from his pocket. Phil shrugged his shoulders compassionately. T. S. Crew knitted his brow in sudden concentration and Tiponi lent me a sympathetic nod.

I had been forgotten.

"I'm Owen Weaks," squeaked the banker. "Vice president and senior loan officer of the Green River Savings and Loan."

"I understand that Mr. Flaner is here with Sophia Curtis," the attorney said. "Does anyone object to him being here?"

Danny raised his hand and smiled at me.

"You don't have a vote," Archie said.

"I have a question," he stammered.

"What is it?"

"Oh, uhm. I forgot."

I hate Danny Hinds.

"Everyone get comfortable," Archie said.

T. S. Crew shifted more in the deep couch. It was plush and low, and he had to look up to see anyone. It might as well have been a beanbag. I could tell he deeply regretted his choice of seats, but it was too late now. There wasn't an unoccupied square foot in the room.

"Is everyone comfortable?" he asked again earnestly. It was very important to him that everyone be comfortable. Sensing a storm, I sat on the edge of the couch, my butt in Crew's face. He shifted.

"Mrs. Victoria Racine asked for you all to be present today, to hear the reading of her will. You will understand why in a moment. I am directed to read the following which is her words and her wishes for her legacy. Her wishes are formalized and notarized."

He produced a piece of lined paper from a folder. I could see hand-written script, Vicky's own words.

"'This town is a narrow-minded, backwater, accidental boom town that should be erased from the earth and forgotten like a cat turd. It has no business existing,'" he began.

Not a traditional beginning to a legal document, but I liked it.

"'Those people who claim to be 'Moab natives' need to shut the hell up or give the land back to the Utes. They are snobs and bigots, and if the newcomers don't chase them away, I can rest easy knowing their inbreeding will kill them off soon enough.

"'I haven't felt welcome here in my life. My husband and son were from Moab and tolerated this nasty place but got out as soon as they could. Now I'm finally free of it as well. May everyone die of radiation poisoning or floods. May the Indians come back and slaughter the lot of you. Rot in hell, Moab.'"

Archie paused to let it sink in. Even Tiponi's practiced stone face showed shock, or maybe hope. Sophia grinned and I caught it like a virus. We choked back laughs. Archie read on.

"'The last Racine died in Atlanta. The line is gone. I carried the name but only the name and stayed in the desert for Thick and for Lance. When I'm gone, even that pretense is gone. Let it all go.

"'It is my wish that my one hundred acres of desert known as the 'Racine Ranch' be auctioned off immediately and all monies from that sale be given directly to Sophia Curtis, one of only a handful of flowers to blossom in this desert. She is to take the money and leave Moab, hopefully never to return. I'd like her to travel to Asia and see Tibet, but she may do as she sees fit.

"'The house on Cottonwood Lane is also to be sold. I doubt there will be any money left after the mortgage, but if there is, Sophia gets that too.

"'It is my wish that these auctions be held as soon as possible after my death. That is why I have asked T. S. Crew, The Ashe Brothers and Tiponi, that Indian guy, to be here. They have all shown an interest in buying the Ranch. If more buyers want in, they are welcome to bid, but I want the auction to be done as soon as possible so Sophia can get the hell out of this bigoted, cruel place she suffered for me, and I for my lost boys.

"'The bidding on the Ranch must begin at $250,000. I will be satisfied with that amount. That much should pay the taxes and fees and still give Sophia all she'll ever need. If that amount is not met, Archie may market the land for up to three months to get more buyers.'"

Archie looked up at the shocked group.

"Are you gentlemen interested in buying the land? Will an opening bid of $250,000 be a problem?"

"Good with me," bellowed Crew so loud, he made me jump.

The Ashes looked stunned. Finally Bill said, "I'll offer that."

"This is an outrage, a travesty!" said Tiponi, slipping out of Indian chop-talk and back to English. "It is not Racine land. It is Hopi land. It is the rightful land of the Hopi Nation and I will not buy back what was stolen. You will be hearing from my solicitor." He pushed his way through the crowd and out of the house. He knocked into Weaks and slammed the door on the way out.

"Mrs. Racine warned me about this," Archie said. "I was hoping he'd be reasonable."

"So when's the auction?" asked Crew.

"Let's say in a week. Next Thursday. I'll let you know the details when I have them fixed. Victoria's death was sudden and unforeseen and I'm afraid I've been out of town. I've been in Washington, free climbing, it was really great. Good hospitals in Portland. Anyway, I'm not as prepared as I need to be, but I will be by Thursday, and I'll be in touch."

Everyone nodded.

"Is there anything more?" asked Sophia in a cracked voice.

"Nothing more about the dispensation of the property," he said. Just a personal note.

"Read it," said Sophia.

He hesitated. "It's personal."

"Give it to Tony," she said. "I can't focus."

"Sophia?" I said.

"Out loud, Tony," she said.

I took the letter reverently and read it. "'Let all the secrets be known. I am ashamed of none of it. It was all done for love. Be free, Sophia. I love you.'"

A silence fell over the group. A tear fell from Sophia's eye.

"I'll be in touch," said Archie as way of dismissal.

The others shuffled out of the house. Archie excused himself. I stayed with Sophia and knelt beside her. After a moment, I laid my head on her lap and misted up for the family I hadn't known, the aunt who'd suffered in silence but screamed from the grave. I contemplated the injustice of distance and distraction and wondered about secrets.

20

SOPHIA TOOK up Vicky's handwritten papers and held them like holy writ. I sensed an exit. Outside I found Archie talking with Danny. I overheard the last of their conversation.

"Probably just kids," Danny said. "Tourist kids passing through."

Danny saw me, nodded to Archie, and marched to his patrol car and got in. He peeled out spitting gravel at our legs per departmental protocol.

"Pesky itinerant tourists bother you too?" I said. "Seems to be a regular pandemic of unsolvable tourist-related crime here."

"It does happen," he said.

"What was it?"

"Just a broken window." He pointed to the window behind his office desk through an overgrown bush. "Nothing was stolen, just vandalism. I reported it a month ago and no one ever even showed up."

"You could use the newspaper," I said.

"Like this?" He held up a paper.

"Son of a bitch." I admired this month's issue of *Family Saving/Family Values*. I stared at my mug shot over "Local Celebrity Private Eye Can't Even Watch a Dog" in triple bold block letters.

"Where'd you get that?" I asked.

"Sergeant Hinds gave it to me. He was passing them out to everyone before they left. He had a stack in his car."

I was dumbfounded. How had a Salt Lake Valley rag made it all the way down to Moab the day after it was released? Then I remembered Lieutenant Herbert Levis, acting police chief, and added the power of FedEx, and I had working recipe for long distance defamation. Danny the delivery boy would be an easy recruit.

I could smell the smoke pouring out of my ears, feel the veins in my neck bulge and thought back on Mark's appeal for clemency.

"I saw your ad too," Archie said. "That was either a good or a bad idea."

He was a lawyer alright.

"I may need an attorney that knows something about libel," I said.

"And I may need a private eye. Are you really a detective?"

"I thought so," I said. "What do you need?"

He folded the paper and tucked it under his arm.

"Victoria thought that Tiponi, the Indian guy, might make things hard. She'd hoped he'd just bid like the rest of them, but it doesn't look that way."

"What can he do?"

"He can delay the auction while experts write reports. That's not what Victoria wanted."

"Can he win the land?"

"I don't think so. The implications of handing land over to native Americans—bless their oppressed souls—on the basis of them having had it in the past or scribbled something on a wall, just won't fly. If he gets the auction stopped, you'll see every landowner in the county out for his scalp, then the state, then the country."

"So ignore him. I'm good at that. I can show you how."

"No. I think he'll try something. I don't know how desperate he is. He's a true believer. He'll do something if only waste our time. Vicky didn't want that."

"What's his claim?"

"I'm not wholly sure about that either. Last I heard, it had something to do with magical writing on a cliff wall."

I had Tiponi's photo in my wallet and showed it to Archie.

"Yeah that's it, but there's more. Victoria had a bunch of photos of the place. I meant to have all this settled with a threatening letter, but there wasn't time. She died so suddenly."

"Murder is usually fast," I said.

"Not always. Are you really her nephew?"

"Yep. I'm not a Racine, though. I'm related on my mother's side."

"Bummer for you then. You get nothing. Do you want to sue the estate? I can't help you, but I know a guy."

"I got plenty," I said to the ethically challenged solicitor. "Is a quarter of a million too low for the land? Seems like a hundred acres ought to be worth more."

"It's too high," he said. "Even before the housing collapse, it wouldn't have been worth that much. There's an old mine on it, possible heavy metal clean-up. That doesn't help development values. Besides, it's all broken in canyons. All the flat land that was any good for human use was sold long ago."

"So why did Vicky think she could get two-fifty large for it?"

"Someone already offered her that much."

"Who?"

"She didn't say."

"But there are at least two parties willing to pay that much now," I mused.

"And Tiponi, the phony. Victoria was pretty sure he'd be in on the bidding."

"If he doesn't kill the auction outright."

"Yes," said Archie. He thumbed through the magazine for coupons from stores two hundred miles away. "What's this about?"

"Stupid rich people."

"Stupid is good," he said, giving me free legal advice.

"I'll check into the Indian thing. Can I see those photos?"

We went back inside. Sophia still sat on her chair, the pages still in her hands. She wasn't crying, only staring.

"Do you want some water or a high-caloric energy drink, Ms. Curtis?"

She shook her head.

He sat down behind his desk and searched through a side drawer.

"It's partially my fault for this whole Tiponi thing," Archie said. "When she was looking to sell the land last year, I sent out feelers."

"She was going to sell it last year?"

"After her son Thick died, she got really sick. It looked bad. She thought she was going to die. She was wasting away. She wanted to tie up as much as she could. The taxes were due, and the state was going to take it anyway, so she made plans to sell it."

"I told you how ill she was," Sophia said. "When I got here, she was frail as a dandelion bloom. 'Bout the same color too."

"Cancer?"

"Depression. It was eating her up. She was weak and could hardly keep down food. She was dying."

"Then you saved her," I told Sophia. "And made her happy."

That brought a sniffle from the old woman.

"Here are the pictures," Archie said, handing over a dozen photographs of a rock wall in a narrow canyon. It was hard to tell scale, but it looked like the wall art was about seven feet long and four high. Scratched and painted. There was some colorful English graffiti too.

"So after Sophia came, she changed her mind about selling it?"

"Yes. When she 'stopped dying' as she put it, she wanted to keep it."

"How'd she pay the taxes? Why didn't the state take it?"

Archie leaned back in his chair and unscrewed the top of a brown jar of sludge and poured some in his mouth. He chewed a bit and then swallowed.

"Someone paid the taxes for her," he said.

"Who?"

He shrugged.

I looked at Sophia.

She shrugged.

"Was it a lot?"

"I think so, low to mid five figures."

"And there's a mortgage on it?"

"Not on the land. She couldn't borrow against that. It's that crummy. She was trying to get one when she wrote the will, but it never worked out. The bank refused."

"Which bank?"

"Green River Savings and Loan," he said. "They also hold the first and second on the home."

"How'd she make those payments?"

"My savings," said Sophia. "I had some social security too. Vicky couldn't have gotten by without it. She needed boarders before I got there, and even that wasn't enough. We were always behind."

I nodded and gulped back a pang of guilt I was so familiar with I'd named it "Guilt Buddy von Sour-Gut." I could have helped her if I'd known.

"How much is owed on the house?" I asked anyone who'd answer.

"In this market," said Archie, "more than it's worth."

"There was a realtor at the funeral. Scabies or something."

"Skingle?" asked Archie.

I nodded.

"He represents flippers and rental converters. He might be interested in the auction, or he might just try to swing a deal with the bank after foreclosure. That's what they usually do."

"Is it in foreclosure?"

"No," said Sophia. "We were way behind before, but we're only two months now. We have to be three before the bank can begin foreclosure. We checked."

Guilt Buddy noted the use of the plural and nibbled my ribs.

"I have to announce the auction to as many people as possible," Archie warned me. "It can't be fixed."

"Well the bank already knows. The more the merrier," I said.

"Mr. Rumbold," said Sophia. "Was Tony mentioned in the previous will?"

"No. She didn't have one beyond the basic do-it-yourself one out of a book. It named Thick Racine as the beneficiary. When he died and she got sick, she came to me about selling the land. Then she got better, and she came to me for the will."

"Have you ever been in the house on Cottonwood Lane?" I asked.

"Yes, a couple of times, before Sophia moved in. Victoria was too weak to come to my office frequently, so I went there."

"What do you get out of this?"

"My legal fees are deducted from the auction proceeds."

"Nothing else?"

He looked at me and raised a suspicious scarred eyebrow.

"Nothing," he said.

"How'd you get that scar?" I asked.

"Which one?"

I quickly counted eight recent visible scars on his face and several that might have been a year or two old. No telling what was under the hair.

"Never mind," I said. "Can I keep these photos?"

"Sure, but I'll need a receipt. And we should probably put together a contract. How much do you charge?"

"For this? A dollar a day," I said.

He thought about the offer for a while, doing long division in his head and gauging his budget against my exorbitant fees. He was about to agree when I added, "Plus future legal work."

"What kind of future legal work?"

"I don't know, but I'm sure to need some. I always do."

"But not to exceed a certain amount."

"But I'm not certain of anything."

"I'll pick a number on a sliding scale," he said.

"When you do, send it to my lawyer for his review."

"Who's your lawyer?"

"You are."

"Oh," he said, the wheels turning again. "Are you kidding?"

"Usually," I said. "I'm taking Sophia home. Here's my card. I'll try to remember to keep my phone on. I'm staying at the Cottonwood Lane house."

He read the card, and everything fell into place in his rock-chipped lawyer mind, which was good. At least one of us had a handle on things.

"I'm sorry Tony," Sophia said in the car. "I don't think she meant anything personal by not remembering you in the will."

"I'm okay with it. It makes things easier, I think. Forgetting each other was a sad two-way street. I didn't even keep in touch with Rick."

"You're the only one who calls him that," she said.

"I know. You going to the Himalayas?"

"Yes," she said. "I saw them in a movie once. Fell in love."

"Going to see the yeti?"

"Exactly."

I laughed.

She didn't.

"Want some lunch?" I suggested?

"Yes, that would be nice."

I was hungry and didn't give much thought to what a seventy-two-year-old woman's diet might need to be, so I pulled into the drive-thru of a greasy spoon called The Greasy Spoon. There's something to be said for truth in advertising. The place is a local landmark and always crowded. I seem to remember a class action lawsuit brought against it a while ago after a local epidemic of cardiac disease was traced to the restaurant. The case was dismissed when they added a fruit cup to the menu and the last original complainant died of a massive heart attack over a plate of cheese and chili fries in booth six.

"What was I thinking?" I suddenly said, remembering frail Sophia. "We should go in."

I escorted Sophia inside on my arm.

Sitting in a booth in a corner, huddled together like spies, were T. S. Crew and the banker Owen Weaks. They were both smiling. I had a sudden urge to hurl a brick at them but didn't know why. I used to carry a brick with me for just such a purpose and regretted not having one then.

With the first waft of indoor air, I felt a cloud of grease anoint me in a thin but ever-growing layer of shining oil. The tile floor was slippery as ice. They had to go through a mop a day trying to save lives on those floors. A path of rubberized carpets led to the counter. I ordered enough calories to feed Sumatra for a week and Sophia asked for a grilled cheese sandwich. No crust.

We sat down with our food and I realized my suit was done for. Forget the gravy stain. Ignore the mustard splotch. It would take an acid bath to get the smell of this joint out of the pinstripes.

The place was crowded but pretty quiet. Low conversation floated over the sound of dipped fries and hardening arteries. We were two tables away from Crew and Weaks. I sipped a drink and turned my head to eavesdrop.

"Independent builders will buy them for sure," Crew said.

"They better, or we're both cooked," Weaks said.

Crew said something I couldn't make out. I think the word "arachnophobia" was involved.

"Why would I tell them?" asked Weaks.

More mumbles. Crew was facing away from me.

"I'll extend it, but you have to flip it in forty-eight hours or there'll be an audit."

"Is there a worse word in the language?" asked Crew.

"Prison," said Weaks.

"Just back me," Crew said, "and we're both winners."

Sophia knew what I was doing and surreptitiously watched them over my shoulder. Suddenly, she laughed. "That is so funny, Tony!" she said. "What happened next?"

We were made.

"Garret hid under the table," I said quickly, "but Critter was all up in his face, calling him a bigoted, narrow-minded, neocon fascist shit-eating

MAGA-head. Critter took one to the jaw. Both of Garret's hands were in a sling for a month."

She laughed again, and I filled my mouth with food.

Crew and Weaks got up quickly and left the restaurant like it was on fire.

"Did you hear anything?" Sophia asked. "I couldn't make out a word."

"Yeah, I don't know what, but I got some."

I pulled out my notepad and scribbled a rough outline of what I'd heard, including arachnophobia. Everything could depend on that. Spiders. Of course!

"These are some awesome onion rings." I offered her one.

"This place is older than you," she said.

"Reminds me of *American Graffiti*."

"Hell, I bet the grease on the wall is older than you."

She dug through a mountain of fries until she uncovered her other half sandwich. I helped myself to the half bushel that fell onto the table.

"You certainly get your money's worth here," she said, eyeing her "triple-decker four-cheese All American Jr. Size" feast.

I had basically the same sandwich but on a bun, with beef, mushroom, bacon, mayonnaise, lard, and a punch card for a free defibrillator after eight more visits.

"So Sophia," I said through a mouthful of heavenly grease. "What did Vicky mean by 'let all the secrets be known. I am ashamed of none of it. It was all done for love.'"

She nibbled the top layer of her sandwich.

"I don't know," she said.

"Really?" I tried to dip a horseshoe-sized onion ring into a thimble-sized sauce cup.

Sophia chewed thoughtfully and, I think, fretfully for a moment, then shrugged. "I guess she might have meant our friendship," she said.

The gentleman in me had refused to follow me into this dive. He waited in the car. I pressed her.

"That would be a secret. Not secrets. Single versus plural," I said.

"Slip of the tongue?"

"She wrote it."

"Slip of the pen. She didn't have an eraser. It's just a figure of speech, for crying out loud." She snapped another bite of cheddar/American/Swiss/nacho sauce-laced bread and chewed.

She was holding back. I knew this as surely as I knew I'd regret this lunch for the rest of the day and probably tomorrow. I remembered the other rumor I was told, the one about Vicky killing her husband, Lance. Sophia had said it was bullshit and I'd believed her. Now I didn't know. Now I had doubt. Suddenly I realized there might be two deaths I should look into. No, I corrected myself. Three: Vicky, Lance, and Rick.

Information was falling on me like dirt on a coffin or bird shit under a bridge. I had to get back into my notebook and some quiet time. Curiosity rose to compete with emotional debt. My guts swirled from Guilt Buddy and deep-fried nausea. I had work to do.

Sophia wasn't talking. We finished our grease in silence.

21

I DROPPED Sophia off at the house.

"I've got some investigating to do," I told her. "I'll call you if I can't make dinner."

"I doubt either of us will want to eat the rest of the day after that meal."

"Amateur," I said and drove off.

I had to stop at a gas station within minutes for the first of a long day's journey into men's rooms. I was no health food nut, but even my body knew when it had been insulted and made me pay.

Twenty minutes later, I drove south out of town. I wanted to see T. S. Crew's land development firsthand. It was a workday and it was a worksite, so I figured I'd be able to talk to a workman.

I was wrong.

T. S. Crew's development project was not being worked on. There was a weather-beaten sandblasted wooden sign that announced "Phase One" of the "Moab Pueblos" coming three months ago and a little map showing where the pool would be in relation to the handball court. There was nothing there. It felt like staring at Ozymandias' foot. Nothing but a few poured concrete foundations littered along gravel roads sprouting weeds in the unused tire ruts. It was an exquisite location for a planned desert community. The view of the mesa across the valley was unobstructed, the access to the main highway direct and convenient. The land itself was inter-esting, leveled in sandstone, dotted by cactus, and trees along a narrow ravine cut by ancient summer storms. The weathered picture on the sign showed a modern, attractive condo, colored and built to blend into the surroundings, a lá Frank Lloyd Wright. It was going to be a first-rate community, but all there was now were potential basketball courts and possible basements.

Off to the right I noticed an aluminum mobile home marked "project office." No cars were parked in front of it, but I was lucky and saw a blue honey pot standing behind it. The door blew open and slammed shut in the rising wind. A storm was coming. I raced to convenience, my bowels lubricated by cooking oil and heavy breadcrumbs.

Once inside, the wind sent sand through the vents and I felt like a pioneer alone on the prairie. I had only this blue plastic-walled stench-bucket between me and the harsh elements. I was just like Jim Bridger, but with a travel-size bottle of Purell Instant Hand Sanitizer hanging on a wire, three fly strips, and double-quilted Charmin tissue. I squeezed the roll for old times' sake. Just like pioneer days.

The internet had told me that T. S. Crew did road work before this little venture. If my windshield told me nothing else, I knew that gravel was a huge part of road building. Was T. S. Crew interested in Vicky's land for gravel?

Gravel is a rock, I remembered. Rocks are minerals. I'd found that notice in the land office about the mineral rights. They'd been leased and would return to the Racines this year. But not yet. Soon. Crew couldn't extract any rocks from the land until the ancient lease was up in a few months. Was he getting a jump on things?

Gravel? Seriously? The fumes in the bathroom must have gotten to my head.

Suddenly the door blew open and a gray-bearded man in a greasy CAT ball cap and denim jacket was staring at my bare knees.

"Ahhhhh!" I said.

"Ahhhhh!" he answered.

So we had an understanding.

I covered my crotch with both hands—yes, both hands—and said, "I'll be out in a minute."

He closed the door. I fixed the lock.

He'd shattered my intimate pioneer pooping mood, so I wrapped things up.

Outside, I found the gray-bearded man standing a respectable six paces from the door, patiently drumming a rolled-up magazine into his open palm.

"What the hell were you doing in there?" he asked.

"You saw me. Don't you recognize ballroom dancing when you see it?"

"Huh?"

"Do you need to use the facilities?" I said, gesturing to the honey bucket.

"Oh. Uhm, yeah," he said. "I do, but I'll be a while. I had Mexican."

"Good for you."

"What are you doing here?"

"Ballroom dancing, remember?"

"Huh? Are you with the state?" he said, admiring my greasy suit.

"I am from the state," I said. Which was true. I was—technically, if not officially.

"You've gotta talk with Mr. Crew about all that," he said. "He told me to tell you that."

"He knew I was coming?"

"He said you would eventually. Told me to send you on."

"So you know about the..."

"I don't know nothing about nothin.' You gotta talk with Mr. Crew."

I took a step away from the port-a-potty. The wind had changed. I admired the view. "This is a great location."

"Ought to be for what it cost," he said.

I nodded. "So is the development scrapped completely?"

"It all might could happen," he said, surveying the concrete slabs. "Economy and all."

"That all will get you," I said. "I'm surprised you didn't even finish a model."

"We did. We had two. One after the other. The designer kept changing it."

"You pulled it down?"

"Twice," he said. "The new one's on the billboard. I got plans in the trailer if you're interested."

"Why didn't you build the third one? Didn't have any bricks?"

"Nah, Mr. Crew said to hold tight. See what happens with the road."

"Oh, yeah," I said. "The 191?" I was looking at the road number over his shoulder. Otherwise, I might have gone with "yellow brick" or "to nowhere." It was a lucky break.

"No, the 95," he said defensively. "We ain't got the contract to do nuthin' on 191. If there're problems with that one, you gotta talk to someone else. You're in the wrong place. Are they behind too?"

"I'm really not at liberty to say," I said.

"Well it ain't us."

"Then I'm in the wrong place."

"You don't wanna see Mr. Crew?"

"No," I said. "Don't even tell him I was here. No need to worry him."

"I hear ya,'" he said.

"What's your name?"

"Verne."

"Of course it is." I shook his hand.

The wind blasted paint off my car door as I fought it open and got inside. Either a storm was moving in or they'd started nuclear testing again. I looked at my clothes. The grease from lunch had acted as glue and my best dark suit had taken on a pink talcum glow from the desert dust. I looked like a Vegas mortician and was probably more flammable than a crêpe suzette.

Red sand blew through the valley and into town like out of a Sergio Leone picture. I'd have to tell Sophia about it. She'd appreciate the reference. I pulled out of the cloud and onto Cottonwood Lane where I was met with a surreal scene of streaking lights darting through the dust. It was like a disco, but the colors were limited to red and blue.

Aunt Vicky's house was surrounded by cops. Three Moab police cruisers were parked elegantly across the lawn, one on top of a rose bush. A white van with official state plates spat out cleanroom technicians like a barfing clown car.

I recognized the subtleties of a police harassment search and parked my car up the street. I had my burglar bag with me, which included a lock pick set that never worked, rubber gloves, a glass cutter, a few Ziploc bags and a place for a brick that I'd been meaning to replace. I had other fun stuff too, like a gun holster—minus gun, and a notebook of cryptic notes any sane person would wonder about and any mad one would devour. I parked far enough away from the house that there was no way they could include my little car in the search without being obvious.

I got out slowly and locked the car. I took a deep breath and marched up to the house. I braced myself for another arrest. I was an old hat at this. I knew my rights like every television watcher. I could recite the Miranda warning by heart but usually had it yelled into my face by irate garlic-eating stormtroopers set on sending a message.

My wrists involuntarily came together as I approached the front door. The white clowns were milling around the front room. No one looked particularly busy. If there was a search, I'd either missed it, it hadn't begun, or this was all just show and intimidation. I knew this dance.

I caught a glimpse of Danny and Lt. Herbert Levis in the kitchen and walked upstairs as if I lived there. I passed a state patrolman in blue latex gloves standing next to the bookcase. He held a heavy-duty Ziploc evidence bag. It was pricier than the brand I used, but he had a state budget financing him. I didn't like the way he pinched it closed. I didn't like the way he walked with a swagger. I didn't like the shape in the bag. I didn't like the smirk on his face.

"Whatcha got there, sport?" I asked him.

He grunted through a slit grin. Not good.

I followed him into the kitchen. I'd hoped to present myself to a junior officer for arrest. They are more likely to make mistakes and breed technicalities like a dog breeds fleas. Following Officer Smiley into the kitchen meant that I'd probably have Danny's cuffs cutting into my wrists for a while.

I paused to admire a white, clean-suit searcher. One had finally gotten into character and squatted over the floor with a pair of tweezers picking up strands of hair fiber and dropping them into a professional grade Ziploc. I was getting plastic envy. When the carpet wouldn't surrender a sample, he produced a pair of stainless steel surgical scissors and took a swatch the size of an eyeball out of the middle of the hall. I admired the underlying pad and wanted to kick him in the head.

I felt terrible. I had brought this on us. Sophia wouldn't be here long. With any luck, she'd be in Tibet in a month, but this disgrace was uncalled for. I worked up real anger against these cowardly cops and decided to take the lead in this stupid farce. I burst in on Smiley and the kitchen crowd with the traditional welcome.

"You fucking tinpot gestapo Nazis make me sick," I said. "You know, if you morons spent half as much time trying to solve crimes as you do committing them, I bet the governor would give you a gold star and a lollipop."

Danny was standing behind Sophia. He actually looked sorry. Sophia's face was etched in silent disbelief. I heard the distinct click and rattle of handcuffs being latched.

I'd interrupted Lt. Levis' stuttering reading of the Miranda warning off a dog-eared card. "Do you understand these rights?" he asked Sophia, probably hoping she'd explain them to him.

Sophia's feet went out from under her. I dashed forward but Danny had already caught her. Together we carried her to the sofa while Levis just watched. I figure he was practicing sums in his head and wishing he could take off his shoes to get above ten.

Smiley was on the phone with the EMTs. "What's the address here again?" he asked.

It was surreal.

"What the fuck Danny?" I said.

He answered with a blank stare, standard Moab police procedure.

"Take those cuffs off," I said. "She's lying on them for chrissake."

Danny immediately removed the cuffs. I laid her hands on her chest. She looked dead. I'd just seen my Aunt Vicky in this same pose, and it was unsettling.

I repeated my question: "What the fuck?"

Levis stepped forward with an evidence bag. He held it up as way of explanation. I saw it contained a long rusty ice pick.

"What the fuck?" I said. I saw no reason to change my phrasing.

"We found this," he said, the sums solved, the shit-eating grin back in place.

"Where?"

"Hidden behind a scrapbook," he said.

"What? In the front room there?"

Officer Smiley nodded. "Behind that big family album," he said. "Looks like we got ourselves a killer."

"How you figure?"

He shook his head in practiced condescension.

"Do you have a warrant?" I said. "Can I see it?"

Acting Police Chief, Lt. Disphit Levis flicked an envelope into my face which caught me on the cheek. Add a paper cut to my list of police-induced injuries.

"Your little stunt made us curious," Levis said. "We got to looking at the case again. We figured you were in line to inherit. So we thought we'd check things out."

"With a raiding party?" I said. "Where's the SWAT team?"

"Right here," a helmeted man said from the hall. "Got lost on the way. You still need us?"

"No, you can go home," Levis said. Three black-clad Tron refugees with automatic rifles high-stepped it out the house. One bounced into the door-jamb where his peripheral vision had failed him. He recovered and followed the team outside.

"What the fuck?" I was determined to have my question answered but changed tact to get faster results. "Why would I kill Vicky," I said. "I wasn't even mentioned in the will."

"Yeah, but you didn't know that," Levis spat. "Criminals like you always prey on good, trusting folk. You won't get away this time."

"Earlier you said it was good she was killed, now she's a model citizen? Get your story straight, you boneheaded, inbred, hypocrite, ooze stain. And what won't I get away with? Am I under arrest?"

"No," said Levis. "Not even a suspect anymore."

He realized his intimidation speech didn't match the facts and glanced at the other officers to see who'd noticed. Everyone had, but when he looked, they suddenly found the floor, ceiling or a fingernail unshakably fascinating.

"So what the fuck?" I said, gesturing to Sophia.

"We have motive and means," Levis said. "Mrs. Curtis is under arrest for suspicion of murder."

"You don't honestly think," I said.

"We'll let the judge look at things," he said. "In the meantime, she'll get three hot and a cot downtown."

"I know you think you cut me off just then, but my previous sentence was complete."

I was being too subtle for him. I was about to say something in slow monosyllables so he'd understand, when he held up the ice pick again. He was close enough that I could see it was not rust on the spike and handle but dried blood.

An ambulance arrived and the room was even more crowded. I was escorted outside while flashlights were shone into Sophia's eyes and her arm was lifted for a blood pressure cuff.

Clem Tucker from *The Moab Picayune* stood in a cloud of cigarette smoke talking with a policeman under the big cottonwood tree.

Thick had told me they used to hang people from that tree.

Clem waved me over. I shook him off. My head was spinning so fast I was surprised it stayed put—no need to tempt fate by lingering under the hanging tree.

The wind had slowed, blocked by civilization, but the smell of cold, dry sand still flavored the air. I don't know how long I sat on the porch steps but eventually Sophia was brought out on a stretcher. She was strapped down and had an oxygen mask over her face. Her eyes were wild, desperately seeking a friendly face in the crowd. She latched onto mine.

I held her hand and went with her to the ambulance. Danny walked alongside and didn't try to stop me. He had to stay with the prisoner, but even he'd grown tired of the farce.

"Tony," she said through the mask. "What's happening?"

"Good things," I said. "After a fashion."

"How? What?"

"They're taking you to jail. They found the murder weapon," I said.

"And that's good?"

"Well, yeah," I said excitedly. "But what's really cool is that I know for a fact that it was not there yesterday."

They slid her into the ambulance. Danny shrugged and got in beside her. He put a hand on my shoulder to keep me out.

"What does that mean?" she asked.

"I don't know yet," I said. "But I will find out."

22

THE CLEANROOM EXTRAS actually worked for a while. The discovery of what even I was sure was the murder weapon, took the police intimidation task-force to the level of actual purpose. No one was more surprised than smug Levis who spilled coffee for the next three hours while everything was boxed and removed. The entire craft room, all the documents were taken. Photos were taken of Vicky and Sophia's bedroom walls, and the drawers were searched and bagged and numbered. If I ever needed to move, I wouldn't hire movers, I'd just make it a crime scene. What they lacked in skill, they made up for in thoroughness. They took a pile of my dirty underwear for reasons best left to them. At quarter past one in the morning I was asked to sign an eight-page inventory of everything they'd taken. I did and they finally left.

I brought up my car and got out a change of clothes with new underwear. I took off my greasy suit and showered until the hot water ran out. I put on some clean BVDs and laid down to contemplate the dark ceiling in my ransacked guest room.

I'd stirred the pot alright. What did I think would happen? The cops had moved off their donut-engorged asses, found an easy suspect and all was well again. Their show last night would resonate through town and they'd sleep better knowing justice was being done. They'd forgive and forget the police beating they'd witnessed before. Their love of pumpkins and flowerpots would dissolve in the name of public safety. An outsider, surrounded by rumors, despised for being different, had been caught and revealed as the villain they all suspected her to be. All was well and right in the world. It wouldn't matter if they didn't get a conviction. The authorities would drag it out for the show and then let it die quietly when proof was required. They'd claim she escaped on some technicality, but the matter would be settled in the minds of the public.

It was so perfect that it took me a long time to discount a total police setup. The search warrant was dated late Wednesday, before the will's reading. They'd been coming for me. They wanted to make a show and cast doubt on my muckraking. A hit job for the mythical town fathers. Sophia wasn't on their radar then. No one thought they'd actually come out of the search with a suspect. It was a show for the town, for the paper. Clem's presence at the search was not an accident. He'd been tipped off, probably ordered to come. This was a countermove to my ad, and it had worked out better than they could have imagined. I knew that Sophia hadn't killed Vicky, but they didn't have to. Hell, compared to the weak evidence usually used to burn people in court, this was a slam dunk. Shit, they might actually get a conviction if they couldn't scare her into some kind of plea deal.

Guilt Buddy joined me the rest of the night as I watched Tibetan peaks melt into iron bars and Sophia's last few years spent in appeals and Gitmo-orange jumpsuits. What had I done?

———

The next morning, sun rays found their way into my eyes through an elaborate course of mirrors and shiny objects strategically arranged by ancient Egyptian tomb makers to piss me off. I pulled a pillow over my head and rolled over.

Suddenly, it was noon. I don't know how long I'd slept but it wasn't enough. It could have been ten hours, it could have been three. Who was keeping score? Guilt Buddy didn't remember. Useless friend.

I called Archie Rumbold. I should have called him last night, but I wasn't thinking. I had to leave a message. I told him a brief explanation of what had happened and told him to get Sophia the hell out of jail. "Right now," I said with emphasis. "It's lawyer time."

The house was a disaster. Every room had been violated. I started putting things back in place but gave up quickly and went downstairs for coffee.

I needed a friend. Guilt Buddy just didn't cut it. I started to call Allie then surveyed the house, drawers open, pictures crooked, Levis' coffee stains down the side of the table and decided to just leave. I'd drive over.

The town was bustling. The LARPers were arriving in droves. Long braided beards and longer velvet dresses flowed along the walkways shopping for whatnots. Cars from all over the country lined the roads and idled in drive-thrus. Many had triangle flags depicting a red dragon on a yellow background on their antennae. Not a few people were head to foot in green face-paint and leather skins. They must be freezing, but their costumes were too good to cover up. Three stopped on the sidewalk, shook their fists and barked at a passing Camry which had an elaborate coat of arms painted on the door. The watercolors were streaked from the drive, but you could still make out a horse, or maybe it was a cow. It might have been a crumbling Corinthian column, but whatever it was, the green-skins recognized it enough to hurl anatomical observations at the driver.

I pulled behind the Camry and followed it through town. The driver waved at supporters and snarled at the Goblins. He drew in behind a stopped row of cars a quarter mile from the LARP festival grounds and waited his turn for a parking assignment.

I swung around the traffic jam and passed them in the empty oncoming traffic lane. I got the usual stink-eyes from people thinking I was butting in line, but they removed their curses when I turned left into Allie's driveway. I was relieved, because I'm sure there were wizards among them. It could have turned ugly—polymorph and fireball ugly.

Allie's ranch was as crowded as it'd been during the reception. A row of vehicles were parked on the driveway and in front of the kennel. A woman in a shimmering blue conical hat and matching gossamer dress carried a white plastic pet carrier from the back seat. Judging from the noise, it contained arguing harpies. I followed the damsel to the barns.

Allie was with a group of seven people ages eighteen to fifty-five, weights from ninety-five pounds to three eighty-six and a quarter. She was demonstrating how to tighten the cinch on a saddle. I held back and waited for her to finish.

When she was done, the damsel handed her hell beasts to Allie who took them with a look that said she'd be more than happy to euthanize them for her. She sat the carrier down and turned to the horse renters.

"All the horses are gentle and easy to ride," she said. "I'll have them ready for you at four. You can get them then. Have them back by ten at the latest."

It was a dismissal. The group broke up and Allie took the rocking pet carrier to a side barn.

I followed.

"They're usually so calm," the damsel explained. "I even gave them each a Valium, so they'd be mellow for the drive."

"How far did you come?" Allie asked.

"Idaho," she said. "They've been acting this way since we left."

"Did you let them out to walk and drink?"

"Yes, but they fell down a lot."

Allie nodded and entered the kennel. She hadn't noticed me.

The left side of the kennel was for dogs. The huge white beast I'd seen before lunged against the wire fence. On its hind legs, it stood taller than me by a head and a half. It was massive, though proportional to what most people consider to be a dog shape, but this thing, white as eggshells and whipping around a foot of pink tongue, was something out of a cave paint- ing. It could be saddled and ridden. Its paws were big as my hands, and its jaw could hold my head and maybe another. I remembered Moab's uranium deposits and knew with grim certainty the power of mutant evolution. What had we wrought?

"That's an Akbash," Allie said sharply from down the hall. The damsel was gone and the animals—cats or badgers—were growling in slurred hisses from a room behind her. "He's called Gandalf. It's a very expensive breed. Are you going to kidnap him too?"

I should have known that my dognapping infamy would have reached Allie. Even if Danny hadn't driven over and personally delivered Levis' libelous current issue of *Family Saving/Family Values*, which I suspected he had, she'd have heard about it by now. Moab is a small town.

"Don't believe everything you read," I said.

Gandalf licked my hand through the fence. I jumped. It barked. I jumped again. The dog's voice was as immense as it was.

"Dog karma," she said.

I took a step toward her.

She planted her arms on her hips and glared at me with withering intensity.

"Allie..." Dog slobber dripped off my hand.

"I trained that dog, you know. I know Precious. I loved that little delicate puppy. She'd never do anything to anybody. How could you?"

"Well, that's an easy question," I said. "I didn't."

"That isn't a picture of you? Your name isn't Tony Flaner?"

"Those things are true, but the story is bullshit with a capital fetid odor."

She glared.

"Wait. You trained that dog? How? Why?"

"They paid me," she said. "It's what I do. I'm good at it. I told you."

"Why you?"

"What's wrong with me?"

This was sliding into terrible territory.

"How do you know the Levises?" I asked.

"They're Herbert's cousins. I thought you were a detective. At least I did before finding out you were a kidnapper."

"Dognapper," I corrected. "But I'm not that. I'm not even a kidnapper. I am a detective. I have a license to prove it. But by that logic, I'm also a fisherman, driver, and disco dancer."

I opened my wallet to show her my License to Boogie. It was from Danceaholics. The club had closed years ago, but the license was still valid—good for a lifetime. I held it up for her to see, but she was too far away to read it. I stepped closer.

She flinched.

I stopped.

"I didn't do it," I said. "I was a babysitter for Precious when someone snatched her. They'd had threats before they even contacted me. If I did anything wrong, it was in not taking the threats seriously, or the Levises. If I could go back, I'd change the first, but still doubt I could do anything about the second. Have you met them?"

"Why didn't you find the kidnappers?"

I was about to correct her again but thought better of it. People love their animals, often more than their own kids, and Allie was coming from that angle.

"Vicky died," I said. "You called me the day it happened. I was distracted. I came down here. Also, the Levises are total assholes."

I caught her making an imperceptible nod. She knew them.

"Mark isn't a total jerk," she said.

"No, he seemed okay." I remembered the pleading drummer in my car after the Comedy Cellar begging me not to sue. "I met him just the day before yesterday," I said. "Before meeting Lt. Herbert-sucker-punch-Levis, I'd only known the irrational Ronald and faint-happy Rosalyn-Janet. And who the hell goes around calling themselves Rosalyn-Janet by the way? This isn't the antebellum South. And even there, I bet they'd have found that name sickening."

There was certainly a nod this time.

Gandalf jumped on the fencing again. A wire sprung loose, and the fence leaned out like a cardboard flap. The big dog wagged its tail and barked. The sudden movement, or more likely the sound waves, pushed me sideways into the far wall.

"He likes you." Allie strolled up the hallway.

"And if he didn't?" I asked.

"I doubt that fence would hold him." She offered her hand to the slithering tongue.

"You really don't believe that rag, do you?" I said.

She hesitated.

"How'd you get a copy, by the way. Do you subscribe?"

"Danny," she said.

"And what does that tell you?"

She opened Gandalf's kennel to inspect the broken wire. The dog leaped out and trotted over to me with a serious desire to sniff my crotch. Since Allie didn't react with liability-related horror, I stayed calm sensing a test of some kind.

Gandalf had to lower his head to poke the family jewels but did so hard enough to double me over. That gave him a chance to finish a posterior inspection before finding my face easily accessible and slathering it up with a quart of high-grade dog slobber, thirty-weight. Satisfied, Gandalf wagged his tail and deafened my left ear with a happy yip.

From far off in a tunnel, barely audible over the buzz of lost frequencies, I heard Allie say, "You've made a friend."

"With friends like this..."

"Heel Gandalf," she ordered, and the dog sat down at her side.

Sitting, it was nearly as tall as she was.

"You do realize this dog is freakishly large," I said. "Is this normal?"

"For the breed, yes. And they're always white."

"Not from around here?"

"No. I'm training him for a rich software guy."

We strolled out of the kennel and into the sunshine. Gandalf was tight on her hip but between us. I caught glimpses of her face over the dog, so I kept talking.

"Is training dogs hard?" I was making small talk, trying to cement the cracks in our relationship Danny and the Levises had hammered open.

"Depends. Gandalf is bright. The breed is trained to help shepherds. Working dogs tend to be brighter but less manageable."

"And cocker spaniels?" I said. "Was Precious hard to train?"

"That breed used to be something special but once it got popular, breeders weakened the line with inbreeding. Precious has epilepsy."

"I know," I said. Then added carefully and softly, "So what did you train Precious to do?"

I was hoping Allie would see this as more small talk, but to be honest, if that stupid dog had graduated with any schooling whatsoever, she'd cheated on her finals.

"Not much," she admitted. "Just the basics. They didn't leave her with me long enough."

"And the dog had epilepsy," I said.

"And other physical problems. I got the basics in. Just barely."

A van drove carefully up the driveway and parked on the shoulder.

"There's no parking here for the festival. We're full," Allie yelled.

A man behind a bushel of wild brown beard stepped out of the driver's seat. He wore a dark leather jerkin, knee-high boots and studded bracers on both forearms. He produced a double-bladed battle-axe from inside the cab and threaded it through a loop on his belt.

"You can't park here," Allie yelled again.

He didn't hear, or didn't care, or had other business. The van side door slid open and a gaggle of children with hair glued to their shoes bounced out of the insides like gumballs from a crashed machine.

"Gandalf, go!" Allie commanded.

Instantly, the white dog lurched forward with a deafening bark. It sprinted toward the trespassers in a cloud of sand, gravel and pounding footpads. It ran at the car like a charging rhinoceros.

The children screamed. The father jumped back inside the van and pulled the door shut, hoping the dog would be satisfied with his kids.

Five yards from the panicked LARPers Gandalf skidded to a halt and then, as fast as it could turn its formidable momentum, it wheeled around and raced back to Allie at full speed.

Now I screamed. The sight of three hundred pounds of white fur and teeth touched an ancient race memory from when we'd evolved from seals. I staggered back.

Gandalf skidded to a stop right in front of Allie. She reached up and scratched the dog vigorously behind its ears. The dog was obviously pleased with itself and shook its huge head in affable slobbery pleasure.

Allie took a silver dog whistle from her lips and called out, "There is no parking for the festival here." She had their attention now. "Do you understand?"

Wide-eyed, the family tumbled back into the van and backed all the way out onto the street.

"They arrested Sophia," I said.

"What?" said Allie.

"The cops raided the house last night. I think it was to intimidate me, as if beating me up wasn't enough. Actually it wasn't, so I guess they knew what they were doing."

"Yeah, I heard about that. Was it bad?"

"It happens all the time," I said, and sadly thought how true it was. "It was in retaliation for the newspaper ad. I expected something, but not what happened. They think Sophia killed Vicky."

"Why?"

"She was the only beneficiary of Vicky's will," I said.

"That doesn't seem like enough to arrest her."

"They found the murder weapon hidden behind a book in the house too. That didn't help. The cops are looking for an easy out. They always have been. I don't know about a legal conviction, but the court of public opinion will be satisfied."

"Tony," she stuttered. "What are we going to do? Why are you smiling?"

"I don't know," I said. "But everything's going to be okay. I'm pissed off now."

She seemed to understand, and my heart melted a little more. Soon, it would be running out over my shoes.

"Can you get away tomorrow?" I asked.

"I'm kind of busy here," she said. "This festival is bringing in a lot of business. What do you need?"

"I thought we could go out."

"Now's probably not the best time."

"I'm going to visit the Ashe winery tomorrow. Poke around. Could use the company."

"I'll see what I can do." She was smiling at me.

Gandalf licked my hand and accidentally sucked it into his mouth. I didn't care. He rolled my fingers around his mouth with his tongue like a lozenge and then spat them out. Then he sniffed my shoes, sensing drops of melted heart pooling on the laces.

23

THE LARP FESTIVAL was a boon for Allie, if not the town. She'd sold parking places, sheltered animals, and rented horses. It would be the last big financial windfall she or the city would see until spring. Guilt Buddy told me that I should have offered to help scare off hobbits and feed stoned cats instead of asking her on a thinly disguised date. Guilt Buddy is a poor wingman.

Allie and I talked on her porch where I convinced her not to believe the trash the Levises had written about me. I may have gone overboard on my sudden saccharin praise for Precious, though. I gushed compliments on Allie for Precious' training. I called her a "magical spaniel-whisperer." I was doing well until the sonnet. I could have done without that sonnet. They're hard.

"I'll call you tomorrow," I said. "See if there's any time you can escape the Fellowship and we'll get some wine and cheese."

"Tell Sophia…" she trailed off.

"I will," I said.

She kissed me goodbye on the cheek. I melted into my car and drove past a caravan of elves and orcs to Archie's office.

I knocked on his back door like I was serving a search warrant. It'd been only hours since I was last here, but it felt longer—maybe a day and half. I was surprised when Archie opened the door.

"What are you doing here?" I said. "Why aren't you helping Sophia? Didn't you get my message?"

Archie's left hand was wrapped in fresh white gauze.

"Yes, I did," he said. "She's still in the hospital. She hasn't even been booked yet. Nothing to do until she's out of there. Then it gets legal."

"How is she?" asked Guilt Buddy.

"She's fine. Being held for observation." He gestured me to come inside.

"What happened to your hand?" I said.

"Rope burn on the Avatar today."

"Avatar?"

"A big, blue, hot air balloon. I was going up with a friend and things got dicey. Just a little rope burn. It'll be fine in a month or two. The Avatar needs a new panel and some sewing. Power to the Lazy L and Mendolin Ranches should be back up within the week.

"It all worked out then," I said. "How long are they going to keep her?"

"At the hospital? At least through today," Archie said. He sat at his desk and gingerly lay his bandaged hand on the blotter.

"You hear what happened?" I asked.

"Yeah, I did. Sounds like it was the biggest police mobilization for an arrest since the Stirps gang. Did they really have a SWAT team?"

"Yes, it was creepy. Who're the Stirps gang?"

"A bunch of two-bit bank robbers who hid out here after robbing a bank in Colorado. There was a final shootout in Peaceful Canyon. Eight hundred sixty-five shots fired over twenty minutes. No one was injured."

"Stirps?" I said. "Like Roy Stirps, the ranger?"

"Yeah his father or grandfather, I think."

"How much did they get?"

"Not much and I think they got it all back. Ask Roy. He'll tell you the story. Sometimes he brags about it, sometimes he's ashamed at how terrible a crook his ancestor was. He's moody about it. Still, bring it up, and I bet he'll bend your ear. It's too good a story."

"If it was anything like what I saw last night, it was a show for the locals and the press. An example of police power and incompetence."

"Sounds right," Archie said. "Did they break anything during the search? Did they hurt anyone?"

I detailed what I'd witnessed the night before. How they cuffed Sophia and she fainted. How I asked Danny to remove her cuffs and how he had. I told him about them damn-near cleaning the place out, leaving me a spoon and a mattress. Then I smiled.

"What?" he said.

"The night before," I said, "I fell asleep in the front room with that big scrapbook on my lap. There was no ice pick there when I replaced it that morning. Then we had the reading of the will and the raid. It was not there before and had not been there long. Hours at most."

"So you think it was planted?"

"Of course I do," I said with as much indignation as I could manage without spitting. "Don't you?"

"Not my job."

"It was a plant. I'll swear to it. The police or the killer stuck it there. Could be the same person."

"Your word isn't exactly gold," he said. "I'm not talking about the dog thing. I mean, you're her family. Any jury would expect you to lie for her. This helps, but it doesn't end it."

"She's not really my family," I said, "but I know what you mean."

"We'll wait and see if the blood's a match," Archie said, trying to open a bottle of water with one hand. I reached over and helped him.

"I have other leads too," I offered meekly.

"What?"

"Uhm...stuff."

Archie smiled and nodded. He tried not to look condescending, but lawyers have a natural talent for that and often use this secret power without meaning to.

"Okay," I said. "I've got work to do. You watch out for Sophia. If the hospital is nicer than the jail, keep her there. Do what you can."

"How're you doing on the Indian thing?" he asked.

"Nowhere yet," I said. "But soon. Does Sophia's arrest mess up the auction?"

"No," he said. "The auction is separate. She asked for her possessions to be liquidated and then distributed. If Sophia is convicted of the murder, she'll lose the legacy, but everything will still be sold."

"Oh," I said.

"And Mr. Flaner," Archie said.

"Call me Tony."

"Tony, if Sophia is convicted of the murder, everything will likely fall to you, after extended probate and such."

It took me a beat to see where he was going with that.

"Motive."

"Yes," he said. "I don't know how it will play out, but you are definitely an interested party."

"Duh," I said, reaching deep into my bag of infinite comebacks, but I knew what he meant. Rumbold had suggested that it could be construed, imagined, and fancied that I killed my Aunt and framed her lover for a hundred acres of lizards and a rose garden. I pretended not to notice.

I made him promise to do all he could for Sophia. I made him swear it on the grave of his dear departed mother and favorite kayak "Rainbow," which was still being repaired after his September life-flight ride. He really loved that kayak. He had a picture of it in his wallet from "before."

I couldn't bring myself to go back to the house and think, so I found a small café hidden behind main street that smelled of coffee, curry and cannabis and did some thinking there. It was called Firebird Coffee. I bought a free trade, double foam latte and left my credit card at the counter for computer time. They had rentals. I was roughing it. I wasn't sure what I wanted to do with it, but I needed to work. Sitting in front of a computer always made me feel productive. It was a habit I picked up while working a call center for three weeks. I beat the the company high score in mine-sweeper while selling eight sets of carbon steel steak knives to a polygamist family in Idaho. I was employee of the month until I quit a week later. There was just no more challenge in that job.

The café was a warm comfortable space filled with old hippies and young hipsters. I counted six Grateful Dead concert posters and three hand-painted watercolors of local hard-to-get-to tourist spots, like Hike Three Days Through Cactus To See This Lame Hole in the Rock Arch, and Gross Water Puddle Canyon, accessible only by teleportation and seven thousand feet of free-style, white-water rappelling. In short, the place was "groovy." I wouldn't have been surprised to see Greg Brady crash in to buy some dope for Marcia and the girls. They had to be stoned in the later seasons. All that singing.

Usually such places are territorial. I expected to feel unwelcome since the smell of high-grade marijuana was not well concealed under the Colombian Dark Roast, but I was accepted after a quick aura check and felt like I'd found a new home.

I surfed Native American Territorial Rights over my coffee and despaired. I was thrust back into my high school days with a twenty-page report due the next day and all I have is a dictionary and a stack of National Geographic magazines to detail the political ideology of the original Congressional Congress. Why did I leave my textbook in my locker?

My mind wasn't on Tiponi as much as T. S. Crew. I'd overheard Crew mention independent builders, so I searched on that. I got a list too long to consider. The computer knew my location and gave me a Yellow Pages list of possible answers. If I wanted a drywall fixed or a kitchen remodel I had a hundred independent builders to choose from within two hundred miles. I found listings for two companies that actually called themselves Indepen-dent Builders. One was in Las Vegas and their website included a very angry open letter to the Nevada legislature complaining about their building permits being pulled on account of not having water to supply their new suburban paradise. Of all the nerve. The other was closer, in Cedar City. They specialized in "inspection services, repair and new construction for the family-valued customer." I wondered if they had a coupon in Levis' rag.

After a while, I got around to searching on keywords "T. S. Crew" and "191." Pay dirt. Literally. The Moab Picayune had a story about Moab's own son being awarded a multi-million-dollar contract to fix some overpasses on Highway 191, a lesser-used road but one "growing fast, like our own little city." After the exciting initial story—a gushing fluff piece destined for framing behind Crew's desk, the Picayune hadn't mentioned the project again. Ever. Not a word.

A Salt Lake Tribune article a couple months later picked up the story.

Investigation into Road Repairs. The State of Utah is looking into complaints that construction work done on Highway 191 is shoddy and dangerous. T. S. Crew Construction from Grand County was awarded a contract last spring to repair three damaged and decaying overpasses along the route. However, motorists have complained of shoddy asphalt peeling up from the road and cracking windshields.

"The job was not merely to pave over the old bridge, but to reinforce the supports and then replace the entire roadbed. It does not appear that this has been done," said Utah Transportation Under-Secretary Assistant to the Commission's Aid's Spokesman, Jeff Jones.

"It is unclear what the state will do about this matter, but an investigation is almost certainly in the works," said Jones. "We'd like to know how all the money was spent."

"You looking to buy?" came a whisper.

"What? A road?"

I looked up. There was no one there.

At the next table, a man had settled into a chair. He cocked a quizzical eyebrow and rolled a paper cup between his hands. He was in his mid-twenties, rugged and fit, with short straight blonde hair and blue eyes. He smiled at me.

For a second I wasn't sure if I'd heard him correctly, then I realized that was the idea.

I picked up my coffee and moved tables. His didn't have a computer. I couldn't stay long.

"Whatcha got?" I asked under my breath.

"Rope. Anasazi Red," he said into his cup.

Sophia had mentioned Anasazi Red Rope marijuana. This was the perfect opportunity to check out her story.

"Okay," I said.

I passed a C-note across the table. He took it and got up. I watched him walk out of the café. He winked at the door, and I said goodbye to my money.

I've been ripped off in drug deals before, but this one was on a whole new level. There was a chance he was just going to his car to get it, but I didn't think so. I'd just paid a hundred dollars to make a guy leave. It was probably a bargain. Hell, usually you have to pay two hundred dollars to experience such local color. I'd gotten it cheap.

I moved back to my table laughing to myself. What did I want pot for anyway? That's all I need is for Danny to roust me and find a lid of the notorious Anasazi Red Rope in my pocket. The country might be embracing pot reformation, but Moab, Grand county and Utah were not exactly on the bleeding edge of the movement.

"Dude." A dreadlocked barista glared at me from behind a steaming espresso machine. "Dude," he said louder. He twitched his head at the table

I'd just left. I looked at it and then back at him. Now he was engrossed in grinding coffee.

I got it. It was uncool to leave a dirty table. My hundred-dollar bill had bought me the rights to play busboy where I'd been robbed. What a bargain.

I picked up the coffee cup the blond had left behind. The weight was wrong. I peeled back the lid and saw a plastic bag of bud stuffed at the bottom. I carried it back to my table and checked my wallet for my private detective license. A more honest man would have torn it up on the spot, put fire to it, and scattered the ashes. Instead, I slid the bag from the cup into my pocket and looked for pictures of cats on the internet.

I've never been much of a drug user. Nancy, my ex-wife, disapproved. I don't think pot is any worse than alcohol, probably less so if you believe statistics and facts. I've never been attacked at a concert by a stoner because I looked at his woman the wrong way. Can't say the same for beer.

I once got Nancy to try it. To be honest, she liked it and we humped like rabbits for hours, but she felt so guilty afterward I knew never to bring it up again. Nancy is too organized and serious for that kind of distraction.

Remembering that brought on a wave of nostalgia and homesickness. Nancy, before the divorce, when we were still in love, those first few months were bad enough, but it came as a prelude for my childhood memories of Rick and Aunt Vicky. Being single isn't all it's cracked up to be. Family is cool. I missed my son Randy. At fifteen, he was old enough to do his own thing, had been for quite some time. He'd shed me like a spent cocoon years ago, the little shit. I wondered what memories he was making now that he'd rediscover in twenty years. I hoped they'd be as good as mine were here in Moab.

Guilt Buddy found the phone in my pocket and dialed the number before I knew what was happening. I saw the name on the screen and held it to my ear.

I have a good relationship with my ex-wife. She wouldn't mind a friendly call. We'd been married nearly fifteen years and we'd got along for most of it once we decided to be roommates instead of lovers. It was her plan to stay married until Randy was at a proper psychological age to handle a divorce. Right on schedule, we'd divorced. It worked perfectly into her strict schedule but came at a rough time in my life.

We'd been split now for over a year. Randy stayed with her because there were fewer shootings at her house than mine. She was a real estate agent of some success and had bankrolled my Peter-Pan life even after the divorce thanks to a fair settlement. She moved on with her life in fits and starts, slipping off her over-analyzed life plan for some dramatic moments of irresponsible mayhem, but she'd always managed to return to the tracks. I'd like to think she missed me, but lately, I think she's been seeing someone new. I hadn't met him yet, which was good since I had little to brag about beyond failed dog-watcher, and one must always have good bragging points when meeting the ex's new squeeze.

The phone picked up. I was taken aback by the strange male voice at the other end.

"Hello, Nancy's phone," he said cheerfully.

Visions of twisted sheets and Nancy's dimpled bum flashed into my brain and a million years of evolution went out the window. The reptile in me said, "So what makes you so special? You a fitness freak? You invent a nano-tech capacitor? Let me guess, you're a fighter pilot and you love long walks on the beach? I bet you clear your browser history religiously every night, am I right?"

"Excuse me?" he said.

"I can't believe she fell for such bullshit," I said. "Why she looks for dates online is beyond me. Hey dumb-ass, there are no beaches in Utah, unless you're talking about some rocky reservoir littered with dead trash fish and tetanus hooks."

"Uhm, do you have the right number?"

"It's on my speed dial, you gold-digging gigolo," I said. "You'll never know her as well as I do. You're nothing but a cheap replacement. If you hurt her, you will pay. Do you understand? If you lay a finger on her, you better know I'll come after you. If you break her heart, you better have a valid passport. Am I making myself clear?"

"Uhm, okay. Nancy's upstairs, should I get her for you?"

"Who is it?" I heard a woman ask in the background.

"Some crazy person for the realtor," he whispered back.

"I told you not to answer her phone," said the woman.

"It's for you," said the man eagerly.

"This is Nancy Flaner," said my ex-wife.

"Hey Nance, whatcha up to?"

"Just showing a house to a very nice couple," she said and then added, "who now look a little terrified. What did you do?"

"Nothing, just thinking of you."

"And?"

"And...family is important, you know."

"And?"

"And I wondered if Randy is doing okay."

"Yes, he's fine. Is there anything else?"

"We need to take him places.".

"We went to Hawaii last summer," she said.

"I know. I wasn't there."

"Have you been drinking?"

"I think he should spend time in the desert. Maybe down here in Moab. Build up some memories. Change his life."

"He'll disown you."

"We can talk about it, can't we?"

"Tony, I'm busy. My clients are trying to leave."

"Okay, I'll talk to you later."

"Oh, Tony," she said. "What's this about a dog?"

"Don't believe the tabloids," I said.

"Typical," she said. "Did Benjamin find you?"

"What?"

"Benjamin. He said he met you at the Comedy Cellar Wednesday."

"And?"

"And I told him you were in Moab," she said.

"Nancy, I love you, but you're going to get me killed."

"What? Oh, I gotta go. They're out the door."

"Bye."

"Where are you going?" I heard her call before her phone cut off.

I swallowed my instant karma with a sip of cooling coffee.

24

I LEFT the café and went walking. I took my notepad, cellphone and a jacket. It was unseasonably warm. I remembered that November from before, when the first thin snow fell and didn't wholly melt until April. Today was in the sixties, the perfect temperature for goblins and knights clad in furs and wool capes.

The hospital turned me away. Yes, Sophia Curtis was still there, but no, I could not see her. Police orders.

I sat down in an empty waiting room and planned a way to see Sophia through the gauntlet of green-clad orderlies and black-clad cops. Everyone was clad for adventure but me. But what would I say to her? I had nothing to report. Maybe silence is better than disappointment.

———

I had learned that from Rick when our first quarter report cards arrived in the mail. He'd skipped his last class for a week so he could ambush the mailman before his mother could get the letter. On Friday, with a growing list of unexplained absences, he'd gotten it. I found him in the backyard when I came home.

"Give me some matches," he said.

"Sorry all out. How 'bout some dynamite?" I said, digging into my bag for effect.

"No, that's too much."

"Looks like I'm fresh out of explosives too."

"Got a spark plug?"

"Let me check. No. Why?"

"I gotta burn this letter before mom sees it. It's my report card. Here's yours. You gotta burn it too."

He gave me the two envelopes. I opened them. Mine was respectable, very good actually for starting a new school, but Rick's was barely passing.

"You got a B in Home Economics," I said. The rest were C's. Low C's.

"Mom ain't gonna like it," he said.

"So tear it up," I said.

"Nope, it's gotta be burned."

There was no arguing with his logic.

We took the letters into the garage and I watched Rick expose the innards of the lawnmower. Deftly, he disassembled the wiring until he had a cable with a spark plug hanging over the blade compartment.

"Put the letter under it," he said.

I did.

He pulled the rope and I saw a spark, but no fire. He tried several more times.

"I'll go see if there're some matches in the kitchen," I said.

Rick watched me go, scratching his head.

"What you boys doing out in the garage?" Vicky asked when I came in.

"Just hanging around," I said.

"Don't let Thick play with anything sharp, okay?"

"Sure thing, Aunt Vicky."

"Is that your report card?" she asked. I'd carelessly carried mine into the house with me.

"Uhm, yeah," I said. "It came today. Rick's must have been delayed."

"Let me see it."

I gave it to her.

"Great job, Tony. Have a cookie," she said. "Take some out to Thick too. They always make him feel better."

I stuffed my pockets with Oreos and stole a packet of matches from a drawer.

The explosion, when it came, wasn't a boom as much as it was a whooshoosh. I was at the backdoor just returning to the garage with swag, when the outbuilding erupted in orange flame. Black smoke poured out from under the door, cracks in the walls and holes in the roof.

I ran to the door and got there just as Rick staggered out. His hair was burning, his face was black, his eyes were wild. But he was smiling.

"Told you it would work," he said. "All it needed was gasoline."

We stopped the fire with a garden hose and an old blanket before the firemen arrived. They reported it as "misadventure," as they had the time before, and the time before that.

Rick was chastised and made to get a very short haircut, but there was never any mention of his first quarter report card as long as I was there.

After finding and disposing of a wildly misplaced copy of *Family Saving/Family Values*, I sat down in the deserted hospital waiting room and read through my notes again. I found the name of the company Rick worked for when he died. All I knew about his death was that it was sudden, accidental, and in Atlanta. It also occurred relatively and coincidentally close to Vicky's. If there's one thing I've learned from reading pulpy detective novels is that I don't get my fair share of femme fatales and scantily clad suspects throwing their tits in my face. But there's another lesson too, and it's that coincidences are suspicious.

"You're Tony Flaner aren't you?"

A gray-haired nurse clutching a packet of files stood in the doorway, eyeing me suspiciously.

"Let me guess," I said. "You're a dog lover?"

"No. Can't stand the beasts. A pack of them rip open my garbage every week."

"Why then, yes. I am Tony Flaner."

"You don't remember me, but I remember you from when you stayed with Victoria and Thick. I'm Barbara Kominsky. I worked at the grocery then. I am so sorry about Victoria's passing."

I nodded.

She said, "I don't believe for a second that Ms. Curtis did it. It's ludicrous."

"That's how I see it."

"As far as I'm concerned Ms. Curtis saved Victoria. I'll testify to that. Victoria was dying before she came, withering away, like from poison. It was horrible to see."

"You saw her?"

"I'd run into her from time to time. I asked after her, and she admitted she was feeling poorly. I always thought Victoria was strong, but losing her boy really ate her up. It even crossed my mind that she might even be helping things along, if you know what I mean. Then Ms. Curtis came, and she was her old self again in no time."

"'Helping things along' how?"

"Oh. Oh, no. It was nothing, Mr. Flaner. I didn't mean to speak ill of anyone. She was a lovely lady and this town treated her badly. I just wanted to say how sorry I was." She withdrew down the hallway.

I stared after her for a long moment and then a longer one until my eyes watered and drool pooled in my lower lip.

I made a note in my book. "Vicky—suicidal? Barbara Kominsky." Then ran through the door after her.

I found the nurse at a nurse's station. Coincidence?

"Mrs. Kominsky," I said.

"Barbara."

"Not going to happen," I said. "I remember you now." Mrs. Kominsky gave Rick and I fruit from the back of the store if we caught her at quitting time. It was stuff they were going to throw away soon anyway, like within a month or so.

"Did anyone ever examine Vicky when she was sick?"

"She came in once but was sent home. She couldn't pay."

Gotta love the American healthcare system.

"Did anyone look at her at all?"

"Yes, she was looked at."

"Can I look at the file?"

"No, that wouldn't be right."

"But I'm her last living relative."

"I can't help you. You'll have to talk to records and arrange something."

"After I talk to records, where might they send me to look at the files?" I asked.

"Probably the records room or a computer."

"And where are they?"

"You'd need a password."

"What password might they give me?"

"I wouldn't know," she said.

"What's yours? Just out of curiosity."

"Not telling," she said, giving me the conspiratorial look I remembered from the grocery when she gave us an opened box of cookies that she'd just happen to find on her way out.

"It's a serious thing," she said. "Someone was fired just this morning for looking at files they shouldn't have."

"What was their password?"

"Hypnotoad." She spelled it for me while showing me to the nurse's lounge where I could get a Diet Coke in private.

"You looked parched," she said. "I'll be right outside." She giggled as she moved the mouse and the computer came to life.

Armed with a notebook, a lookout, and a 'hypnotoad,' I leaped to the computer and brought up Vicky's hospital records.

She'd been looked at in the Emergency Room claiming exhaustion, aches and pains. They'd checked her pulse, which was slow, weak, and erratic, her blood pressure, which was low, drew blood and ignored her normal temperature and loose bowel movements. She looked jaundiced but they ascribed that to her bad diet and vomiting. There was a mention of her son recently dying, but she claimed symptoms preceding that. Her heart was strong, and at first pneumonia was suspected. An X-ray came back negative and it was about then that she overstayed her financial welcome.

She was told to visit her regular doctor and take vitamins, eat better, and try to relax. Stress was the short diagnosis, and they sent her home with a pamphlet on grief counseling. That was it for the visit.

On a quick timeline, I mapped out her symptoms, Rick's death, the ER visit, Sophia's arrival and then her returning health.

A later note in her file recorded the blood test results. If anyone looked at the findings or contacted her about them, there was no mention of that. It found poor clotting in her blood due to high levels of Phenylquinoline carbonic acid.

I scribbled down the name, careful to check the spelling for future Scrabble games, and hurriedly logged out.

Mrs. Kominsky was having a coughing fit outside at the nurses' station. The door opened and an intern came in. He found me sipping a Diet Coke and reading a *People* magazine like I belonged there. I ignored him. He ignored me. He got something from a locker and left. I followed him out.

"Mrs. Kominsky," I said. "Have you ever heard of this?" I showed her the words in my book. I wasn't about to try and pronounce them.

"No."

"Can you look it up?"

She could. She found it listed in a book the size and shape of a green brick at the end of her desk.

"It's used in Atophan," she said. "A medicine to treat gout. That's a disease of the joints. Really painful."

"Can it kill you?"

"Gout?"

"No, Atophan."

"Most medicine can if you take too much."

"Or if you take it when you don't need it?"

"Yes," she said conspiratorially and read further. "It's listed as toxic if used improperly over time."

She looked over her shoulder, tapped on her keyboard and brought up the report I was just looking at.

"Doesn't say anything about gout," she said. "But they might not have gotten her whole history. They were in a hurry to get rid of her. See that code there? That means uninsured, but you didn't hear that from me."

I thanked Barbara, finally bringing myself to call her by her first name and left the hospital.

Sophia had mentioned Vicky was sick, but she hadn't named it. Nor had she mentioned medicine. She'd nursed her back to health with bacon and tea she'd said. Maybe she was hiding her gout from Sophia. She'd do that. Vicky hated to have people worry about her. She'd martyr herself that way. I remember once Rick threw a baseball into her ribcage by accident. She said it didn't hurt but the bruise was from her waist to neck. I caught a glimpse of it the next day. I put Vicky's gout on the back burner and thought of Rick.

In the still vacant waiting room, I called the Sherman Janitorial Service in

Atlanta Georgia where Rick had worked and died. I navigated the telephone menu until I found a choice to speak to a human. The human was unavailable, so I left a message.

"Hello," I said. "My name is Tony Flaner. I am—was—the cousin of Rick —Thick Racine. I'd like to talk to someone there who knew him. Not in the Biblical sense necessarily, though that would be fine too. It's personal." I left my number and instructions to call any time. It was a shot in the dark. I wondered how long it would take me to get past an insurance company stooge to someone useful. If they smelled a lawsuit, and everyone did these days, this could take years.

I should have gone back to the house, but I recalled it looked like it had been tossed by crack-addicted toddlers on a scavenger hunt. Okay, maybe not that bad, but close.

A muddy-green troll walked by me in the waiting room. He had a nasty gash on his forehead. A nurse informed him he had to check in at the front desk first. Reluctantly, he stumbled with his two elf friends back up the hallway. One of the elves had lost the point of an ear and the other wore a ski vest, but otherwise the illusions were complete.

In reception, the vested elf sat at an outer chair looking concerned but noble. The other elf sat with the troll and filled out paperwork. The troll's prosthetic forehead was torn and bleeding.

"I'm so sorry," said the elf. "It slipped."

"Lucky blow, lowly elf. Troll stronger than that. Get armor round yourself, and prepare for Troll's attack," he rhymed.

The elf regained control.

"Noble troll, you fought well and are brave," he said bowing. "My people salute your strength."

The troll grunted a response, stood up and took the paperwork to a confused nurse. He was a tall troll, probably six foot four without the additional three inches of "troll boots" and five of "troll hair." His arms were as big around as phone poles and his belly, which was real, I'm sure, was firm and huge. He could wrestle professionally with folding chairs and trademarked flying-troll elbow-gaugers. Any idea I had of LARPers being all nerdy and effeminate was dispelled when the headpiece was pulled back and I saw a six-inch slash at the hairline. A nurse poked it with a gloved finger. The troll only growled. It was a good growl.

They took him back with one elf. The other remained in character at reception.

"Do you guys know how lucky you are?" I asked her. I saw that this one was a woman. It's hard to tell at a distance, elves are like that.

"What do you mean?" she said.

"The weather. It was freezing the other day. It gets cold here."

"Our enchantress has foretold that the weather will be fine for the festival."

"Well if she's got it under control, why worry?" I said.

"The festival ground fees were also very reasonable," she added.

"I bet they were."

"Do you think this will take long?" the elf asked me. She could have been twenty or twelve. Only the down vest over her long robe kept her in Moab instead of Mordor.

"Looked like some stitches. At most an hour," I said. "It's empty in there."

"Then we shall not be late for the opening celebration."

"What time is that?" I said. "I'd like to see that."

She looked at me critically and suspiciously. "It is not open to the denizens of this world," she said.

"If I buy a ticket?"

"You'll have to come in character and costume."

"Ah, yeah, of course." I said. "I'm Tony."

"I am Summerleaf, that was Stagwind and Mog, the Great Troll."

"Nice to meet you," I said, standing and bowing.

Still suspicious of condescension, she smiled at the gesture, nonetheless. Maybe sixteen years old. Maybe eleven.

I left her sitting as nobly as a summer leaf, which was exactly what she was going for.

Outside the air was cooling. I could smell wood fires and saw billowing columns of gray-brown smoke rising from the festival grounds. The enchantress had slipped a bit. It was in the fifties now; the night would probably freeze.

I got my car from the café and drove to Main Street. It was quiet again. The parade of fantasy characters was over for now, assembled in the "reasonably priced" festival grounds by Allie's ranch.

"The grounds" was just an open field when Allie, Rick, and I played there. It was Rick's favorite place to let wild animals loose. He'd catch them around his house, play with them until he needed a rabies booster and then reluctantly set them free in the big field so he could visit them again. Even if he didn't see them, he said they saw him and that was enough.

On our walks, Rick would often find animals who'd made the acquaintance of a jeep or a camper. Most didn't survive the experience, but once we found a hare with a broken leg and another time a stunned rattlesnake. Both we carried to Allie's barn.

She set the rabbit's foot in a splint and the three of us brought it food every day—lettuce, radishes, and carrots—icky vegetables we snuck from the table. When it could hop away, we took it to the field and it did just that.

Allie wouldn't touch the rattlesnake though, so Rick brought it home, named it Rattles and put it in a splint too. It took the better part of a day and two rolls of masking tape to straighten that snake out on a two by four, but when it was done, we had one unhappy snake.

From past experience and emergency room visits, Rick knew to put the first piece of tape over the snake's mouth. But that didn't stop Rattles from lunging at us. It hit so hard it bruised us and raised snake head-size welts all over our bodies. I got a big bump over my left eye and Rick was covered in one-inch bruises from head to waist.

We left Rattles overnight to calm down but the next day the snake was gone. It had worked its way off the board.

"Must have been that old tape," Rick said. "It wasn't sticky enough."

"I don't think it was as hurt as we thought," I said.

"Or we fixed it up with the splint, and he went home to tell stories about the good people he met."

"Or went to raise an army and seek revenge."

"Nah. Animals know when you're trying to help them," he said. I felt the bump on my head and together we searched for Rattles for a couple hours, but never found him.

25

"I HEARD ABOUT THE AUCTION," said Guy Skingle. "But I don't think it'll sell; the house is so far underwater, I doubt anyone will bid."

I didn't think much of Skingle when I'd met him at Vicky's funeral and nothing during this visit had so far changed my mind. It's not uncommon for Moabites to have a tan, but his was unnaturally orange. I didn't know the brand, but it wasn't cutting it. In fluorescent light, he reminded me of a jack-o-lantern. In black light, I bet he glowed like an open furnace.

He chewed Altoids like they were food, crushing them between his teeth in little pyrotechnic sparks until his breath was so minty it nauseated me. Between Altoid shots he drew his fingers through his hair to refresh his failing pompadour.

"I thought you said you had buyers?"

"I do, but they're not stupid." I could see chemical vapors on his breath. It cleared my sinuses. "They'll wait for the bank to repo it and then make a deal with them. In this economy they'll do much better that way. When the market rebounds, it's a prime flipper, but now it's not worth what's owed on it."

"What was your plan before?"

"Pick it up at a short sale," he said.

I squinted.

"It's done all the time," he said. "You don't own it. What do you care?"

I left Skingle's office and heard the motorcycle before I saw it. The sound of throaty engine rage is a common sound in Moab at certain times of the year, but this wasn't one of them. The burping din that would enrage my Sugarhouse neighbors into a lynch mob was as welcome as money out here.

I glanced up the highway and caught a reflection of winter desert sunlight off the belt buckle. I ducked behind a sandwich board in front of Skingle's office.

Out of the badlands above Moab, across the frozen desert expanses, rode the villain into town.

It must have been a long, horrible, frigid ride. Underneath the frostbitten face, tear-frozen eyelids, and crippled blue fingers was Benjamin James Ulrich, Delores' ex-husband. He had on a pair of ice-caked jeans and a worn leather jacket that looked awesome but as warm as chain mail. His hair was frozen in place and his ears were past blue, moving toward a nice shade of coal.

He rode past Skingle's office without turning his head. I'm sure his neck was frozen solid or else he'd have noticed my little green car in the driveway. It was a missed opportunity. I could probably have taken him then. One smack with a lunchbox and he'd shatter like an icicle. I needed to buy a lunchbox.

I lost sight of him around some cheap motels. Night was coming on. If only he'd left a little later, I'm sure he'd have gone all *Shining* frozen solid on the road shoulder, malevolent grin on an ice-covered face, hands clutching the motorcycle handles, murder in his eyes.

But he'd made it to Moab alive. He'd need at least the night to thaw, so I was safe for now. I considered calling the police and letting them know about Benjamin but thought better of it. With my popularity, they'd probably give him an escort to the house and a complimentary stun gun and sap.

I went home to Vicky's and hid my car in the garage behind her house.

I tossed in some toaster cookies and began cleaning up. To help things along, one way or another, I opened a bottle of Ashe wine and dipped my pastries in it.

I rolled a joint from a sheet of notebook paper and a pinch or five of the famous Anasazi Red Rope. I was home for the night. I was in a safe place and I was a consenting adult. None of that would matter to the cops, but it was enough for me. Even before lighting up, I recognized a hint of sage, fruity and full-bodied . I was no connoisseur; I just recognized the smell from the café. Phil Ashe also smelled like this, and to my slow recognition, I remembered that Mark Levis had been smoking the same stuff in my car.

I lit up from the gas stove.

Soon I was in a cleaning frenzy. In Rick's room, I retrieved a boom box and some old 80s mix tapes. To the cheerful tunes of REM, U2, Madonna and The Beastie Boys, I rearranged furniture, closed cabinets, straightened shelves, and vacuumed walls. There was a good reason for the last thing, but halfway through the hallway, I forgot what it was. It must have been important, so I Vogued up the stairs vacuuming around picture frames and hanging quilts.

Around midnight my phone rang. I'd come down by then; just an afterglow remained. I'd eaten all the Pop-Tarts and two cans of peaches. The bottle of wine was gone. I needed salt. A homicidal desire for pretzels gripped me. I stared out the window guessing the distance to the nearest 7-Eleven when the call broke the spell.

Never answer the phone when you're high. It's an obvious rule and easy to follow, unless you're high.

"Hello," I said. "I really need some pretzels."

"Is this Tony Flaner?"

"Do you have pretzels?"

"Probably."

"Good, we can deal," I said. "Can you bring them over? I'm in no condition to drive."

"I'm in Atlanta," said the man. "I'm calling about Thick."

"Thick?" I said.

"Yes. Returning your call."

"Hold on."

I put the phone down and ran to the sink. I stuck my head under a cold water faucet. When I felt adequately water-boarded, I stood up and slapped myself across the face several times. That shit never works, by the way. Don't believe the movies. You always pull your punches. Self-preservation. But the water helped me focus. Two minutes later, I no longer needed pretzels. I wanted them but didn't need them.

"Yes, I'm Tony Flaner," I said. "Sorry, I've had a bit to drink tonight. Who's this?"

"My name is Sherman, Tim Sherman. I worked with Thick. I knew him in the army too."

"Rick—Thick—was my cousin," I said.

"Yeah, he told me about you. You're the one he'd let call him Rick."

"We lost touch," I said. "Can you talk?"

"Yeah. I've been drinking too," he said. "It's pretty late out here. What time is it there?"

"Blurry past twelve."

"Sorry."

"No problem. I'm up. You were in the army with Rick? Tell me about it."

"Thick was a nice guy. We met in basic. He was like that dumb guy in *Full Metal Jacket*, stupid but kind-hearted. It wasn't like the movie, though he got through intact—dumb, but still kind. Shit. I'm sorry," he said. "I shouldn't call him dumb. I don't mean it as a put-down, he was just, you know, a little slow."

"I know." I found my notepad and a pencil and wrote large, so I'd have a better chance of deciphering my writing later.

"We got along. He was accident-prone. He spent a week of basic in the hospital for self-inflicted damage. You know that drill where one guy's gotta throw himself on the barbed wire while his platoon uses him as a human bridge? Well that was Thick every time. Problem was, he'd go out after hours and practice. He tore up his forearms pretty bad once."

"Ouch."

"Once out of basic, we were sent straight overseas. It was hairy. We were assigned to the back, kitchen, and clean up. Janitorial work. I had experience and Thick just wasn't safe with a gun. He got his first purple heart two months into deployment when we came under mortar attack. Thick ran to the kitchen to save the blue cleaner. It was hard to get, and we'd just got some. It really worked on the grease. He took a piece of shrapnel to his leg. The wound wasn't bad, but the blue cleaner had spilled into the wound and poisoned his system."

"He got a medal for that?"

"Purple heart, not a Bronze star," he said. His voice was slurring. I wondered if mine was.

"There was this one asshole who dared Thick he wouldn't walk naked around the outside perimeter of the fence. He took the bet. I wasn't there. I'd have stopped him. But once the firefight started, I was at the wall. Thick was hit in the shoulder, just a graze, but his side was covered in blood. He ran, and I lost sight of him. An hour later, he reappeared coming from the opposite direction toward the gate. We were using flares by then and had air support. We pounded the shit out of a hill but had new hot spots appearing all around us. Thick crawled through the gate and then a couple of medics dragged his naked body to the hospital. He won the bet. Another purple heart and he sent the money to Utah, to his mother."

I didn't know there was a financial element to medals. Sounded like a racket. Or I misunderstood. I was in the frame of mind to misunderstand, so I left it alone.

"I'd made an off-hand promise to Thick that after we got out, I'd give him a job. After a few false starts in Louisiana and Florida, he followed me to Atlanta and became a janitor. He was working for me when he died. I kind of feel like it was my fault. Like I got him killed."

"Mr. Sherman…" I said.

"Call me Sherman. It's what I go by," he said.

"Sherman, Rick's mother died recently. I'm wondering if there could be a connection." I didn't want to distract him. The fewer details about Vicky's murder, the better. "What happened to Rick? I need to know."

"It's my family's company, so I'm in management."

I heard the rattle of ice in an emptying glass near a Georgian phone.

"I put Thick on a high-rise detail. It was pretty cushy. Emptying trash cans, cleaning toilets, nothing hard or heavy. He did alright. No problems, though once he mixed the wrong chemicals and increased our insurance premium twenty percent."

The clang of a glass against the receiver. A gulp. He went on.

"One night he was working with a crew to clean up a remodel on the thirty-fifth floor. New tenants had pulled down some drywall, and we had to take it away.

"As I heard it, one of the guys, a new hire, was afraid of heights and wouldn't go near an outside window. The building had a great view, looked out for miles.

"Thick teased him and made the new guy feel foolish. When he saw that he'd hurt his feelings, he tried to apologize. He claimed to have read how safe the building was, how the glass could withstand hurricanes, and how the windows were as good as a reinforced concrete bunker. To prove his point, he threw himself into one. He bounced back with a 'ta-da.' The guy wasn't convinced or Thick didn't think he'd done enough, so he took a long run at the window and threw himself into it again. That time, the window didn't spring back."

There was a long pause on the line.

"We put it down as an accident. Misadventure. Our attorney said we could have slipped the claim, shown egregious employee behavior or something, but I insisted we let it stand. I sent the money to Utah," Sherman said. "To his mother in Moab."

"That was good of you," I said. "Really good of you."

"Yeah, he was a buddy. I just should have put him someplace safer."

"Sherman, is there any chance that it was not an accident? That Rick was killed on purpose somehow?"

"No," he said. "It happened as I said. My guys are still seeing therapists about it. There was no malice. Just...just stupidity." I heard the slosh of a bottle over the long-distance line.

I remembered Rattles and I had no reason to doubt that Rick could have flung himself through a high-rise building and died by "misadventure" or less politely, stupidity, particularly if he was trying to comfort someone.

"He was a good kid," Sherman said.

"Yeah," I agreed. "A real good kid."

"How come he let you call him Rick and no one else?"

"I'm not sure. I didn't know it was only me."

"It was."

"Thanks, Sherman. If you're ever in Utah, let me buy you a drink."

"Will do, Cousin Tony. You take care of yourself."

"I'll be fine," I said. "Once I get some goddamn pretzels."

26

I DON'T USUALLY TAKE drugs, so don't get started because you read it here. I won't be responsible for your vacuuming the walls, which by the way, actually brightens up a room nicely. Nevertheless, from what little experience I've had, I can say that Anasazi Red Rope was first rate. It was the first designer weed I'd ever encountered. I didn't have a sales brochure, but the hint of sage was not an accident, nor was it natural. It might have originally been intended as a masking smell, but it had failed to cover the potent aroma of the grass and only complemented it. It would have gone well with pretzels, but I didn't find out.

I slept well that night thanks to the Rope and woke up refreshed in an oddly cleaned house. My work hadn't been particularly thorough. The drawers were closed, but all my clothes had been stuffed into a single one that fought like a pissed squid when I tried to open it. I've never actually fought a squid, but I'm sure they'd fight that hard. Squids are creepy. Don't get one pissed.

I'd emptied the house of all easy-to-make food and unless I felt like making something that included flour and turmeric, I was eating out.

The LARPers had suffered a cold night, but the day promised to be warmer. My magical smartphone said today would reach into the sixties before dropping below freezing tonight with possible snow. The Enchantress better get busy.

Denny's was crowded with elves, goblins, heroes, and knights of all kinds. I was surprised to see real swords, daggers, and bows. No Nerf stuff here. The noise was happy and excited. I noticed that the groups didn't mingle. Orcs were at one end of the restaurant and barbarians gathered at the other. It was fantasy apartheid.

The elves I'd run into yesterday were eating pancakes with six other slender gender ambiguous teens. Mog, the troll with the head wound, was eating with the orcs. His bandage was covered in blue arcane runes. He looked tougher and meaner for it. He was having a salad.

"Hi Summerleaf," I said with a bow.

She smiled.

"And hail to you Deerfart."

The table froze.

"Oops," I said. "I mean, hail to thee, Stagwind."

I use association tricks to remember names, and well sometimes I'm careless, and sometimes the joke is more important than people's feelings.

He nodded hello and goodbye in one deft jerk of his head, and I was off. Contagious giggling spread over the table and to the next.

I found a seat at the bar counter, a dying luxury for the socially challenged.

"Hail Mog," I said. "How goes the wound?"

"Do I know you, human," he growled.

Live Action Role Playing it may be, but the game didn't end when they left the festival.

"I saw you at the hospital yesterday," I said. "With Summerleaf and Deerfart."

Hearing that, the table of green-skinned baddies burst into deep loud laughter. It was too good a joke not to have a callback.

"Has the Prince heard that name?" Mog asked.

"Yeah, it kinda just slipped out."

"You may eat with us!" he yelled, pushing a lesser creature aside to make room.

I sat down. Maybe I was still stoned.

I ordered the meat lovers breakfast with yogurt and listened to stories of glory and plans about how the greenies were going to disrupt the games and make off with the princess. It was a good plan, but they didn't like the horses the knights had.

"What you need is a dire wolf," I said, gnawing on a piece of rubber shaped like a link sausage.

"Yes, Lord Mog," said a sniveling little goblin. He sniveled well. "Why don't you have a dire wolf?"

Mog barked at him.

He jumped.

The waitress kept away.

The cooks peaked out from behind the swinging door.

Love to see this group drunk, I thought. Or maybe not.

"I know where there's a dire wolf," I said. "Or rather, the biggest dog you've ever seen. Big as a bear, and white as an elf's courage." I was getting into character.

"Where?"

"The horse mistress Allie Braise who supplied the steeds also has a great dog. She is not loyal to one side over the other and I know her. I bet I can make a deal for Gandalf."

"Gandalf?" hissed the crowd.

"That's the beast's name."

Mog roared in a great laugh. "What is your name, stranger?"

"I am Flaner."

"A tradesman?" said a woman troll with a serious latex skin infection around her neck.

"Of a kind."

"Get me this wolf," said Mog, "and the trolls will be pleased."

"I'll see what I can do."

They got up before I was finished. The women among them produced small compacts and reapplied green makeup around their lips and helped touch up their friends.

Mog strolled over to the elves who were just getting up themselves.

"Fare the well, Deerfart," he said.

Stagwind shot me a glance that cost me 2d8 hit points, but I saved against ongoing damage.

I drove to Allie's after breakfast. It was early for me, before ten, and she was surprised to see me. How quickly she'd picked up on my slovenly habits. My heart fluttered.

"How goes the festival?" I said.

"Good. Making money. Nice little surprise this time of year."

"Is this the first LARP festival?" I saw Gandalf standing against the wire fence. I reached up to him and was met with a meter of tongue.

"And the last. Everyone's complaining about the cold."

"It's winter," I said.

"They thought the desert was immune."

"Oops," I said. "And it's going to freeze tonight. And maybe snow."

"Do they know that?"

"I'm sure they can read a smartphone as well as me."

She saddled the last of four horses and left them tied to a hitching post.

"Have you had breakfast?"

"Ate with a bunch of trolls this morning."

"Coffee?"

"They preferred Diet Coke," I said.

"Do you want a cup of coffee now?"

"Sure. What about the horses?"

"They don't like coffee," she said.

I could have kissed her.

"The knights or whatever will come get them later. I arranged it so I can be free today."

"So you can come with me?"

"I haven't had a date in a long time."

"What about the other night?"

"No kiss. Barely qualifies as dinner."

Her house was warm and homey. Even without a crowd of people it seemed small. When I was a kid, it was bigger. How the years had shrunk it.

We sat at the table and sipped Folgers. Déjà vu except with hot cocoa.

"Did you see Sophia?" Allie asked.

"No. The cops wouldn't let me in, and I didn't have anything to report anyway."

"So no luck in the sleuthing?"

"Well I'm developing a picture, but I'm not there yet."

"Tell me what you have," she said. "Maybe I can help."

"You sure are prettier than my notebook," I said.

"What kind of compliment was that?"

"I'm a sweet-talker. My Sharpies don't hold a candle to you."

"So what do you have?"

"I have Sophia's story of an earlier break-in. I have a clumsy, unnecessary lock picking at the back door. I have a broken vase for no good reason and a dead lady stabbed by an ice pick in the darkest hallway of the house. I have said ice pick miraculously showing up just before a police raid."

"And what do you make of all that?"

"A calculated, cold-blooded murder by someone local," I said. "If I had any doubts, they evaporated when that ice pick appeared."

"So how do you think it happened?"

"Well, I think the perp—that means 'perpetrator,'" I said.

"Don't condescend," she said. "That means 'talk down to someone.'"

"The perp put the pick in a place I previously perused perfunctorily," I said and waited for applause.

She glared behind a smirk.

"That alliteratelly means it was an obvious plant and proves that it was someone who's still around. Only a person who read the paper and might have known about the raid would plant the knife there."

"Okay, so who was it?"

"That comes down to motive. I'll check alibis once I figure out why she was killed."

"The land?"

"That's the best lead. It was the only thing she had of any value. Her house isn't worth what she owes on it, but the ranch is something. At least people are willing to pay for it."

"So how would killing Vicky get anyone the land?"

"Did everyone know that Rick died?"

"Of course. It's a small town."

"So maybe the perp thought that without Rick in the picture, she had no relatives and killing her would put the land up for sale. No one knew about me. This was just a way of putting the land up for sale."

"The old-timers knew about you," she said. "But why not just buy it from her?"

"She wouldn't sell it. She wouldn't let it go while there was a Racine still alive."

"Would the perp know that?"

"I think so. Three parties are interested in the land and all three visited Vicky about it before she died. I don't remember Vicky being the kind of woman to mince words. She'd have told them."

"Who were the three?"

"Tiponi the racially ambiguous Indian, T. S. Crew the developer, and the Ashe brothers, wine makers."

"And we're going to see the Ashes today," she said. "Cool. Do we get code names?"

"I'm Buttercup. You're Sal Monella."

"Reverse them. It'll be easier to remember."

"Good idea," I said. "If I can figure out why they want the land, I can assign a motive and then look for means and opportunity."

"Wait. What about the will?" Allie said. "What about Sophia? Wouldn't they have suspected Vicky would leave everything to her if not you?"

"Most people aren't that good about making wills. The perp probably didn't know she had one."

"They might have. It's a small town."

"Maybe," I said. "The cops are saying Sophia killed Vicky because of the will, but she said she didn't know anything about it. I believe her."

"So they gambled there'd be no will?"

"Or they knew there was one and knew it would lead to an even faster sale."

"You think Archie is involved? He's a masochistic X-games nut, but I don't think he's dishonest."

"No, just a hunch. He said his office was broken into. Maybe it was to read Vicky's will."

"Nice hunch. What do you have for evidence?"

"I don't need evidence," I said. "Yet."

"You better hurry. The auction is Thursday."

"Yeah." I'd forgotten that. "Oh, hey. Is Gandalf trained well enough to let a troll use him for a while?"

"What are you talking about?"

"The trolls at the festival, or maybe it's the entire goblin nation, who are going to make off with the princess, but they are afraid of your horses. I said you had a dire wolf that you might lend them."

"He's a sweetie," she said. "He could use the exercise, but I'd need to teach the handler a few commands or things could get rough."

"Groovy," I said. "Oh, wait a minute. What about the owner?"

"When he pays me, he's the owner."

"Stuck you bad?"

"He's a month behind in payments and the last one was short," she said. "Do you know how much that dog eats?"

"But he's a sweetie," I said.

"Yeah, he's a sweetie."

We finished our coffee and went to the festival. We weren't required to pay because everyone knew Allie. Since most of the denizens had covered their elaborate costumes with heavy coats, no one said anything about our modern clothes. We did, however, get more than a few stares as we led a four-foot tall dog through the camp.

It was like fairy Burning Man. There was a center arena with a royal viewing box. The different factions were each given a quarter, their particular royalty facing the middle, while the minions were kept behind in elaborately decorated tents. Flags were everywhere but luckily the wind was still. The day was warming, but I could see the effects of a long cold night on the faces of many players.

I waved to the elves. Summerleaf waved back. Stagwind did not.

Green and blue creatures huddled around fires drinking from steaming mugs while others spooned out huge globs of gruel into wooden bowls at a peasant soup line.

Clem Tucker from *The Moab Picayune* held a tape recorder under the chin of an acned youth with a see-through beard, a yellow and red robe, and a sequined crown.

I waved at Clem. As he nodded back, an inch of cigarette ash fell from his lips and made a little mushroom cloud at his feet.

"You going to be here all day?" I asked him.

He nodded. "What else is there to do?"

At the orc camp, we met the goblin royalty. A tall green woman with brambles in her hair and a broken tusk in her mouth demanded to know who we were. She wore two dozen rabbit pelts crudely but strategically stitched together as a furry dress. She clutched a sheepskin cloak around her shoulders but dropped it to show her full height and muscles when addressing us. She worked out.

"I am Flaner," I said. "I have business with Mog."

"You may enter, Flaner," she said, looking at Gandalf.

Mog was easy to find. He was at the ax range. Three ply-wood figures sat against hay bales at the end of the orc enclave. One showed an elf with exaggerated pointy ears and a dumb expression. Another showed a man in armor but not pants, his unarmed hands modestly held over his nether regions. The last was a barbarian man, draped in wild animals like the dress of the war chief, but the animals weren't dead. Each had its fangs dug into the dopey barbarian whose cartoon face showed pain and confusion. A couple of paces away, green-faced people in ski-jackets hurled axes and knives at the figures.

"Mog," I called.

He'd put sticks in his hair since breakfast. It was a good look. His eyes beamed when he saw Gandalf. The dog was not so pleased.

"Mog, this is lady Allie," I said in way of introduction.

The troll bowed low. The first bow I'd ever seen any orc make.

"She will lend you her beast provided you harken to her instructions." I could get into LARPing. I put it down as a potential new hobby.

"Step up to the dog," Allie commanded. "Let him smell your hand, don't look right at him, three-quarter profile is good."

Mog did as he was told.

Gandalf smelled the hand but didn't lick it. The green grease paint probably wasn't appealing.

"To command the dog," she said. "Say his name, Gandalf, and the command. Gandalf sit."

The dog sat down.

"Gandalf is a sweetie, but if he's messed with, teased, or otherwise upset, he'll be more than you can handle."

"So he's dangerous?" Mog asked.

"I won't tell you the attack command, and don't try to guess it. There's a reverse attack command that you'll find first that brings him on to you. You won't get a second chance, so don't even try it."

"Sure thing," Mog said, rethinking his decision.

"Really, Gandalf is a sweetie. Some good commands you can use are 'heel,' 'sit,' 'bark,' and 'quiet.' The last two are really dramatic. Should go far. Don't let go of the leash. Don't let him out of your sight."

"Cool."

"Even so, he's a puppy and he might chase after a rabbit or something. If he gets away, use this whistle." She produced the silver whistle I'd seen the previous day. "It's ultrasonic and Gandalf is specially trained with it. I will need it back so don't lose it. If Gandalf gets away, blow this hard and he'll come running to you like a shot."

"This is going to be so epic," Mog said, scratching behind Gandalf's ears.

The dog rolled over, showing his belly and nearly took Allie over with him.

Mog scratched it and they were pals.

"Good luck," I said.

"How much do I owe you?" Mog asked as we were leaving.

"I'll let you know when I need something," I said and winked. I had an "in" with the orcs. If I ever needed to get rid of a ring, I had people to call.

27

"THAT WAS REALLY NICE OF YOU," I said. "You got me in the gang."

"Gandalf needs to learn to be around people. I couldn't ask for better conditioning than that."

"He's huge and scary."

"He doesn't know how big he is, but he's really nice. He might knock someone over, but he wouldn't hurt anyone. He's just a puppy."

"That's a puppy?"

She nodded. "It's a big breed."

"What about the attack commands and the reverse attack commands? Are those real?"

"Could be," she said.

"Isn't that dangerous?"

"I haven't gotten to the violent part yet. Right now, it's all about play. If he guesses a command, someone might get licked to death, that's all. I'll start the mean stuff next month."

"What are the commands?"

"Attack is 'swing.' If I do the 'attack the speaker' command, it's usually 'attack' or 'sic-'em' but I don't usually teach that. It's a gimmick. It gets people to hire me, but it's not useful. I usually talk them out of it. Still, it should keep those goblins well-behaved."

"That's why you get the big bucks."

Allie changed into more formal wear. Considering she was in jeans and three layers of flannel, it didn't take much. She put on a clean pair of pants and a long-sleeved blouse that would keep her arms warm but not her upper chest and cleavage. It was yellow, I think. Maybe green.

"What do you know about the Stirps gang?" I asked Allie to take my eyes and mind off her blouse.

"You've been talking to Roy," she said.

"No. Archie."

"Well Roy is the one to talk to. I'm not sure how he feels about it. On the one hand, it's a bit of local color. On the other, it's a sad tale of stupid criminals."

"How so?"

"Stirps, some relative of Roy's, and a couple of other guys held up a bank in Colorado. They ran west all the way to Moab while the FBI chased them. They hid out all summer here. Stirps got a job, but the other two just sat around in a cabin on top of Center Street. Everyone thought they were weird, but since they were outsiders, no one really talked to them to find out."

"Not a lot changes."

"No, not really. Anyway, one day, one of them tried to buy some groceries with a bucket of coins. That got the sheriff called. He went up to the cabin and knocked on the door. Story goes that one of them, possibly Stirps himself, calls out, 'We didn't rob that bank in Colorado. That was three other guys.'"

I laughed out loud.

She chuckled and nodded. "The sheriff rounded up some men and went back up there. The three jumped in a car and sped off but ran out of gas at the mouth of Peaceful Canyon, the police behind them the whole way. They jumped out of the stalled car and ran up the canyon where they hid out on a cliff."

"A box canyon?"

She nodded. "Actually not. They just stopped and tried to hide. There was a long shootout that ended when the sheriff agreed to take a two-hundred-dollar bribe to let them go. Stirps marched down with the cash and was arrested. The other two lost heart after that and gave up. All the money was recovered and 'Stupid Stirps' became a folktale."

"How much they take?"

"Like ten thousand dollars," she said. "Story is that most of it was in pennies."

"I can see why Roy is of two minds about it." I thought about Rick.

The Ashe Winery is up the river from Moab. You pass it if you approached the town from the northeast desert side or were a downed fighter pilot crazy from exposure. It is a space of green in the middle of red. Where the pioneers were thrilled to get corn or squash out of the ground, the Ashes had figured out how to grow grapes.

Their fields crept up the steep hillsides and were visible long before the buildings were. A winding road circled the hills like the river I knew was behind them. Off the highway, a great wooden arch made of woven willow branches towered over a two-lane entry. At the zenith hung a hand-carved sign proclaiming Ashe Winery on a weathered wagon plank.

Past rustic wooden fences, a long gravel road wound through more low, vine-strewn hills and past an abandoned house that looked worse than it should have for its modern construction. The hills sloped down toward the river which flowed beneath a western-pink, sandstone plateau and brought smells of water and wood. On the banks of the river sat a huge manor house, three stories high with wings reaching forward around a marble fountain like embracing arms. It was a monument to white stucco and red Spanish tile, but with Western Americana juniper timbers extending out the walls. Plenty of Pueblo Indian mixed with Spanish. It was majestic and rustic and probably cost more than the space program.

There was valet parking in the courtyard, but there was no need. In the summer, tourists would line up for free tastes, but not now. We parked beside three other cars and together Allie and I went in.

"Ever been here before?" I asked her.

"Never. Strange, isn't it, not to have seen the sights of your own town?"

We passed a tasting room in the right wing. A woman in a business suit, tight hair bun and flat shoes appeared.

"Would you like a tour?" she asked.

"Can we get sloppy, fall-down-the-stairs-naked drunk when it's over?" I asked.

"Yes."

"Lead on."

The woman led us through the factory part of the manor house, including some outbuildings where machinery was kept. There was a short PowerPoint presentation discussing the technology of hydroponics where water and nutrients were delivered directly to roots in little hoses like hospital IVs, thus overcoming any erosional deficiency the soil may have. Where the dirt was better, the vineyard used the old fashion irrigation method of drip hoses with minimum computer interference.

All the vines were lovingly cared for by undocumented Mexicans who earned just enough to pay the coyotes for biannual visits to their families.

We got to see where the grapes were washed and squashed and put in big silver barrels before bottling. We got to see the Arthur C. Clark climate-controlled storage room and the *Matrix* control pod. The shipping center used only organic African Serengeti buffalo grass for padding and the wooden crates were bamboo, the fastest growing wood the guide could think of.

"This is a slow time for us," said our perky guide. "Most of our workers are on vacation or visiting families. These stalwarts here now are mostly long-timers who have been here since the beginning."

She waved to a couple of workers carefully packing bottles into crates amid a haystack of loose yellow grass. They waved back at us and twisted their faces in unpowered compulsory smiles before returning immediately to work.

"I know that guy," I said to Allie.

"Who?"

"The blond surfer. I met him in a café in town."

"What's his name?"

"No idea. We aren't that close." If he remembered selling me illegal drugs in a paper coffee cup, he didn't show it.

The tour ended when we passed through a hall decorated with pictures of the winery's evolution. It started in the '90s when the Ashes built a little house in the desert, the one we'd seen sandblasted for effect on the drive in. There was a sudden expansion in the late 90s with the construction of the villa and new grapevines.

"Now Ashe Winery produces some of the best wine in the country, if not the world."

I hope nobody got paid for that tagline.

"Where are the Ashes today?" I asked. "I'd like to say hello."

"Oh, they're around. Maybe they'll drop by the tasting room later."

The tour ended at a long buffet table with a wine tasting. A nuclear family with one point five children fed from the free cheese and crackers tray while drinking pink alcohol. Their three-year-old was bored sick and had his head down on the table. The infant in the carrier chewed on a cork.

Allie and I helped ourselves to a glass of château de gratis grape and a plate of glorified stone rolled Wheat Thins and strong cheese. I avoided the brie.

Mute servers poured wine in little splashes and tastes. There was an ornate spit bucket at the end of the table, dry as a bone. After I demanded my fifth splash, the server gestured hard at a display of bottles for sale. I bought one of whatever it was he was pouring.

While we munched, a group of non-goblin LARPers shambled in for some local color and free booze. They remained in character as they toasted the slaughter of the "green-skins." I worried about the tensile strength of the crystal. There were two maidens, a knight in fabric chain mail and a Viking with a braided beard and fur vest. When he caught himself slip out of his Scandinavian accent, he'd overcompensate until he was unintelligible. It was like eavesdropping on The Muppet's Swedish chef.

"Ja, Durgi dohofra. Ve gonna get den gublins."

"Hear hear, my good sir," toasted the knight.

"I'm getting tipsy," said a maiden.

"Is this cheese or pudding? It's loathsome."

"It's brie," I mumbled with a shudder.

Two spandex models with antennaed bicycle helmets and wrap-around glasses promenaded into the tasting room. One took off her helmet and shook out her long blonde hair like she was in a conditioner audition. The other flexed his abdomen beneath the biking shirt and surveyed the room without drawing breath.

"We've just biked twenty miles," the woman said, pointing her boobs around the room as if scanning for aircraft. "And I'm not even tired."

"Would you like a tour?" our bun-haired guide asked them.

"Oh no, we're just here to rehydrate," the woman said.

"Do you have any mineral water?" asked the man.

She gestured to the tasting table, and the two strutted over.

"We were on a tour with other bikers, but they were too slow, so we went out on our own. I'm not even tired. That's how good shape I'm in," said the woman to no one in particular. She was in her thirties, mid to late, but masochistically fit and surgically altered. Her over-plump, collagenated lips would serve as an emergency flotation device. Her wide, big-eyed stare said Botox. Her slenderness said cocaine.

"We'll meet up with tour at the end of Castle Valley. We'll beat them by an hour, as fast as we go," the man said. I'd yet to determine who they thought they were talking to. "We should beat them by an hour."

"You gave them a hell of a head-start," said someone.

The pair stopped talking and located the voice. It was Allie. They were talking to her apparently.

"We're not worried. We just biked twenty miles nonstop, and I'm not even tired."

"We just stopped to hydrate," said the man.

"Castle Valley turn-off was back down the road," she said.

"That's where we left those losers," said the woman. "We'll take the back road over the rocks and still beat them by an hour."

"No you won't. Besides the turn off you missed, the only other way into that canyon is around the mountain. Maybe fifty miles. Maybe more."

"No. There's a back road just a mile past this winery."

"Left or right side?"

"Left," they said together.

"Who told you about the back road?"

They hesitated.

"It was that girl with the thing in her lip," the woman finally said.

"And her boyfriend, the one with the tattoo," added the deflating six-pack man.

"Some of the losers?" I inquired.

They didn't say anything, but they moved closer to our table and their smiles had slackened.

"Over a bridge?"

They nodded.

"If you take a left in a mile and go across a bridge, it takes you northeast of Arches. It's about as far from Castle Valley as you can get on a bike without wings. Not only is that road on the wrong side of the highway, but it leads to wild country. People die out there."

They paused their hydration.

"If you hurry," I said, "you might be able to meet the tour coming out from the valley on their way back to town. Maybe. If you hurry. It is twenty miles."

The room was quiet except for the sounds of spreading grins and fading egos.

The two carried their water outside without another word.

"At least they're not even tired," Allie said.

We munched crackers and chewed cheese. Drank a little wine. I was happy.

Remembering why we were there, I said, "The ranch is just south of here. It shares a border with the Ashe holdings."

"So it makes sense that they'd want it," Allie said. "To expand."

"Even with hydroplaning," I explained, "I doubt they could grow old on that land."

"Was that sentence on purpose?"

"You get my meaning." The wine warmed my ears. "Look at this topographical map. It's all canyon and cliffs."

I pulled out my drawn-on USGS map and together we studied it. I snuggled in close to study the detail. When I misread the scale, I added water to my wine.

"This winery is big," I said, taking in the vast tasting hall and its three-story vaulted ceiling. "They did all this from nothing?"

"Quite a success story," she said. "Rags to riches."

"Where are they from?"

"California," Bill said, standing behind us.

"Jez-uss! Don't sneak up on me like that. You want me to go all ninja cat on you?" I said.

"Ninja cat?"

"A hydroplaning ninja cat," Allie explained. "He's been drinking."

"Sit down, Bill," I said. "Where's Phil?"

"Phil's in the field communing with nature." He sat down and poured himself some water. "Lose any dogs lately?" he asked.

"Just the one," I said. "Wait? Does today's count?"

"Not yet," Allie said, suddenly worried.

"How do you know about that?"

"Lt. Levis brought a stack of coupon books over for our reception area."

"I didn't see them," I said.

"I threw them away. I don't like Levis much, and I can recognize a crap hit piece when I see one."

"Thanks for that," I said.

"What's with the map?" he asked, studying my poorly drawn property lines over the intricate elevation lines.

"Where in California?" I said, taking control of the conversation, like a boss.

"San Diego," he said.

"Why come here?"

"Am I being interrogated?"

"No," said Allie. "We're just—"

"Yes," I slurred. "I am a detective and I am investigigating. Is that a problem?"

"What are you investigating?"

"I'll ask the questions, thank you very much," I said. "My aunt Vicky's death."

"You don't think we had anything to do with that, do you?"

"Remember what I said about me asking the questions?"

Allie's elbow caught me on the floating rib and sobered me up a glass and a half.

"I'm just checking things out," I said.

He poured me a mineral water.

"Why do you want to buy Vicky's land?" I asked in a more civil and chest-bruised manner.

Bill nodded, understanding the intricacies of my question or maybe my eyes just thought he did.

"It abuts our property," he said.

"Yes, about that. You can't grow anything on it."

"Probably not," he said. "But developers could try to put condos up there. It'd spoil the entire southern view."

He pointed to the ridge to the south through a wall of stained glass. Through the clear sections, we could see a high wire fence marking the end of the estate and the beginning of Vicky's land. On this side was flat fertile green land, on the other, rock and sand. For effect, tumbleweeds were piled against the fence as if trying to climb over on the backs of their brethren.

"Who'd put condos up there?" I asked.

"T. S. Crew, for one," he said. "Not right away, but with his connections and a better economy, eventually he'd get it done. It overlooks my vineyard and the river."

"You want to buy it to protect your view?" said Allie.

"Yeah, mostly," he said. "A buffer zone of nature, so to speak. But if it doesn't sell for condos, then maybe mining again or a landfill will be there. It's self-defense. We can't exactly move our operation."

"Why pay so much for it?" I asked.

"Because we have the money, and when we made the offer to Victoria, she needed it. Much of Ashe Winery is on land that used to be the Racine ranch. We didn't buy it from them, but from others who had. The Racines got shafted by hard times, and Phil wanted to garner good karma by helping out Victoria."

"A quarter million dollars buys a lot of karma."

"Money is relative," he said. "If she was going to sell it, we wanted to own it."

"So you're going to bid on Thursday?" Allie asked.

"Oh yes," he said. "If the auction comes off."

"Why wouldn't it?"

"Tiponi will try something, and Crew is just sleazy."

The LARPers were arguing about critical hit mechanics in *Dungeon & Dragons*.

Phil appeared through a side door and scanned the room. Seeing us, he walked over.

"Phil," said Bill, "you remember Tony Flaner, ace detective, and the lovely Allison Braise."

The map drew his eyes and held his gaze. "Hey again," he said, not looking away.

Having had not only a whiff but a taste of Anasazi Red Rope, I recognized the odor on Phil instantly.

"What's with the map?" he asked.

"Flaner wants to know why we want to buy the Racine Ranch."

"Karma," he said instantly.

"See," said Bill.

Phil reeked of weed but he was maintaining very well. I'd be a bloodshot, hallucinating, poo-flinging monkey if I'd have smoked half of what I smelled on him.

"So what brought you here from California? Edward Abbey?"

"Exactly," said Phil before Bill could say anything. Phil sat down and finally took his eyes from the map.

"What did you do in San Diego?"

"Waited tables," said Bill.

"I did three years for possession," said Phil fessing right on up.

Bill shot him a look.

"It's not a secret," he said. "And Tony's a detective. I read about him on the internet. He's famous on two continents. He'd figure it out and I wouldn't want him to suspect we were hiding anything from him. You're here about Victoria's murder, right?"

"It's not the brie." I sensed a headache making reservations in my skull for a wedding party in twenty minutes unless I slowed down now.

"I hope you catch the fucker," he said.

It was the most direct and articulate thing I'd ever heard Phil say. Something in his voice, something in his tone and intensity made me believe him. Bill had guile, but Phil, at least in that statement, was as truthful as a priest. Okay, bad example, but I believed him.

"We needed to get out of the city," explained Bill. "It held bad influences for Phil."

We stared at him.

"Cocaine and heroin," Phil explained. "I'm off that stuff now, though. Just wine and the occasional cigarette now and then."

"It saved Phil's life, coming out here," said Bill. "And it offered a great business opportunity."

"You've done well," I said.

"Yeah, ironic isn't it. Now that I can afford a serious habit, I don't want it."

"Really?" I said.

Phil looked hurt, then shrugged. "Well, okay, I may want it, but I'm strong enough to resist."

"Some things," I said.

"Some things," he said with a wink.

28

WE LEFT Ashe Winery in the late afternoon warmth of what was probably the last nice day of the year.

"Was that useful?" asked Allie.

"I had fun."

"Did you learn anything?"

"Nothing springs to mind."

I slowed by the turn-off that I knew went to the Racine Ranch. The road looked like it hadn't been used since Vicky drove us out there that once. I considered wrecking my car on its rocky, sage-grown, sand trap length but thought better of it.

Ten miles out of Moab, we passed a police cruiser going the opposite direction.

"That was Danny," said Allie.

Sure enough. I saw brake lights and the cruiser swung wide for a U-turn. I floored it. Why make it easy?

"What are you doing?"

"Getting away," I said.

"Why? What have you done?"

"Don't know yet."

My car roared with silent electric acceleration as I pushed it to fifty. Danny was already behind me. So much for ecologically-minded getaway cars. He flashed his lights and we found a scenic pullout overlooking a fishable bank of the Green River.

I watched Danny in my side mirror and slowly reached under my seat. Allie's eyes grew big as I slowly withdrew an orange canister.

"What are you doing?" she whispered. "Are you going to mace him?"

Danny knocked on the window.

I stared straight ahead, waited until he leaned in close to the window, then lowered it with a button.

Before he could say anything, I turned to face him, lifted the can and squirted a wad of Cheez-Whiz into my mouth.

"Got any crackers?" I said through a gooey orange mouth of squirt cheese. I smiled broadly to display the adhesive effects of modern design dairy products.

"Hi Danny," said Allie.

"Hi Allie," he said. "Out for a date?"

"You out arresting old ladies?" I said, or rather spat.

"Flaner, I'm sorry about what happened to Sophia. It wasn't me."

"Aren't you an 'acting detective?'" I blabbed. "Act like one."

He pointed down the road to emphasize some point I didn't let him make.

"Even a disgustingly handsome blockhead like you knows Sophia didn't kill anyone. You know this is all about image. If you'd have done your job, I wouldn't have needed to get beat up by your boss and the sweetest movie buff in the county wouldn't be spending the last years of her life in a prison hospital. You are so lazy it makes me sick." I'd spat most of my orange cheese-product on his uniform. I took another hit of cheese and my head grew a little dizzy. Nitrous oxide propellant—laughing gas now to go with intestinal gas later on. Clever marketing.

Danny dropped his hands, paused and pondered.

"Why did you pull us over, Danny?" asked Allie.

That brought him back.

"Sophia asked me to give this to Tony." He found an envelope in his green police jacket and handed it over. There was Cheez splatter on it.

"She gave this to you for me?" I asked, trying not to gag.

"Yes."

"And you took it?"

"Obviously."

"And you didn't read it?"

"No. That would have been an invasion of privacy."

"No, that would have been investigating," I said. "But thanks."

"What are you talking about?"

"Is she still under arrest?" I asked.

"Yes."

"Then she doesn't have a right of privacy with anyone but her lawyer. It was probably the second paragraph of the policeman's handbook. I can see how you missed it."

"Tony," reprimanded Allie.

"Can't win with you," Danny said.

"Never could. You should stop trying."

He stormed back to his car.

Allie glared at me.

I sighed hard enough to force a cheddar substitute into my sinuses. I got out and walked to the cruiser.

Danny tensed up behind his door. His hand slid to his holster.

"Thanks," I said.

I could see him dissecting the word for hidden meaning. I sucked some more cheese for the nitrous.

"Okay," he said timidly.

"BFFs?" I said.

He pondered.

I said. "There's a guy on a motorcycle staying in one of the cheap motels. He's a felon breaking parole. It would be a good collar if you nailed him."

He paused and pondered. The change in topics confused him. It didn't take much.

"How do you know this?"

"Because I think he came down here to hurt me."

"So he hasn't done anything yet," Danny said.

"He's violated his parole by leaving Salt Lake City."

"I'll wait until he does something."

"You mean you'll wait until he beats me up."

He smiled.

"Dick," I said.

Danny smiled. "What does he look like?"

I described Benjamin Ulrich to the best of my ability, including the strong possibility of frostbite deformed head and hands.

Danny listened and then waved goodbye to Allie before driving off.

"What's with the cheese?"

"Keep him off-guard," I said. The nitrous had made friends with the alcohol and the headache they were planning would be the event of the season.

"Why are you so hard on Danny?"

"You know why," I said.

"Well, he got more tolerable after you left. He's still stuck on himself, but he's not overtly mean like he used to be."

"And he's a rival."

"Oh, please," said Allie. "That's just juvenile."

"You do understand me." I fluttered my eyelashes.

"How old was that Cheez-Whiz?"

"Oh god," I said. "I'm afraid to look."

I opened the letter Danny had given me. In an elegant hand learned before "word processing" was even a phrase, was written, "Don't let them sell the house." I showed it to Allie.

"What do you think this is about?" I asked her.

"She's probably thinking of where she'll live."

"What about Tibet?"

"That's when this crap is over," Allie reminded me. "If she has to hang around for a trial, she needs a place to stay."

"But the bank? Foreclosure?"

"It's easier to teach a cat to come on command than it is to evict a tenant. I've seen it."

I remembered terrible tales of squatting renters in houses Nancy was trying to move. It took less legal machinery to start a war in the middle east than to evict a tenant. Significantly less.

"I'll talk to Archie."

———

We made it back to Allie's ranch at dusk. We bundled up and wandered to the festival where there was a commotion. The goblin/orc/troll encampment was empty. The elves stood around like noble, emotionless, androgynous lampposts, and the humans, both knights and barbarians, screamed for battle.

"We will save the princess!" boomed a stout Viking. He was wider than he was tall, and he was nearly six feet. His horned helm was impressive, but I knew it was inaccurate. Vikings didn't really have horns on their helmets. That's all propaganda started by the traumatized survivors of their bloody massacres.

I bought Allie and I elephant ears, which are big-ass deep-fried bread, some call them scones. They were usually reserved for carnivals but were strangely appropriate for the LARP festival. We found a log bench to watch the action.

In a few minutes, Allie's four horsemen rode into the arena. They carried poles with colorful banners and their horses looked positively sick of their riders. They saw Allie and whinnied beseechingly for her to save them. Allie cringed but didn't move.

"They paid for the day," she said.

Six trotting barbarians followed the riders and doubled over to catch their breath as a sixty-year-old man in a crimson robe and gold sequined crown stepped out of a tent.

"What news?" he proclaimed. He didn't talk. He proclaimed.

"The goblin army approaches!"

Led by Gandalf on a ten-foot rope leash, the green-skins scampered into the center arena. The princess had her hands tied in front of her. She wore a long flowing dress three sizes too small for her double D's. She was led by a hunched goblin with red warpaint on his green-fanged face. The female war chief, fur-clad but goose-pimpled with the setting sun, stepped forward.

"Surrender your throne to me, and I will give you back the princess," she demanded.

Two knights advanced.

Gandalf barked.

One knight fell over. The other just ran. The entire assemblage retreated, even the goblins.

That dog could bark.

"Send forth your champion," commanded the king.

Mog stepped up carrying a huge foam-padded club. He'd picked at his head bandage until it bled again, and a little live stream of crimson dripped down his cheek to very good effect.

The king called for his champion.

From the tent behind the king stepped C-3PO's lesser brother. Clad in silver plate-mail armor from head to foot, his plumed helmet under his arm, he looked the quintessential Lancelot, with a pointy goatee, pale blue eyes, and sparkling white teeth.

"Sir Nicholas Smallberries," said the king. "Defeat this goblin champion and save the kingdom."

"If I were king," I whispered to Allie. "I'd set up a royal commission to vet these character names."

The arena cleared.

Allie got up to help with the horses.

The elves were trying to one-up each other in disinterestedness, but still jockeyed for position, just not as violently as everyone else. Goblin drums rose loud and menacing behind the war chief. Trumpets erupted behind the king, almost together, but not quite. The barbarians blew battle horns made from cow parts and tuned by Helen Keller. One elf stepped forward with a small harp. He/she/they/it strummed its strings but couldn't compete with the din of the horns, drums and Gandalf who yipped and ran in circles entangling a half dozen greenies in the overlong lead.

The combatants stepped forward. Sir Nicholas Smallberries donned his helmet. A page ran forward and gave him a padded two-handed sword. Each faction sent forward a judge. Each held a fluorescent orange traffic flag that made me think of Cheese Whiz. I gagged.

"For the king!" yelled the knight.

"Warrggh!" answered the troll.

The knight circled counterclockwise. Mog stood tall in the center and rotated to face him. All attention was on the battle. Even Gandalf calmed down to watch.

The knight lunged forward, but the troll was a step too far away to be touched. He dropped his padded club on the knight's helmet and Sir Nicholas Smallberries was down. All four judges' flags went up signifying a hit. Mog roared and made space for his opponent to get up.

Sir Nicholas Smallberries rolled over on his ass, took off his helmet and cried, "No fair! That hurt."

A pathetic disgust quieted the embarrassed crowd, broken only by Smallberries' sniffles. They began to hiss and boo. The King covered his face with his hand. Mog walked up to the sitting knight and pushed him over with his club. Four flags went up. The troll tapped him two more times with the club and planted a foot on his chest.

The green-skins roared with delight. The humans who weren't screaming every foul name invented over the past ten centuries were dumbstruck.

The smug elves just watched.

The war chief stepped up to the platform, took the king's crown, and sat down on the throne. The princess was released.

"Let the feast begin!" the goblin queen commanded.

Cheers and merriment ensued.

I found Allison behind the Viking tents.

"Did you see that?"

"Kind of a letdown," she said.

"Oh yeah."

"Hey, I've got to put the horses up and feed the critters. Can you get Gandalf and bring him back to my place?"

"Sure thing."

The sun was behind the mesa and the grounds were in shadow. Cold was coming fast, but everywhere was movement. A huge bonfire blazed in the center of the arena. Each faction laid out food and drink, some dainty and fine, some bloody and still part of the beast it belonged to. Some burgers and hot dogs. Potato salad. Coleslaw, black bread, and ketchup.

A Renaissance quartet warmed up on stage. The war chief had gone back to her tent for her cloak. The former king and Sir Nicholas Smallberries were nowhere to be seen.

"Flaner!" cried Mog. "Friend!"

Monosyllables meant the mead was already flowing.

"I need the whistle," I said. Mog took the chain from around his neck.

"Without the white warg, we'd never have captured the princess and forced the duel!"

"Hail Mog!" someone yelled.

The cry was picked up and carried through the crowd.

The war chief peeked out of her tent enraged.

"And Hail the Chief!" Mog added quickly.

The others picked that up too. There was something truly savage about the scantily clad, tall, green woman that said crossing her would be bad, and I joined in the chant.

Mog started a new chorus. "Flaner! Friend of Trolls! Friends of Orcs and Goblin-kind!"

"Padding the resume," I said.

"Join us for meat!" he yelled. Anything less than shouting just didn't fit the occasion.

"I'll try!" I yelled. Everyone raised a glass of frothy warm home brew and I gathered up Gandalf after a toast.

I walked with the dog back to Allie's house afraid that he'd see a squirrel and pull my arm off. I contemplated climbing on his back, but I didn't have spurs.

I found Allie brushing the horses in the barn. I put Gandalf back in his pen and poured him half a ton of Purina mutant chow before joining her. Together we put the tired horses away for the night, and probably the season.

"We have to go back to the festival," I said. "It's going to be a helluva party."

"You go," she said. "I'm pretty tired. I've been up since four."

"Why so early?" I said before thinking.

"So I could go with you today."

"Should I come in?" I asked casually.

"Not tonight. I'm still half drunk and wholly tired."

"I don't see the problem," I said. Casanova has nothing on me.

I walked her to the door, and I kissed her good night on her porch. It was the second time I'd kissed Allison Braise for real. The first was unforgettable, a sweet rite of passage into near manhood shared with a friend. This second reached back twenty years to that moment and rekindled a magical fire undiminished by time. I lost my balance when all my blood fled my already dizzy head, and I staggered away before I fainted or Allie noticed my erection.

"Call me," she said.

"Uhma, bluhnuh gubb adabo," I said.

Casanova has nothing on me.

29

I WAS TOO excited to go home and too much of a gentleman to beg, so I went back to the festival to burn off some energy. I hoped to run into Clem Tucker. My little research project into T. S. Crew had been thin on details and thick on silence. After a big opening splash, *The Moab Picayune* was suspiciously quiet about Crew's dying development and road work.

I found parking easily. The festival was still crowded but some had left, and many had broken camp and loaded their cars already. They'd rather wake up in a warm motel a little poorer than under a blanket of desert snow, grease paint frozen to their eyebrows. With the sun down, the temperature had failed its morale check and was falling fast. Still, I could feel the heat of the bonfire from the parking lot.

Mingling with woodsmoke were the seductive smells of greasy barbecue and curry which made my stomach gurgle. There was music, laughing, singing, boasting and barfing. A revelry worthy of the name. A drunk elf slapped me on my back while a balding barbarian insisted I drink mead from his handmade, silver-trimmed horn cup which gave the drink a decidedly musky, marrow flavor, not unlike sucking warm beer through an aged jock strap.

An orc offered me another horn of drink, this one made from a yak. I passed. His makeup was a memory, but his costume would make Sting glow.

The knights had a keg, and the goblins had home brew. The elves sipped vodka and cranberry juice which they called "fairy water." I was a guest of the goblin-kind, so the heavy beer was free but left an aftertaste akin to tar and the aforementioned jock strap. More technologically advanced than the other races, the elves had discovered plastic and sold fairy water for seven dollars a cup. They'd also invented cash registers with credit card support.

Fourteen dollars and much troll love later, I found myself arm in arm between a ten-year-old hobbit and a sixty-year-old wizard dancing around the fire in a medieval line dance Shakespeare would have found quaint.

Collecting hobbies is one of my hobbies. My ex-wife, son, friends, lovers, strangers, government agencies, and poultry distributors all tell me that I'm basically an immature boy in a man's slightly overweight body. Who am I to argue with a chicken handler? LARPing was not something mainstream grown-ups would understand, but I did. I could see why folks would endure Moab in November to live a Tolkienian fantasy.

A buxom barbarian maiden handed me a paper of lyrics for a song challenge. On cue, I joined the trolls in the first verse:

> *A dragon has come to our village today*
> *We've asked him to leave, but he won't go away.*
> *Now he's talked to our king and they worked out a deal.*
> *No homes will he burn and no crops will he steal.*

The Knights picked up the second verse:

> *Now there is but one catch, we dislike it a bunch.*
> *Twice a year he invites a virgin to lunch.*
> *Well, we've no other choice, so the deal we'll respect.*
> *But we can't help but wonder and pause to reflect*

Everyone jumped in for the chorus:

> *Do virgins taste better than those who are not?*
> *Are they salty, or sweeter, more juicy or what?*
> *Do you savor them slowly? Gulp them down on the spot?*
> *Do virgins taste better than those who are not?*

I was in heaven. My head swam with spirits and hops, my body froze and cooked at once and I'd found a leg of something artery-hardening and ripped huge chunks of meat from it with growling teeth. I couldn't wait to throw the bone nonchalantly over my shoulder.

Elves danced with Celts who danced with trolls. Maidens and kobolds slipped out together for the trees and there was an overall sense of belonging. It was playful and pretend, usually hidden and denied, schoolyard bully-bait, but given full rein in that cold Moab night.

I never found out about the virgin. I saw Clem Tucker walking unsteadily toward the parking lot and caught up to him.

"Clem, wait up."

He turned and squinted his shaggy eyebrows at me. "Who's there?"

"Tony Flaner," I said to the newspaperman. "Can I talk to you for a second?"

"That's my line," he said. "I'm going to my car for more cigarettes."

I followed him.

His car was a twenty-year-old American box, more rust than faded white paint. When he opened the door, the stench of resale impossibility billowed out. Even in the darkness, I could see the smoke stains on the upholstery and a constellation of cherry burns on the seats, dash, floor mats, steering wheel, safety belt, ceiling, blinker wand, and gear shift. Tucker dug the last three packs of Lucky's from a carton and tossed the box to the passenger side floor where it caromed off two just like it.

"Things didn't turn out the way you wanted, did they?" he said, lighting a fresh cigarette off his previous one.

"Things aren't over yet."

"Maybe you should have left things alone."

"Is that you talking or the Town Fathers?"

"Me, but they'd agree."

"Tell me about Moab Pueblos," I said.

He leaned against his car and took a deep draw on his cigarette.

"T. S. Crew, huh? That's where this is headed?"

"You don't seem surprised."

"T. S. Crew is in trouble. His development's already cost twice what it was supposed to, and they don't even have a model yet. He bought the land at the height of the market and his original bid didn't take into account how much dynamiting would be required just to lay the foundations and plumbing. Then he fired his architect who turned around and sued him. And won. All this while the market crashed like Stevie Wonder on a Harley. Some of his investors are the proverbial Town Fathers but others aren't local and have bent noses and East Jersey accents, if you know what I mean. None of them were happy when the biggest single development in Moab's history cratered. He's made peace with most of them, but where he got the money for all of it is a mystery."

"But not a big enough mystery for you to look into it?"

"Who do you think I am? Woodward and Bernstein? I run a feel-good paper for a tourist-centric backwater. I only ran your ad because it was slow, and I was stupid. I wouldn't do it again."

"You got heat?"

"I got heat."

"So why were you at the house during the raid?"

"I was told to be there, to report how good the police are, etc. Besides, it's a real story now. Even if I don't dare publish it locally, other papers might pick up the piece."

"Written under a pseudonym?"

"Of course."

"So this mystery with T. S. Crew's money," I said, "might it involve the rodent Weaks and Green River Saving and Loan?"

Tucker smiled and lit another cigarette, flicking the burned filter ten yards into the darkness. "So you are a detective," he said.

"And you're a goddamn litter bug."

"Guilty."

"Tell me about the bank."

"It's owned by an oil family in Houston. Owen Weaks is the nephew of the owner. Rumor is they put him in charge of it to get him as far away from Texas as possible. They didn't even make him president or manager. He's a vice president."

"Why?"

"Easily manipulated," Clem said and grinned. "The bank's nearly failed a dozen times since I've been here. Several big boys have been sniffing around to buy it but keep getting scared away because it has so much non-collateralized money out. The family finally forbad new loans last year, but I know it's been lending anyway."

"Forbad? Is that a word?"

"Look it up."

"Don't tell me what to do. I'm my own man."

"Whatever."

"So he's been lending to Crew?"

"Among others. But, yeah, Crew mostly. He's gotta be into them over a million. Probably two. Maybe three. You didn't hear it from me though."

"What about the bridge work on the 191?"

"You've found your calling, Flaner. I don't know anything certain, but the money he got for that bridgework is probably the only thing that has kept his debt to Green River under control. The timing is perfect. Just when he got paid, his investors' torches and pitchforks went away."

"Can I get a list of the investors?"

"It's not public information," he said.

"You looked?"

"I was curious."

"Could the Ashes be involved?"

"They don't get along with Crew, but they might be. They have money now."

"Now?"

"You didn't look into them? I was just thinking you knew what you were doing. The Ashes didn't have a pot to piss in when they started. Now they can probably buy and sell Crew. They're one of my biggest sponsors," he added.

"I was out there today. Nice place."

"Yeah, a real Horatio Alger story. They planted grapes, and boom, things took off."

"Boom?"

"That's how things often work." He lit his third cigarette of the interview, stomping out the butt of the last one under his foot. A small improvement, I guess.

"Has anyone ever told you that smoking is bad for your health?"

"What? Really? Oh my God! What have I done?" He sucked half a cigarette into his lungs, and I decided I liked Clem Tucker, litterbug that he was.

"I'm going to go in and drink," I said. "I'm curious about how virgins taste."

"I think there are some in there," he said. "Mostly the boys though. Now that would be a story they'd like me to print." He waved his hand, glazing the headline. "'Tony Flaner, Local Troublemaker Arrested for Statutory Rape.'"

"I meant the song."

"Be careful, Flaner. You are unpopular in Moab right now."

I headed back to the festival as Clem fired up his American wreck. It burped a cloud of gray smoke which mingled with the tobacco for a carcinogenic cocktail of nighttime poison.

My phone vibrated. I grabbed it and turned away from the noise for a better place to talk. I hoped it was Allison. That would have been awesome, but it wasn't.

"Hey Tony," said Standard Flox. He sounded like he was at the Comedy Cellar. I could hear the loop of filtered upbeat background pop music noise they made people suffer through between acts.

"'Sup, Standard," I said.

"Where are you?"

"The Shire. What do you want?"

"I just got a call from Dara. She went to see Perry down in Arizona."

"Oh yeah, he's got that gig at the Indian Casino. How's it going?"

"Opening night, he killed," he said. "But tonight he had a meltdown. Someone's gotta get down there."

"What are you talking about?"

"It's Perry. Dara said he was three minutes into a six-minute bit and then someone took a picture of him with their phone, and he goes paranoid. Accuses the guy of being a MIB, that's a 'Man in Black.'"

"I know what an MIB is," I said. Everyone who knows Perry, who sees him unmedicated, knows what a MIB is. They're the guys following Perry around, tapping his phone lines and rounding out a dossier for later "action." Or so Perry believes when he's not on his medicine. Maybe when he's on his medicine too, but he's quieter about it then.

"Perry is refusing to go back on. Dara's sitting on him in his suite, literally, to keep him from making a break for it. If you're still down south, you are closer than me and I can't get away in any event."

"What about Garrett and Critter?"

"Critter's game, but Garrett can't go."

"Send Critter," I said but I knew it was impractical to send a puppet without the puppeteer, cheaper probably, but still ultimately impractical.

"We'll have to if you can't go. Can you go? He's blowing his big chance, man. We gotta help him. He's family."

Twain said you can pick your friends but not your family. But sometimes your friends grow so close they become family which means deep down inside you come to loathe them. It's a paradox, but he was right. We were a tight group. Perry would take a bullet for me. And I'd let him.

"Where is he?" I said.

I didn't have a pen, so Garrett said he'd text me the information when Critter got back from the bathroom. I didn't ask how he'd got there.

I checked my sobriety against the drive to Arizona, my new green-skinned friends against my old crazy one. It was no contest. I had a duty. Time for farewells.

"I thought that was you, you rotten sack of shit."

It's common practice for the less cultured species of LARPers, like orcs and barbarians to insult you as greeting. It's in character, a game of witty, clever insults like the Dozens of yore; *your mama's so fat, she's got her own zip code*. What I'd heard however was not particularly clever, so I vanquished my foe with a little nugget I'd heard earlier.

"Rot in a spider bowel, you spawn of goat sex," I said, easily winning the challenge.

"What did you say?"

"Oh dear." It wasn't a LARPer. I recognized the skull snake tattoo above the balled fist too late. A waist high Eisenhower flashed in the dark with reflected firelight.

I heard the horrific sound of splitting skin and cracking bone before I felt the blow on my forehead. I staggered backward.

"Son of a bitch!" I yelled, more in surprise and pain than in challenging insult, but it worked for that too.

I stumble into camp. My hand was up to my head and I felt warm blood between my fingers.

Benjamin James Ulrich marched after me, a terrible grimace on his prison pale face. He had a new welt down the side of his chin which I figured had been applied by a dog leash in a parking lot a couple days earlier. His nose was off-color from the cold motorcycle ride and his lips were more scab than flesh. He shook his right hand as if shaking the pain out of it. The third finger dangled unnaturally, but on he came.

"So I'm a son of a bitch, am I?" he said.

"And a leprous bugbear!"

I felt the fire behind me and heard the singing stop.

Benjamin was a hardened criminal. Just looking at his wild eyes, short hair, and scabs, you could tell he'd learned to fight in a prison yard. If I had been hoping the crowd of gossamer elves and hobbits would slow him down, I was sorely mistaken.

He swung at me with his other arm. I ducked and toppled back, catching my heel on a tuft of unkind grass and fell beside the fire.

The heat singed my hair and coagulated my forehead. In the flickering orange flames, Benjamin James Ulrich looked demonic, the wrath of hell itself.

"Time to teach you a lesson right now," he said. He pulled back his leg to kick me into tomorrow via the bonfire.

I felt hands on my shoulders and a sudden yank.

Mog, the troll champion, the very one who won the kingdom for the war chief, pulled me away before my coat melted onto me.

Benjamin stopped and stared at the wild-haired troll and laughed.

Mog, for as big and mean as he looked and for as well as he'd fought Sir Nicholas Smallberries, was visibly frightened of Delores' ex-husband. Trolls aren't as dumb as they look.

"This doesn't concern you," Benjamin said.

The goblin war chief stepped forward. She'd tossed off her fur cloak exposing her rabbit skins and ripped biceps. She stood by her champion and looked down at me.

I looked up her skirt, but it was an accident, I swear.

The fire melted away the goose bumps on her thighs. She barked twice then let out a long howl.

Benjamin hesitated. Then he pulled a knife from his pocket and flicked open the blade with his thumb. With a click, it locked into place.

Before the click was done and the howl over, Benjamin was surrounded by green-skins. They murmured and yapped, kicked dirt like a bull preparing to charge.

The elves disappeared, too frail to be so close.

The humans surrendered the battlefield to the fighters and Mog stepped forward, unafraid of the knife or the man behind it.

"How bad you want him hurt?" Mog asked me.

"Keep him down long enough for me to make it to Flagstaff," I said.

Mog glanced at the war chief who gave a single nod.

A dozen goblins and orcs jumped Benjamin from all sides in a single act. They pushed and shove. He fought back, but his knife flew out of his hand in the first crush. The chief kicked it into the coals and the handle lit up in blue flames of burning plastic.

Mog landed a hard blow to Benjamin's belly that bent him over but not before Benjamin head-butted a little orc. The orc wore a steel helmet so didn't notice the attack. Benjamin did however and tore open a frostbite scab on his cheek and cracked his chapped lips open like a torn zipper.

They dragged him away into the night, away from the others, to a dark place where orcs do what orcs do. Barks, howls, and human cries echoed off the cliffs and then subsided as the music kicked up again.

The war chief helped me up with one arm. I admired her muscles.

"Thanks," I said.

"We look after our own," she said, leaning over to kiss my forehead. As she pulled back, she licked my blood off her lips and howled again.

"Do virgins taste better than those who are not? Are they salty, or sweeter, more juicy or what?" she sang and was immediately joined by the entire ensemble who danced more furiously than before; primal and proud.

I was led away by two maidens to the healer's tent. A monk in a long brown robe and cowl sat me at a bench and looked at my forehead.

"How many leeches do you prescribe?" I asked.

"Three," he said. "On your testicles."

"Sounds about right."

He threw back a brown fur and revealed an aluminum suitcase. Inside were modern medical supplies.

"It's just a scratch," he said. "I could bandage it or stitch it. Bigger scar if you just bandage it."

"Stitches," I said.

He raised a disapproving eyebrow. "Do you want local anesthesia or a piece of leather to bite on?" he asked.

"Local."

He rolled his eyes again but turned to the trunk and dug out a syringe and small glass vial. He poked my head a few times with a needle and swabbed the area.

"Feels like more than a scratch?" I said as he cleaned the wound.

"Head wounds bleed a lot. Two stitches," he said. "Or, I could go with one and leave you a narrow scar."

"I'll go with four."

He sighed disappointedly. "Missed opportunity," he said, setting up a steel tray of sutures and needles.

"I'll have more chances," I said.

"What's this about you kidnapping a dog?" He pinched the cut closed.

While he stitched up my forehead with dissolving sutures, I explained my innocence. I assured him I bore dogs no ill will beyond the usual suburban loathing of mowed dog shit and all-night barking serenades.

"Who was your friend?"

"Ex-girlfriend's ex-husband."

The monk turned out to be a doctor from Wyoming, a general practitioner by day, neutral monk healer by night. "Brother Miro, I am called," he said and signed the bandage with a stylized "M."

"I don't take sides," he said. "Besides, it's about time the goblins got the kingship."

"How often do you meet?"

"Locally, every month. This big, once a year. The knights will be ready to retake the crown next year. Should be a good gathering. I just hope they get it organized earlier so we don't have to freeze."

He gave me a prescription for some antibiotics if it showed any signs of infection and wished me well.

The moon had risen above the cliffs but had been followed by thick black clouds that crossed it and hid its light like a skyward shell game. I had a six-hour drive ahead of me. If I started now, I might be able to beat the worst of the storm.

I left the LARPers dancing and singing, drinking and beating the snot out of Benjamin James Ulrich and went to my car. My head felt funny under the anesthetic and my elbow reminded me of my earlier police beating. I felt like a detective.

As I pulled out, Guilt Buddy took shotgun and wanted to know how long I'd be in Arizona, distracted from the case.

"Not long. Besides, there're Indians in Arizona." I turned south. "I'll check up on the Indian thing there."

"You better," he said.

"Or what?" said I.

"Or I'll make you feel really guilty, fill you with self-loathing, and make you hate yourself."

"You wouldn't dare."

"Watch me."

I shouldn't have been driving with so much fairy water in my veins, but at least I had Guilt Buddy to keep me company. Maybe I'd let him drive for an hour or so while I slept.

30

IT WAS JUST before dawn when I pulled into the Lucky Arrow Indian Casino and Convention Center an hour north of Flagstaff. I don't remember much of the drive. Guilt Buddy must have taken over after Blanding and woke me as we pulled into valet parking.

"Checking into—Ahhh!" said the costumed valet.

"What?" I yelled back.

"You're covered in blood," he said. "Do you need a doctor?"

"No, I'm good."

"What happened?"

"Sorry," I said. "The first rule, you know."

I tossed him the keys eight feet too high, and they flew over his head into a cactus garden.

"Sorry." I put a ten on the dashboard.

This was the grand opening weekend for the casino and the smell of new carpet was a nice change from stale tobacco, which is the signature stench of casinos all over America.

The rooms were to the right above a bank of six gleaming gold elevators. Directly ahead was the entrance to the "The Pueblo People Museum" exhibit and gift shop beside the reception desk. To the left was the casino, the Indian's economic revenge on the white man, stretching as far as the eye could see. It began simply with slot machines and Keno runners then morphed into Twenty-One tables, a sports book, poker rooms, then a dog track, and probably an unmarked back room with Vietnamese Russian roulette; "MAU! MAU! DIDI MAU!" All games of chance in ascending order of seriousness.

A sandwich board placard announced, "Comic Genius Perry Whitehouse live in the Cactus Room all month."

I saw myself in a mirrored column and wondered why they'd let me inside. Head wounds bleed, and I'd just had one. I was scabbed, caked, and covered in gore to prove it. Miro had left me gory for effect. Among the clans, it was a sign of power. Here in the casino, it reeked of highwaymen, loan sharks, and poor security. What kind of rent-a-cop would let Carrie's prom date walk into a grand opening of a billion-dollar resort? Distracted ones I learned.

A gauntlet of security swarmed around a middle-aged man in a plaid shirt. His comb-over had flown up vertically to become a mohawk due to a screaming shit-fit he was still working through.

Four costumed guards with imitation bone breastplates surrounded the man but gave him his space. A thirty-year-old woman trying too hard to look eighteen popped gum a few steps away. She showed much too much mid-drift under her unseasonal tube top.

"She'll tell you," the man said, pacing a circle in front of a Triple Cherry slot. "It was all a mistake. Tell them, honey."

"Sure," she said. "Just like that."

"Once the money's in the machine it's the casino's," a guard explained.

"I'll replace it," he said. "Give it back!"

"Maybe you should go have a lie-down," said another guard.

The man turned and rushed the machine. He shook it violently like he was trying to beat a confession out of it. The guards pulled him off it in an instant. He broke free and rushed the girl.

"You stupid bitch!"

She yelped and ran into the casino.

A guard tackled him.

"Excuse me," I said, stepping forward from the gawking crowd. "I'm covered in blood. Perhaps I can help."

"That stupid broad put my quarters in that machine!" the man yelled, satisfied with my credentials.

"How much did you lose?"

"Eight thousand dollars!" he yelled.

"That's a lot of quarters without a payout," I said, raising an accusatory eyebrow at the guards.

"It was ten quarters," he cried.

"Two-fifty? I don't follow."

The man made another dive at the machine from his knees, but a guard had his belt. He gave up when his pants were down to his knees.

"They were valuable," he howled.

"Most money is," I reasoned.

"They were silver," he said, his eyes searching mine for comfort.

"Yes, I know. Were they shiny too?"

"Silver! 1932-D Washington silver quarters," he howled. "They're worth eight hundred bucks apiece, and that bimbo put ten into that machine!"

"Oh," I said. "Ouch."

"Mister, this is a casino. There are no refunds," explained a guard.

"It's robbery," he said.

"It's a casino."

He lunged at the machine again. His pants went to his ankles, his boxers had cupid hearts on them and needed to be changed. He grabbed the coin return tray on the machine and yanked. Already off-balance, the machine toppled over and onto the man.

The crunch was loud enough to silence a casino. Even the chirping of idle slots paused in horror for a moment as the machine settled into the crook of the man's shattered arm. Then like a distant train whistle coming out of the dark, the man moaned and then screamed, and then blubbered snot down his face. Three guards lifted the machine off him and carried him toward an unmarked door, his pants trailing around his ankles, his sobs fading behind them. The bimbo, and I think I'm safe in using that term here, was nowhere to be seen.

Robbers and robbed alike returned to their income redistribution routine, and I went to the counter for check-in. The rush of excitement had been good to sharpen my sleep-deprived senses, but they were dulling again by the second. I'd missed the snowstorm, and the sun was bright outside, but that was our little secret because once past the doors of the casino, windows were rarer than a cocktail waitress at the nickel slots.

"I'm Tony Flaner," I told the receptionist.

Her perky plastic smile melted as she took in the bloody gore of my ensemble. "Do you have a room for me?"

She tapped a hidden keyboard and watched a secret monitor.

"You have a reservation on the fifth floor, suite 529."

"I do?"

"Yes, you called and reserved four hours ago. Special guest of Perry Whitehouse."

"I did?"

"Says you called from a cell phone en route."

"If you say so."

"We have a nurse on duty. Should I send her up?"

"I'm too tired right now. Put me down for a French maid tomorrow."

———

I woke up late that afternoon with no memory of entering my suite. It crossed my mind that maybe I'd received a concussion from Benjamin's broken finger but dismissed the notion when a squirrel ran under the window.

"Hey, look. A squirrel."

I was still caked in blood and needed a shower. A porter had brought my stuff from the car. It was everything I'd brought from Salt Lake, my clothes, my suit, and my burglar bag with pistol, sans bullets. I wonder if I'd tipped.

It was easier to shower with my shirt on. It was cemented to my body with dried blood. Peeling it off too soon would cost me more hair than a hot wax demo. Steaming hot water melted the scabs, and I gingerly tugged off the garment and let it fall into the tub where it clogged the drain. Ankle deep in rusty blood water, I scrubbed the rest off with a complimentary loofa.

Refreshed and no longer looking like an extra from *The Walking Dead*, I dressed. A blinking light on my phone told me I had a message waiting. It was Dara.

"Glad you fucking made it," she said. "Get your ass up here. I'm in 540, Perry's in 502. Get over here and do something!"

It was past five o'clock when I left the room. I went first to 540, but there was no answer. 502 was at the other end of the wing and I followed the unnaturally bright-patterned carpet down the hall until I had an over-whelming subliminal urge to dump my savings onto a craps table. *Put it all on the horn!*

I knocked. No answer. I knocked again. Still nothing. Most people would give up at this point, max out a credit card for chips and play red until it evaporated, but I was made of stronger stuff. I was a trained investigator. I knocked again, and this time, I called out too.

"Perry? It's me, Tony. Let me in. The carpet is melting my medulla oblongata, and if I don't get away from it soon, I'm afraid the damage will be permanent."

The door opened, and an arm quickly pulled me inside.

"God, yes. I forgot about the carpets." Perry bolted the door behind me.

"Where's Dara?" I asked.

"I don't know."

The suite was identical to mine except more lived in. The couch pushed up against the door was a homey touch so few tourists take advantage of.

"Tony, you're the only one who'll understand," Perry said. "It's about the moon thing."

Perry is a brilliant man, a potentially first-class comedian with intelligence and timing that makes me think of Pryor. But unlike Pryor, or much like him, depending on your view, he's insane. His usual daily dose of medication keeps him stable enough to blend with the population at large, but when he's off it, he sees spies in every corner and writes really intense poetry.

"You're off your medication?" I asked.

"I cut it back," he said. "I needed an edge. This is supposedly my big chance, you know. They're paying top dollar and all kinds of people are going to see me. They said there'd be folks from Hollywood. New York. London."

"Moab," I added.

"But it's all a scam, see? They tricked me. They've trapped me."

"How much did you cut back your meds?"

"Completely. You should have seen me opening night. I got two job offers."

"And last night?"

"Not as many." He peeked through a curtain onto the same lawn where I'd seen a squirrel earlier.

"What happened?" I asked. "Can I order room service? I'm starving."

"I wouldn't trust it."

"So it's okay then?"

I called down for two club sandwiches, a pot of coffee, and a piece of pie. I love pie.

"You want anything?"

"I'll try some of yours. Maybe."

"Make it three clubs."

I helped myself to an eight-dollar bottle of orange juice from the minibar.

"This is all comped, right?"

"I think so," he said. "But I don't know. They're threatening lawsuits and shit."

"What did you do exactly?"

He rushed over to me and looked me in the face hard as if his eyes could peel back the *Mission Impossible* mask. He said, "Okay, I was in my bit about lunar cycles, you know, the one about periods and werewolves?"

"Great bit," I said.

"Well, when I said 'moon,' this guy raises up a phone and snaps my picture. I didn't think anything of it, but then I said moon again, and again up comes his phone, and he takes my picture. It's not like I can miss it. He's got a table right up front and the flash on. I can see him in the spotlight bleed. He's sitting with one other guy. Both are in black suits, thin ties, and sunglasses. I think, Perry, you're seeing things, and press on. You know, 'cause I have my edge now. With no meds. Then I say moon again, and up comes the camera! He's keying on the word moon, and every time I say it, he snaps my picture. Neither one of those two laughed the whole show, and I know that ticket wasn't cheap. I pause and say moon. Just moon. No lead-up. No context. Just moon. Up comes the phone. I look right at the guy and say Pluto, nothing. Then I say Nereid. Nothing. You know Nereid is a moon of Neptune, right?"

"Who doesn't?" I said.

"So he's not looking for just any moon, just 'The Moon.' I step forward and shade my eyes to get a look at these guys. The audience knows something's up, but I don't care. The one with the camera looks familiar, but I can't place him. The other guy gets up and scampers away. Him I know. I've seen before but don't get a good look."

"Didn't get to the finale then?"

"No. I stare at the guy at the table for a minute. He stares back through his sunglasses. I can't see his eyes. I say moon, and up comes the camera. Snap. That's it. I'm done. I leave the stage and came up here. I haven't left the moon—er, I mean, room, since."

"Where was security?"

"Paid off, I'm sure."

"Who do you think they were?"

"Spooks. Men in Black. It's about my moon blog."

"I must have missed that post," I said.

Perry contributes to several conspiracy blogs, or rather, all of them. He'd send me links to them now and again, but I seldom clicked on them. Most required a more encyclopedic knowledge of the Illuminati and Operation Blue Book than I possessed.

"It was about the dark side," he said, looking for recognition on my face.

"You better walk me through this one."

"The dark side of the moon is always pointed away from the Earth. It's a perfect place to hide an alien space base."

"But of course."

"NASA released some recent satellite photos of the dark side. But they've been airbrushed to hide the existence of an alien base. Several of them, actually."

"How can they take pictures without light?" I asked.

"It's not always turned away from the sun," he said, and I felt stupid.

"So the photos were doctored?"

"Blatantly. So I linked a couple of old articles from retired Air Force personnel who swear that their job was specifically to airbrush out signs of life on the dark side of the moon. One of the whistleblowers was found dead just last year. He was only seventy-three years old. Pretty suspicious."

"And a drinker?"

"Smoked two packs a day. But that doesn't matter. He was offed, and I linked to his near-deathbed confession. The spooks are trying to send me a message. It's a conspiracy, and I'm getting too close. They're warning me."

"Well that's the answer then," I said.

"Yes. Uhm, what is?"

"The counter move to this move is to be more famous. They're trying to keep you small, so you won't get reputation enough to blow the lid off all this. All you have to do is just keep going, take your meds so they can't throw you off, and eventually, when you do *The Tonight Show*, you can tell it all on primetime, and there's nothing they can do about it. If they disappear you, then it'll only back up your story."

"I'll be a martyr for truth," he said, glassy-eyed. "Like Matt Anderson."

"Who?"

"He was killed after he claimed to have incontrovertible evidence the

Mayans created an extra-dimensional portal to the middle east during the reign of King Two Hat Llama."

"I must have missed that one too."

"It got covered up deep," Perry said.

There was a knock at the door. Perry ducked into the bathroom, where I heard the sound of a shotgun shell being racked up. The door was ajar, but I couldn't see Perry.

"Take it easy, Perry. It's just room service."

I pulled the couch away and opened the door.

"Fucking Flaner. About time." Dara pushed me aside and climbed over the sofa.

"It's Dara! It's Dara," I shouted, saving at least one life.

"What the fuck?"

"Perry's in the bathroom with a loaded shotgun," I whispered.

"The fuck he is." She stormed to the bathroom door and kicked it open.

"My mistake," she said, backing away.

"Perry, it's alright. It's just us. Leave the gun in there, and we'll work this out."

He peeked around the door.

"Tony believes me," he said to Dara.

"You do?"

"I just heard the story."

"If it went down as he said, security would have hauled them out by the hair," said Dara.

"Not if they were bribed," Perry said. "Or in on it."

There was another knock at the door. Perry retreated to the bathroom, and racked another shell into the gun. I heard the previous one rattle around in the bathtub. Dara hit the floor and rolled under the bed.

"Room service," I said, taking the tray in the hall. "Anyone got a tip?"

I was talking to an empty room.

I signed for it and added a gratuity.

"Good. Food," said Dara, taking a sandwich before I could put down the tray.

Perry skulked out and sat on the bed.

"Thanks for coming down here, Tony," he said, forcing his breath to near calm. "If anyone can figure this out, if there's something to figure out that I haven't figured out already, it's you."

"There's a thought in there somewhere," I said. "It might even be a good one."

"I got the tape of last night's show," Dara said, tossing a disk beside Perry. "The security guy wasn't easy to convince, but when I got through with him, I had to give him the name of a good shrink. He's a very visual thinker. I may have hurt him."

I grabbed the last sandwich before Dara could. She'd started a second one before I saw her finish the first. Marking territory.

"Perry, just get on your goddamned drugs," Dara said, spitting bread and cheese. "Don't fuck up your big chance. I can't believe you let a heckler ruin your show. Fucking amateur."

I slid the disk into the player and ate my sandwich trying to figure out the controls. I finished a cup of coffee and slice of pie before I got the thing working.

Dara continued berating Perry. I wondered if she remembered there was a loaded shotgun in the next room. "For fuck's sake, it's not a conspiracy to fuck with your mind!"

"Or that's exactly what it is," I said.

"You're not helping Tony," she said.

I rewound the security tape to the aisle camera where the one spook hurried from the table and out of the theater. His glasses were off.

"Didn't I hear that Perry had to audition against Matticks for this job?" I asked.

"Fuckin'-a," said Dara into the freeze-framed face of Wayne Matticks.

31

I KNEW Wayne from the Comedy Cellar when he was on the circuit looking for enough notoriety to land him a job like Perry had now. He'd made some bones on my misfortunes at the time but that wasn't the reason I wanted to get him now. Well, not the only reason.

Perry calmed down when he realized the conspiracy was between a disgruntled agent and a dick comedian. We even got him to take his meds and ordered more club sandwiches while we planned. There are times in your life when you should go the extra mile and plan an all-out war against a conniving little weasel like Wayne Matticks. For the next hour, we planned helicopter strafings, back-room brutalities, whoopee cushions, blue-laser brain reprogramming—Perry's idea—waterboarding, and the ever-popular middle school trilogy of terror: Indian burns, noogies, and swirlies, the last is where you hold the victim's head in a toilet bowl and flush. Oh, the humanity.

After much debate, during which Guilt Buddy took a controlling role at the end, it was decided to alert the casino and have them deal with them in their own Navajo-gangster manner. Dara saw no harm in starting a Twitter slander campaign but promised not to mention Perry's vulnerability to men in black suits and sunglasses. Perry promised to lose his edge and soldier on.

I love my friends, and under normal circumstances, I would have relished an opportunity to put together an elaborate practical joke that would leave Matticks sterile and bound up in a straightjacket, but my thoughts kept going back to Moab. Everyone has their own problems. You can't measure yours by anyone else's or you quickly realize how stupid and superficial you are. Like when you can't find a parking place or mislay your cell phone. There are places in Africa where there are no valets and cell phone coverage is like two bars at best. Most people have it pretty good and when the universe looks at what they think of as problems, galaxies face palm and new black holes are created just to show what real shit is. But nobody looks.

What struck me as strange, while Guilt Buddy explained how I just didn't have the time and resources to "eviscerate the fucker" right then, was what I'd thought of as 'my problems,' weren't actually my problems. What I had going on in Moab was just an interesting detective case without pay. My personal involvement, an involvement that I felt all the way to my core like a Capulet insulted Montegue, was fueled by a loyalty to a family I hardly knew. And now my hurry to return to Moab was centered around an old woman I hadn't even met two weeks before and had no ties to me at all. But still, I knew I had to get back as certainly as I knew the truth of lunar base cover-ups and blue-laser mind-control experiments. Actually, more so.

I realized that if I hadn't gone to Moab, if I hadn't stirred the pot, and run the ad in the *Picayune*, things would be better, which is a roundabout way of saying I'd made things worse. What Vicky wanted most was that Sophia to be free. She had it handled fine without me. Thanks to my Mensa reasoning, I'd put the love of my aunt's life into jail for the foreseeable future. This fact ate at me like leeches in my undies or Guilt Buddy at my frontal lobe.

Dara was not pleased that we weren't going to personally deal with Matticks. "This is fucking bullshit," she said succinctly. "It's an honor thing, for fuck's sake."

Perry was calm. It was his career that had been threatened but when he realized he wasn't going to be disappeared, it was like Christmas to him.

"This is decided, Dara," he said. "Tony will tell the management. They'll handle it."

"We should chloroform the fucker like we discussed. The third elevator cameras aren't installed yet. It's perfect."

"Kidnapping is a felony," I reminded her.

"You'd know, woof woof."

"That was low," I said.

"What does that mean?" said Perry. He'd missed this month's issue of *Family Saving/Family Values*. Glad someone had.

"Tony got some bad press for losing a fucking dog."

"True story?"

"True story. Not what was written, but that's the gist of it. They got the dog back, though."

"Ten thousand dollars later."

"Well it all worked out then," Perry said.

"Sure, but now Tony attracts packs of rabid dog owners to the Cellar and Barry banned him until this thing with the dog blows over."

"I didn't know that."

"Well, now you do."

"Great," I said. "Well, I'll go talk to the management. You get Perry ready for his show. Make him throw up if you have to and then re-medicate."

"Gotcha," Dara said, winding her finger toward Perry's mouth.

Perry had eaten a whole sandwich and we were worried that a full stomach would prevent his pills from working. It was Dara's idea to go all bulimic on him.

Perry cringed.

I left before the shotgun reappeared to hunt down some authority.

Casino director sounded right. I found an office so named on the second floor above a very Indian name.

"Mr. Twinbear?" I said, peeking in the door. There was no secretary.

"Yes?" The man behind the desk was an actual Native American. Besides a few dealers, guards, and vendors in the casino, everyone I'd seen there was of European invader stock. I couldn't guess at his age. The weathered creases in his cheeks could have said thirty or sixty. The long braid down his back was shiny, neat, and black as obsidian.

"I need to talk to you about Perry Whitehouse and Wayne Matticks," I said and took a chair.

The director listened to the story. I livened it up as best I could. Never waste an audience.

"I don't want to tell you your business, but it would be best if he didn't get another chance to disrupt the show," I said.

"I'll handle it," he said. While I'd talked he'd tapped at his computer and now turned the monitor toward me. I saw a color picture of Wayne and his agent entering a room on the third floor.

"Is this them?" Twinbear asked.

"Yeah. Do you have cameras in the rooms as well?"

He smiled. "Of course not."

I didn't believe him.

"Nice casino," I said.

"It's our fourth. The first this far north."

"Expensive?"

"Yes. If we hadn't the income from the other three there'd be no way we could build such a place so quickly. We'd have to work out of tents to get a savings first."

"Couldn't you just get investors?"

"It's not a sure thing. If something goes wrong, you have to scamper to pay the money back you've already spent. Investors are seldom forgiving. The wrong ones can really make life hard."

He was probably talking about Jack Abramoff, but I thought about T. S. Crew and what he faced with a town of angry fathers and east coast investors.

"Good you're in a position to work like that," I said.

"We learned the hard way."

"I noticed you have a museum downstairs," I said.

"Yes. It's a cultural outreach program. It's another attraction to the resort and it offers a different portrayal of the Pueblo people than what is usually available."

"What portrayal?"

"Exactly."

"Hey, no offense, but is it just for show or is there an actual historian involved? I need to talk to somebody about Indian land claims."

He pinched his brow but then shrugged. "No, it's a real museum. It's the jewel of the Lucky Arrow. Five thousand square feet with rotating exhibits. It's run by Tanner Pinion, PhD"

"Can I talk to him?"

He looked at his watch. "He's gone for the day. Try tomorrow."

———

I had an hour to kill before the show and made the mistake of wandering into the casino. I sat in on a Blackjack game and pondered whether to split sixes when Wayne Matticks sidled up beside me.

"Flaner? Is that you?" He dropped three one-hundred-dollar bills on the table. My stack of thirteen white, one-dollar chips wasn't as impressive as the green and red ones they slid over to him.

"Matticks. What are you doing here?"

"Catching Perry's show," he said.

"Did you catch it last night?"

He turned away and grabbed a waitress' ass.

"Two Jack Daniels, babe," he said.

"No alcohol, sir," she said, controlling the urge to slap him with the utmost effort.

"Ah, right. Never mind."

"Card, sir?" asked the dealer.

"Sure," I said.

A four. I had sixteen. From two sixes to a sixteen, I had the crappiest hands in the game.

"Give me another," I said.

He dropped a five in front of me.

The dealer had twenty. I was the only winner.

"Well look at lost dog Flaner make—what? Five dollars?" Matticks put up fifty dollars in chips. "You gotta have money to make money, chump."

I said, "It is a wonder that with that kind of wit, you're still in the mediocre echelon of dead-end comics."

"Very funny," he said.

"Ouch, that was a zinger. Nice suit," I said. "Are you going to a funeral?"

"Yeah, yours."

"That's your best? I set up a tee ball and that's all you got?"

Matticks busted with twenty-three and the dealer took his chips with a practiced scoop.

I held at eighteen. The dealer couldn't hit his seventeen. Another five dollars for me.

"You know what your problem is?" Matticks asked me.

"I'm too tolerant of morons, wannabes, and idiots in public places?"

"You don't know how the game's played. The dealer had a king. You have to put him on a twenty. You should have hit."

"You must have been having one of your delusions of grandeur," I said. "You missed it. I won; you lost."

"Luck only goes so far." He pushed a hundred dollars out in front of him. "If you don't know the game, how to work all the angles, you'll always end up the loser."

"You'd be the expert on losing," I said. "Heard you were up for Perry's job here. What happened? They didn't like fart jokes?"

He flushed and signaled for a card. He got a king and leaned back and smiled.

I flipped over an ace on top of my jack.

"Blackjack," I said.

Push, said the dealer, turning two fives to their ace. Wayne's hundred was scooped away when his twenty didn't cut it.

"We'll see how long Perry keeps this job," he said. "I heard he's unstable."

Wayne pushed all his remaining chips forward this time.

"You mean he's prone to rage? Goes full tilt after a losing streak and makes stupid decisions?"

Wayne split eights and had to fish another hundred fifty from his pocket. This time it was all small bills, nothing above a ten. It took the dealer a minute to unfold it all and count it. He slid it into a memory hole and put chips on the table.

The first eight got a queen, the second a five and then a jack. Busted, scoop half.

I hit on a fifteen and landed another five and stayed. There were a lot of fives in this deck.

"Nineteen," said the dealer. "Pay twenty."

Wayne was busted.

"Just luck," he said. "A string of bad luck."

"It's not over yet," I said.

Two burly men appeared on either side of Matticks. They'd had the courtesy to wait until he was out of money. Nice touch.

"Sir, the director would like to talk to you," said the smaller, three-hundred-pound one.

"What's this about?" Matticks said.

"Just come with us."

"I haven't done anything. I just lost four hundred fifty bucks. What? Is losing not allowed in this casino? What the fuck?"

"We don't like that kind of language," the first one said.

He pulled out a stun gun and jabbed it into Matticks' neck. Matticks flopped to the floor like a dropped fish. He relieved himself, which offered his gills some moisture, but probably not enough.

"Was that necessary?"

"No," the bouncer said. "The waitress is my sister."

They picked up the soiled Matticks and dragged him away. I grabbed my chips and quickly followed them, hoping that they'd lead me out of the labyrinthian gambling maze before eight.

We emerged into the lobby and they took Matticks behind the door where I'd seen them disappear the manic coin collector earlier. Upon closer examination, I noted a small brass plate by the door. It said merely, "Room 101."

I found Dara in the theater sipping Diet Coke.

"Sucks there's no alcohol here," she said. "I mean they're Indians, right? Where's all the firewater?"

"I think that's the point." We settled in for the show.

Perry killed. His opener was a juggler, always a good warm-up for a wordy comedian. The front table where Matticks and his agent had intimidated Perry the night before was vacant, though it still had a reserved card on it.

We were the first to stand and applaud when he'd finished, and the crowd, being shamed by our enthusiasm, followed suit.

"Everyone," said Perry from the stage. "I'd like to introduce two of the funniest people I know. Two loyal friends who are as close as family to me; Dara Sutter and Tony Flaner!" He gestured to our table and the spotlight fell on us.

There was scattered applause and murmurs of "dognapper." We waved and sat down the instant we could.

"What are you going to do about this dog shit?" Dara asked when everyone was filing out.

"I'll worry about it when it's a problem."

"After the other night, I'd hate to be around when that happens."

"You saw the fight?"

"Only the last of it. That tattooed guy got horse-whipped by a gray-hair with a studded leash."

"Yeah, I saw him."

"Where?"

"Moab. He followed me."

"Not just there," she said.

"What?"

I looked behind us where she pointed. Coming down the aisle, fighting against the tide of exiting gamblers, was Benjamin James Ulrich.

32

BENJAMIN LOOKED like the mummy's curse. He had a new tattered bandage around his head, several peeling Band-Aids on his face and arms, a mud-splattered splint on his swollen finger, two black eyes and a definitive limp. These were above and beyond his already frostbitten face, leash welts, and freely bleeding lips. I noticed the stylized M signature on the bandages from the LARP physician. I bet he went for the scars.

"Am I trailing breadcrumbs?" I grabbed Dara's arm.

We ran up onto the stage and into the wings. Two bouncers with earpieces stepped forward but let us by.

"Good thing Perry introduced us," Dara said.

"Yeah, that was swell." I glanced at Benjamin who was now at our vacated table.

Backstage we found Perry's dressing room as the bouncers intercepted Benjamin.

"Great show," I said, barging in on Perry. He was half naked down to his drawers. He'd sweated a lot on stage. I'd have done worse. I'd have had to change mid-show.

"Can we hang with you?"

"Sure," he said, stripping off the boxers. I looked away. Dara didn't.

Perry took us to The Cooking House, the best restaurant in the resort. I was dressed up for me, which meant long pants, closed shoes, and a clean Bjork tee shirt. They let us in anyway. No one has standards anymore.

The restaurant had more atmosphere than light. Table candles offered the greatest illumination. The track lighting artistically arranged on the domed ceiling was of the five-watt variety and two floors above us.

"They have wine here," said Perry. "But I can't have any. I'm contractually obligated not to drink."

"Why?"

"Standard contract. They've dealt with comedians before."

"Not many twice, I bet," said Dara.

A waiter materialized with three two-foot tall embossed menus bound with gold cord. Unlike most restaurants this expensive, their menus listed prices. I wish it hadn't.

"Remember the three-dollar milkshake from Pulp Fiction?" Dara asked. "Here they're eighteen."

"They're good," said Perry.

The waiter reappeared, thin and regal in his vest and clean apron.

"Tonight Chef Bencini is here in person," crooned the waiter. "He recommends the bisque followed by the pesto pasta Bencini."

"Okay," said Perry.

"Sold me," said Dara.

"Do you have wine?" said I.

"I'll send over the wine steward. And for you?"

"The same. Bisque us up."

"Tony," whispered Perry, "I can't get you any discount on alcohol."

"'Kay," I whispered back.

The waiter disappeared, his hands never coming from behind his back. In a minute, an elderly man with a silver cup around his neck emerged from the gloom.

"How may I help you?" he asked.

"Have you heard of Ashe Winery?"

"Yes sir, they're a winery in Utah. What are you having tonight, I'll recommend something appropriate."

"They're kind of new, aren't they?"

"Yes, they've had only one good year, to my recollection, but it's aged well and still earning prizes."

"How long does it usually take a vineyard to get good wine?"

"It depends on the acumen of the winemakers. I've heard it done as quickly as a decade, but usually much longer."

"Ashe's took about a decade," I said. "They've acumen then?"

He hesitated. "They found a good grape," he said.

"What does that mean?"

"I'm no expert on growing to be sure, but I'd suggest that much of Ashe Winery's success came from the acquisition of the Tolanto Rimini grapes."

"Come again?"

"Ashe Winery purchased and transplanted the entire vineyard. The grape's pedigree went back to Caesar."

"Cheap?"

"Oh no."

"Recent?"

"About five years," he said. "Wine from those grapes is appearing now. But as I said, they did have one excellent year before that."

"We're having the bisque and pesto pasta?"

"Shall we look at Spanish wines then?"

After we settled on a reasonably priced Californian wine, the steward left.

"What the fuck was that about?"

"A case," I said.

"You learn anything?" asked Perry, breaking a piece of bread off the loaf the waiter had brought us.

"Actually, I got lucky."

We talked about friends, loves, and careers and the lack thereof, and then we called it an early night. Perry confessed to not having slept since the previous night's moon crisis. Dara, happy to have had some wine, wanted to find someone "fuck-worthy" in the casino. I told her about the taser-wielding bouncers, and she laughed.

"Better than a shotgun," she said.

In the morning, I prepared to leave. Moab was heavy on my mind, but I was not sorry for coming to The Lucky Arrow. Things were coming together. I could feel them settling into place in the back of my mind like the round peg in the round hole and a star in the star. I didn't see them yet, but I could feel fittings.

The Pueblo Indian Museum Exhibit and Gift Shop opened at nine am. I was back to my old self so I didn't show up until after ten. I bought a ticket and wandered the exhibits. They had models of mud dwellings with little brown people lifting pots and scraping pelts like a 3D photograph. The exhibit included all of the Pueblo Indians from Utah to Mexico and described their evolution from the oldest peoples to the current nations of Hopi, Ute, Paiute, and Navajo. There was a lot on the Anasazi and long disclaimers about "the cannibal" myth littered with phrases such as "isolated occurrence," "few bad apples," and "following orders," that made me think Carl Rove was their copywriter.

I was pleased to find an exhibit of Native American Resistance in the twentieth century and beyond. There was a tasteful montage of protesting Indians, sit-ins, and even the occupation of Alcatraz. There was a list of current lawsuits against the American Government from Pueblo Indians and other tribes throughout the country. Most demanded the return of ancestral land. A lot was made of the Taos Pueblo getting back their sacred Blue Lake Mountain in 1970, setting a precedent for territorial recovery by legal means. A good news story that boded ill for the Racine Ranch.

I studied the maps closely. They showed the many overlaps of Indian peoples in the southwest, frequent migrations, and the effects of European encroachment from the Spanish to the tourism boom.

I bought a Kachina Doll for Allie and asked to see the curator, Tanner Pinion, PhD

"Do you have an appointment?"

"Do I need one?"

"He's busy."

"Mr. Twinbear, the casino director and head of the stun gun brigade, sent me," I said.

The mention of stun guns got her moving because it wasn't my shirt. I was still in Bjork. I followed her through a door behind the gift shop and down a short hall to a door that hung ajar.

"Mr. Pinion, someone here to see you," she said.

I poked my head around and showed him the kachina doll.

"Can I help you?"

"Yes." I sat down. I'd brought the maps and photos of the ranch I'd collected in a paper sack and started rummaging through it.

"Mr. Twinbear said you might be able to help me."

"Who are you?"

"Tony Flaner."

"The dognapper?"

I stared. "Perry Whitehouse's friend. The comedian."

"Are you the detective that lost the dog?"

"They got it back."

"I can't stand useless dogs," he said. "If they don't work, they don't eat."

"We can be friends," I said and put a pile of photographs on his desk. He picked them up and looked at them.

"Here's the deal," said I. "My aunt Vicky, a wonderful woman, was murdered in Moab a couple weeks ago. I'm looking for the murderer. Don't worry. You're not a suspect. Yet."

He shot me a glance.

"Well, I think she might have been done in for this little bit of land she has north of Moab. It's really a miserable place." I unfolded the map and pointed to the area I'd outlined. "I'm trying to figure out why it might be valuable enough to kill for."

"Moab is a tourist village," he said. "Development."

"You know a lot about that?"

"No, but I know someone who does." He picked up a phone and dialed an extension.

"Glenn, come down here. We have a mystery." He hung up and said to me, "Glenn is our development planner."

"There's one guy who says he's a Hopi but he's blonde as Leif Erickson's inner thigh."

"Tiponi?"

"You know him?"

"What a freak," he said.

"Yep, that's him. He says that he has an ancestral claim on the land because it's an ancient holy place as demonstrated by those pictographs. He's trying to stop an auction on the land that will free up what little my aunt left as a legacy."

He looked at the pictures and then the map.

"Where on this map are these pictographs?" he asked.

"I'm not sure," I said, "but by the background, I think it's probably around this area." I pointed to a corner of the property.

"You haven't seen these yourself?"

"Not yet," I said quietly.

"Some detective," he said under his breath.

There was a knock. A tall slender man with a loosened tie walked in. "What do we have here?" he said.

"What do you think of this piece of land?" said Pinion.

Glenn, the newcomer, took the map and studied it.

"You selling it?" Glenn said to me.

"No, just curious. I'm Tony Flaner, by the way."

"Dognapper detective?"

"Fuck."

Glenn produced a magnifying loop like I'd seen jewelers use and bent down over the map and studied the contours.

Pinion found a magnifying glass in his desk and studied the photos. I was the only one without a magnifying glass and I called myself a detective. Fuck.

"It's worthless," Glenn said. "For development anyway."

"Why? Can't there be condos? Just there overlooking the vineyard? Be a great view."

"No way. I know the geology there. Look at those lines. You'd have to blast those cliffs down just to get a road up there. You'd have to raze it all just to pour foundations. No way any planning commission would allow such damage."

"How about a corrupt one?" I asked.

"Possibly, but that's just the start. Any environmental group could challenge such a project and tie it up for years. But the true problem is cost. It's a soft market and even at its height the cost of building there wouldn't make sense. Not even close. Unless someone's looking decades or even centuries down the line, I can't imagine this ever being developed."

"Tiponi is full of shit," said Pinion.

My head was reeling from Glenn's announcement which made liars of a few people, it also invalidated my hunch.

"Why do you say that?" I asked Pinion. "Beyond the obvious, I mean."

"Okay, Moab wasn't exactly a popular area with the Pueblo Indians. Some lived there, but the canyons were too rough and the mosquitoes too thick for anything serious. It was a place people passed through."

"What about those pictures?"

"First of all, the Hopi were hardly there. Way back when, they wandered up that far, but that figure there, it's on top of the others, see?" He handed me the magnifying glass.

"It is actually the most recent carving, not the oldest."

"How recent?"

"A couple of years. At most. Could be months."

"Son-of-a-bitch," I said.

"And those others, it's like layers of writing. Under the Hopi one is some half rubbed off graffiti. 'Blake was here 1962' and under that is a date, 1902. Then there are some Ute signs, some more English, Paiute, Ute again, more Paiute, English, Paiute, Ute, Spanish, Ute, Paiute."

"So it has archaeological value?"

"This is all pretty crude. Nothing here is more than a couple hundred years old. Around here, that's yesterday. And there's absolutely no dominance of any one tribe over another. I record this area as being Paiute, but the Utes wiped them out in the 1800s, and then the Utes were chased away by the white settlers. This area, in modern times, has been traded around more often than a bounced check."

"So who has a claim to it?"

"Whoever owns the title now," he said. "These pictures prove the opposite of ancestral lands. It proves recent habitation, post-European, and a mishmash of tribes who, contrary to what you saw outside in the exhibit, don't really get along that well. Of all the tribes who might have a valid claim on that area, and there are none, the Hopi would be the last on the list. Besides, the tract is tiny. It's surrounded on all sides by non-Indian property."

"So Tiponi...?" I stuttered.

"Is an idiot."

This was good news, I guess, but I hadn't expected everyone's story to collapse today.

"Why would he claim it then?"

"He has a sense of guilt that goes beyond white shame, while I'll admit is the very emotion we try to foster in our exhibit. But he's gone mental."

I turned to Glenn. "And the land is worthless?"

"I didn't say that. It's just a poor—a very poor choice for homes. It might be a great place to climb or make a slick rock trail. Looks like there's a mine entrance. Maybe there's gold in it."

"It was a potash mine. And the mineral rights were leased. But they're coming back."

"Potash, huh? Oh, well. Sorry," he said.

"Is there water?" asked Pinion.

Glenn answered. "A couple of deep canyons would catch all the runoff, but I don't see any springs."

Pinion leaned back in his chair and stretched. "What about water rights?" he said.

"You said they were leased, right?" Glenn said to me.

"The mineral rights, not the water."

"Same thing," he said.

"Really?"

"Yeah."

"Oh, well then. Yes. They were leased but are coming back."

"A hundred acres of pioneer water shares is okay," Glenn said.

"But you said you couldn't build on it. Can you farm it?"

"Hell no," he said. "Have you looked at these contours? You'd need an act of God to flatten that enough to push a plow. No. But water rights are a commodity. There are plenty of people who'll pay for them, people downstream are thirsty. Builders in Las Vegas are buying all they can get. Water shortage is slowing down their expansion, which is bad for them, and good for us."

A jackpot siren erupted in my brain, lights and rattling coins, envious onlookers and the sudden appearance of scantily clad prostitutes rubbing my chest between my buttonholes.

"How much would a thousand acres of original water rights be worth?"

"Along the Green?" said Glenn. "In this market? Maybe ten million dollars. Maybe more if it was auctioned."

"You have a thousand acres or water?"

"Someone will," I said. "I gotta go. Dr. Pinion, would you write up and sign what you told me today? Something I can use in court? About the petroglyphs and land claims?"

"What, you don't trust the word of an Indian?"

33

DARA MET me for brunch at the buffet. It was the second biggest room in the casino. Only the gaming area was larger. The theater Perry performed in was a third of the size. The parking lot was smaller. You could work off the calories of the meal just hunting for a suitable dessert up the three miles of ethnic nooks and culinary curiosities. By the time I got my prime rib, my pasta was cold. They needed reheating microwaves at the tables. I filled in a suggestion card while we ate.

"So this was all damn lame," she said. "I could have handled it. You didn't need to drag your ass down here."

"Nah, I needed a break. Besides, I was being chased by a felonious sociopath."

"Where is he now?"

"Still here, I guess."

"I'm staying for the week. If I see him, I'll do what I can."

"Tell him I've gone to Houston. No—Miami. Wait, no. Someplace colder. Tell him I went to Nome for the winter."

"Will do."

We shoveled ungodly amounts of high-fat food into our mouths and washed it down with diet soda.

"Dara. Do you remember your first kiss?"

"Of course."

"Was it good?"

"Fuck no. Six years old on the playground."

"Okay, do you remember your first real kiss?"

She sucked on a crab leg and thought.

"Yeah."

"Was it good?"

"That's what made it the first real kiss," she said. "Don't get sentimental on me, Flaner. I'll have to kick the shit out of you just on principle."

"What principle?"

"The principle that I kick the shit out of you, so you don't get sentimental."

No arguing with her logic.

We finished our meal and I checked out. I had a long drive ahead of me and wanted to drive it in daylight. I said goodbye to Perry, who was just getting up at one and called for my car. The valet handed me my keys, and I was stabbed by cactus thorns stuck in my leather fob.

I had absolutely no recollection of the road that I retraced back to Moab. I had been so tired and out of it, driving on autopilot with Guilt Buddy, I was lucky to be alive. It was a miracle I'd made it. Magic—Fairy Magic maybe. Perhaps I owed Deerfart an apology.

It was dark when I got back to town. The drive had exhausted me. My body had absorbed more butter in one buffet meal than it usually does in a month, and I eat a lot of butter. I needed to rest. I pulled into the Cottonwood Lane house driveway and saw that it had snowed but not too much. About an inch remained, mostly in the shadows. It was dry and crunched under my feet as I dragged my gear up to the back door.

I dropped my stuff on the step and went to the white rose bush for the key. I was not the first to have done so.

In the dim illumination of the weak porch light, I saw footprints around the bush. Someone had tried to erase them with a broom, but the crusty snow wasn't to be fooled. Being slightly smarter than snow, neither was I.

The key was under the broken pottery as it should be, but I was sure it had been disturbed. With the key in one hand and an empty revolver in the other, I opened the door to the house.

"I have a gun," I said. The hall was unimpressed, but I think the living room was concerned.

I flicked on a light. The dining area to the right was clear. The kitchen to my left was clear. The hallway in front of me was clear. It was a small house. A few steps forward and I saw the living room was clear and turned on the light to the front hallway. Also clear. The hall to my left, where Vicky had died was clear, but I couldn't see into the washroom where the killer had waited for her.

"Did I mention I have a gun? It goes well with my concealed weapon permit, black market cop-killer bullets, and insatiable bloodlust," I called. "If you come out now, I won't shoot you. If I find you hiding, I'll put two in the hat in honor of Eddie Coyle and his friends."

Silence. The easy chair may have been less easy, but I couldn't be sure. The house seemed deserted. I really wish I'd bought bullets.

I moved along the wall until I was beside the doorway to the washroom. I cocked the hammer back hoping the click would echo.

I sprang into the doorway, both hands extended, pointing the gun.

Click.

I'd pulled the trigger. There was no one there. I was suddenly glad I didn't have bullets. I'd have blown out a window. If someone had been there, I'd have blown out his ribcage.

Shaken, I went upstairs, turning on every light in the place. No one was there.

I brought in my stuff, put my gun away, and locked the door. I did not put the key back under the white rose bush but added it to my cactus fob.

I found a flashlight in a kitchen drawer and tried to find footprints in the carpet and looked around to see if anything was moved or missing. After about an hour, I found something and thanked Anasazi Red Rope for the clue.

There was a dusty smudge on the wall in the corner. I'd vacuumed that wall. It hadn't been there before.

I stared at the smudge, tilting the flashlight, looking for anything useful, but it was just a dusty smudge. No usable fingerprint, if it had even been made by a finger. Just a smudge. I triple-checked the locks in the house before going to bed wondering what the hell was going on.

In the morning, I called Archie and told him about my interview with Dr. Pinion at the Lucky Arrow.

"I'll tell the judge," Archie said. "He's filed some papers. I don't know how much weight this will carry, but I'll try to make him come up with a precedent or something. Luckily, Tiponi is not well-liked."

And thus American justice took sides along the lines of popularity.

I had two days before the auction. I had information but no theories.

I'd heard the banker Weaks and Crew in the diner mention that an "independent buyer" would buy "it." That was a big missing piece. I needed to visit Crew or the banker.

Then there was the house burglary. What did I make of that? What could someone have been looking for? The police had everything. Did they know that? Who was "they?"

I called the Moab police.

"This is Lt. Levis," said an unwelcome voice.

"Hi, uhm. Is Danny there?" I didn't know who to talk to, but somehow I figured Danny would be better than Levis.

"Tony Flaner," he said. "Calling from the Racine house."

"Nice police work. Did you have to take a class to learn to read the caller ID, or did you pick that up from TV?"

"I've been asked to write a letter requesting your private investigator's license be revoked."

"By your cousin?"

He paused a moment, then went on. "I'll mention how much trouble you caused down here. Interfering with active cases and all that."

"By 'all that,' I suppose you mean being the victim of police brutality while other officers watched and abetted."

"You crossed the wrong people, Flaner. The Levises don't forget."

"Forget what?"

A pause.

"Oh, did I mention this threatening phone call is being recorded?" I asked.

A pause.

"You can't do that?" Levis said.

"Are you sure?"

Another pause.

"How about you play desk jockey cop and take down a report of a break-in."

"Why should I?"

"Can I quote you on that?"

Another pause.

"What is it?" he said.

"There was another break-in here while I was away."

"You were away?"

"Good to know you keep up on things," I said, actually pleased he wasn't aware of my movements.

"What was stolen?" I could hear papers shuffling and an electric pencil sharpener grinding down an inch of innocent graphite.

"Nothing stolen but signs of intrusion."

"What signs?"

"Footprints, smudges."

"But nothing was taken?"

"Right."

"And all you have is smudges and footprints?"

"Outside footprints."

Levis let out a satisfied sigh. "Okay, I'll write it down."

"And that's that?"

"That's that," he said. "Oh, I hear that the Salt Lake Chief of Police has three German Shepherds. He shows them. I'll be calling him later about things."

While I was chasing a killer in Moab, my reputation was being savaged in Salt Lake by some stuck-up, rich, persecution-complexed snobs. I'd have to deal with them before the damage was irreparable. I put it on my list.

I drove to the Green River Saving and Loan to see Mr. Owen Weaks.

There was an unfortunate time in American architecture when round, whitewashed stone buildings were considered neat. It was long ago, when cocktail parties dulled all aesthetic senses. Such was the Green River Savings and Loan building. Someone with less sense than the original architects had added a brownstone drive-up window wing to the saucer. It looked like someone had put a log in a meringue pie.

Mr. Weaks, vice president, had his own little cubed office with a blinded window and locking door. He was a man of medium importance.

"Mr. Weaks?" I stepped into his office, closed the door, and sat down before he could answer. The look of fear on his face told me something was up, but hell if I knew what it was.

"Do you want to tell me about it now?" I said. "Or should we wait for the authorities?"

His jaw dropped like an upside-down cigar box and hung there. His tongue wiggled like a drowning worm on a hook. No sound came out.

"I know what you and Crew are up to," I said. For punctuation, I examined my fingernails in detail, the way Hollywood said it should be done. My nonchalance was overwhelming.

"What are you talking about?" Weaks finally said.

"You know what I'm talking about." I fixed him with a Sam Spade stare. "You know."

His face flushed. His ears looked about to ignite.

"You're stuck in this godawful blancmange of a building. I can see why you want to get out. But believe me, this isn't going to work."

"What?" he said, his face was cooling. I'd come close but missed.

"Crew will turn you over like a pocket ace. Blackjack. Then where will you be?"

"Turn me over to who?"

"Whom," I corrected him, frantically trying to continue the bluff. "Who do you think?" I said.

Normal color returned to his face. I was losing him. I'd played this wrong, but when in doubt, double down? Sure, why not.

"We're talking prison time for fraud and conspiracy, but murder? You want to face death row?"

There we go. Blood again found its way to his ears.

"Murder? What murder?"

"I'm not saying you did anything. You might not have even known about it, but will the jury believe you?"

"You mean Mrs. Racine? You think I killed her? Why? Because I wouldn't give her a loan?"

"Why didn't you give her the loan?"

Now his veins were throbbing. I'd either get answers or a *Scanner's* head pop redux. I was good with either one. Weaks didn't fill me with warm fuzzies. No banker did. The humanity is removed from them before they're allowed to sign their first usury document. How else could a bank function?

The door crashed with a splintering kick. "Freeze!"

I was grabbed by the back of my shirt and pulled to the floor. The chair shot out from under me and into the desk.

Weaks shrieked.

I joined him.

My unobstructed view of the bank ceiling was interrupted by a gun pointed between my eyes. Above the gun I saw Danny Hinds.

"What the fuck, Danny?"

"You have the right to remain silent."

"Danny?"

Lying on the floor searching for answers, I saw a wire leading from the back wall, up the inside Weaks' desk, and ending at a sweaty black button.

Danny rolled me over and snapped cuffs on my wrists.

"Panic much?" I said to Weaks.

34

"I GET A PHONE CALL," I said. "I saw it in a movie."

Levis laughed and walked away, leaving me in a holding cell in beautiful downtown Moab. No windows.

Weaks must have pressed the button the second I walked into his office. He claimed I threatened him but was unclear on details. He hadn't decided to press charges yet. No one was hurrying him. For the time being, I was being held on suspicious charges.

"That's 'suspicion,'" Danny had corrected me.

"I think I got it right the first time," I said.

They didn't have to charge me for a while, and since I wasn't charged, I didn't get a phone call. Thus it was explained to me.

I didn't have a watch, so kept time by singing Christmas carols until I was told to shut up at the end of a pepper spray can. By my calculation, it was four Rudolphs past Silent Night when I had to find another way to pass the time.

The fools had left me my shoes, so I made a noose from the laces. In fact, I made two. They were short and could barely hang my wrists, but now at least I had options.

Several times over the next few hours, Levis walked past the cage I sat in and taunted me.

"How does it feel to be behind bars?" was his first witty rejoinder.

I countered with, "Were you born this stupid or did you have to practice?"

The next time, he said. "You've messed with the wrong people, Flaner. We take care of our own."

My counter: "If you bathed and saved a wad of twenties—a big wad—I know a blind prostitute who might be able to help you. You'd have to get her drunk first. And buy her rubber gloves. She may not have eyes, teeth or legs, and is pushing ninety, but she has standards. Wait, you know what? Forget it. Better just keep doing it yourself."

He knew he'd been insulted, but I don't think he knew how. He scoffed and left.

He brought Danny back with him the next time, probably as an interpreter.

"You know we can keep you locked up here a long time."

"Javel, mein Kommandant," said I.

"You're a bad egg, Flaner."

"Are you just coming from a Buford Pusser marathon or making this up as you go?"

"Flaner, don't mouth off to me," Levis said. "People die all the time resisting arrest."

"I've flushed smarter things than you," I said. "I'm keeping a running list of your abuses, by the way. Once word of this gets out, the all-powerful town fathers will hand you your ass in a basket."

He knitted his forehead like a lemur taking a trig quiz.

"Can you see the newspaper headline?" I asked. "Innocent Man Abused While in Moab Police Custody—Tourism to Picturesque Village Plummets. Entire town goes on food stamps. Acting Police Chief Levis unavailable for comment after late night visit from torch-wielding lynch mob?"

That got him thinking. I could tell it hurt.

"You're not innocent," he said.

"Well, until I'm charged with something, we'll never know, will we?"

He leaned over to Danny and whispered poorly. "How long do we have to charge him?"

"I don't know," said Danny.

"You could Google it," I said. "Or give me a phone. My lawyer will know."

"Crew said to hold him at least overnight," Danny said. "But I think he gets a phone call."

"Don't tell me my job, Poopy-Pants," he spat at Danny.

Danny flinched from the insult, an old open wound poked with a stick. For an instant—just for an instant—I felt sorry for Danny.

"I better look this up," Levis said and left.

"So you're working for T. S. Crew? This is not going to end well. When my publicist gets done with this, you guys will be cleaning radiation tailings with a sponge."

Danny moved to follow Levis but paused. He regained a look of handsome confidence that'd been dented by his superior. He unfolded a chair and sat down. "You have a publicist?" he said.

"I am in show-business," I exaggerated.

"I thought you were a detective."

"I do some stand-up comedy. I was just down at the Lucky Arrow Casino over the weekend." It was true. Whether the last sentence was a continuation of the previous thought or a new paragraph, I'd have to let Danny decide.

"You think your publicist could help me?"

"I don't think anyone can help you, Danny."

"I'm just doing this job until I'm discovered. I want to be in movies."

"It's that kind of job dedication that sets the level for Moab Policing," I said. "How long have you been working this 'day job?'"

"Ten years," he said. "Maybe more."

"Ah, the attention to detail. The sign of a true professional." I was lashing out, but he showed no signs of caring or catching on.

"So can you give me his number? The publicist?"

"You need an agent. That's first."

"I had one," Danny said. "Actually, I've had a couple. They cost me plenty and then dropped me."

"You paid the agent out of your pocket?"

"Yes. Isn't that how it works?"

"Eh, actually, no. They get paid when you get paid for doing a job they helped you get."

"Oh?"

"Oh."

"Do you have an agent?"

"Why am I being held here?" I said. "I didn't do anything to Weaks."

"If I tell you, will you call your agent for me?"

"For fuck's sake, Danny."

"He's not going to press charges. He said he panicked."

"So why am I still here?"

"Lt. Levis doesn't like you."

"And this is how things work here?"

"Yes."

"What about Crew?"

"I don't think I should tell you."

"Do you have a headshot? Agents need headshots."

He beamed. "Yeah, I do."

"What's this about Crew?"

He glanced down the hall before he said, "Crew is a big deal around here. He suggested we keep you in jail as long as possible."

"And you're going to do that?"

"Not my call."

He flipped his hair back with a twitch of his neck, and light sparkled off his full, conditioned locks. There wasn't a split end on his head.

"How often do you get haircuts?" I asked.

"Every week. Unless there's something special coming up."

"Floyd's best customer," I said earnestly. "The auction is Thursday. In two days. I've got to figure out what's going on."

"Something's going on?"

"Danny, you need to act a bit more like an acting detective. Think of it as an audition for competency."

"I don't follow."

"Of course you don't." I sighed. "Danny, there's been a murder and several burglaries and some beatings. I smell fraud and a touch conspiracy, theft of some kind, civil rights violations, blatant police harassment, and unlawful detention. And I'm just getting started with this list. Since the Moab police are otherwise distracted, someone has to get to the bottom of this. That someone has been me so far. I can't investigate behind bars, now can I?"

"I can't help you," said Danny.

"What about my phone call?"

"Levis says no. Maybe tomorrow."

"You mean I'm here overnight?"

"At least."

"Danny, will you call Allie for me?"

The hopeful look on his face fled, and he twisted up ashen and ugly.

"Levis is right," he said. "You are a troublemaker. I won't help you."

"I should have said 'Archie.' Will you call Archie Rumbold for me?"

"You know she's my girl?"

"Not according to her." I wasn't helping my cause, but it was chest pounding time.

"What did she say?"

"You're a shallow mutton puff."

"She said that?"

"No. I did. It's catchy though, don't you think?"

He paused and pondered, the Danny I knew.

"Danny, you've got an opportunity here. Maybe if you just, like, did some of the homework, followed up a few things, took a little initiative, you could actually help solve a crime."

"I'm not really a cop," he said.

"I've noticed."

"I'm an actor or something."

"Or something," I said. "In the meantime, how about acting like you're a detective."

"No can do."

"Then at least call Archie."

"I can't help you. I could lose my job."

"But it's not your real job," I said.

Synapses fired to little avail.

"Besides, Rumbold is in the hospital," he said.

"Someone tried to kill him?"

"No. He fell off a rock in Peaceful Canyon trying to free climb. Sandstone gave way. He busted a leg."

"How's Sophia, by the way," asked Guilt Buddy.

"She's still in the hospital, but Levis wants her in jail by Wednesday."

"That's tomorrow. Where will she go?"

"Here. Well the other side, where the real cells are."

"Not cool," I said. "She's an old lady."

"She killed someone, Flaner. Don't do a felony if you can't sit in jail."

"That's not how I heard it," I said. "You don't actually believe that sweet old thing could have killed anyone, do you?"

"Women kill all the time. Mrs. Racine killed her husband, they say."

"What do you know about that?"

"Just what everyone says," he said. "That Mrs. Racine killed her husband and hid the body on the ranch. That's why she won't sell it."

"And you believe that?"

"Sure," he said. "Everyone says it."

"You're right, Danny. You have no future in police work. Hollywood is definitely the place for you."

"You really think so?"

"With your morals, hell yeah."

"So you'll get in touch with your agent?"

"Who'd I talk to about Vicky's alleged murdered husband? See what I did there? I used 'alleged.' That's police talk."

He absorbed the information like notes from a director.

"Was there a police investigation?" I asked.

"No. It's all rumors. Mrs. Miller might know. She was around then. So was I, but I was a kid."

"Mrs. Miller? Haggy? I mean, Haddy Miller? She's still alive?"

"She's in the Sunset Home Assisted Living Facility, 'restful and exciting, catering to the needs of the greatest generation.'"

"You get paid for that plug?"

"No," he said. "Just seen the commercial so many times."

"Danny, I've got to get out of here. Now. Tonight. I'll call my agent if you help."

"If you promise, I'll do my best."

Danny's best meant that I had a bad night sleeping on a steel banded cot, tissue-thin blanket, and piss-smelling pillow.

The next morning I was treated to an Egg McMuffin. Danny brought it in a bag with a bar of hash browns.

"This is for you," he said. "Since you didn't get to leave last night."

"How about now? Can I leave now?"

"I'll check."

Danny brought me Burger King for lunch. Around four, he showed up with a box of Ding Dongs.

"You doing your best?" I asked, restraining the urge to grab his throat through the bars and bite an eyebrow off.

"You know I am," he said.

"I thought so."

It was six o'clock when the door finally opened.

I was angry beyond words, so I barked in Levis' face. It was an impersonation of Gandalf and for not practicing or workshopping it, I thought it came off pretty well. He took a greater, more threatening meaning than I intended, probably connecting Precious to my yelp, but I was going for more troll than canine. Still, it made him wince and step back.

I collected my things and checked my messages.

"Why don't you fucking answer your phone?" Dara said in the recording. "Anyway, this place is getting boring without your drama. That tattooed guy left this morning. He had help leaving. You can thank or blame Perry for that. They look after their own here. He tried to get in to see Perry and didn't make it. I don't know where he went. Maybe he got the message about Alaska, but I don't know. He was unconscious when I last saw him. Laters, schmuck."

Levis put on his game face, took his seat behind his desk which fit him like a diaper, knitted his fingers and gave me an apologetic face.

"On behalf of the Moab Police Department and the City of Moab itself, we are sorry for the misunderstanding and your short..." He glanced down at a printed sheet on his desk. "Your short visit to our facilities. The health welfare and safety—no. The safety and health. No. The *health, safety, and welfare* of our community is our greatest goal. We thank you for understanding and respecting our perseverance in this matter. Have a nice day."

"You've got to be kidding me," I said. "How many people helped you write that?"

He stared daggers. I saw the fax headers and knew it'd come from Texas. Long distance mayoral damage control at its finest.

I stormed out.

Danny made to follow me.

"I'm not in the mood," I warned him.

He stayed back.

I walked in the cold winter twilight to the pastry-shaped bank and collected my car. At least they hadn't towed it. I noted the bank closed at six, which was exactly the time I had been released from jail. There was no one there to talk to, threaten, or insult.

I got into my car.

Making an honest but critical analysis of other drivers, I managed to vent much of my rage before I arrived at the hospital.

35

ARCHIE WAS SPENDING another night "on the floor" for observation. The doctors wanted to observe their titanium bone graft. It was a marvel of metallurgical medicine. X-rays of his bionic leg hung like family portraits on the wall of his private room, and hospital personnel wandered in regularly to gawk at them. Doctors would come in without a word and shake their heads at the pictures and leave. Nurses would come in and count the screws. Kitchen help, janitors, drug reps, patients dragging chrome IV stands, homeless people, and Swiss tourists all came in to stare at the pictures like they hung in The Louvre.

"I'm going to be laid up for the winter," Archie said. "I think this is actually the worst injury I've ever had, metaphorically speaking. No worries though. It's below the hip and above the knee. Just a new femur, better than before. Everyone should have their bones replaced with metal."

I laughed.

He didn't.

"Oh, yes, a great idea," I said. "So the auction is canceled?"

"Oh no. It's on. I'll be there in a wheelchair."

"What about Sophia?"

"They took her to the jail this morning. She's been refused bail and has limited visitation. Don't even bother trying. You're on a list."

"How'd you let that happen?"

"I was in here," he said.

"Are you up to all of this?" I said.

"A murder case? No, but I can walk us through preliminaries. I'll get her out, it'll just take some time."

"I think we should cancel the auction," I said. "There's more here than meets the eye."

"Out of my hands," he said. "At this point, only the judge can do anything about it. It's seven o'clock. Everything's closed. There might be time to file something in the morning if it was already done, but I have nothing. It'll be fine, don't worry. The auction is a good thing."

"For whom?" I said, hoping Archie wasn't counting on this commission for his new medical bills.

He couldn't give me a good answer, so I went home to the house on Cottonwood. It was dark and cold, and I smelled like a pee pillow. I called Nancy in Salt Lake for some real estate investment assessments.

"If the house is that far in hawk, it's a push at best," she said. "I don't know what rentals are going for down there, but you'd be lucky if you could make the payment during the summer. What would you do in the off-season?"

"Cry?" I suggested.

"Unless you're planning on moving down there, buying a house is a bad idea."

"No flip possibilities?"

"The market is soft now. Maybe it's better in Moab, but I doubt it."

I remembered Crew's vacant lots of blown out building pads and sighed.

"Why do you want to buy it?"

"Family honor," I said.

"Please..."

I made her give me a quick guess of how much I could reasonably expect to pay at the auction, and she threw in a dire warning about being unreasonable, foolhardy, and impulsive for free.

"Don't worry," I said.

She took a breath. "Oh, god. Tony, don't do it."

––––––––––

The auction was held at the courthouse in a meeting room usually reserved for lawyers to negotiate a plea deal moments before a trial. It reeked of despair and injustice. I found the room after a visit to the county recorder and a very expensive photocopy. It's free to see records. Using the only photocopier in the building, not so much.

I'd tried to call the judge the night before, beg for time, cast aspersions, but she'd been unavailable past six o'clock as I'm sure my captors had known.

Archie was in a motorized wheelchair. His leg was cocooned in a fiberglass cast with steel reinforcing probes poking out of it like an erector-set bridge.

T. S. Crew sat at the table, as did Bill Ashe. Phil stood in the back. Weaks, the banker, sat next to Crew and as far from me as he could. Tiponi, in a leather shirt with dangly fringe, stood ramrod straight next to the judge, pleading his case. Allie was there to watch, as were several people I didn't know or like. Danny was there playing cop/actor, Roy Stirps in ranger garb, and Lt. Herbert Levis, acting police chief and poster child for police brutality and law enforcement inadequacy. I showed him one of my middle fingers, then the other, so he could compare. I waved to Clem Tucker from *The Moab Picayune*. Guy Skingle huddled with two other realtors at the end of the table. Their plexiglass smiles and polyester coats gave them away as the vultures they were. Two uniformed marshals stood in the corners and several court-related people in suits flanked the judge. Finally, there was me.

I sat next to Skingle. He blinded me with a bleach-produced seizure-inducing smile that left tracers on my retinas.

"Judge, this Indian land," said Tiponi. "Sale no good."

The judge was no more impressed with his grammar than I had been.

"Bailiff," she called in that special kind of tone that summoned up visions of handcuffs, fines, and awkward showers.

Tiponi quickly found a chair and sat down. His face went beet-red under his sunburn, finally giving him the complexion he wanted.

"It's time to begin," said the judge. "I am Judge Shepherd. We are all assembled here for an estate auction of two properties as requested in the testament of Victoria Racine, deceased." The judge spoke with authority but there was an urgency which implied a busy schedule. "I have been asked to oversee this auction as a courtesy to a longtime resident. I expect everything to go smoothly and I will not indulge disruption." She cast a sidelong look at Tiponi who actually scowled back. "Mrs. Racine asked for an immediate auction of her real estate for the benefit of her sole beneficiary. I understand there are some legal issues surrounding the beneficiary, but that does not touch upon this part of Mrs. Racine's last request."

I glanced at Levis. He met my eye and slid into a shit-eating grin that made me yearn for pliers.

Allie dabbed a tissue to her eye, absorbing the significance of this last act of a dead woman. Danny glanced at Allie and then looked at me. He smiled like we were old friends, but I could read his jealousy.

"We will begin with the house on Cottonwood Lane." The judge nodded to a court person who picked up a stack of papers. "I don't know if we have enough for everyone," she said. "Don't take one unless you're serious about bidding."

I took one.

The judge went on. "As you can see, according to two independent assessments, more is owed on the house than it is worth. The discrepancy is between thirty-five thousand and fifty thousand dollars. As such, the primary lien holder, Green River Saving and Loan, will assume the property by this debt unless there are bids in excess of the amount outstanding. Are there?"

"I'll bid the amount owed plus a dollar," said Roy Stirps. In answer to my unspoken question, he said, "I like the house."

"A thousand more," said Skingle.

"Five thousand over amount owed," I said.

Roy flushed. Skingle looked shocked and conferred with his people.

"Ten thousand," said Roy.

"Fifteen thousand," I said quickly and then clenched my jaw. Nancy would never let me live this down, but I wanted that house. I'd have to mortgage my Sugarhouse home and find a way to be in two places at once to justify the purchase, but I couldn't just let that fragment of my childhood and my lost family slip away without a fight.

Roy could see I wasn't going to back down. Skingle glanced around the room, looked at Roy and then at me, and then shook his head.

"Any more bids?" asked the judge.

There were none.

"Mr. Flaner," said the judge. It scared me she knew my name. That wasn't good. "I pray this is not some attempt to subvert the proceedings here. You'll be required to make satisfactory financial arrangements immediately after this meeting or I'll hold you in contempt."

"I understand, Judge," I said. "I mean, your holiness—Your Honor."

"We'll register a backup bid," said the judge to the recorder. "Just in case."

"Thanks for the vote of confidence."

A bailiff's hand slid to his Batman utility belt, but the judge only shot me a "shut-the-hell-up-before-you-get-in-serious trouble" look. I am very familiar with that look. I knew it was coming, but I didn't expect it so soon.

"We'll move now to the one-hundred-acre Racine Ranch," said the judge. Again packets were handed out. There were many more this time. Everyone got a copy. I scanned it over quickly and prepared to misbehave.

"There is nothing owed on this property," said Judge Shepherd. "All back taxes were paid earlier in the year. However, I understand that Mrs. Racine asked that the bidding start at a quarter million dollars. Two independent reports state that the land in question has a normal retail value of half that amount. The court acknowledges this difference and wants to make it clear that the wishes of Mrs. Racine will be carried out. If the property does not sell for this minimum amount today, other options will be explored, bearing in mind Mrs. Racine's final wishes and reality."

"Two hundred fifty thousand," blurted out T. S. Crew. "I bid the quarter million."

The judge hadn't finished talking and took the outburst with calm, quiet understanding. Just kidding. She rapped her gavel and raised her voice.

"I have not opened the bidding yet. The courtroom will be quiet."

"It's not a courtroom," said Phil a little too loudly.

More rapping. Real anger on her face. The judge had a short fuse. More of a button, really.

When everyone shut up, she went back to her notes.

"Since there doesn't seem to be a problem with the minimum bid, we'll get to it."

"A quarter million," said T. S. Crew again tentatively.

The judge hadn't actually asked for bids and picked up her gavel but then laid it down.

"Three hundred thousand," said Bill.

"I object," said Tiponi, standing up. "This sale is illegal."

"Three hundred twenty-five thousand," said Crew.

"We've been over this, Mr. Tiponi," said the judge.

"Three hundred seventy-five thousand," said Bill.

Tiponi looked around the room for support. His pale blue eyes beseeching someone to do something to save the Indian's claim.

"Four hundred thousand," said Crew, glancing at Weaks, who winced a little but remained calm.

"Four hundred fifty thousand," said Bill immediately.

Clem Tucker stared slack-jawed at the mayhem. The judge raised an eyebrow and looked again at the report.

T. S. Crew's ears went red.

"Half a million dollars," he shouted, hoping to stop the bidding by sheer volume. Weaks shifted uneasily in his chair.

"Fraud!" I yelled before Bill could answer. "Fraud. Fraud I say. Fraud!"

The room quieted. Clem grinned. Everyone looked at me.

"Judge, there is fraud here. I think you can see how it's playing out, but you don't understand why this is happening."

"Bid or shut up," said Crew, sweating now.

"What do you have to say?" said the judge.

"Yeah, what's up, Tony?" said Phil behind me.

"These independent surveys of the land failed to include the mineral rights," I said.

"No, they're right here," Bill said, pointing to a paper. "It says the mineral rights have been leased off the land and are due to return at the first of the year."

"Exactly," I said.

The judge shook her head as if getting a ringing out of her ears. "Are they included or not, Mr. Flaner? Fraud is a serious accusation. Against whom are you making it?"

"Uhm, well, uhm. Let me finish." I could feel the cuffs closing around my wrists and another week of sleeping on urine pillows.

"The surveyors, either by ignorance or design, failed to include the value of upcoming mineral rights when assessing the land."

"No, Tony," said Bill. "It's right here. There's even a geology report. No useful minerals present." No uranium and what potash is left is too expensive to mine. It's there."

"You're not helping, Bill," I said. "Or perhaps that's exactly what your plan was all along."

Bill looked hurt and confused.

"You're not making any sense, Tony," said Allie behind me.

The judge glanced at a bailiff who took a step toward me.

"Water," I said. "The mineral rights include water. And the mineral rights for the original Racine Ranch are all concentrated on this last one hundred acres. There're a thousand acres of original homestead water shares that come back to the land on the first of the year."

"Six hundred thousand dollars," yelled Crew, real panic in his voice. Weaks put a hand on his arm which caused him to immediately increase the bid. "Seven hundred thousand!" screamed Crew.

Weaks whimpered and pulled back his hand as if it'd been burned.

"I think some of the bidders here are aware of the real value of the land, or rather the water shares, while others may not be."

Bill looked shocked. Phil started to laugh. Archie looked sheepish. The judge, irked.

"To be fair to my dear departed Aunt Vicky," I said. "An accurate assessment of the land's value should be made public prior to any auction. Maybe we should allow some independent builders a chance to get the land."

The blood drained from Crew's face leaving it a mask of horror, rage, panic, and constipation, maybe even the suggestion of an alien egg hatching beneath his sternum. None of it was good. He looked at me with such hatred that I pulled back from the table, readying myself for the mad-man lunge I knew was coming.

"Wow," said Bill. "Just wow."

"Ah, shit," said Phil, laughing maniacally. "Not good."

The crowd burst into conversation, accusation, and demands to complete the auction.

"The bid is seven hundred thousand dollars," said Weaks through gritted teeth. "Are we done here?"

"Seven fifty," said Bill without a pause.

Archie remembered his job and raised his hand.

The judge looked at him.

"Forgive me for not standing," he said.

"We're not in court, Mr. Rumbold," she said.

"Right. Habit," he groveled. "There is a precedent that the auction could be overturned if the estate can prove that the assessment was deliberately falsified or accidentally grossly miscalculated. It might be best to pause the proceedings until this matter can be looked into."

"Mr. Flaner, do you have any proof of this, or are you going to jail again?"

"Here it is, your honor." I pulled out the very expensive copy I'd made that morning and passed it toward the judge.

"I can't speak to what the water shares would be worth, but I'm pretty confident it's in the millions of dollars."

Archie nodded. Skingle nodded. Crew buried his face in his hands. Weaks looked sick. Bill looked shocked and worried. Tiponi looked confused. He, at least, looked normal.

"How was this not discovered in the survey reports?" she asked the room.

"Who did the reports?" asked Clem Tucker, holding a pencil in his lips like the cigarette I knew he sorely wanted.

"Mr. Rumbold, you were in charge of the surveys," said the judge.

"Yes, Your Honor. You don't think that I..." he stuttered. "I engaged Mr. Weaks' bank for the services. Green River Savings and Loan maintains land experts as part of their business."

"Mr. Weaks. Is this true?" said the judge.

She knew who everyone was. Small town.

Weaks froze. It was as if he was staring into the face of the Gorgon. Only the growing rhythmic pulse in his temple suggested he was still flesh. He didn't answer immediately. The room grew quiet. Everyone looked at the mousy little man.

"Mr. Weaks, I asked you a question."

"Your honor," said Crew. "I'm sure that—"

"I wasn't talking to you, Mr. Crew," she said. "Mr. Weaks. I was talking to you."

You could hear the pressure in his veins approaching stroke level as he spoke. "Yes, we did the report," he said slowly, drawing out each word to buy time. "I sanctioned our surveyors to do it. And they did it."

"So how did they miss the water rights returning?" Bill asked.

In slow motion silence, Weaks shrugged.

"Who did they give their reports to?" I asked. "Are these the exact reports presented to you or have they been edited?"

Weaks snapped his head around to look at me. I could hear Crew's hard and labored breathing. Weaks had stopped breathing altogether and looked about to topple over.

He took a sudden deep breath and righted himself on his chair. His nostrils flared, but his eyes objected to the change of plans, preferring the canceled fainting spell to this consciousness.

"I think...I...should..." he said so slowly that I could hear punctuation in each syllable. "Talk to an attorney...before answering any more...questions." Then he returned to Plan A and fainted into a heap on the floor.

No one said a word. No one moved to help him.

Crew glared at me with cruel venom.

Phil laughed and broke the tension. The room erupted in noise, accusations, gossip, and more laughing. No one took a step to help Weaks.

"We will postpone this auction," said the judge.

"Your honor," said Roy. "Does this mean that the house will be auctioned again?"

I was surprised she could hear him over the noise.

"No. That stands," she said. "Unless there's something suspicious about its value." She looked square at me.

I shook my head, knowing I was on thin ice.

I'd stirred the pot again, kicked the anthill, and piñataed the hornets' nest. Investigations, publicity, and arrests would probably follow my little disclosure. Town fathers and land developers would not be happy with a scandal in the desert, and I'd thrown a gritty one in their faces. Time to sit back and enjoy.

"This meeting is adjourned," said the judge. "Mr. Rumbold, talk to the city prosecutor after lunch."

The judge exited through a door behind her seat and was quickly followed by the court people. The bailiffs stayed back, ushering folks out through other doors. One of them finally got to Weaks and broke a tablet under his nose. He shot up with a scream.

Crew pushed me into a chair. "You ruined me, Flaner. I'm going to ruin you."

"With that breath, you're well on your way," I said.

He balled up his fist but thought better of it when he realized the entire room had stopped to watch. "This isn't over," he said. "You'll regret this."

"Like I haven't heard that before," I said, and sadly, it was true.

36

"WHAT HAPPENED TO YOUR HEAD?" Allie cupped my cheeks in her hands and bent forward to inspect Benjamin's love tap. "And you were in jail?"

"It's been a fun couple of days," I admitted.

The courthouse overflowed with mumbling onlookers. Clem waited nearby looking for an entrance and an interview. The Ashes whispered between themselves in a corner. Crew stormed out of the building looking to knock someone down as he went. He only found Levis and thought better of it. Asshole professional courtesy, I thought.

Allie pushed me hard in the chest, and I was on my ass.

"What was that for?"

"You just up and leave? No call? Not a word from you? Then you get thrown in jail? Are you some kind of Unabomber loner?"

"Uhm…"

"I was really worried about you," she said. "You could have been hurt or in jail, and I wouldn't have known."

"No arguing there." I got up.

"So?"

It'd been a long time since anyone cared enough about me to be worried, probably as long as it had been since I cared enough about anyone to check in with them. I was out of practice, and I'd screwed up. I knew it. I had that horrible feeling you get after that dream of walking through your middle school naked on test day when you haven't even looked at the book yet.

"Allie, I got distracted, and I'm a jerk, and I don't have much in the way of an explanation except to say that I'm sorry, and I will make sure I wear clothes to school from now on. And I'll study."

"You are so lucky we…we're not going together," she said. All sympathy for my wounds and jail time justifiably evaporated. "If so, I'd lay you out like Tyson."

"You did," I said.

Her arms fell akimbo, and she took a step back. I could tell she was comparing my childish charm against my childish sense of responsibility.

"I had to help a friend down in Flagstaff," I said. "It was kind of an emergency. The CIA was about to assassinate him. But even before that, I ran into a frozen biker who wanted to beat me up so he could go back to prison. He jumped me, but I got away thanks to a pack of stoned trolls. A plastic surgeon who likes scars patched me up by candlelight, and my imaginary friend drove me to Arizona. I saw a Mohawk taken down by Navajo after he lost his life savings—two dollars and fifty cents in a slot machine. But rules are rules, and he was swallowed behind a door, never to return. After I slept, I showered in my clothes because it was easier than picking the scabs. I found my friend holed up with a shotgun in a bathtub. He let me in because the carpet could induce seizures. I recognized the spook as a jerk, so everything was copacetic. I told the director, who produced the waitress' brother, and that was that. Zap and taken to the Mohawk door. Jerk-be-gone. See?"

Her expression was unreadable, but I was sure it wasn't understanding.

"I got you a present," I said.

"What?"

"I bought you a kachina doll."

"I like those," she said. "Is it nice?"

"It's in the car. I'll go get it."

Before she could come to an unsatisfactory conclusion about my story, I ran to my car for the bribe.

I was ashamed that I hadn't called her. It was like Moab existed in its own dimension, a fantasy world where marvelous and meaningful things happened daily but faded like half-finished dreams when the sandstone was out of sight. How much of what I am, what I became, was forged when I was ten and abandoned in the desert? How had I lost touch with Rick and Vicky? How could I not have thought enough to call Allie from Flagstaff? Would I spend every moment atoning for my short attention span and ingratitude toward this desert oasis? Would Crew be waiting for me outside the door to beat me up?

He was.

"Flaner," he said, marching up to me.

"Before you say anything dumb, which in your case is anything," I said, "let me just agree with you. This isn't over. Fraud will get you a few years in jail, get you kicked out of the country club—maybe, but murder will get you ass-raped for the rest of your miserable death row existence."

He stopped as if I'd slapped him.

"What?"

"How low can a person sink, you greedy pus-mouthed, pasty-faced dick-head? You murdered a wonderful woman for your miserable condos."

"I had nothing to do with Mrs. Racine's death," he said. "She was going to sell me the land."

"But it was easier to kill her and win at auction. Only you knew about the water."

"How would I know about the auction?"

"You broke into Archie's office," I said.

"What are you talking about? Archie who? Rumbold? What break-in?"

"The one where you saw Vicky's will."

Stunned disbelief hit his face like the coconut cream pie I wanted to throw at it. My guts fell to the ground as I read sincerity there. Was I wrong?

Crew looked around to make sure no one else could hear.

"Do you know how much trouble it was to forge those stupid reports? To keep it quiet? Do you have any idea what I had to go through just to be humiliated in there today? It was a long shot, at best, that I'd be able to win the auction. Why would I do all that when Racine was going to sell me the land anyway?"

"What about the Ashes?"

"I could have made an arrangement with them. They don't want the water. They don't need it."

"Why do they want the land then?"

"It's hit and miss with you, isn't it, detective?"

"So where were you when my aunt Vicky was killed?"

"I was in Las Vegas meeting with some people."

"Independent Builders?" I asked.

He started. "Yes, as a matter of fact. Independent Builder of Nevada, LLC. I needed to get some guarantee from them that they'd buy the water rights if I purchased them. I said *purchase*. Victoria and I were getting close to a deal."

"And you have witnesses?" I said, feeling I was knee deep up the wrong creek.

"Oh yes. And I'm sure every one of them will be called down here to testify at my trial."

"So you didn't murder anybody?"

"Not yet, you little shit."

"Uhm, yeah, okay. I'll consider that."

"The only murderer I know was your aunt," he said in a deliberate and not ineffective attempt to hurt my feelings.

"See you in jail," I said. "Consider it a little long-term payback for the police hospitality you engineered for me. I better make a formal complaint to the DA about that. It won't make me more popular, but it might add a year to your sentence. So it'll be worth it."

He balled up his fist.

I moved away. "Nice chatting with you. I have to go." I ran to my car, leaving the fuming developer standing alone in front of the courthouse like an abandoned bride. He looked like he was going to cry. Then he did.

I waited for Crew to leave before coming back with the doll. I found Allie on a bench talking with Roy Stirps.

"Here you go." I handed her the doll but leveled my jealous reptilian eyes at Roy.

"That was quite a show in there, Tony," Roy said, edging away from Allie a couple of inches. Message received.

"I have my moments."

"Roy invited us to dinner," said Allie, overhearing the message. "I think it's nice."

"Double date?"

"Sure," he said. "I'm a good cook."

"Sounds great," said Allie. "We could all use more friends."

"Particularly you," said Clem Tucker, barging in.

"Isn't there some ethical thing about reporters eavesdropping on private conversations?" I asked.

"You just defined the entire job," he said.

"I'll call you," said Roy, sensing an exit.

"So are you still looking for Mrs. Racine's killer or are you just pissing in the fountain?"

"You have a way with words. You should consider writing."

"Well?"

"Motive, means, and opportunity," I quoted from the detective hand-book. "I gotta think that this entire thing revolves around her land. I looked at who would benefit from it and got a short list. Crew was at the top."

Clem wrote furiously in a notepad. Old school.

"That's good," he said. "Can I quote you?"

"Seriously?"

"Sure. Why not?"

"Because you'll get Tony into a libel suit," said Allie.

"Good point," I said. "I'm already pretty despised. Don't make it worse."

"I doubt I could," said Clem.

The Ashe brothers were gone, having exited through some unseen door. Danny was gone too, as was the rest of the police presence. No loss there. Tiponi had walked past stoically, his spine straight as a laser.

"Greed is the only thing that motivates white man," he said with more grammar than he was used to. "Sacred places mean nothing."

"No that's not true," said Allie.

He raised a blond eyebrow.

"Tony bought Vicky's old house."

For a couple of months, when we were kids, adolescent and innocent, becoming who we would be, I knew this girl, and now thirty years later, she knows me better than I do myself. I'd rationalized buying the house as a favor for Sophia, but Allie knew it was for me all along. At that moment, in those eyes, it all flooded in on me. At a time in my life when my family fought ruin, I was safe and blissfully ignorant of the struggle, safe with my cousin and aunt who welcomed me and loved me unconditionally. When my life should have been a mess, full of fear, doubt, and dread, my family crumbling under debt and stress, I was in a magical oasis of adventure and possibilities. Yes, the house on Cottonwood Lane was a holy place. I had an overwhelming urge to buy candles and gold leaf kits.

"You talked to Dr. Pinion," Tiponi said.

"He called you?"

"I called him for support. He no give."

"You gotta choose your battles," I said. "I hear there's a significant archaeological find in Maine. A buried Nordic ship from the 1300s. You could start a petition."

He frowned.

"Have you had breakfast?" I asked Allie.

"Yes, but it's nearly lunchtime."

"Good with me."

I took Allie by the arm and left Tiponi and Clem Tucker in the foyer. I knew Clem had more questions, but already had more than enough information for a sensational story, one big enough to get him and his paper noticed outside of town. Maybe even the county. Besides, he had Tiponi for some local, off-color.

"So Tiponi is out," Allie said over a burrito.

"I think so. He wants the land as much as the others, but Vicky's death didn't help him at all. His only card was Vicky's guilt. Without that, it forced his hand, and it is pretty weak. I'm coming from the angle that whoever killed her knew about the will."

"Why would they need to know about the will? Wouldn't it just go up for sale when she died because of her debts?"

"No," I said. "If there'd been no will, the property would have gone into legal limbo. There was absolutely no hurry to sell at that point since the taxes were paid up. It could rot in probate for decades, or at least five years until the tax liens came up again."

"So it was Crew. He needed the land and the water shares right away."

"He was in the biggest hurry. Sophia told me that he'd been courting Vicky for some time. Crew said they were close to a deal, but then the Ashes appeared and made it harder."

"Crew has friends all over this town. He might have known about Vicky's will."

"Maybe, but I don't see it. Archie is still an outsider. He and Crew don't move in the same circles. Crew barely remembered Archie's name and the look on his face when I accused him of all this was pretty convincing. I just don't think it's him anymore."

"So the Ashe brothers?" Allie said, crunching a tortilla chip.

"Crew made a cryptic remark about them. Said they didn't need the water shares. They're doing really well. I can't see them killing for money."

"I've never met anyone who has enough money," she said.

"True, but they looked as shocked as anyone when I burst the water balloon."

"You trust in appearances too much. Aren't detectives supposed to be cynical?"

"Yeah, but I'm more of a hunch kinda guy. Still, they're the only ones I can't figure out yet."

"Tiponi? You've figured him out?"

"There's no figuring Tiponi. That's how I figure him. He's not a bad sort, just confused."

"Appearances again?"

"Well, I have some facts to back that up," I said. "His only play this morning was to beg for the land. He had no money, no lawyer, no resources to make a real attempt at getting it. And again, the water thing surprised him. Worse, I don't think he understood what it was about. He's a kid playing Vikings and Indians."

"That leaves the Ashes," Allie said. "We going back to the winery? Will you behave this time?"

"No. Something more obvious. The ranch."

"That's a good, if not an obvious, idea," she said. "You're the Tony I remember."

"Maybe it's not the ranch," I said. "Maybe Vicky was killed for revenge."

Allie stopped eating.

"What did that woman ever do to anyone?" she said. "She was a saint."

"Kill her husband?" I said.

"She didn't."

"You know that?"

"That's just an ugly rumor."

"The lesbian rumor was correct. Why not this one?"

"Because Vicky was about love, not killing. I knew her, Tony. I knew her better than you. Don't get your feelings hurt, but I did. She'd suffer anything before hurting anyone. There's no way she could have done anything like that."

"You weren't there," I said.

"I was. I lived here. It was before you came. That's when the rumors began."

"What were the rumors exactly? When they were fresh?"

"I don't remember. I was too young. But I do know they've changed over the years, so that should tell you something."

"Changed how?"

"Stories get bigger with the telling," she said. "Once, she shot him for running out on her. Later, she fed him to Thick's animals in the yard. One story says she buried him in the old potash mine. And of course there are stories that he's still alive. I don't believe any of them. I do know that Vicky would never have killed Lance. She loved him almost as much as she loved Thick."

"I know someone who was there. Someone who'll remember."

"Who?"

"Haggy Miller."

37

THE SUNSET HOME Assisted Living Facility was a new building, about ninety years younger than its average tenant. There wasn't a stair to be seen. Long ramps led to the doors in such shallow slopes that you could shoot marbles on them. The yard and plants were immaculately cared for, making you feel like Edward Scissorhands had come down from his mansion and given up on plant menageries in favor of eggs and boxes. A parking lot able to accommodate fifty cars had one parked in an employee spot and two in handicapped stalls.

It was a cold afternoon, breezy, and slightly overcast. There was a possibility that the dried crust of snow that still lingered under trees and against buildings would be sprinkled with another layer, but I didn't think so. It was too cold. The storm would blow by and drop on a warmer place.

It was like setting off a grenade when we opened the door. Heat hit us like a shock wave. Outside, it was too cold for snow; inside, it was a broken-thermostat blast furnace, a difference of at least a hundred twenty-two degrees.

"Shouldn't we have had an interview with St. Peter before going in here?" I said.

"Come on, Dante," said Allie. "It's not that hot."

"Yes, Beatrice."

She pushed me forward and we fought our way through a second airlock to an even warmer hallway inside. Did I say warm? I meant hot. Crayon-melting hot. The kind of heat that cooks food on the counter and glues hard candy together. That kind of hot.

Faster than newlyweds, we stripped out of our coats. Allie wouldn't let me strip down to my underwear, which I told her was unfair because I'd have let her.

Beyond the entranceway, we found a counter. Behind the counter, we found a *Cat Fancier* magazine. Behind the magazine, we found the sweaty bored stare of a young man more asleep than awake. He looked at us with unseeing eyes, half-boiled in his skull.

"Can I help you?" he whined.

"We're here to see Satan," I said.

Allie bruised my rib with an elbow.

"We'd like to see Mrs. Miller," she said.

"Didn't I just say that?" I braced for another shot.

"Haggy? I mean, Haddy Miller?" the man said, surprised.

"Yes," said Allie. "Is she here?"

"Has she melted?" I asked.

"Her room is 15, down the hallway, but she may be in the game room. Down that other hall to the left." The receptionist leaned back into his chair, expending as little energy as possible.

The air was still and as thick as paste as we moved away. We'd sucked all the moisture outside when we breached the door, but deeper in, it was the tropics in a heatwave.

Room 15 was empty and smelled of antiseptic and evil, so to the game room we went. There we found half a dozen people sleeping in front of a television set to a soap opera with more pregnant pauses than a *Twilight* marathon. At a table, three men in sweaters played dominoes.

A prune man slammed one down and shouted, "Fifty-five, bitches," and then added up a new score.

The sleepers stirred but returned to oblivion quickly enough as a blissful housewife danced around her kitchen with an animated cleaning genie.

Mrs. Miller sat alone under a woolen shawl at a card table working a jigsaw puzzle. She didn't notice us come in. No one did. I leaned over to Allie. I smelled her hair and got distracted for a second, but then said, "I probably should mention that Haggy never liked me."

"She doesn't like anyone."

"I don't like her much either."

"No one does."

"Mrs. Miller?" Allie said, stepping to the table. I held back remembering the police call she made that grounded Rick and me for a week.

"What do you want, girlie? I'm busy." She'd almost finished the edge of a five-thousand-piece puzzle of a Monet painting. "You one of those bulimics who puke up your supper so you can be thin? Got no use for trash like you."

"Do you remember me?" Allie said to her softly before I could punch the old lady in the face.

She looked me up and down.

"I know that one. That one is Thick's ignorant cousin, Timmy," she said.

"Tony," I corrected her. "Tony Flaner. I was hoping you could tell me a little about Vicky Racine."

"Don't correct me, you little bastard," she said. "Show respect."

She was on the wrong side of eighty in age and weight, but I wanted to slap that face into next Tuesday.

"You come from a bad gene pool, Timmy. Bad people, the Racines. Stupid as wood. Thick dumber than a bowl of soup. I baked him cookies once with laxative for chocolate chips. He ate the whole plate and came back the next day for more, but he couldn't stay long without soiling his drawers. What an idiot." She laughed.

Allie grabbed my wrist before I got arrested again.

"What do you remember about Victoria Racine and her husband?" Allie said through gritted teeth.

"You're the Braise girl, aren't you?"

"Yes, ma'am."

"Thought you died out with the rest of your clan. Good riddance to you all. That ranch of yours was nothing but a rabies colony. Killed half the town's dogs in one spring. Should have run you out of town on a rail."

I drew a deep breath and opened the doors of insult, picked a few prized gems, but before I could spew—and spew was a'coming—Allie touched my arm and I hesitated. Magic gesture, that. Her years of dealing with dumb animals had endowed her with an unearthly patience. I understood her meaning. If I wanted to get information from this musky monster, I needed to be nice. There'd be time for holy water and stakings later. If not, I'd make time.

I let my breath out slowly, feeling sweat pour down my back from the ambient lava-level thermostat. It was a smelly sauna of unwashed-shawl-scented musk and melted hard candy.

Haggy Miller ignored Allie's peacemaking. She sucked down her upper bridge and played with it on her tongue, showing us the porcelain dentures in slobbery detail. Allie and I could only stare and fight to keep our lunches down.

Finally, she fit a puzzle piece into a corner and said, "Victoria Racine killed that husband of hers, I know it."

"What do you know?" I said. My hair was saturated and sweat ran into my eyes freely. I finally wiped my face with my coat. The superheated nylon burned my cheeks.

"I know that Victoria was a goddamn liar. She lied about everything. She lied the day she got married. She lied when she said she loved Lance, the last real Racine, still dumb as a stump, but old blood. Now all dead and good riddance."

"When she was married?" I coaxed. My hand hurt and I looked down to see my fingernails digging into my palm, so tight was the fist I was making.

"Victoria was a sophist, a dyke, a carpet muncher. She had no business ruining an already troubled family. But her type can't be happy unless they're ruining things for others."

"Imagine that," I said.

"Then she had that stupid child. Even as a baby, Thick was dumb. He wouldn't cry when he needed changing, just laugh. When he was hungry, he'd wait for food. Surprised he didn't starve to death. Then Lance ran away from his wife and that retard. Who could blame him?"

"Did they fight?" asked Allie after a calming breath. "Vicky and Lance?"

"Hell no," she said. "That's how I knew their marriage was a sham. They never had a crossword for each other. It was unnatural. Some thought they were just so much in love that they never bickered, but I knew her lesbianism sins and figured out that it was all an act to fool everyone. Lance figured it out soon enough too but just kept quiet. Proud people the Racines, always have been. To their damnation."

"So you think it was a loveless marriage because they didn't quarrel?" I asked.

"I didn't say it that way, but yes, that's some of it. They were sick to watch. People didn't cotton on to Lance Racine marrying a newcomer, and he wanted you to think he didn't care what everyone said about them, but he did. I know he did. How could he not? He'd hear people talking about how uppity he was when he went out. He couldn't miss it."

"I'm sure you raised your voice to make sure," I said.

"The whole town thought it," she spat. "I've just always been a better person than most. I'm honest."

"When did Lance leave?" Allie asked. Her face was red, I don't know if it was out of frustration, anger, or heatstroke. Even money.

"Oh, the first time was when Thick was seven or so. He left for a year. But he came back. God knows why. He stayed for a while then left again when that boy was nine or ten. No one ever saw him again."

"I heard that Lance left after Rick's tenth birthday," I said. "He went looking for a mine in South America."

"Who's Rick?" Haggy said. "That was all a lie. He just ran off somewheres to get away from those two."

"Okay, so he ran away. Why do you say Victoria killed him?" I asked.

"Because she did. I heard it. I was there that night. Just across the street when it happened."

"What happened?"

"Mind you, I didn't know what I was hearing at the time. I pieced it all together afterward."

"What happened?" Allie said.

"It was late at night, past one o'clock, maybe one-thirty. I heard a clatter across the street at the Racine house. They had all kinds of Roses in front to hide the house back then, like they do now, but they were better cared for then. Part of the deceit, no doubt.

"It sounded like someone tripping over a wood pile or maybe kicking a paint can. It was noisy. I thought it was an animal at first. Then I heard it move around the back of the house and thought it was a burglar. Victoria never kept any lights on at night. Probably too poor to pay the electricity bill. Served her right, I thought, that she got burgled. All the rest of the street kept lights on to protect each other, but not Victoria–stuck-up–Racine."

"And the burglar?" I coaxed.

I'm not a violent man, and I don't usually fantasize about beating parchment-skinned, blue-haired old ladies into hamburger, but talking to Haggy Miller took me there and fitted me for brass knuckles.

"Well, I heard a pop, like a cork. It wasn't loud, but I heard it. Then it was quiet. I rolled back to bed not wanting to waste any more of my sleep thinking about those stupid neighbors."

She fiddled with her bridge again and fit it back into place like a cow working a cud.

"About an hour later. I was woke up again. I heard another kick at the woodpile. I got up to get a glass of water and saw a couple of lights on at the Racines. I thought of calling the police about all the noise, but the police didn't always believe me. So I went back to bed again.

"The next day I walked by that house and saw that Mrs. Racine had been out that morning. I saw fresh gravel kicked up. She almost never drove. Couldn't afford the gas. I walked down beside the house and found her in the backyard planting another damn rose bush. She looked like she'd been crying.

"'Good morning, Victoria,' I said. 'How are you doing today?'

"'Allergies got to my sinuses,' she said.

"'You have any trouble last night?' I asked. 'I thought I heard something in your yard late at night. Almost called the police thinking it was a burglar. You really need to keep your porch light on dearie, if not for you then for the neighbors.'

"'I didn't hear anything,' she said. Then she turned her back to me and went on with her gardening as if I wasn't even there."

"That's some pretty damning evidence," I said. "Surprised she didn't swing." I made to get up and sorted through the growing list of nasty things I wanted to say to Haggy as a parting shot.

"My cousin worked up in Price at the bus station," Haggy said. "I ran into him the next month. He told me that he saw Lance Racine get off a bus in Price and then hitch a ride south. The date fixed to that night I heard the commotion behind the Racine house."

"Did you tell the police?" asked Allie.

"After that, of course I did," Haggy Miller said. "I figured the whole thing out and laid it out right in front of the sheriff. Lance comes back to town late at night. He walks in on Victoria and maybe a lesbian orgy with the stupid kid watching and everything—I never did find out who she was seeing then, but it was a good theory. There was some arguing, and then she shot him dead. She dragged the body into her car and disposed of it."

"Let me guess," I said. "The police didn't believe you?"

"Hell no. They said I had it in for her because I suspected her son Thick let skunks into my garage and filled my bathroom with wasps. Twice."

"And your cousin?"

"He told the police that he couldn't be one-hundred percent sure it was Lance he saw. It could have been someone that looked like him. But he was sure when I talked to him, so I know the police were being bribed or something. My cousin's not above changing his story if another one helps him better. By the time I got him to man up and swear that he had seen Lance Racine get off the bus that night, it was three months later, and he didn't convince anyone. I told the police to drag the river and check out the old mine on the Racine ranch, but they didn't."

"So, let me guess," I said. "You let the whole thing drop?"

"Hell no, stupid. The police didn't believe me, but the rest of the town did. With all the talk, eventually they got around to questioning the bitch."

"That's a strong word," said Allie.

"It's the very one I was thinking of," said I.

"The police might have been fooled, but I wasn't, and I made sure she knew it too."

"You confronted her?"

"No. That wouldn't have been lady-like."

This was a test. God had sent me this woman, at this time, in this place, to test my patience. God should know me better than that.

"You sniveling, shriveled-up, conniving, banshee from hell," I said. "You're a rat with the black plague. You made a wonderful woman's life miserable. You slandered her with baseless rumors. You evil bitch. You are, and always have been, a miserable, cruel, shallow, black-hearted cow. You were born without a soul, Haggy Miller. That is why your husband left you, and your children won't visit. You're toxic gas." I'd raised my voice. Actually, I screamed right in her face, spittle condensing on her reading glasses.

Before she could respond, and she was going to respond, the room erupted in applause. The sleepers had awakened and the dominoes were set aside. The others cheered my verbal assault on the heinous woman.

The receptionist we'd left behind a magazine peered in the door.

"I think you need to leave," he said. His blue scrubs were soaked at the armpits from the exertion of walking from the desk. He wiped his forehead with a wad of tissue, leaving a smear of torn paper on his brow.

"We're leaving," I said. "Someone's likely to drop a house on this thing. I don't want to be here when she dies. She needs to do that alone."

Haggy Miller's jaw quivered, and I knew my guess about her husband and children had been right on the money.

Outside, back in the freezing dry air, Allie and I steamed like a couple of escaped lobsters.

"Well that was fun," I said.

"You know," Allie said as we walked to the car. "I half expected Lance to show up at Victoria's funeral."

"No, he's dead," I said. "He wouldn't have left his family here among people like that if there was breath left in his body. No human could."

When we got to the car, I dropped a handful of Monet puzzle pieces on the ground. I hadn't heard about the wasps before. Good job, Rick.

38

ALLIE HAD to get back to her place. The animals needed looking after. I went home, my home, my Moab home that I wasn't sure how I was going to pay for, and turned on every light, except the outside ones to spite the old hag who no longer lived across the street and still spat venom like a colicky cobra.

Once settled in, I reached for the photo album again and looked at pictures of my lost family. I turned the pages backward seeing Rick flipping off his mother from Atlanta, from Iraq, from a mess hall during Basic Training, from the step of a bus taking him away from Moab, away from Haggy Miller. There were few pictures of Vicky. She was behind the camera most times, but there were some of her. A birthday party where she blew out candles at the very table that stood in the next room. She sat alone with two small, poorly wrapped presents awaiting attention.

Deeper in, I found photos of Lance and Vicky in the backyard, scraping up a garden patch of vegetables where the white roses grew now. Christmastime, and there were three in the picture—mother, father, and child in a posed and timed photo. The three of them immortalizing an offensive gesture and two happy adults wrapped in each others' arms, kissing with joyous abandon. Rick and his presents, a shirt, a pocket knife, and his new .22, with his dad pointing out its parts. Vicky with a new dress, blue but faded now in the old photograph. Lance showing off his new watch, grinning broadly and proud, his son's middle finger extending into the frame from the right.

Pictures of Rick as a baby. Birthday parties, first steps, hospital. Vicky staring into the face of her newborn, oblivious to the photographer across the room, rapt in the little face hidden in a blanket, pride and wonder.

Someone was cutting onions and dust fell from someplace I hadn't vacuumed. I sniffled.

Vicky and Lance's wedding. My mother was there, holding a bouquet of white roses. Wreaths of white roses framing the wedding party. I didn't know the man beside Lance. I didn't know Lance. A glimpse of my father eating a piece of cake talking with Lance. Neither looked comfortable in their suits. Vicky aglow with youthful enthusiasm, young love, and promise. My own wedding was not as joyous as this one. White roses on the table, one pinned to my father's breast, a bouquet held in my mother's hands. Rick and I are yet to come, but already linked by white roses. Family.

I cracked open a bottle of wine. Ashe Winery drunken Kokopelli, two years old. Guilt Buddy and I toasted our lost families. When I had a good buzz on, I did what every good drunk does. I called my ex-wife.

"Hey Nancy," I said. "How ya doin'?"

"Oh god, Tony. Are you kidding me? I was just telling Karen that at least my ex-husband never called me up drunk in the middle of the night."

"It's required for unemployment benefits. Don't blame me. Blame the system."

"Are you alright?"

"I'm feeling lost, I guess. I'm thinking of my folks, of Rick and Vicky. About us."

"Us? Tony, we're as close as we've ever been."

"Are we?" It was an automatic question. I really hadn't considered it.

"Time gets away from us. It happens to everyone. It's how things are. Remember what Dr. Seuss said?"

"'I won't eat green eggs and ham?'"

"'Don't cry because it's over, dance because it happened,'" she quoted.

"I've met someone. Or rather met her again?"

"Allison Braise," she said. "I thought you might look her up."

Fourteen years of marriage. Nancy and I didn't have many secrets. Of course, she knew about my first kiss as I knew about hers. Does a cousin count though?

"So is she single or divorced? Or are you involved with a married woman?"

"She's single, and I'm not involved."

"Yet."

"Okay. Yet. Does this bother you?"

"Of course it does," she said. "But this is the way of things. That's why we have the rule not to tell each other about our affairs. Remember? Do you remember Tony? The rules?"

"Uhm, yeah, but I, uh. Guilt Buddy is such a nag."

"Who?"

"My drinking friend. Guilt Buddy. He hurts my feelings. It's what he does."

"Go to bed, Tony. It's late."

"How's Randy?" I asked.

"He's fine. I don't know if I can handle his drumming much more. It was great when he got involved with something not connected to the internet, but the noise. Oh, the noise. And now he's talking about taking the next step in his musical career. He thinks his current drum set is holding him back. He wants me to fork out ten thousand dollars for a Yabuchi X98-Z Alpha electric drum set. He's mentioned it so much that I've actually memorized the serial number. I think he should move his drums to your place. Are people still shooting at you? Can Randy and his drums come live with you for a while?"

"A ten-thousand-dollar drum kit?" I said. "Seriously?"

"I know you can't afford it, but if he moves all his drums to your place, I'll consider buying it for him."

"Revenge?"

She didn't answer.

"I know that drum set," I said. "Someone told me about it. It's supposed to be really good. But I don't know why I know that."

"Randy must have hit you up for it too," said Nancy.

"No. He knows I'm broke. It'd just hurt my feelings if he asked me."

"You're not broke. You just don't have any income," she corrected me. "And you have your savings."

"Not anymore," I said, catching myself too late.

"Oh," she said. "Oh. Today was the auction, wasn't it? What did you do Tony?"

"I bought the house. I needed to own it."

"You can't afford two houses, Tony."

"I said I was broke. Didn't you believe me?"

She sighed heavily and long into the phone.

"Tony, when you're sober, we should really have a long talk. Maybe we can hook up with a rental agency and recover some of your investment. It's not a good time for vacation properties but the market will turn. Eventually."

"What colors were the flowers at our wedding?" I asked. It was the natural sequitur to where my mind was spinning.

"Carnations, pink and blue," she said. "Don't you remember?"

"I don't remember the details, only the mood."

"That's enough," she said.

"Thanks."

"Go to bed, Tony."

"Give my love to Randy," I slurred.

Drinking alone in a cloud of nostalgia is the kind of thing that gets you free coffee and stale donuts in the church basement every Tuesday and Thursday, but it's also a good cleanser. Seuss was right about the Lorax, but Socrates was right when he said, "the unexamined life is not worth living."

Actually, he said something in Greek that was later thought to mean this. Who knows? It's a good sentiment, though. "It's hard to be sure where quotes originate," said Abraham Lincoln to Caesar after the Battle of Waterloo.

Guilt Buddy, Bacchus, and I invited the Greek philosopher for a final drink and then we all went to bed.

I was woken up by knocking at the front door. I rolled over and opened the window. Cold rushed in but my blankets protected everything but my face. Below me, at the front door, were Allie and Gandalf. The big white dog saw me, barked, and began climbing the side of the house along the brick quoins as Rick and I had, not that he had far to go. He could almost look into the second-story window by standing on his hind legs.

"Didn't you say nine o'clock?" Allie called.

"I say a lot of things."

"Open the door. It's freezing out here."

Still wrapped in my blanket, I went downstairs and let them in. I braced for a dog attack or the sound of breaking furniture, gnawed glass, and piles of poop bigger than a sofa falling from great heights on hand-woven antique rugs, but Gandalf heeled to Allie and was a perfect gentleman.

"I got a little melancholy last night," I explained. "I slept in."

She saw the empty bottle on the table and the scrapbook on the chair.

"I'll make some coffee. You clean up."

"Okay," I said and went back upstairs.

My life is a series of poor decisions I decided as I tried to wash away the hangover I so richly deserved. Today we'd planned a long, dry, cold, steep hike into the Racine Ranch. I remembered the topographical maps with the contour lights so close that they looked to have been drawn with finger paints. My head wasn't going to hold me back as much as my legs would. The closest thing I'd had to regular exercise for months was taking Precious to the park. God, I thought. I still had that to deal with.

I came downstairs dressed and feeling surprisingly well. Either I hadn't overdone it, or the wine was the kind of wine that didn't kick your ass the next day as hard as you deserved. You know, good wine.

"You don't have much food here," Allie said.

"Yeah, I actually haven't been here much." I sat down at the table. "Besides, I figure I should eat out as much as possible. I'm an economic asset to the city."

"Town," she corrected.

"Town."

Gandalf strolled over and sat directly in front of me, blocking all sight into the kitchen where Allie was coming from with coffee.

Sitting square on his haunches, Gandalf flattened his long face to his chest to look down at me expectantly. I had to crane my neck to look into his eyes. When I did, a meat slab of tongue splatted against my chin and nearly snapped a vertebra.

"How nice. He kissed you." Allie said, pushing Gandalf aside.

"I think I've been water-boarded."

I washed my face before drinking my coffee. I'd given up dog slobber for cream and sugar years ago.

"We should grab a bite on the way," I said.

"We'll have to," said Allie.

In the kitchen, Gandalf bent down and drank out of the sink.

"So are you an alcoholic?" Allie asked.

"You only ask that because I'm always drinking. No. I'm not an alcoholic. But lately, I admit, I haven't passed on many opportunities to imbibe."

"Like the winery?"

"Yeah, and the LARP. And a bottle at a casino."

"And last night?"

"Friends dropped by."

"Who?"

"Ghosts of family past, imaginary friends, a Greek god, Dr. Seuss, Socrates and white roses."

"Something specific eating at you?" she said.

"Missed opportunities. Gratitude. Un-repaid kindnesses. Losing touch. Legacy."

"You're not upset about the land, are you? About being cut out of the will?"

"Hell no," I said. "If anything, I'm angry Vicky didn't know how rich she was. She had to open her house to strangers to get by when she was a millionaire. She should have used the money to leave and get the hell away from Haggy Miller and this town."

"I don't think she'd have left."

"Why?"

"She wouldn't move. She wouldn't sell. Even if she knew what it was worth, I doubt she'd have let it go. She felt a debt to Lance and the Racines. She had to keep it through her lifetime, thereafter she didn't care what happened. She told me that. It was like she was a caretaker. She'd have given it to Thick, maybe, but I think she was happy when he got out. You know, for years there was a joke that Moab's primary export was its children. There was no future here. Then Moab was discovered, and the outdoor craze brought jeeps and people. Moab is a tourist boom town now. But like mining before, tourism will eventually peter out. Besides, it's a kind of servitude when your entire economy is based around catering to strangers. Look how they swept Vicky's death under the carpet."

She took a sip of coffee.

"I'm sorry," she said. "I'm rambling."

"I get it," I said. "I wish I'd been here for Vicky."

"Oh, don't even go there," Allie said. "Didn't you hear what I said? Vicky didn't want you here. She was glad you had a life up in Salt Lake. The last thing she'd want is for you to be here or feel guilty."

She looked at me hard, making me see the truth in her eyes.

I nodded.

"Still," I said.

"Still, get over it."

Gandalf bumped his head on the upper cabinets, and I heard a wine glass crash and break inside it.

"We better go," I said.

We grabbed food at a drive-thru. For the hike, Allie had collected a box of crackers, three summer sausages, and gallons of bottled water in nylon saddlebags.

"Gandalf," she explained.

Under gray skies, we drove to the ranch in Allie's white Chevy SUV. The air was still and cold. Gandalf was scrunched in the back, his breath fogging the windows.

Allie took the turn-off onto the road that led to the ranch. The ranch itself was not on the highway. That might have made it even more valuable. We had to follow an old rutted mining path through someone else's property and then another's by virtue of a grandfathered easement. The road was worthy of the Jeep Safari, the Moab tradition where every year thousands of people drive off-road vehicles worth more than their houses off cliffs and into ravines trying to surmount boulders nicknamed "axle breaker," "tire popper," "the wall" and "what the hell was I thinking?" Allie navigated the ruts, bushes, and drop-offs like a stoic Mars rover, and soon we came to a gated fence.

"I think this is it," I said, checking the map.

"It says no trespassing."

"What? Now you're scared? You flushed us down a gully that ripped off both mirrors simultaneously, and you're worried about a no-trespassing sign?"

"The sign's new," she said.

I looked closer.

"Oh." The detective in me dope-slapped the other me to move aside.

I got out and walked to the gate. It wasn't exactly new, but neither did it date from the days I'd last been here. The cement columns that held it and a new chain were firm and unmovable, effectively precluding any chance of driving around by virtue of a large boulder to the left and a thirty-foot drop to the right. Barbed wire ran in both directions. The fencing was higher than usual, at eye level instead of chest high, which kept cattle out.

"I'd say it's been here about five years," Allie said. "There's some rust, but not much."

"Looks expensive," I said.

"Oh, yeah. Forget the material. The labor costs would be sick. Most of these fence posts were drilled into the stone."

"That's razor wire," I said. "On the top. Not barbed wire. Nasty."

The chain holding the gate shut had links bigger than my thumb. No normal bolt cutters could work through it. It'd take a cutting torch to break that chain, not that I had one of those either. I had a Leatherman tool and an empty pistol.

We followed the chain to a steel box on the right hand post. A key was needed to get into the box where, through a crack, we could glimpse a padlock the size of a salad plate waiting inside.

"This is very interesting," I said, feeling the unloaded weight of my pistol. "Did you get a chance to teach Gandalf those attack commands yet?"

"No," she said. "Just hop and lick."

"That'll do."

Allie synched the nylon saddlebags around Gandalf, turning him into the biggest, scariest, whitest pack animal I'd ever seen.

We left the vehicle and walked around the boulder and along the barbed wire fence. Ten yards from the road, the fence ended in the side of a steep cliff. We clambered up, kicking rocks behind us in crackling avalanches until we reached the top. Gandalf was waiting for me when I dragged my sweaty ass up. The fence began again, but the endmost post had fallen over and hung on wires like an open magazine page. We crossed under it and onto the Racine Ranch.

One hundred acres sounds like a lot. It is if you're building a house or planning a garden, but in terms of farming and ranching in the desert, it's nothing. This was less than nothing. From atop the next hill, we could see pretty much the entire property or at least the peaks of it. The one hundred acres was probably more like ten thousand if you included vertical area. It was like a brain with ridges and arroyos, some sandy, some stone, some with vegetation, all steep and unusable.

We'd seen some of the north side from the Ashe Winery, so we turned south and followed the tops of the ridges as far as we could, then slid down a hill before climbing up another.

"Why didn't we just follow the road?" Allie asked forty minutes into our hike.

"I want to see the petroglyphs," I said. "The ones Tiponi found."

I pulled out a map, and Allie gave Gandalf a gallon of water and us each a quart.

"I think it's a little farther west," I said.

"Okay," Allie said with a smile I wouldn't have worn if the roles were reversed. I'd be bitching up a blue streak if this were her errand, and she'd dragged me up and down the calf-crushing hillsides.

"You're a good egg," I told her.

"Glad you noticed."

Allie threw a bundle of aluminum rods on the ground. With a clatter and a snap, they sprung together like magic into long poles. She quickly threaded them through plastic hoops in a sheet of nylon fabric and tossed the whole bundle on the ground, where it popped into a tent. It was small but cut the wind.

While I racked my brain for clever Harry Potter references, she crawled inside, unrolled a foam cushion on the floor, and unwrapped a silver reflective survival blanket that she draped around her shoulders.

Instinct quivered my nethers, but my stupid brain denied the obvious.

"Planning on staying here a while?" I said, unable to come up with anything suitable or sufficiently funny.

"A while," she said.

Under the silver sheet, she leaned over on an elbow and signaled me to come over with a twitching index finger.

My brain searched for less fortunate but more plausible explanations of what was happening, but my feet listened to the smarter animal in me, and I shuffled forward. I kneeled, kicked off my shoes and crawled into the little tent.

Before my unbelieving brain could apologize or ask for a written disclaimer of some kind, Allie kissed me. All the blood from my head mercifully fled away. I glimpsed the gray winter clouds through a gap in the zippered door hovering over ember-orange sand cliffs and became giddy and lightheaded. I closed my eyes and lost myself in the heat of Allie's breath and the smoothness of her skin.

I shuffled off my pants in kicks and wiggles and held Allie as she squirmed out of hers. Her shirt was off before mine, and I kissed her lightly on the neck. I tasted gooseflesh and nipped her ear.

She moaned and shivered.

I gasped.

I pulled her naked body to mine and tucked the foil blanket as best I could. She rolled on top of me, throwing it off, hot and eager. Our breath had warmed the tent, and it was enough. I looked up into Allison Braise's face and thought I was dreaming a dream I'd dreamed before.

39

"THAT WAS the best three minutes I've had in years," I said.

"Minute and a half."

"Still the best."

"The best." Allie leaned over and kissed me. "You owe me."

"I look forward to repaying the debt."

We kissed again, long and warm. It was nicer than making excuses. I'd offered a few already and was readying a new barrage: it was the cold, the sand, the strangeness, sun spots, never happened before, I have a brain tumor, please forgive me. I tuned out my worry, but when the kisses stopped, my insecurities came back.

"Really," I began. "I'm usually—"

A crash echoed up the canyon behind us.

Gandalf barked.

Deafened by Gandalf, we silently got dressed. That dog could bark. A moment later, we were pulling down the tent and watching the white wonder run into a canyon.

I dug Allie's dog whistle from her jacket pocket and glanced at her. She nodded and stuffed the spring bars into a sack. I blew the whistle. I heard nothing from the whistle, but far away, I heard giant paws skid across slick rock as Gandalf returned like a boomerang.

We packed the saddlebags, loaded them on the dog, and headed up the canyon.

We had walked for maybe ten minutes when Gandalf stopped. We followed his gaze to a ledge on the canyon wall. Above sat a blanket-wrapped figure looking down at us. Between the soles of his dangling feet, I recognized the blond braids of Tiponi.

"How'd you get up there?" I called.

He pointed up the canyon. We walked farther on and found a narrow trail that led up the cliff face. I went first. Allie followed and then Gandalf like a clumsy goat.

The trail ended in a six-foot-long ledge, two and a half feet at its widest. Below, was a drop of maybe forty feet. Above, the top was invisible behind the overhang. On the wall behind Tiponi was the mural of petroglyphs I'd seen only in pictures before.

"Are you fucking kidding me?" I said.

"What?" asked Allie.

She stepped out on the ledge and laughed.

The petroglyphs I'd come to see were not as awe-inspiring as the photos had suggested. I'd been told they were junk, and I was still disappointed. What I saw was not a grand gallery but a tiny band of pictures none larger than three inches high. The entire panel is about eighteen inches long.

"You must have used a fisheye lens," I said, digging the photo out of my pocket and holding it up to compare. I noticed the curved angles of the rock and the careful framing to exclude anything that would give it an accurate scale.

"It's still valuable," Tiponi said. "Maybe it isn't as grand as other carvings, but it's here, and it's historic."

Gandalf nearly pushed Tiponi off the ledge as he crossed to the far end and stopped. He was too big to turn around there, so he backed up until he had enough room to sit behind Tiponi.

"That is a very large dog," Tiponi said.

"Your powers of observation amaze me," said I.

Allie took the photo and tried to find the angle from where it'd been taken. She was on her stomach and almost rolled off the side before she did.

"I talked to a historian about this land," I said. "Dr. Pinion, you remember? He said this land has changed hands more often than a bundled mortgage. This little artwork doesn't prove a thing except that the Hopi weren't here."

"That black figure there," Tiponi said, indignantly pointing.

"Was painted by you," I said. "I'll run DNA to prove it if you argue."

He shut up. He wasn't the brightest man I'd met.

"What's with all the fencing, Tiponi?" Allison asked.

"I assumed it was to keep people from finding this ledge," he said.

"Seriously?" I said.

He furrowed his brow. "Why else?"

"Why do you want this land so much, Tiponi? You had to know you didn't have a chance. Did you know about the water?"

"You mean the water shares you talked about at the auction? I honestly don't know what that all means," he said. "I just found these here and thought I'd made a major discovery. I added the black dude, so my people, the proud Hopi, would be interested."

"I don't mean to upset you," I said. "But you aren't a Hopi. You're not an Indian. You're a pale Norwegian from north of the Arctic Circle."

"No. I am," he said. "I traced my ancestry, and my great-grandfather married a Hopi woman."

"And that makes you Hopi?"

"By marriage. Yes."

"By marriage?"

"Yes," he said. "My family disowned him, like they did me. But roots are roots and family is family. I have a claim to my birthright. I have a right to be part of the Hopi Nation. But I got the same reaction from them as I'm getting from you. That's why I thought I'd prove my worth by getting them this land. Mrs. Racine wasn't opposed to it, at least not until people started coming by with money."

"You were trying to get the land before they were?"

"Oh yes, for a couple of years. I'd visit and drink tea, and we'd get along. She'd only say she'd consider it, but I think I was making real progress. She liked my company. Then that Roy Stirps moved in and her son Thick died and finally Miss Sophia moved in. She didn't have a lot of time for me then. Besides, I couldn't offer money the way those others could. When I wouldn't go away, they got mad at me. Crew threatened me on Mrs. Racine's own doorstep one day and Ashe's men chased me off this ledge several times. Actually, I thought you were them at first. I figured I'd just stay here in protest. You know, like the tree-sitters? I'd draw attention to the situation by civil disobedience."

"When did you decide to do this?" I asked.

"After I heard the dog bark when I nearly fell off the ledge."

"What were you going to do for food and water? Shelter and heat?"

He looked confused. He was good at it.

Gandalf licked Tiponi's face and nearly pushed him over on his side. I grabbed him before he could tumble off the ledge.

"You say Ashe's folks chased you off the ranch? From this area?"

He nodded.

"But this is at the opposite end of the property from the Ashe's Winery. Why would they care? How did they see you?"

"I don't know. I've looked down on their grapes before, but the last couple of times, I just came up here to burn sage and do a medicine dance, but they found me."

"You danced here?" Allie asked.

"Small steps."

"And they found you?"

"They were serious. Had guns."

"They point them at you?" I asked.

"No, but they didn't need to." He tried to wipe the dog spit off his face. It dripped down his neck under his jacket.

"How'd you know it was Ashe's people?"

"Ashe Winery hats," he said. "With the drunk Kokopelli staggering around."

"Did you tell the cops about this?" Allie asked.

"No. I'm trespassing. It's just more white man bullshit."

Allie passed him a canteen, and he drank thirstily and splashed some down his cheek where dust clung to dog saliva.

"There might be some historic value in this panel," I said. "Maybe it can be saved somehow."

This didn't please Tiponi like I thought it would.

"Wouldn't that be good?" I offered as if consoling a sad child.

"Hopi want ancient ancestral land, as was before white man come."

"Don't start," I said. "If that's what they want, you might want to go to those lands. This ain't them."

"The Hopi are a Pueblo people, like the Utes and Paiutes and those other guys. Their ancestors were here."

"You mean their cousins were."

"Same thing."

"Not really," Allie said.

"Aren't Indian people practical?" I asked.

"Proud people," Tiponi said.

"And practical. What is practical about this land? When the white settlers came, there was no one here. This is crap land. No use to anyone except for hiding. That's what Moab has always been, a place to hide. This place is useless unless you're on the lam."

I could tell there was no consoling Tiponi. I made too much sense and he shut down rather than hear it. Again, he was good at that. How else could a Norwegian Hopi by marriage get along in life?

"Let's get down from here," I said. "Gandalf will lovingly push us all to our deaths."

We all followed the trail down and back to the wire fence on the north.

"I'm going back town, white man Flaner," Tiponi said. "Me cold."

He disappeared through a hole in the fence. A motorcycle roared, and a red dust cloud rose against the gray clouds as his bike sped away.

"What now?" Allie said.

"We find what the Ashes are hiding here," I said.

We circled the property, following the fence line, admiring the workmanship and regular no-trespassing sign placement.

"Someone with money put these fences up," I said. "They were put up recently and for a reason."

"So what makes you think it was the Ashes?" she asked.

"Well, we have reports of armed guards wandering around. The fence line goes along the Ashe estate. Remember we saw it from the tasting room? The tumbleweeds were attempting a prison break? Phil, or was it Bill, pointed to where impossible condos could ruin their view. There's no way anyone could build condos up here. And the fence itself is weird. The Ashes spent money to decorate their estate with weathered wood right out of a John Ford film. This demilitarized zone feng shui does not support that image. The Ashes would have seen this fence going up and done something about it. Unless, of course, they were the ones doing it."

We found the southwest corner of the fence and then set out in a diagonal toward the northeast corner. The hills were steep, and our legs ached. After an hour of this, we found ourselves in a canyon and decided just to follow it down. Even Gandalf was dragging so we stopped for food a few minutes later.

We pitched the tent again and fought to keep Gandalf out of it. He wouldn't have fit even if we weren't in it. It was cozy for two. Mammoths need not apply.

We ate sliced sausage on crackers, trail mix, and a bagel. Gandalf just had sausage and another gallon of water.

After lunch, I sat against a rock in the cold shadowed canyon with my arms around Allie, the survival blanket over our legs. Gandalf wore the tent like a hat.

Allie slid her cold hand under my shirt and wiggled her fingers into my manly chest hair which made me a fire hazard at Hawaiian luaus and Fourth of July picnics.

I kissed the back of her head and got a mouthful of desert sand. I swallowed it with my last cracker, thinking that now this place is truly a part of me.

Eventually we had to get moving if only to get warm. The clouds had finally decided to do something and an occasional snowflake hovered and bobbed in the air, mischievous and menacing, too light to fall, too heavy to return.

Forty-five walking minutes later, we crested a hill and heard voices in the canyon below. Allie's hand went to Gandalf's muzzle before he could alert us, them, and passing satellites that something was happening.

Carefully, we crept down the hill to the bottom of the canyon.

Besides the voices, we heard the sounds of liftings and droppings, grunts and motors echoing between the narrow walls like a cough in a wind tunnel. Making as little noise as possible and keeping to the darkest shadows of the shadowy gully, we crept forward.

There was sunlight ahead. It was bright and warm and strangely out of place. It shone not from the sky, but a cave.

A moving truck was parked beside a pickup with the Ashe Winery logo stenciled on its side. The surfer who'd sold me pot at the café appeared at the mouth of the cave. He had a big black rifle slung across his back and pushed a handcart laden with plastic crates up a ramp and into the truck. Behind him, Phil Ashe appeared carrying a potted plant which I recognized to be an actual pot plant. He put it in the truck.

Then Bill Ashe emerged. I'd never seen him not wearing a tie, but his demeanor and haircut made differentiating the twins easy. He spooled a long green extension cord over his shoulder and called back into the cave.

"Don't connect the detonators until we're sure we're done. Don't even think about it," he commanded.

The surfer came out of the truck with an empty cart and headed back inside. That's when Gandalf barked for no apparent reason.

The rifle was in the surfer's hand before the cart stopped its momentum. He fell to one knee and scanned the shadows where Allie and I hid behind a rock.

"Is that a bear?" I heard Phil ask. "An albino bear?"

"I think it's a pony," said the surfer.

"Too big for a pony," said a voice I didn't recognize.

"It's a dog," Bill said. "I saw it at the Braise place. Allison, is that you, dear?"

Allie stared at me. There was something really creepy about the way he said dear. I gripped my empty pistol and asked myself earnestly why I hadn't bothered to buy bullets.

"Tony Flaner?" called Bill. "You've gotta be out there too. Come out so we can see you."

"We've got you surrounded," I yelled. "Maddy Ross and Rooster Cogburn are up the ledge behind you. If you drop your guns now and leave, we'll delay the marshals for six hours."

Phil laughed. It wasn't a cruel evil mastermind kind of laugh, but a genuine laugh every comic yearns to hear from an audience.

"It's Tony, Bill," said Phil. "He's cool."

"He's a detective," said his brother.

"He's a what?" said the surfer. "Shit, I sold him, bud."

"When?" asked Bill.

"I dunno," he said. "You know, like the other day. Maybe last week. I dunno."

"So he parties," said Phil. "That's a point for him."

"Phil, you have no idea about federal drug laws," said Bill.

"I think I know them better than you do," he said. "Tony, are you with the law or just out for a stroll?"

"Which answer won't get us killed?" I yelled.

His laughter returned.

"What do you want us to do, Mr. Ashe?" said the voice I didn't know.

"Bill," said Phil. "We are not killing anyone, for god's sake. Call off the dogs."

There was a pause that lasted sixty-eight days, but was probably not that long in retrospect.

Finally Bill said, "He's right. Put 'em down, boys. Get back to work. Make sure we're out tonight."

"Come on out, guys, and bring your yeti. I want to look at him."

I looked at Allie, and she at me. I shrugged my shoulders. She shrugged hers. I put my gun in my pocket and peeked around the rock. Phil was lighting a cigarette. Bill finished winding the cable. Both waited for us to move.

We stood up, and followed by Gandalf, we walked into the light of the cave.

40

I CREPT up with my hands in front of me, fingers spread, displaying no weapons. Phil reached out and put a joint between two fingers of my right hand.

"This will calm you down," he said. "Anasazi Red Rope. About to be in short supply."

An older man with long hair held back in a ponytail carried out a three-foot-long fluorescent grow light and loaded it into the truck. He glanced at us with worry and tried to turn his face so we wouldn't get a good look at him. I guess he forgot about the Grateful Dead tattoo on his neck. Identification would not be hard.

Bill watched Gandalf carefully. The dog looked back at him. They were about the same height.

"That is the biggest dog I have ever seen," he said. "Does he bite?"

"He has a mouth," Allie said. "He can if he wants to."

"I mean, are we in danger?" Bill said.

"Are we?" countered Allie.

"No," said Phil. "We just need a couple more hours to clear out then there won't be enough to prove anything."

Beside the mouth of the cave, I spied a wooden box with the word "explosives" stenciled on the side.

"I thought those only existed in cartoons," I said.

"It's pretty old, but it still works. We'll make sure to use enough so the cave falls in."

Suddenly, I recognized where we were. It had changed since I was last here, a new side road showed recent signs of use, but the opening was unmistakable.

"This is the old potash mine," I said.

"Yeah. We kinda needed to borrow it," Phil said. "Pass the dutchie."

I lifted the joint to my lips and then recalled Allie asking about my chemical intake and passed it to her. She was on my left after all.

She drew a puff and sent it to Bill, who passed it directly to Phil.

"This is how you could afford the Tolanto Rimini grapes," I said. "And the house. And the water system."

"You know a lot about us," said Bill with more menace than I was in the mood for. Luckily, I thought, drug dealers aren't usually violent. Oh, wait.

"What are you talking about?" said Allie.

"The rags to riches story of the Ashe Winery has a lot to do with having money to make money and being able to buy an entire Italian vineyard."

"Our grapes are decent," said Phil, a little hurt. "We had a good year. They just needed more time to mature."

"And we've crossed the Tolanto Rimini grapes with our own Moab Rouge for an exciting new wine to debut in three years," said Bill.

"Save it for the brochure," I said.

"Tony, did you not see the nice people with automatic weapons?" asked Allie.

"I can't wait to taste the new wine," I said excitedly. "I'm sure it will be delicious."

"This is messed up," said Bill. "I knew this would happen."

"Chill, bro. I don't think Tony's out to get us. And Allison's always been cool. Haven't you?"

"Oh yes," she said, as excited as I was about the wine.

"We should have shut this down last year," Bill said, shaking his head. "Moved it to Colorado. Hell, they'd give us tax incentives. A few miles over the border and we'd be legit. Here we're drug runners."

"You said we didn't want to be associated with it," said Phil. "Said it would spoil the winery image."

"Then we should have just shut down."

"We're legendary," said Phil. "Best grass in the world. And besides, we needed the money. Your suits weren't free."

"We could have started a dummy corporation."

"Oh? And no one would be able to pierce the veil?" said Phil. "No fed would link us with decades of illegal growing and come after us? Utah would forgive and forget? It's just barely legal for medicinal use."

I could tell Allie and I had entered into a pre-existing argument. I shifted on my heels uncomfortably, hoping they would notice we were there before something too personal and icky came out.

Bill said, "The taxes were a smoking gun. I told you it was too obvious."

"Oh yes, way too obvious," I said. "What are we talking about exactly?"

Phil laughed again and slapped me on the back hard enough to confirm his lack of coordination but not so much as to break anything beyond repair.

"You want to see the operation?" asked Phil.

"Make sure you remember to show me the one button that will cause the entire underground lair to explode," I said.

Laughing, Phil said, "Actually, we just installed that."

Bill stepped aside, and with a grand gesture, swept us toward the mouth of the cave. "It was Phil's idea," he said. "I was confident the winery would take off, but the cost of startup was much higher than anticipated."

"And we didn't know shit about wine," Phil added. "That was costly."

"Yes, we had a few false starts."

Phil passed me the joint again, and I took a small taste, just enough to confirm that it was, indeed, the famous Anasazi Red Rope as everyone had already said it was. It was.

"How'd you get the sage in it?" I asked.

Bill stopped. "You can taste that?"

"Hell yeah," said Allie a bit too loud. "Are you kidding? This stuff is famous for it."

"He won't believe me," said Phil. "It was his idea. He really does have a knack for crossing plants. Back in Fresno, he once crossed pot with clove and mint. It was practically a menthol hash. Two hundred an ounce and that was twenty years ago."

"Well, it just seemed natural out here," Bill said. "Marijuana is not my thing. I prefer grapes, but I know how to grow."

After a narrow anteroom, I remember being boarded closed when visiting with Rick and Vicky. The cave turned and opened up. Along the narrowest part of the cave, dynamite was roped to the walls like garlands in a rose arbor. Grow lamps had been hung by wires on climbing pitons over the corridor, offering full spectrum light. Past the curved corridor, a dozen yards under the mountain, the cave opened up again.

"I got the idea from *Pineapple Express*," said Phil. "The watering is mostly my work. I was an engineer for a while. Before dropping out."

The room was the size of a school gymnasium, but the ceiling was lower. It was sandstone and crisscrossed with wooden supports. They didn't support the ceiling. They were for hanging grow lights and narrow plastic watering tubes. Many of the lights had been removed, and there were obvious gaps in the pattern. Some were in the hallway we'd come through, others already in a truck.

The plants were in all stages of development from seedlings to three-footers, to six-footers to the seven-footers hanging upside on clotheslines along the right wall.

"Only ninety feet below, we hit an aquifer," said Phil. "I think it's why the potash mine failed. It's too much trouble to deal with if you're looking for minerals, but just right for this kind of operation. We built a silent turbine generator and bang, the whole thing was set."

"Please don't say bang," I said.

"We usually keep the front boarded up and camouflaged. We only drive up here when we absolutely have to. Usually we use mules, horses, and hikers. It's way cooler that way."

"*Treasure of Sierra Madre*," I said.

"Isn't that the one with Bogart?" Allie asked. "I think he's cool. Loved him in *African Queen*. Vicky, Sophia, and I watched that just last month."

The mention of the two other women cleared my head a little. It occurred to me that the Ashes were leading us deep into the mine where our bodies would never be found. Gandalf was skittish, and any gargantuan menace he might have offered was diminished by his hesitancy to follow. With a clearer mind, I had to agree with him; there was a pressing sense of doom and claustrophobia I hadn't sensed the moment before.

"What's wrong, Tony?" asked Phil. "What's got you spooked?"

I knew I had to play my cards close to my chest if I had any hope of getting us out of the mine.

"You brought us down here to kill us, didn't you?" I said. To be fair, I didn't start crying, though it crossed my mind. I just whimpered.

"You think that's what we're doing?" Phil was hurt. Bill didn't act surprised.

Allie picked up on it too. She blinked and looked at the two brothers, and said, "Oh no. Gandalf, ready!"

The dog recognized the command and the strange urgency Allie spoke it. Forgetting his spelunking distress, the dog clung to Allie's side and the hair on its back bristled. I knew the dog hadn't been trained to actually hurt anyone yet, but I hoped he'd read ahead and could save us.

"Shit," said Phil, taking a step back and another drag. "Dude, we're just proud of this. Wanted to show someone before we nuked it."

"It's a great operation," I said. "Very expensive, very lucrative. You should be proud of it. It's great. Great enough to kill for."

"Tony, we're not going to kill you," said Bill. There was disappointment in his voice either because we thought so ill of him and it hurt his feelings, or he regretted not being able to kill us. Even money.

"I know you aren't," said Allie, her hand on Gandalf's neck, the dog looking for all the world, ready to rip someone's head off and chase it like a tennis ball.

"You killed Vicky, didn't you?" I said. "You killed her so you could buy the land and keep your operation going. It was an extension of the fence you built around the ranch to keep it to yourself."

"Ah, hell no," said Phil.

"Oh no, Tony, don't even think that," said Bill with disappointment. "We loved Vicky."

"You had the motive. Boy did you have the motive," I said. "This operation has got to be worth a million a year."

"Two million a year," Bill said. "That's wholesale. With a little retail we do on the side, the number is closer to three."

"That's a lot of motive."

"The winery brought us five last year," said Bill. "Net."

"We're building a school in Guatemala," said Phil. "Really. A school."

"Tony, why would we want to kill Vicky?"

"I told you."

"No way. It was much better for someone else to own this property. If we're caught, Jedediah and Brian are ready to flee as scapegoats. They'll take the heat and live like kings while we just blame bad employees. Isn't that true, Brian?"

The surfer appeared with a hand cart loaded with mulch and fertilizer. "That's the plan. I'd rather not go yet; my Spanish is still a little weak."

"If we owned the property, it would make things worse for us, not better. It was perfect for Vicky to own it. She never came out here. Anyone else, and it'd be too dangerous."

"Kinda like it is now," said Phil. "People will be poking around here for sure after what you did at the auction."

"We knew the time would come when we'd have to pull up stakes," Bill explained while keeping an eye on the dog. "We thought we'd get a few more years in, but we're good with leaving now. Nobody got hurt."

"But you knew she was going to sell it."

"I don't think so. She said she had to keep it until she died. Some kind of debt of honor. But even so, had it come for sale, we would have bought it. Really. We have money. Plenty of it. The hard part would have been explaining where it came from if the price went too high. With the water shares, it went too high. We knew T. S. Crew couldn't come up with more than a million on his best day. We have twice that in our American banks right now. But bidding against real developers, desperate for water in the desert, we'd be found out. That's why we're shutting down."

"So you didn't know about the water?"

They shook their heads.

"But..." I stammered.

"We wanted Vicky to keep it. That was Plan A. Plan B was to buy it. Anything that touched our land is good to have even if we had to close down or limit our operation. Plan C was to move out quick. We're on plan C. Really it was only a matter of time before some hiker found the operation or, like you, someone traced the tax payments back to us."

"You paid the taxes for Vicky?"

Phil nodded and toked. "Yes."

Bill said, "And we brought her mortgage current so she wouldn't have to worry. You didn't know that?"

"No."

Phil laughed. "I told you it wasn't obvious."

"He'd have figured it out eventually," Bill said in his defense. "Any detective worth his salt would have."

"Oh yeah," I said. "I was just coming to that."

"We paid the taxes so Vicky would own the ranch and continue to ignore it. We got greedy, maybe, trying to keep it going longer than we needed to, but the product was good, and Vicky kept her asset. It all worked out until someone killed her."

Brian and the Dead-Head, who I assumed was Jedediah, passed us carrying a steel table between them.

"Truck's getting full," Jedediah said. "You want us to make another run? How much time do we have?"

Phil and Bill looked at Allie, me, and Gandalf in turn.

"Dude," said Phil. "We are not about killing. That's not us."

"We can just walk out of here?" I said.

"Of course," said Bill.

Allie took a step backward. No one made a move to stop her.

"Come on, Tony," she said from behind the big dog.

Phil dropped the roach on the ground, and Bill slid his hands into his pockets. It was warmer down here than it was outside, but with half the grow lights taken down and moved, the temperature was dropping.

"You're going to blow up the mine?" I said.

"That was the plan."

"I'd rather you didn't blow up the mine," I said. "It'd look suspicious."

"Better than the alternative—us in jail."

"You've never even been in jail," said Phil. "It's not that bad."

"We won't say anything," I said. "Empty it. Leave it. Board it up. Have a nice day."

Bill looked skeptical, but Phil smiled broadly and stupidly behind blood-shot eyes.

Allie shrugged.

We walked out of the cave and followed the overgrown main road back to our car. Gandalf found it hard to match our slow pace with his long legs, and with empty saddlebags on his back, he had more than enough energy to run ahead and then trot back.

"This has been one really weird day," Allie said.

"You talking about my one-minute marathon back on the ridge?"

"That's part of it. The weed is still in my head. Are you okay to drive?"

"Yeah, I'm pretty good."

We climbed into the cab after Gandalf clawed his way into the back seat.

"It sure was nice of the Ashe's not to kill us," Allie said, cuddling next to me.

The setting sun showed between cracks in the clouds and shone down in streaks of orange and red, setting the matching landscape aglow.

I turned the car around and slowly drove back the way we came. My mind cleared enough to navigate the road and even allowed a couple of brain cells to ponder the mystery.

"Oh, fuck," I said.

"What?" Allie said, coming awake. "What's going on? Are we stuck? Do you want me to drive?"

"No. Well, maybe that would be a good idea," I said. "I was just thinking that I believed Bill and Phil. I don't think they killed Vicky."

"I agree," she said. "Isn't that a good thing?"

"Yes and no," I said. "It's good they didn't kill us, don't get me wrong. I'm happy about that. Damn nice of them not to execute us gangster-style and leave our bodies buried in a collapsed sandstone mine. Damn nice. But it's bad too, because now, you see, I'm out of suspects."

41

ALLIE DECIDED she should drive back. Even half-stoned, it was safer than letting me try to climb the rocks back to the highway. I took over once we were on asphalt. Allie fell asleep as soon as the car hit forty, and I fell into my thoughts.

I tried to tell myself that it was a good thing that I'd run out of suspects. That meant I was doing my job. It also meant that I was falling into familiar patterns, and any moment now, things would fall into place, and all the previously supposed meaningless things I'd seen and experienced would gel together and flash through my skull like a bolt of burning lightning. In a gush, I'd figure the whole thing out. But I had to remind myself, or Guilt Buddy did, or one of his cousins, Insecurity-Pal, Self-Loathing Chum, Never-Be-Good-Enough Playmate, that it also meant I was a shitty detective. I'd followed every false lead and red herring into the wall before looking where I needed to, wherever that ended up being.

I took a quick inventory of what I'd accomplished so far. I'd gotten beaten up and become one of the most hated tourists in Moab's history. That sentiment had dragged a nice old lady to jail and away from her lover's dream of freedom for her. I'd ruined a real estate promoter's dream of wealth, a lost Indian's dream of acceptance, and come close to destroying the most profitable enterprise in the county. All this in about a week.

On the other hand, I'd actually slept with the girl of my dreams. It had been cold and sandy and windy, and only slightly disappointing. When every sexual fantasy you have revolves around a single subconscious figure, any reality has to be a letdown. However, the reality wasn't far from my imaginings. I experienced my schoolboy fantasies, and just like a schoolboy,

I'd finished before we'd even begun. Like a grown-up, she'd forgiven me and promised to give me another chance. I cuddled her dozing body against me and smiled at my good luck in that at least. Moab wasn't all bad. Actually, I liked it. I think Rick liked it too. It was Vicky who suffered unbearably and hated this place. Maybe Lance too. He was one of the children exported from the town. He just hadn't managed to take his family with him.

Lance Racine. There was a thread I needed to follow. With all of my other leads dried up, anything became hopeful. Sherlock Holmes said that when you've eliminated the impossible, whatever is left, no matter how implausible, must be true. I used the argument once to prove the existence of Cthulhu at a party. I think I did permanent damage to a couple of Mormon missionaries who'd happened by and got pulled in with the promise of free cocktail wieners.

Lance Racine was probably dead. I remembered the pictures in the album, those faces staring into each other's eyes, filled with hope and wonder at a big wide life stretching out ahead. The proud expression of a new father holding his son in his arms for the first time and taking him fishing. The fishing came later of course. A newborn could hardly bait a hook. Duh. Vicky's constancy of staying in Moab told me she was waiting for something. Or mourning. The specter of death hung around the memory of Lance like a cologne. Rick was dead. Vicky was dead. And, because they'd died without Lance, I knew he too must be dead.

I tried to figure a scenario where some angry, murderous extended family member would kill Vicky, believing Haggy's rumors, but I couldn't. There were no others. It smelled like another herring and I was tired of fishy leads.

I pulled into Allie's driveway and carefully jostled her awake. Gandalf was eager to get out, the call of nature calling hard. I opened the back, and he skipped away to the greenest patch of lawn on the estate and put an end to that.

"Do you have Roy's number?" I asked her. "We better call and beg off."

"What time is it?" she said, startled.

"It's six thirty."

"We have an hour. Let's go take a shower, and we can still make it."

"I like how you phrase things," I said.

She giggled.

"Are you sure you want to go?" I said since I wasn't.

She was.

I'd made a better showing in the shower if anyone's counting, though in truth, I nearly drowned. I'd never been so ready to accept death as I was then.

"You know that feeling you get before you go someplace you don't want to go, but you know it'll be okay?" I said.

"Yeah," said Allie.

"I have the first half of that feeling right now."

"Want to skip it?"

"Yes."

"No. It'll be fun. I like Roy. He's a newcomer and needs all the friends he can get. Unlike you, Mr. Popular, he's planning on sticking around."

I hadn't thought about it, but Allie had. Was this a fling? Could it be more? How long would it last? What were my plans? Would I ever get the taste of soap out of my mouth?

I never make plans. Plans are for suckers. I kicked myself for even thinking about the possibility of planning a time to make a plan. I go where the wind blows, and right now, it was at my back and into Moab. I kissed Allie, and it said something that made everything better, except her lipstick which I'd smeared across her face and into her ear. I like earlobes. So sue me.

"Hasn't he been accepted?" I said, thinking how much better Allie's house would be than Roy's tonight. "How much of this small-town prejudice is still going on?"

"Enough," she said. "There are plenty of newcomers, though. Natives are a dying breed."

I thought back on what I knew about Moab. Native was a very relative term. Everyone was passing through, whole people hanging out just long enough to carve a stick figure on a wall or plant a squash between mosquito attacks.

Allie knew the way to Roy's place. It was only a couple blocks from Vicky's old house, my new one. It was not as old as Vicky's, didn't have the architectural details mine did, nor the second floor. It was a late 70s rambler in need of paint and shingles if the shadows of the headlights were to be believed. The yard could use some work. It was too late in the season to mow, but a rake wouldn't have been useless.

A green forestry truck was parked in the driveway. A little white Honda, freshly washed, was parked on the curb. Allie collected a bottle of Ashe Winery award-winning Italian Grape-transplant ganja-funded desert-red-burgundy and we rang the bell.

A short, dark-haired woman in her early twenties and fitter than I have ever been, opened the door with a broad grin.

"I'm Julie," she said. "Roy's in the kitchen."

She showed us to the living room. We sat down on a futon couch and Allie put the wine on an end table which was a poorly camouflaged wooden cable wheel. It matched an overflowing dormitory-style cinderblock bookcase on one wall but not the Ikea television stand and thirty-inch boat anchor CRT TV on the other. The house smelled of Italian spices and steam.

Roy appeared from the kitchen clad in a red and white checkered apron and a hairnet. In one hand, he held a wooden spaghetti fork, and in the other, two iced local beers.

"Hey guys," he said, giving us the bottles. "Dinner's almost ready. Hey, you brought red wine. Great. It'll be right out." He disappeared back to the kitchen, and I cracked open the beers with my manly Leatherman tool which made me look a little stupid when I realized they were twist-offs.

"So how do you guys know Roy?" said Julie. She sat across from us in a mismatched chair, not that anything matched. It was a bachelor's house, that much was certain.

"Friends," said Allie.

"And you?" I asked Julie.

"From work," she said. "I'm a ranger too. I graduated from Michigan State in forestry and got hired here last year for the summer. I got moved to part-time for the off-season but I saved up enough to stay. So you're from here?"

"She is, I'm not," I said.

"Beautiful place. Really draws you in," said Julie. "I write poetry. You want to hear some?"

"Sure," I heard myself say. What I'd meant to say, what every thinking person in the world should say to such a question, was "No. Hell no. Goddamn hell no. For the love of decency, in the name of the Pope, the Bard, and the Supremes, NO NO NO! Fuck no." I'd doomed us. May God forgive me.

But we were saved. "That'll have to wait until after dinner," Roy said, carrying a bowl of steaming pasta. "Time to eat!"

We followed Roy into his dining room. My family had had the same steel and linoleum table when I was growing up. I recognized the shape and the spindly steel legs and the ripped rubber casters. It fit in our apartment before I learned its weight limit was significantly less than a six-year-old. Roy must have reinforced his somehow. It felt sturdy as a stump. We took our seats.

Roy carried out breadsticks, sauce, and a colorful salad. It all smelled and looked great. I was hungry. I opened the wine and poured glasses for everyone.

"I'm into retro," Roy said when he caught me feeling under the table for wads of old chewing gum. "I believe in giving old furniture a second chance."

"Especially with what the National Park Service pays," said Julie. "Slave wages."

"The job's not for everyone," said Roy, passing the salad. "You've got to love it. It's like being a teacher. If you don't have an innate love of what you're doing, you can't get through all the bullshit."

"Like the stupid tourists who don't know how to read, won't listen, and have no sense at all," said Julie. "I had one last year who sent her kids up to climb on Double Arch for a Christmas card photo. I tried to stop them, but this fat old cow in a bathrobe just told me to shut up, saying this was her park. All that taxpayer bullshit."

"What happened?" asked Allie.

"Double ambulance," she said smugly. "Greatest moment of my summer watching the whale scream for me to call an ambulance after both her kids slid down the cliff. One broke an arm, the other an ankle."

She beamed in delight at her own story.

"I'm not sadistic. I saw them fall. I knew they were hurt and not dead. It was schadenfreude, you know? I'm only human. I wanted TV coverage of their stupidity, but it was hushed up so as not to scare tourists. We need more movies about idiots cutting off their arms in these canyons. That got some people thinking about how stupidity can have consequences."

I thought of Rick falling down the stairs, being attacked by all sorts of animals, and finally flinging himself through a high-rise window. I had to change the subject.

"So Roy, you've got to tell me the story of your notorious bank-robbing family," I said.

He examined me for sarcasm, but for once, it wasn't overflowing.

"It's a good story, in the way a story that begins with "me and my buddy were drinking one day" is a good story. Embarrassing, but good."

"Let's hear it," said Allie.

"I'm sure you've heard it, Allison, but since Tony hasn't, okay." He settled back into his chair. He fell into a scripted monologue showing all the signs of a hundred command performances. It wasn't that he resented the story, just that it was so familiar that he fell into a zone when he relived it. Comics did the same thing to keep their shows fresh. The first time a joke is told, everyone, even the comedian, enjoys it. By the twentieth time, the joke is as stale as Mayan crackers. The performer needs a performance to bring back the fire. It's no longer a joke, there's no joke anymore. It is a show, an act. Roy told the story with practiced timing and the learned emphasis of a trained performer.

"Only after they were in the vault did they realize that the tip wasn't about a cash transfer, but a coin transfer to the Denver Mint," he said. "Instead of piles of high-denomination paper money, they faced a hundred paint cans of pennies, nickels, dimes, and quarters. A ton of it."

We groaned on cue.

"They grabbed all the paper they found and then started a sweaty bucket brigade of cans into their car until there was no more room and the sun was coming up. Their Ford sagged so low the bumper dragged sparks as they sped off."

It was a good beat, and the table laughed.

"They'd taken too long, and the car was too heavy. They crossed into Utah on the quietest roads they could find. The canyons devoured the old Ford's transmission, and the way I heard it, the sedan rolled into Moab in neutral, without a gear left. They pushed it to a gas station and agreed to hide out until things cooled down.

"My grandfather was a brick mason and found work in a couple of days. They were afraid to spend any of the money. The radio had said the money was all traceable. Using my grandfather's wages, they rented a house and stayed out of sight until one of them, not my grandfather, had to go buy cigarettes with a can of quarters."

Julie hadn't heard the story and was rapt in the telling. Roy could go on stage with this, jazz it up, exaggerate a bit, and maybe color his grandfather a little less heroically. He came off as a smart, even-keeled gang leader who was just unlucky.

"Eight hundred and sixty-five shots were fired in Peaceful Canyon and absolutely no injuries reported. The gang just ran out of bullets before the police did. By about ten shots, I think."

We all laughed. Roy joined us.

"I've tracked down everyone I can find. I'm working on a book about it, but I'm not much of a writer."

"It'd make a great book," said Allie, sopping up sauce with a breadstick.

"And you tell it well," I said.

"That's my legacy. It's the only inheritance I got. My family left me nothing but that story." He said it with a bitter edge. "A family should leave you more than just an embarrassing headline, don't you think?"

Yes, there was definitely bitterness there, a deep-seated resentment I was happy to have Julie gloss over.

"So was the money really traceable?" she asked. "How can you trace coins?"

"Oh, there was some paper money too, but yeah, the coins were identifiable," Roy said, returning to his affable demeanor. "But that's not what got them caught. It was carrying a paint can full of 1932-D Washington quarters to the drugstore for some Lucky Strikes. The papers said paint cans of coins had been stolen. It was a no-brainer. Besides, I'd be surprised if the locals didn't already suspect the gang up there in the cabin. Moabites are suspicious by nature, and gossipy."

"Amen, there," I said.

"No offense, Allie," Roy said quickly. "I didn't mean—"

"It's okay," she said. "I know what you mean. Small towns."

"So what happened to the money?" asked Julie.

"Oh, I forgot, you don't know the story. All but three hundred-fifty dollars was recovered. A fifty-dollar bill they used to repair the transmission and a bucket of dimes they probably jettisoned in the desert to lighten the car."

I was going to ask Roy why his grandfather didn't just abort the heist when they saw the coins or ask him how long the prison sentence was, but I knew those were the embarrassing questions he did not want to answer. The answers would show a fool bank robber. I held my tongue.

Julie didn't. "How long was he in jail?" she asked.

"He served fifteen years and came out with tuberculosis. Bank robbery is a hardcore felony."

He said it in the resentful tone I'd caught earlier. A wasted life, a boy who didn't get to know his grandfather. Family disgrace.

I needed cake.

"I have tiramisu for dessert," Roy said, collecting the dishes.

"Let me help you with those," Allie said, getting up.

I sat with Julie as the table was cleared.

"Poor Roy, I can see where his money problems come from," said Julie.

"What do you mean?"

"He has no sense for money. Misses opportunities everywhere."

"Money isn't everything," I said. "If you love what you're doing."

"You know what his nickname is at work? Stirrups, for Stirps," she whispered. "It's because if you want to advance, just step on Roy-Stirrups. He's got seniority but won't be transferred. I'm surprised he can live out here full time."

"You made it work. Maybe he likes it here. Money isn't everything," I said again. I don't know why it bothered me so much that Julie's previous sentiment about the majesty and wonder of the desert was so easily put aside. "Why are you still here?"

"It's not forever," she said. "Lifers are rare."

"So Roy's rare."

"I guess so, but get him drinking, and you'll hear about how unfriendly this town is for anybody but tourists and how the National Parks are being privatized. He'll tell you about going to Patagonia."

"What about Patagonia?" Roy said from the door.

"You want to move there," Julie said.

"Yeah, it's a beautiful place. The dollar goes a long way in Argentina. One day," he said. "One day, I'll go."

The dessert was as good as the meal.

"You don't get along with the locals?" I said to Roy over coffee after dessert in the living room.

He looked at Allie in shock and then Julie in accusation.

"They can be snobby," he said carefully. "I mean, you'd think after five years the grocer would know my name and not require ID on every damn check I write."

"It's because you bounced one," Julie said.

"Three years ago. This town is expensive. Getting worse every year. My rent went up three times in the last two years. How is that cool?"

"It's not."

"Is that why you bid on Vicky's house?" I asked. "To get out of renting?"

"Damn straight," he said, pouring a little Bailey's into his coffee and offering us some. "It's a great old house. Much better than this dive, but it's all I can afford."

The house was warm and cozy, and I had the sense of being around new and old friends. Allie cuddled beside me on the futon and my arm naturally went around her shoulders and fit like it was made for that purpose.

"How were you going to pay for the house?" I asked Roy.

"I'd get a loan," he said after a moment. "I know the house really well. I stayed there for months. I figured I could let three rooms out each season. That, plus what I've been paying here would more than cover it."

"It'd work," said Allie. "Vicky let out rooms, and that kept her going."

"Actually, that's why I wanted you over here tonight. What are your plans with the house? You live in Salt Lake City, don't you?"

"Yeah, I do," I said. "I'm not sure why I bought the house. I don't have any plans yet."

"Nostalgia," said Allie, but I could sense she didn't like that I had "no plans."

"Just seemed right," I said.

"Well, I could look after it for you while you're gone. I could take my old room and I could show you the plans I drew up for the simple conversion for more tenants. The bathrooms are the problem, but with the big garden in the back, it could be a really cozy bed and breakfast."

"I'll think about it," I said.

"I'd do it for a room," he said. "Or I could pay rent if it's not too much."

"Generous," I said. "Let me think on it."

Julie told us about how expensive a one-month rental was on Maui. She and two girlfriends stayed in one after high school graduation. I zoned out on her conversation, concentrating on Allie's occasional chin nod and the sweet coffee.

My eyes scanned the bookcase. You can tell a lot about a person by what they read. Roger Waters said that if you go to someone's house and they don't have any books, not to fuck them. Roy could get lucky with Roger. His bookcase was mostly non-fiction, books on local history, coin collecting, and writing guides, but there was a shelf of mysteries and thrillers that look to have been bought secondhand and read a half dozen times.

"My folks had to wire us money after a week just to get groceries," Julie droned. "Everything was so expensive there."

"It's like that here," Roy said dreamily. "Everything has to be imported. My grandfather said bricks were so costly here that no one local knew how to lay them. That's what he did those months he was hiding."

I stood up. "Roy, where's the little boy's room?"

"Down the hall by the kitchen." He pointed.

On my way to tinkle, I glanced in the kitchen and felt like I was looking back in time. Congress passed a law in the early eighties outlawing harvest-gold kitchen appliances. Unfortunately, the law was not retroactive, so existing harvest-gold appliances were not confiscated by the decorating police. It was assumed that the remaining kitschy kitchen devices would die a natural death within a few years and be replaced with something less dated. They hadn't counted on cheap landlords and far away rural towns.

One look at coiled burners, rust streaks, and paint bubbles told me that they were original equipment to the house. The cabinets were just as old but had been painted more times than a freeway bridge. Thirty years of paint filled in the routing work on its edges as effectively as putty, leaving just the hint of its former features. The floor was yellow linoleum. It might not have started that way, but that's what it was now. There were deep scrapes where heavy things had chiseled up the plastic strips and the yellow wasn't uniform; lighter where the sun could reach it, darker under the counters. I had a new respect for Roy having made such a nice dinner in such a shitty kitchen.

The bathroom was serviceable but just as dated. Cracked white tiles framed a more modern cream-colored sink beneath a cracked mirror. Pill bottles for depression, joint relief, and hair loss stood in a little orange pyramid by the faucet. The hot water was molten, the cold ice, each controlled by its own spigot. I felt like I was tuning an old radio as I dialed in a temperature that wouldn't destroy my flesh.

When I came back, Julie was standing up reading from a moleskin notebook:

> *What is fire, but briar and spires*
> *Above the desert, deserted*
> *Of life except where there is some.*

I'd been seen. It was too late to retreat. I sauntered over slowly, taking the long way around. To keep as much distance as possible from the literary crisis. I paused by the bookcase and perused some old photographs and a newspaper clipping declaring the *Stupid Stirps Gang Captured After Hour-Long Shootout.* "*The penny thieves couldn't hit the inside of a house while standing in it," says police chief.* The mugshots of the criminals stared out at me from fifty years before. A memory stirred but was then squashed when Julie changed her voice into a low reedy register to give emphasis to the most important passage of her poem so far.

> *"The sage is wise and the varmint cuddly*
> *But will he nip at my toes?*
> *Or my nose? No one knows."*

There was a thudding on the door. It wasn't a knock. I recognized the door-denting sound of a flashlight on the other side, the calling card of vandalism of a police visit.

Roy answered it, probably to get away from the poetry.

"Hello Mr. Stirps, I'm here to see Tony."

"Well if it isn't Acting Police Chief Lieutenant-Fuckwad-Herbert Levis, of the little brain, littler dick variety," I said loud enough to be heard in Flagstaff.

"I'll pretend you didn't say that." He pushed his way past Roy.

"Pretending is something you're good at," said I.

"I'm not here officially," he said.

"Oh good. Look, an intruder. Quick, get a gun." I looked at Roy expectantly. Levis' eyes widened then narrowed.

"Flaner, can I talk to you outside?" he said.

"Do I have to?"

"No."

"Then no."

"Okay, Flaner, if it's like that," he said. "I got a call from my cousin Ronald up in Salt Lake. He asked me if you've been down here the last few days. I didn't know for sure."

"Score one for truth, justice, and the American way."

His face blushed, but he carried on.

"It seems that his dog was kidnapped again."

"Couldn't have happened to a nicer person."

"He needs help," he said. "Why don't you go up there and find his pooch for him?"

"Why would I even think of doing that?"

"As a personal favor for me," he said. "They're family."

"They're not my family."

"No, but Sophia Curtis isn't either," he said.

"What's she got to do with this?"

"Nothing. It's just she might have things easier if you cooperate with me. You know, medicine delivered on time, sheets washed. Maybe even get a visitor. You know she hasn't been allowed any."

"You sack of shit," I said. "You just want to get me out of town."

"That's a bonus," he said. "The way I see it is you owe Ronald and Rosalyn-Janet. This is a chance to pay your debt. There's been some talk about transferring Sophia down to St. George. They have more room down there. Our little jail is so small."

It wasn't small. This man was.

I thought about Precious and the Levises. It did irk me that I'd lost the dog, but it pissed me off more that I'd been libeled by the Levis' rag of a publication. I remembered Sophia's terrified face under the oxygen mask and how I was responsible for putting it there.

"Okay," I said. "Sophia gets a visit from Allie tomorrow morning and anyone else from then on."

"According to policy," Levis said.

"Yeah, we'd hate to be treated differently than other citizens." I was being too subtle, or he ignored my slight.

"Fuck it," I said. "I'll leave in the morning."

42

HERBERT LEVIS LEFT.

"Is this about Precious?" Allie asked.

"The case of the kidnapped dog. Part two," I said.

"Not the missing dog?" said Julie. "I thought you looked familiar."

"You saw that, did you? Yeah, that's me, but look, I have a chance at redemption." I turned to Allie. "I gotta leave first thing in the morning. With any luck, I'll be back in a couple of days. A week at the outside."

We said our goodbyes. Julie packed up to leave too. The party was over, and Roy and Julie's relationship wasn't one that would invite a sleepover; a free dinner, but no sex. Not even a kiss goodnight.

I walked Allie to her door and kissed her goodnight. I kissed her long and passionately on her doorstep. Well on her lips, actually, we were standing on her doorstep. I'm not a freak.

Gandalf boomed a hello/goodbye, and I went back to Cottonwood Lane alone. I called Ronald Levis and arranged an appointment for noon the next day. That would give me enough time to sleep and drive. He praised the Lord and said that I have a chance at "atonement," a thing rarely offered to people like me. So I had that going for me.

Once at home, the day's many events blurred into swirled pudding and threatened to keep me up all night with a spoon. But I was beat. I fell on my bed. Fatigue from my sore hiked-legs spread up my body like a paralysis. Six hours later, I woke up in the same position I'd laid down in.

The sky was cloudless and bright which meant the air would freeze the tits of a mastodon. My car heater wasn't up to the task of the long drive, so I dressed warmly and pointed north. Before I-70, my brain was spitting out ideas like a belt-less tilt-a-whirl tosses children. I pulled over and found my beloved detective notebook, sadly neglected. So much had happened so quickly. It'd been two days since the auction, less than a week since Sophia was arrested. Guilt Buddy reminded me that I hadn't visited her in jail. I responded I couldn't have, Levis hadn't allowed her visitors.

"You could have tried harder," he said.

"So?"

"So you're a terrible friend."

"I've been busy."

"There's one you haven't used before."

"Shut up."

"Make me."

We had a heated argument at the side of the road. It got ugly. Passersby slowed to see what was wrong but sped away when they saw only me and my wild, angry eyes in the car.

"I won't be productive visiting her in jail!"

"Are you sure? What about that cryptic message about not losing the house?"

"I got the house, you snot-nosed scab-biter!"

"Do you kiss your kid with that mouth?"

"I'll punch you in your fat, ugly face if you don't shut up and let me think."

And so it went for twenty minutes until my voice gave out. Guilt Buddy had totally made me forget what I was going to write. I headed down the highway again, searching for that mental groove that made me fetch the pad to begin with.

An hour on the other side of Green River it started coming back to me, and soon the tilt-a-whirl was ready to throw toddlers against the chain link fence again. Then Guilt Buddy spoke up, adding comments like, "If you'd talked to Vicky in the last quarter century, I bet you'd be farther along now."

I shut him up with a Culture Club CD.

When he'd decided he didn't really want to hurt me, I turned it down.

A handful of mysteries I'd cracked—Crew, Tiponi, the Ashes, but I still didn't have the answer to the big one, the one I was looking for. I tried to congratulate myself on sleuthing the water ruse and the pot plantation, but it didn't help. I turned my mind to Salt Lake.

I should have told Ronald Levis where he could stick his mop dog, but Herbert Levis had me by the heartstrings with Sophia. It was extortion, and terrible, and I had witnesses if it came to that.

I acknowledge that there was also a sick masochism swimming in my overfed mind that made me agree to it. I hadn't given the Precious case any thought in a week beyond mentally spending a seven-figure libel payout, but nonetheless, gears had been turning behind the scenes and I felt hunches coming on like an Igor casting call. The Precious mess was unfinished, and

I'd sworn off not finishing things. I'd have to turn in my chip if I didn't do something.

I had a nagging feeling that I'd seen something at Roy's that was important, but I couldn't figure it out. Where do you get big wooden spools like that? Construction sites? Mines? IKEA? I didn't know what was eating at me or what it fit with, but I'd heard a click like a pajama snap in the dark. I thought hard about it, but it wasn't ready to come out yet. I was out of leads in Moab and hitting the detective wall. A little time and distance might help. Most of my best ideas come when I'm not really thinking. Sad, I know.

I stopped to replenish my bladder with truck stop coffee and found Gandalf's dog whistle in my pocket. It made me think of Allie, which was good, and then Precious, which was not as fun but also good.

With fresh caffeine, my mind found another gear. The pieces of the Precious mess bubbled and popped like mud farts in a Yellowstone pool, leaving me in a stink cloud with clear sinuses. I made notes in my Detective Notepad®.

I didn't know too much about the new mess the Levises were in. Ronald had only said he came home from slandering innocent people while espousing family values and the dog was gone, taken right out of his backyard. A phone call, like the one before, asked for $12,000 this time or they'd get a paw in the mail.

I wrote down $12,000 and then $10,000 nearly hitting a motorcycle I hadn't seen. Big numbers for a five-hundred-dollar dog, no matter how well Allie had trained it.

A smile crept onto my mouth. I felt like the Grinch sewing his red suit. I reached for my phone. It was early, eight o'clock, but I knew she'd be awake.

"Tony? What are you doing up this early? Are you in trouble?"

"Actually, Nancy, I've been up since five. It's hell, but I'm doing it."

"Doing what?"

"I'm coming back to Salt Lake to work on that stupid dog case again."

"Did you finish down in Moab?"

"Not hardly. Watch the road, you maggot!"

"I will if you will."

"Damn SUV with a trailer forgot he was twelve feet longer than usual. He passed me on a double line besides. Man, I've got to remember to buy bullets for my gun."

"What do you want, Tony?"

"You said that Randy wanted a set of drums, right?"

"Yes, very expensive electric ones."

"They were Asian, right? Cost about ten grand?"

"Yes. The Yabuchi X98-Z Alpha. I have the brochure. You aren't seriously considering buying them, are you?"

"Hell no. Where'd he hear about them?"

"Mitchell's Music, where we got the original drum set. The same salesman, more aggressive than ever. He would talk about nothing else but the Yabuchi electronic drum set. You'd swear he had stock in the company. It is the only electric drum set they have, and he talked it up like it was the second coming."

"Guaranteed to make you a great drummer?"

"Put Phil Collins to shame in a week; Ringo in two days," Nancy said. "He claimed to be the only retailer in the whole state that carried it in stock, but they were hard to keep in. Buy now. He was really pushy. I mean, I'm standing right there and he's talking to Randy in whispers, telling him how parents don't get it and how he should do whatever he had to for his art."

My grin widened as I tied an antler to a dog's head and prepared for Whoville.

"Thanks, Nancy."

I drove straight to Mitchell's Music in Salt Lake City.

I arrived just after eleven when they opened. I stretched away four hours of driving and stumbled to the door.

"Tell me about your drums," I said to the salesman I remembered from last summer. He wore a goatee that wouldn't have been out of place at a live Kerouac reading, but could get you slapped anywhere but an Apple store today.

"I have the best in the world right here." He pointed to a strange sculpture of white platforms and black dials in a web of chrome bars under a myriad of brass cymbals. It looked like a stick figure robot-spider juggling plates. "The Yabuchi X98 Zed-Alpha. On sale today for ninety-nine ninety-nine."

"How much is it usually?"

"Ten thousand."

"What a deal," I said. "You sell a lot of these, do you?"

"Enough."

"Where are they made?"

"Asia."

"You mean China."

"That's in Asia."

"You have some kind of pipeline to Chinese drum sets?"

"Are you from Customs?"

"No, you sold my kid a kit last summer. Now he thinks he needs one of these."

"He does."

"You remember him?"

"Not at all."

"But you're sure he needs a ten-thousand-dollar drum set?"

"Oh yeah." He grinned. "Absolutely positive. You need one too."

He stepped behind the set and selected a pair of drumsticks from a quiver taped to a chrome support. Memories of the aural beatings I'd received at Randy's school made me cringe and draw my hands to the sides of my head. He flicked a switch and a familiar Hammond organ polka beat issued from an unseen speaker. He raised the sticks. I raised my hands.

"I think I've heard them already," I said. "Didn't you sell a kit to Mark Levis?"

"Mark Levis? Oh, yeah. Goth-emo guy. One of the Entitled Offspring," he said. "That's the name of his band, not his situation."

"Works for all occasions. You sold it to him last week for ten K. Am I right?"

He nodded.

"Cash?"

He nodded again.

"Seen him since?"

"Yeah he has a Gibson guitar and two amps on layaway."

"Twelve thousand dollars?"

"How'd you know?"

"Slow-acting little gray cells," I replied.

I'd never been to the Levises' home before. When they hired me, they'd come to my place to inspect it. They wanted to make sure it was good enough for a dog. And it was. Just. They lived in a new McMansion in a new development of McMansions. There wasn't a house on the block with less than six thousand square feet inside and more than a hundred out. Outside living was so last century. It's not as if anyone could plant a garden or even a bed of grass. It'd die in the shade of the neighboring stucco monument twelve inches over the property line.

The circular driveway had a granite rock pile imitating art in the middle of it. Similar rocks were cemented to twelve-foot high pillars on the porch which flanked a narrow stone staircase ending in an arched door that could have kept out crusaders for a month. I found a little white plastic nub between two rocks and pressed it. From inside, I heard classical music chime from a tinny speaker.

Rosalyn-Janet opened the door. I recognized her blue hair in the pink curlers. Her makeup was postmodern grief, vertical streaks of mascara and foundation flooding under her eyes to pool in the folds of her neck.

"Mrs. Levis. Don't you look wonderful," I said.

She sniffled and stepped aside for me to come in.

The house was professionally decorated. Everything in each room matched everything else in that room and nothing looked welcoming in the least. It had the look, feel, and smell of a furniture showroom. The feeling was encouraged when I went from a Western American entryway into a Japanese-themed living room. I glimpsed a French Colonial dining room through a Moorish arch. I knew nothing was older than the brand new house, even though every piece had been masterfully scratched and marred to imitate antiques. Someone had gone overboard with crackle paint on the white pioneer cabinets by the closet. It looked like the canyons of Rosalyn-Janet's neck.

I saw a dozen photos of Precious, the missing American cocker spaniel. Many were professionally done in a studio and Precious stared at the camera under a birthday hat in one and a ballerina tutu in another. There was a wall of photos of other dogs I didn't know. Precious' predecessors I figured. I didn't see a single picture of Cousin Herbert, son Mark, or any other human not in my direct company.

"Mr. Flaner," said Ronald from the couch. He wore a dinner jacket that was five hours too early and fifty years too late. "I'm so glad you came."

"You have learned extortion," I said. "Herbert was persuasive."

He frowned.

"You know your little libelous newspaper has caused me trouble," I said. "And I haven't been paid."

"Water under the bridge," he said.

I gotta remember to buy bullets.

"I think I can solve this case, but it'll cost you," I said.

Rosalyn-Janet snorted. Ronald looked at me hard.

"What do you want?" he said.

"I want a glowing, and I mean glowing front-page apology for your previous libel. Five pages of groveling. If you do that, my attorney and I might not pursue you in court."

He stuttered, surprised by my intensity. "What I said in the paper—"

"Could cost you millions," I said. "I've got nothing to lose here. You do."

He thought about it. More sniffles from Mrs. Levis.

"And," I said, "I want five thousand dollars. Cash."

"That's extortion."

"I learned it from you."

"How do we know you aren't behind all this to begin with?"

"Because you may be evil clowns, but you are also totally stupid." He wasn't convinced. "Why'd you call me then?"

"Mark said he didn't think you did it. He said we'd set ourselves up for a legal mess for last month's paper. We thought we'd show goodwill by giving you a chance to fix things."

"You think I have things to fix?" I said. "Why haven't you thrown yourself under a bus?"

"Redemption," he said like it answered both questions.

"Yeah, you mentioned that on the phone. I'm not sure it applies here. I know the word."

There was an awkward moment of sniffling. I glanced at my watch and thought of Allison.

"Show me where the dog was taken," I said.

Ronald showed me the laundry room done in dental-bleached white panels. A muddy white flappy ten-inch dog exit was inset into a wooden door that led to the back yard. We went out.

What they considered a backyard, Allie would call a planter. It was five feet deep and twenty feet wide and paved with plastic grass undimmed by the hot Utah sun or cold Utah snow. A row of plastic twirling sunflowers stood like statues rusted in place in the stale unmoving air of the enclosure. I could glimpse sky between the houses, but not much. The "yard" was surrounded by an eight-foot-high vinyl fence. At the far end, a single gate with a ridiculous three-pound padlock hung on a fifty-cent hasp. The hinges would pop from a ragweed sneeze. I congratulated the salesman on selling Ronald the lock.

"Who has a key to that lock?" I said.

"There's one in the cabinet. That's the only one I know of," said Ronald.

"Is it still in there?"

"Yes. I checked after Precious was stolen."

I stepped carefully over little Precious landmines and examined the lock and gate. It had not been kicked in or sneezed at. The lock could be reached from the other side if there was something to stand on, but the fence was easily climbed anyway. I hoisted myself up and saw a row of municipal plastic garbage cans the perfect height to scale the fence.

I carefully walked back across the yard and into the house. The Levises followed me. We were joined by an unpleasant smell. Someone had not been as careful walking as I had been.

"When are you supposed to pay?"

"Monday. The same way we did it last time. Bag in the mall."

"Very *Jackie Brown*," I said. "You planning on paying it?"

"Of course we'll pay it," shrieked Rosalyn-Janet. "She's my baby."

Ronald was not as sure. "If we have to," he said.

"What's to prevent them from doing it again?" I asked.

"They promised this would be the last time," Rosalyn-Janet said.

"It will be the last time until the next time. Unless I solve it."

"So you'll take the case?"

"Do you agree to my terms?"

"Five-page groveling apology and five thousand dollars?" Ronald said indignantly.

"Yes. Yes we will," inserted Rosalyn-Janet.

"Put it in writing right now and I'll get working on it. Go ahead and write the check while you're at it."

"I can't just write five pages now," Ronald said. "That's a lot."

"Just put in writing that you'll write it, and that I get final approval over what's said, up to and including writing it myself if I have to. You'll publish it in your *Family Values* coupon rag next month. And don't forget the five big ones."

"Mr. Flaner—" began Ronald.

"Would you recognize Precious' severed paw, Mrs. Levis? I mean, if it arrived by mail in a cardboard box and bloody Kleenex? Would you know it?"

She shrieked and staggered to a chair, her arm over her forehead like a silent movie melodrama. She flopped into it, not fainting yet, but on the verge.

"Alright, alright," said Ronald. "But you get nothing unless you catch the creeps who did this. And we get our dog back—without us having to pay the ransom."

He was so clever with his details. "Deal," I said.

He went over to a desk you could land a plane on and scribbled on a yellow pad.

Mrs. Levis slumped in her chair and hyperventilated.

Soon Ronald got up and gave me the letter. I asked Mrs. Levis to witness it. I don't know what good it would do, or even if this document would stand up, but it didn't matter. They'd do as I wanted, or I'd drop the five thousand on a lawyer's retainer and sue the shit out of them.

"And the check?" I said.

"When you solve the case," he said.

"Pull out your checkbook," I said. "You can date it for tomorrow. One more thing."

"Something else?"

"Yeah, aren't I a pain? It must be awful for you."

"What is it?" asked Ronald.

"Tell that inbred, kissing-cousin cop of yours down in Moab to be nice, and I mean really nice to me and mine. If he isn't, if he lays another hand on me or bends a hair on my Aunt Sophia's head, I will drag him through the mud with you. You can explain in your newspaper how you perverted the course of justice, had your policeman cousin beat me up and threaten me on your behalf."

"We didn't—"

"Tell it to the public after I tell it to the papers," I said. "The real papers. And the judge."

"Who's Sophia?" asked Ronald.

"Just do it or I'm walking out, and you can get your dog back by parcel post once a week for a month."

"Do it," shrieked Rosalyn-Janet.

Ronald wrote a check and promised to call Herbert right away.

I inspected the check holding it up to the light for effect.

"You know it's a federal crime to write checks you don't intend to honor?"

He stared at me, hatred, fear, and loathing—but not the cigarette-holder, acid-head kind that pursued the American Dream to Las Vegas. This was just nasty. I'd gotten to him, which was really nice. I savored it for two uncomfortable excruciating minutes while Ronald squirmed, and Rosalyn-Janet wept. Who the hell calls their child Rosalyn-Janet? What adult lets themselves get called Rosalyn-Janet? I was suddenly so sick of the Levises I wanted to firebomb the block. I thought of Allison and her soft earlobes and put aside my petty torture after only another long squirmy minute.

"Mark has Precious," I said. "Go to his apartment, I'm sure that's where he has her."

"Mark? Mark who?" said Ronald.

"Mark Levis," I said. "Your son. One of the Entitled Offspring."

"What?" said Rosalyn-Janet.

"That's the name of his band. He has your dog. He wants to buy a guitar to go with his drums."

"I don't understand?" said Rosalyn-Janet.

"I'll call him," Ronald said, reaching for a phone.

"Don't," I said. "You have one of these, right?" I held up Gandalf's whistle I still had from the Ranch hike and swung it like a hypnotist's watch. The couple followed it earnestly and nodded.

"You will be better people," I droned. "You will stop being total douchebags and value your human family." Maybe the suggestion lodged in their subconscious, maybe it didn't. I wanted earlobes.

"Okay, take your whistle and go to Mark's apartment," I said while moving toward the door. "Do it now. If you call him, he'll panic, move the dog, maybe cut off a paw if he's feeling really hardcore. I doubt he'd do it, but why risk it? When he won't let you in, blow the whistle and your Precious will come running like Gollum after a fish. Just like she ran from me to the car in the park. Allison Braise trained the dog to do that so it wouldn't get away. Mark knows that. He picked up Precious for you in Moab. Did you know that? Doesn't matter. It'll work. Even if the dog's in a closet, it'll go bat shit trying to come to that whistle. Understand?"

"Mark has Precious?" Ronald said.

I exhaled a long, loud, exasperated sigh and put the check in my pocket with the whistle.

"Okay," I said. "I'll go over it again. Get me a piece of paper and some colored pencils. Glitter and string wouldn't hurt either. I'll draw it out for you, then, if you're good, we'll have crackers and juice."

43

AFTER A LONG, detailed description of my clues and reasonings, I finally walked the Levises to their car and sent them to Mark's.

I drove to Nancy's house. It was a nice Saturday afternoon, and I felt a powerful urge to see my son. I needed to wash my palate of the terrible parenting that had put dog photos on the wall and not a son's. I slipped into woolgathering. I remembered the photos of Rick on Vicky's wall, her photo albums, and her devotion to her boys.

Rick had struggled in school, continually ignoring consequences but was happy and loving. They were poor in money, but rich in love. Clichéd but true. Vicky always had time for Rick. When we'd come home from school, she'd give him a big hug and then look him over from head to toe. She might have been looking for new injuries and bruises, but there was also a sense of pride and a moment of sheer pleasure in looking at her son. If he had new wounds, and he often did, she'd tend to them carefully and lovingly, offering only a single word of rebuke for his carelessness and then soothing the wound's emotional and physical injury with a mother's care. She tended many wounds. There were deep scratches he'd earned by a shortcut through a rose bush, a pencil stab where he'd sat on his backpack, and a new dog bite from his attempt to make friends with the poodle down the street. That damn poodle nearly took a finger off me when it'd finished with Rick. Each time, Aunt Vicky would drop whatever she was doing, turn off the stove, put away her crafts, collect the first aid kit and ask about his day. One of my best days was when the poodle nipped me. Vicky tended to me with the same care she gave her son, and I felt truly loved. It occurred to me that Rick might have deliberately injured himself so he could have those moments. He wasn't dumb at all.

I remembered one Saturday we went to the park to play Frisbee. I was pretty good, and Rick was learning fast. Vicky knew the things existed but had never touched one before that day. We made an ever-shrinking triangle until she could just hand the disk to Rick. She finally got tired of chasing her missed ones and sat down on a blanket with a bucket of chicken she treated like gold. Rick dove for a catch and landed in the river. I felt bad because I hadn't even tossed it yet. The air was cold, the water colder. We bundled Rick up in the blanket and sitting on the grass, had a feast of the Colonel's best. Guilt Buddy connected my memories and showed me that Vicky had bought that chicken because I'd wanted it. It was expensive, and she didn't eat any of it, letting Rick and I gorge ourselves in grease. I'd let myself think she'd had some, but she hadn't. The smile on her face was not contentment from food, but from family. There was so much warmth there. Maybe that's what poverty does to people, makes them appreciate the little—no, the big things in life.

Mark felt entitled to something from his family. He wanted money from them now, felt he should get it and maybe he should, but any psychology major with dreadlocks and a questionable career path would tell you that he was seeking more from his parents than cash for musical instruments. The Levises were too stupid to realize their failure, and it was probably too late to fix it if they did. I wondered what they'd do to Mark. He'd struck me as a lost but nice kid. His parents were an unpleasant vindictive couple. Would their wrath extend to their own son? Of course it would. Only their pride would keep them from pressing charges, well that and the fear of bad press. People in glass family-valued houses and all that.

Randy was home and came down to see me when Nancy let me in. He still had a hint of his Hawaiian tan.

"Come on," I said. "We're going to the park to play frisbee." I included Nancy in my invitation.

"It's forty degrees," she said.

"Yeah, Dad, it's pretty cold."

"Forty-three," I corrected them. It didn't have the desired effect.

Nancy looked at me with long-knowing eyes but said nothing.

"Okay, how about a board game? *Settlers of Catan*?"

"Now?" Randy said.

"Why not now?" said Nancy. "Your father is a busy man, and it's a Saturday afternoon. And if not a board game, I think he'll make us freeze outside."

"You know it," I said.

We sat at the kitchen table and played half a dozen games. Randy won them all. Even the last one where Nancy and I openly teamed up to defeat him. It was embarrassing but fun. We ordered Chinese Food, and I stayed for dinner. I told Nancy I couldn't sleep over. She wasn't going to offer, but I thought I'd make it clear that I was spoken for.

"Allison Braise?"

"Maybe," I said. Nancy blushed. She hadn't been overly jealous in our entire marriage, if you could call it a marriage. It descended into a room-sharing arrangement pretty quick. However, she knew my childhood past in Moab and knew that Allison Braise held a special place in my life and my heart. I don't think she was jealous of Allie as much as of me for fulfilling a lifelong desire. I couldn't help it, I smiled. She scowled just a little before she caught herself and set the table.

My phone rang during a mouthful of moo goo gai pan.

"Oh god," I said, noting the blocked extension. "This could be bad."

I expected to hear Ronald Levis on the other end of the phone screaming at me for besmirching his family name with wild accusations. I was pretty sure Mark was behind the Precious-napping, but I'd been wrong before. Many many many times before.

It was Allie.

"They're going to let Sophia out tomorrow," she said.

"What? When did this happen?"

"Danny just drove by to tell me. Levis was holding up her appearance before the judge and he backed down. She'll go before the judge in the morning and the prosecution will allow release on her own recognizance. That means she won't have to come up with bail."

I knew what released on your own recognizance meant. I'd heard the phrase often, usually with the word "denied" after it.

"That's great," I said.

"When will you be back?"

"Tomorrow."

"Is the house a mess?" she asked.

"The walls are clean."

"Would you mind if I went over and tidied things up?"

"You saw the house when you picked me up yesterday," I said.

"Yeah, I did. That's why I'm asking."

"Oh. Well okay. Make it nice. Get some flowers and stuff. And Pop-Tarts."

"She likes Pop-Tarts?"

"I don't know. But I do," I said. "What time will she be released, you think?"

"By ten for sure," she said.

"I'll try to be there by then. If I'm not, could you pick her up?"

"Of course."

"Don't let her be alone."

"I won't. Do you think you'll be delayed?"

"No. It's a good sign that Levis relented. It means that either he found a conscience or his cousin called him."

"I don't think he has a conscience."

"Which means my machinations have worked. With any luck, there's a family in counseling right now."

"You'll have to explain all this when I see you again."

"Count on it."

"I gotta go," she said.

"See you soon," I said. "Love you."

It was an automatic response. I'd said the same thing to my dentist's receptionist when he called to confirm an appointment. I'd said it to insulation installers when scheduling an inspection. I may have said it to Ronald Levis when he was in Florida. All on accident. All without meaning. Just a habit. A slip of the tongue, a Freudian sleep with your mother.

Nancy caught it and stopped chewing. She watched me closely.

I rolled my eyes in exasperation but then, across hundreds of miles of desert and mountain, Allie said, "I love you too." I felt my heart skip a beat and then race triple speed to catch it up. My face went red. Nancy's white. My whole body surged with pumping blood and adrenaline and even my arms blushed. My hands were wet and clammy, and my ears burned hotter than my cheeks which threatened to ignite my eyebrows. Nancy scowled ever so slightly, then turned to look at Randy savagely biting an egg roll.

"See you soon." I hung up. I scooped some more rice onto my plate. "Well, that was good news."

"Looked like it," said Randy.

"Aunt Sophia is getting out of jail tomorrow," I said.

"Who's Aunt Sophia?" asked Nancy.

"Why is she in jail?" asked Randy.

"Oh, right."

I told them the long story of my adventures in Moab, careful to leave out the sex in the sand and the shower, and other specific events, like me getting stoned with people I thought were going to kill me.

Nancy served coconut ice cream as I finished the side tale of the Levises and their son Mark who needed drums so badly he'd commit crimes to get them.

Nancy and I both glared at Randy.

"Okay, okay. I don't need the drums that bad," he said. "But I shouldn't ignore my art."

"I thought your art was computers?" I said.

"Can't an artist have several modes of expression?"

"Well, yes, I guess they can. People can be many different things. A father and a detective, a mother and real estate broker, a ranger and a grandson."

"That's not what I meant," he said.

"A ranger and a grandson," I repeated, wheels turning.

"Yeah, you said that."

"Sorry. Great ice cream, Nancy."

"It's homemade," she said proudly. "Mother, million-dollar real estate broker, and ice cream maker."

We finished the evening sitting around the living room telling stories and just hanging out. It was a moment we'd never had while I lived in the house. There'd been walls and barriers that being divorced somehow took down. We laughed and told lies and embellished tales. I told them about Rick and the rattlesnake, the skunks, and the hornets. I told the forgotten tales of our family and the newer iterations. I felt a connection reaching across time and people, or maybe it was the Chinese food not sitting well. Who knows how long that fried rice had sat out? Randy wanted to know if Haggy Miller had an email account so he could fill it with porn. I said I'd find out.

A little past nine, I got up to go. Randy went up to his room to his online friends and computer games after giving me a good, long, enriching hug. Nancy gave me a kiss on the cheek.

"Thanks for today," I said. "I know I should have called and arranged it. I took up your whole day."

"I'd have ducked it if you'd given me the chance. It was good you just dropped by. Really good. I could tell you needed us, and it was really good to have you."

Nancy had been a meddling wife, but she was a great friend.

"Take care of yourself," she said. "Say hi to your adopted Aunt Sophia for me."

"And Allie?" I said before I could stop myself.

"Some people have all the luck." She pushed me out the door.

I left my old home with a new skip in my step. I felt grounded but ready for take off. My thoughts bounced between Randy and Allie, Salt Lake and Moab, the snow and the desert.

Allie's words, well, four of them, ran through my mind as I pulled into my driveway. I was two hundred-fifty miles away when I lowered the garage door and threw my bag into the hall. I'd left some lights on, I guess. My neighbors had probably left me a nasty note explaining how every time I forget to switch off a light another rainforest dies. Or is it an angel gets its wings and a kitten dies? I'd check the note in the morning.

He jumped me in the living room. He slammed me across my easy chair with a high-sticking hockey check. Without a plexiglass wall to smash into and drunk fans to chuck cups of stale beer at me, there was no way I was going to get the call. Where's a referee when you need one?

I tumbled onto the floor. I was careful not to hit my bruised elbow or my stitched brow. The back of my skull broke my fall against the coffee table. Plenty of padding there if I didn't need to know algebra.

I stared over my feet and saw Benjamin James Ulrich advancing on me with my metal detector. He'd obviously had some time to search the house. A quick glance at the open drawers and modern confetti motif proved that. He'd been in my hobby collection. I'd been suckered into buying a top-of-the-line metal detector at a survivalist show I'd paid twenty dollars to get in to. Between taste tests of freeze-dried chili and posters of edible fungus and lichen, one guy promised riches galore waiting to be found in every park, beach, and trail in the country. Millions of dollars in lost diamond wedding rings, rare coins, and Aztec gold had been lost in these public places. All were waiting to be found like Aladdin's cave with a twelve-inch Deepsearch Spider Coil Pulse Induction Tech Treasure Hunter 8000. And don't even get him started on geo-caching. I'd paid five-hundred dollars for that thing when I could spend five hundred dollars on a whim like that, i.e., married to Nancy, the real estate millionaire. I'd spent two months fighting other treasure seekers for territory at Liberty Park. It got ugly, so this wasn't the first time I'd been attacked with a metal detector, it was however, the first time I'd been hit by my own.

"What is your malfunction!" I yelled, pulling my feet off the chair, the better to put them beneath me and propel me away.

"I'm going to mess you up." Benjamin knocked the chair over. He tossed the precision magnetic device aside and raised his foot for a gut stomp. I rolled aside, and the foot slammed the floor behind me.

I scampered behind the chair, holding it between us. I looked up at Delores' ex-husband and felt pity for my assassin. His nose was swollen from goblin pounding and black from frostbite. His clothes were torn and dirty. Dried blood caked his shirt down his chest where his nose had poured open. His eyes were sickly yellow plum holes. The splint on his finger was now wrapped with an inch of silver duct tape and included his entire hand and wrist. He favored his left leg, hopping around the chair, first right then left as I shifted. The leash welts across his face, neck, and arms had gone down and were just ugly red bruises now, but I noticed a pair of neat new burns on his neck under his ear, the recognizable love bite from an Indian Casino stun gun. The burns oozed infected puss onto his already stained collar like he was an unfinished vampire lunch.

He looked at me with his two black eyes which made me think of Mog as I'm sure Benjamin did too every time he saw them in a mirror.

"No one's here to save you this time," Ulrich said.

"Why are you doing this?"

"I'm going to mess you up."

"I got that part. I'm looking for a deeper motivation. Look inward. Why do you want to hurt me so bad?"

With his untaped hand, he ripped the chair away and tossed it in the other direction of the metal detector. I turned to run, but he was quick.

He had me by the back of my shirt and pulled me down with a prison-muscle tug that made guards keep their distance.

My feet flew out from under me, and I crashed into his chest. I'd surprised him by being so easy to catch and he stumbled to keep his balance. His bad leg gave way beneath him with a terrible popping sound as we both fell backward in a heap. He screamed. At first, I thought it was his knee, but as his grip released and I rolled off him, his hands flew to his crotch where my heavy blunt skull had landed in the fall.

Amid terrible howls of unspeakable curses from my attacker, I crawled to my bag. My own loins puckered and tried to pull back in masculine sympathy.

I dumped my stuff. I saw Benjamin limping toward me, tears running down his cheeks, his teeth gritted so hard I could smell the crushed enamel. He had the metal detector again but was using it as a cane. He dragged himself toward me.

My hand fell on my revolver. I grabbed it and scooted back against the garage door. I raised it with both hands and aimed right between Benjamin James Ulrich's swollen eyes.

"Did you notice this big-ass gun pointed at your fat head?" I asked.

He paused and wiped tears from his face. He squinted at me.

I reached up and turned on the light. My shiny silver revolver sparkled in the environmentally friendly, low-watt LED bulbs.

"Oh, shit," he said.

I got to my feet.

Benjamin just kind of swayed there.

"Back up, Benji," I said. "Back all the way to the living room."

He did.

As much as he could, he kept his eyes on me and my gun, but they teared up. He nearly fell several times when the five-hundred-dollar aluminum cane he had kept slipping on the carpet.

"Sit down on the couch," I said.

He did.

"Keep your hands where I can see them."

He did this too.

He was visibly relieved to get off his feet. He breathed easier. Instead of short bursts of inhalation and sudden exhales, he fell into an almost human rhythm.

My phone was still in the car.

I righted the chair. Keeping the gun pointed level and true at my attacker's chest, I dug through a pile of spilled papers until I found a cord which eventually led me to a docking station where I was able to signal a telephone handset to chirp behind a curtain. Benjamin had tossed my house pretty well, but to be fair, I remember ditching the phone behind the curtain myself. Damn telemarketers.

"Can I lower my arms?" he said.

"Why? You look strong enough to keep them up forever."

"I want to rub my balls."

Who was I to interfere with a man's personal pleasure?

"Okay."

I dialed the police while he rearranged his gonads into a less painful position.

"The cops are on their way," I said. "They're going to lock you up, you know? You've broken your parole."

"Yeah, I know that. That was the plan. I'll have to serve out the rest of my sentence, a year. They'll tack another six to eight months for the violation and if you press charges, that'll be another eighteen months. Maybe two years. Are you going to press charges?"

I looked around my wrecked house. "What do you think?" I said.

"This is just trespassing and vandalism," he said. "I've got to get an assault and battery if I want the two years."

"What the hell are you talking about?" I said.

"Mind if I take off my belt? I gotta get my hand down there."

"Sure. Go take inventory. But I'm watching," I said. "Eww."

He snapped open the Eisenhower dollar belt buckle and opened his pants. I saw again the stern face of our thirty-fourth president. He had the good sense to look away as Benjamin slid his better hand between his spread legs and moaned.

"You know when I was a kid, I used to keep quarters in my shoes in case I needed to make a phone call," I said. "Is that what the dollar's for? An emergency McMuffin or something?"

"Are you kidding? This is an actual silver dollar," he said.

"So a Happy Meal?"

"It's a collector's item. A genuine 1976-D Type 1 Bicentennial Eisenhower dollar coin. ANACS MS67," he said. "It's worth a couple grand at least."

"Oh. Wait, we're getting off track here," I said. "Why are you trying to kill me?"

"I'm not trying to kill you," he said, surprised. "What makes you think I'm trying to kill you?"

I pointed to the stitches above my eye.

"I did that?"

"Yes."

He blinked several times and squinted at my head.

"I don't know if that's enough," he concluded.

"Start making sense, or I'm taking your buckle."

"You can't do that. It was a gift from my daddy. It's the only thing he left me. It's my inheritance."

"Did he abandon you or die?"

"Both. In that order," he said. "All my people are dead. I got nobody. Nobody but Delores."

"I don't mean to talk out of school, but weren't you two divorced? Years and years ago?"

"Yeah, but she is still my wife."

"Ex-wife," I said.

"Same thing."

"Not really. If you love her, why'd you divorce?"

"We didn't love each other."

"But you do now?"

"No. Can't stand her. She hates me too."

I scratched my ear with the barrel of my gun and shook my head.

"Then why are you beating people up for her?"

"Delores is the only family I got. I gotta fight for her, don't I? You fight for your family. Right or wrong, it's your blood. You do whatcha gotta do for your family. Besides, since I gotta beat up somebody anyway, it might as well be her new boyfriend. Make sure he's good enough for her."

"You're nuts. You know that?"

He shrugged and pulled his hand out of his pants and leaned back.

"Prison's not so bad," he said. "Free room and board. Exercise, friends, discipline. It's a good life. I've been taking these correspondence courses for inmates. When I get out next time, I'll have a Bachelor's Degree in Social Work with a minor in Developmentally Challenged Children's Education, all but the work training. I'll be rehabilitated and ready to start a new life-affirming career helping out the less fortunate and retarded."

"You got it all worked out then?" I said.

"Except you haven't been hit hard. I don't think that little love tap there will get me what I need." He leaned forward.

I raised the gun and cocked the hammer.

"Wait a goddamn minute," he said.

"What?" I tensed up.

"You got no bullets in that gun."

"Yes, I do."

"No. I can see nothing but empty chambers."

That was a problem with revolvers. They're very reliable, stylish, and cool, but you can see into the chambers. I considered asking Benjamin if he'd run across my bullets while trashing my house.

"There is one bullet in the gun," I said. "And it's sitting under the hammer right now."

"No, there ain't," he said. "I saw the empty chambers before you cocked it. That there is a paperweight. You're empty, boy."

"I'm older than you," I said as he stood up.

I stood up too.

We stared at each other, Benjamin sizing up two years' worth of damage on my jaw and me calculating the steps to the door. Just then, we heard the distant wail of oncoming police cars.

He limped toward me, and I bolted for my bedroom.

I slammed the door and locked it. I pulled up my mattress and leaned it against the door. It didn't add any strength to the barrier, but I figured my yellow duckie fitted sheets might confuse him long enough for me to climb through a window.

I waited for the door to be knocked down, but it didn't happen.

After a few minutes, the phone rang. I picked it up.

"Mr. Flaner?"

"Yes," I said.

"This is the police. We're in your living room. You can come out now."

44

"LOOK AT THIS MESS. Isn't this a crime?"

"No one's here. Nothing's stolen or broken."

"But he broke in," I said. "Breaking and entering is still illegal, isn't it? Because if it isn't, I see new career opportunities opening up."

"There's no sign of a break-in," said Policeman Petersen. He was the same cop who'd hassled me about Precious' non-stop yapping serenade the day I first heard from Allie. It seemed like a million years ago. It was more like a fortnight. Maybe a fifth.

"Look at this place."

"That's messiness. For all we know, you did this yourself. Actually, Tony, I do know you did it yourself. I was here."

"You live like a slob." It was the other policeman. Two cars had come to my rescue. My nice Sugarhouse neighborhood, full of upper-middle-class, election-donating white people, brought two police cars at speed to my door. I didn't know this cop, or maybe I did and didn't remember. His name was Perez, and he acted like he knew me. His cold stares and amused smirks made me remember the deep-seated loathing I hold for all policemen, which I'd developed from firsthand experience with beatings, taser burns, and gunshot wounds.

"Do you keep a hidden key around the house?" asked Petersen.

"Yeah," I said.

Perez chortled. I hate chortlers.

"Have you checked it?"

Like all good fathers, drunken bachelors, and stupid homeowners, I keep a hidden key so I can't lock myself out. Mine was kept under a concrete gargoyle at the side of the house. It was gone when I checked it.

"Well, he didn't have permission to enter," I said when I came back.

Perez chortled some more. "Trespassing," he said. "Or maybe you invited him here and told him where the key was. I assume it was under that obvious gargoyle by the side of the house. Maybe this is all just a lover's spat or a drug deal gone wrong and you're trying to get even with a vulnerable ex-con just trying to start his life over. Seen it before. It's a low snake-like thing to do, but the world has all types." He squinted at me. I hate squinters.

"Petersen," I said to the other cop. "Ulrich said he's got to beat me up, so he'll get sent back to prison. He threatened me. Aren't you going to do something about this?"

"Likely story," chortled squinty Perez. "There are plenty of better ways to go to jail than messing with a turd like you."

"He had it planned, measured, and timed," I protested.

Chortle.

Petersen stepped in when my ears went red. "Tony, come down to the station tomorrow and make a report. If we run across him, we'll question him. We're not going to throw a dragnet over the city because he rearranged your pillows."

I stared in disbelief.

Petersen looked apologetic. Perez looked pleased.

"Isn't it your job to protect taxpayers like me? It's not like I'm sending my kids to climb a bone-breaking arch?"

"What?" said Petersen. He must have missed the earlier chapter.

"We all have jobs to do," said Perez. "Sometimes we can be bothered to do it, other times we're just too lazy and let an adorable cocker spaniel be snatched right under our noses to the torment of its loving owners."

"So you clip coupons," I said. "They got the dog back, you know."

"No thanks to you."

"I'll take a report of vandalism," said Petersen, "but you'll have to come down tomorrow and swear out the rest. Maybe you can get a restraining order against him."

"He's broken parole," I said.

"Allegedly," said Perez.

"Okay, wait. He stole my metal detector. It cost five hundred dollars. That's theft. That's illegal."

"No, he didn't. I saw it in the driveway when we pulled up. Next to the motorcycle tracks."

"Come in tomorrow, Tony," said Petersen. "Lock your doors. You'll be safe here. I don't think he'll come back tonight."

Perez winked.

I signed the paper, and they scuttled away. I waved at my neighbors, who scowled at me with blepharoplasty-brightened eyes.

"Go haunt a house," I said.

I broke the head off a broom and slid the handle into the tracks of my sliding door. I locked it and X-ed masking tape across it to minimize the shatter when it got smashed in later. I checked all the doors and windows and then packed my bag. No way in hell was I going to stay there that night. The cops might think that Benjamin would stay away, that was the reasonable thing to do. But I'd talked to Benjamin. Reasonable had nothing to do with it. He'd be back. Besides, I had a cleaned vacuumed house down south and the company of Allison Braise. Sophia would be out in the morning. Guilt Buddy seconded the motion that I should be there when she was sprung.

I was up for another drive and more thinking time. I still had a good stinging adrenaline buzz going, part fear, part anger, part frustration. A little caffeine in Provo should get me home if they sold it there. I made sure I had ID.

New input greased old gears and my mind spun up with new questions for old answers. I wrote that down in my notebook. What a great detective line.

I left the porch light on and barricaded the front door with my rag-doll easy chair. I spared only five minutes looking unsuccessfully for bullets then threw more socks on the pile and re-crammed my bag, empty gun and all.

I nearly backed over my Treasure Hunter 8000. I caught a glimpse of an aluminum pole in my mirror an instant before I ground my old hobby into the driveway. In a crouching serpentine dash, I hauled the machine to the car and tossed it in the back seat. I dove off, expecting to hear a bullet ricocheting off my hood, but there was nothing.

"Calm down, Tony," I said to myself. "He's just going to beat you up. Not kill you." That realization didn't offer as much consolation as you'd think it would.

Ducked low, barely able to see over the dashboard, I drove south and didn't turn on my lights for three blocks.

It occurred to me around midnight when I left the snow clouds behind me and sped across a deserted highway under clear frozen skies, that I could be a long-distance driver after all. I could make money while I worked on my cases. I'd need the money if I couldn't figure out a way to pay for the house. The bank had been pretty lax about accepting me as buyer. I expected a pile of forms, but Weaks was quick out of the auction. His replacement would want some assurance I'd make payments. The fucker.

I couldn't wrap my mind around Vicky's house being mine. It was Vicky's and Rick's. I was a visitor and probably always would be until I got the old people smell out and hung some black light posters in the bathroom. Still, they'd always be there. And that, I knew, is why I bought it. I'd remember the time Rick tried to climb through the ducts under the house and had to be cut out by a fireman with a grinder. That happened before school started. There was the time Rick ate his own homework when he couldn't find a dog to do it. The hospital wasn't so formal in those days. I remember when Vicky made spaghetti three days in a row because it was our favorite and school started in three days. Those were great times, full of Band-Aids and memories that fit into a compartment of my life I'd boxed and sealed and kept hidden way too long. Too many years had gone by without me thinking of those days. I needed more days like them to keep them alive.

I stopped around Price for a coffee. It was two in the morning, no longer Saturday, and the truck stop was hopping like a nightclub. Freshly showered truckers walked through the convenience store from the trucker's bathroom to their idling vehicles, their hair freezing solid before they opened their cabs. Loud music played in the café and two couples danced in the dimmed light where tables had been pushed aside. It was another world. I stood behind a black-bearded cap-wearing trucker with blazing bloodshot eyes and a stack of romance books-on-tape at the register.

"You need some NoDoz," the cashier asked me, looking at my tired face. The adrenaline was long gone.

"I think the coffee will do it," I said.

"Are you sure? I have NoDoz," she said. "And other stuff."

"Okay, I'll take some other stuff," I said just to make the joke.

She rang up the coffee and slid a breath-mint tin across the counter after surveying the room.

"That'll be eighty-five dollars," she said. "Coffee is free."

I looked at the tin and then at her. She smiled and nodded approvingly. Her hair was sculpted to her head with enough aerosol plastic hairspray to waterproof a schooner, but she was friendly and retro in just the way my thoughts floated.

"Oh, nuts," she said, looking at the hundred-dollar bill I gave her.

"What?"

"I don't have change," she said. "I can't ring this up normally. Do you mind if I give your rolls?"

"Rolls?"

"Dimes." She put three five-dollar cylinders of coins next to the tin. "I'm out of quarters. The boys use those for the laundry."

"These are fine."

I sat down at a plastic Subway booth chair and watched the orange running lights of a dozen semis twinkle outside in the cold.

I sipped my coffee and opened the tin. It contained five clear capsules with a pink powder inside. I caught the eye of the clerk who was piling cartons of Camel no filters ten high. I mouthed, "How many?"

She winked at me, which I took to mean as many as I wanted. I swallowed two pills.

There are some people who'd say buying unspecified tablets from a big-haired truck stop cashier in the tiny hours of a Sunday morning in Utah was foolhardy. Those people might also think that eating those same pills then, and there was the ultimate act of stupidity, a cry for help, sad proof of a lingering unhealthy drug habit, but to them, I'd just say, uhm...what's your point?

I waited for the pills to do something while sipping coffee hot enough to blister. I rolled the dimes across the table and then held each in my fist, transforming my hands into deadly dime weapons.

When I started seeing noises, I got up and stretched.

I felt pretty good. Actually I felt great. I no longer needed sleep. I don't think I needed food. Air was also optional, but since it was free, I helped myself. I moved to my car at speeds just below sound so not to wake the sleepers. I got in, turned the car south, and following the aura signatures of the familiar road, I drove back to Moab.

My thoughts were fast and electric. Bright bursts of insight, answers and understanding appeared and then dissolved into something else. For a brief instant, it all made sense. Everything. All the connections were made, all the players revealed, the plots laid out for me to see. I knew who killed Vicky and why. I fit Ulrich in with Mog in with Precious and the Lucky Arrow casino. Skunks and dogs. Summer nights and winter love. It all fell together like the pieces of an old lady's jigsaw puzzle. But then, like a receding thunder echo, it was gone, replaced by Perry's moon conspiracy. Of course, there were alien bases on the dark side of the moon. Where else would they be?

Low of answers, but high as a kite, I crossed the bridge into Moab after three in the morning. I had no intention of sleeping. Again. Ever. Once back at the house, I sat in my car contemplating the nightlife options of Moab in the off-season and realized there were none unless I wanted to toilet paper someone's house. I remembered where Danny used to live and recalled I'd just bought a twelve-pack of Quilted Northern bath tissue "soft and strong." I went inside to get it.

My legs were unsteady. The drug took on a new dimension making me sloppy stoned, drunkish but with an electric boogaloo electrocution sound-track. I suspect my tiredness, caffeine overdoses and adrenaline hangover were altering the flight plan. Better living through chemistry. I was glad I wasn't driving anymore.

At the door, I reached for my key and held it in my hand before I realized the door wasn't locked. My spidey senses tingled the boogaloo. Then I remembered that Allie said she'd be by to make the house presentable for Sophia's return. I pushed my way in and saw she'd left a lamp on in the living room.

I tiptoed into the house, past the kitchen, not wanting to wake her up. I figured her to be on the sofa but didn't see her there. She must be upstairs. Maybe she was asleep in my bed. Sophia's being too soft and Rick's old mattress too hard. I'd make her porridge in the morning.

She hadn't cleaned much. The kitchen was as I'd left it. Coffee cup and grounds still on the counter. She must have started late.

I stepped into the living room to see if she'd done anything there. I had only guessed where some of the pictures and books went on the shelf after the police search. I was hoping she'd remember and make them right. They were as I'd left them too. Nothing was different. Well, almost nothing.

I walked behind the easy chair to where I'd found the smudge before and noticed small holes poked into the wall. I wouldn't have noticed them if the single lamp hadn't been on casting angled shadows in the corner. They were chest high punctures, like nail holes after you take a heavy picture down. I counted four on each wall and three directly in the seam. That was eleven holes I calculated. My mind was racing, and that kind of math came easy to me then. Other things, as you can guess, were slower to register. I looked down and found another set of nine holes just above my ankles. Termites? Indoor pygmy woodpeckers? Stirges?

Strange chemicals filtered the world. My body moved in jerks and starts. Information passed slowly up nerve endings while my mind fired plasma streams of consciousness across the universe while a guitar gently wept somewhere.

I heard something behind me and turned to look.

My arms flailed like lifeless tentacles splattering and splashing on my chest and nearby furniture. In my altered state, I'd forgotten to activate any muscles in them. My right arm flopped into the lamp and smashed it to the floor. The room went dark.

I marveled at my limp limbs, cold and numb, slow to react. I felt the distant control of my body like a pilot of a steamship, calling down orders and hoping someone was there to hear them and make adjustments.

Someone in damage control screamed that there'd been a breach. We'd been hit. Harpooned. Attacked. I took in the news before I felt the pain in my arm.

My left bicep burned and twitched like someone had stuck an ice pick through it. My right hand shot up to help and found an ice pick sticking through it. I was right. It was dark, but I could feel the square wooden handle on one end and the steel spike poking out the other. The point had stabbed clean through my arm and into my ribs but hadn't buried itself so deeply as to pin my arm to my side or pierce my heart—its stated destination.

"Battle stations! Evasive maneuvers!" I yelled.

My attacker kicked me in the Benjamins, and I went down. I fell against the easy chair. I was spending a lot of time getting battered around easy chairs today.

Before my fanny found the cushion, I grabbed a pillow and held it in front of me. My left arm didn't much care for the command but did its best. A fist hit the pillow and folded it in like a net catching a mythical animal.

I screamed in pain as my muscles flexed around the embedded steel spike, but I held on to my snipe.

Another hand—the bastard had two of them—found my face and pushed me backward, chair and all.

I let go of the pillow and tumbled.

"I thought you weren't trying to kill me," I yelled. "Okay, okay. I'll press charges. Happy now?"

Illuminated by only the green microwave display, a figure bolted past the kitchen and out the back door.

I was the captain, pinned under a fallen girder. The ship was listing. First Lieutenant Instinctive Adrenaline took command, signaled three bells to the engine room. The crewmen below responded with full boilers.

"Ouch!" I yelled.

45

BEFORE THE BACK door had even slammed shut, I was already reliving the attack at super chemical speeds. I calculated the attacker's height and shape, stride and hands, had it fixed, matched, correlated and then lost it all to left side pain throbs.

I slumped in the chair and lost track of time. I demanded my brain to pay attention. This was insubordination. Mutiny. I need you now. I know you're tired and wired, but now was no time to look at all the pretty, pretty lights and butterflies, or trace the interesting aches from my heart to my arm. Damn your shock and terror! Focus. I had to focus. I had to focus now. What did this mean? The rainbows could wait. Pretty, pretty rainbows.

I tried to right the chair and brushed my new ice pick jewelry against the wall. That did it. The crew appeared for muster. The rainbows disappeared in a sharp intake of breath. My happy place returned control of my higher functions to pain management and I knew something. I knew who hadn't attacked me.

It had not been Benjamin James Ulrich. The stabber had moved too fast and had no limp. My attacker's hands had been free of duct tape. Plus, the ice pick was aimed at my side, between the ribs, a straight shot for the heart. It was attempted murder, a death row attack, not a bachelor's degree assault. Ice pick to the heart. Just like Vicky.

Thank you, floppy arms.

I started to shake. I felt myself shutting down from shock and exhaustion, chemical poisoning, and violence. I allowed myself a little time out. I think I fainted, but in the darkness, who could tell? I slumped against the wall.

When I asked for sensory input again, the room was still dark. I knew the pain was excruciating, but luckily it was happening to someone else. I got a telegram now and again describing the sensation of having six inches of pointed steel poking through my arm, but I filed it away for later attention. It didn't concern me at that moment.

I put the chair back and blessed its kind for helping me twice that night. Easy chairs are a good and noble race. I sat in it and slid my right hand down my trousers to check for damage. The kick had missed the most sensitive bits. Pointy shoes would have been crippling, but lucky for me, I'd been kicked in the crotch by blunt-toed boots. I never thought I'd say that.

I slowed my breathing and admired the flashing lights on my retinas for a moment. Blood trickled down my side from the hole under my arm, but my bicep was nicely corked and just hurt. The telegrams were becoming more urgent.

I got up and turned on all the lights in the house, checking each room. Nothing out of the ordinary except the punctures in the wall and my body. Allie wasn't there and there were no signs that she had been unless she'd been the one playing darts in the living room and *Gangs of New York* charades in the dark.

The electricity that had dimmed my senses before sharpened them now and led me to a mirror to admire my new kitchen accessory. I considered pulling it out but didn't. I could barely keep up with the flow of blood from one unstoppered hole in my chest. Why add two more?

I drove to the hospital remembering how they used to keep rattlesnake antivenom in a jar marked "For Thick Racine." I've been to hospital emergency rooms before and collected my notebook expecting a long wait in a M.A.S.H. triage where colicky children cried in one corner and ice-picked victims huddled in another. Writing down clues and keywords could keep me focused and alive.

I was not to have the chance, however. The new modern Emergency Room could accommodate two dozen injured vacationers with efficient ease, but in the middle of a cold off-season November night, I was the only one there. Five people, one of whom I hoped was a doctor, and one I knew to be the janitor, buzzed around me with bandages, scopes, questions, and gawking stares.

A male nurse congratulated me on my calm.

"Most people would have just pulled it out," he said.

"I thought that would have been bad," I said.

"I don't know about that. But this way we get awesome, great x-rays."

"I think he's in shock," a woman said after blinding me with a pencil flashlight. "His eyes are messed up and his lips are pale."

"Save the medical jargon," I said. "Will I be able to play the banjo?"

"Are you on drugs right now, son?" asked a child in red scrubs.

"'It is by will alone I set my mind in motion. It is by the juice of Sapho that thoughts acquire speed, the lips acquire stains. The stains become a warning. It is by will alone I set my mind in motion.'"

"Call the police," he said.

It was my luck that Danny Hinds took the call. He stumbled into the hospital half an hour later in a wrinkled slept-in uniform. He talked to the medical folk in the hallway.

Across the room, I read his lips.

"The Baron will not be pleased," he said. "Send in the Sardaukar. For the father, nothing."

I pondered this, laid back, and let the local anesthesia turn my arm floppy again. I craved the Lortab someone mentioned earlier, but it hadn't arrived yet. I closed my eyes and saw electric spice-driven flashes behind my eyelids. How many pills had I taken?

The day was a blur, a continuous string of surreality and unless they put me under, it wasn't going to end anytime soon. I tried to bring back the drive between Price and Moab when I'd figured it all out, but I couldn't remember. It was a cluster of images, noises, and inferences with alien moon bases figuring prominently. Then something began to gel. A color.

"So what happened you to, Tony?"

"Shut up, Danny," I said. "I'm thinking."

My tone was sharp enough to shut up an intelligent man, but he shrugged it off.

"The doctor said you're on drugs," he said. "Maybe I should arrest you."

Rust? Lemon? Silver?

"I'm talking to you," Danny said.

Eyes still closed, I felt a stiff finger jab my sternum.

I opened my eyes.

"Thanks," I said. "That was one place on my body that didn't hurt."

He looked me over. "Look at the lines of blood everywhere."

"Bloodlines?" I said.

"Down your shirt and pants," he said. "What's the story?"

"Someone jumped me at the house," I said distractedly. "And stabbed me. And kicked me. And hurt my feelings."

"Who'd do that?"

"Probably just another random ice pick attack on Cottonwood Lane," I said. "It happens all the time."

"No," he said slowly. "Maybe this is connected."

"Ya think?"

"Yeah. Do you know how to take fingerprints?" he said, bending down to examine the bloody ice pick on a tray.

"Doogie Howser over there wrecked any fingerprints there might have been when he yanked it out of my arm."

"Nuts," he said. "Our first real clue."

"Really? That would have been your first clue?" I said. "What about the first ice pick? Didn't that count?"

"What did I miss?" A cloud of tobacco stink preceded the *Picayune's* editor's arrival by three steps. "You look awful, Mr. Flaner. Tell me what happened." Clem Tucker pushed a button on the recorder, pointed it at my face, and waited.

"How'd you hear about this?" I asked.

"Going into work and scanning the police band," he said. "It's not like people bring me stories of stabbings."

"You're not supposed to do that," Danny said.

"It's not illegal."

"It isn't?" He looked surprised.

"No."

"Well, okay then."

"So what happened?" said Clem.

"I just got stabbed in Vicky's house," I said. "It has a history of that, you know, a family legacy."

Fireworks. Sparking synapses. Amphetamine-accelerated, late-coming, little gray brain cells laying out party favors on a checkered summer picnic table—all smiles and noisemakers.

"I was about to make a statement," Danny said to Clem. "I was here first."

"Then ask him."

"So, what happened?" Danny asked. "What did you see?"

"Yellow," I said. "Harvest-gold yellow."

"What?"

"Oh," I said. "It all fits together. Or might. Only one piece left."

They stared at me.

I grabbed my coat from the chair and pulled it. Rolls of dimes spilled out of a pocket and onto the floor. One broke, exploded really, and scattered money everywhere like a firework.

"Shit, coins are all over the place," Clem said.

"Coins? Yes, of course. Where else?" I laughed, then screamed when I tried to straighten my arm. Doogie ran back and put me in a sling that Velcroed my limb to my chest.

"I got it," I said.

"Got what?" said Danny.

"An idea. Clem, I need your help."

"What about me?" said Danny. He wore a sad, pathetic expression that would get puppies table scraps and virgins laid. It was an expression that Rick could have worn every day of his life when he was passed over for dodgeball or teased mercilessly by this very guy in front of me. But Rick hadn't felt sorry for himself, not like Danny did now. I remembered Herbert Levis teasing Danny about his involuntary bowel movement a lifetime ago. Levis hadn't been there, yet the story had survived, and Danny had to live with it every day. Rick had suffered the same, but he had been comfortable in his own skin, not as handsome as Danny, not as strong, not as wealthy or smart, but happier and a much better person.

What would Rick do now?

I wanted to burn Danny and the entire Moab Police Farce, but that was petty. Usually I'm pretty petty, so I wrestled with my inner demons for a long moment, Guilt Buddy and twelve-year-old Rick each having a say.

Allie said Danny had gotten better after I left. He'd learned a little humility after the shitting episode. For any jealousy Danny may have had for me and Allie, for any long-seated hatred he had for me from school, he had tried to help me. He'd delivered Sophia's message on the highway, tried to warn me before my police beating, and did his best, sad as it was, to spring me from jail. The face I saw now was not the mean little bully I remembered, but a lost supermodel, flailing and failing at everything in his life and begging for a lifeline.

"Okay, Danny," I said. "We gotta check this out. Handle the hospital for me. I'll be at the *Picayune* with Clem for a while. Make sure Sophia gets home alright. She's due to be released in a couple of hours. Keep your cell phone on you, and I'll call you when it's time."

"Time for what?"

"Time to catch a killer," I said.

"Can you give me a hint?"

"Vicky was killed for her property," I said. "She was killed, so it'd be auctioned off cheap. Just as I thought—just not as I thought. The killer broke into Archie Rumbold's office to see the will and then hatched a diabolical plan."

"Are you suggesting that if the Moab Police had taken the burglary of a local attorney more seriously, they might have prevented a murder?" coaxed Clem.

"Maybe."

"Nothing was stolen," said Danny defensively.

"That was a clue. Probably the first one. No, not the first one, but a big one."

"So who did it? Crew?"

"Not telling. Give me your cell number."

Danny did, and Clem helped me off the bed. Danny puffed up his chest and went to battle medical bureaucracy on my behalf. He robustly explained to the doctor-child that I had permission to go. "Police business," and all that. I grabbed a surgical mask from a box by the bed, stuffed it in my pocket and collected as many dimes as I could before following Clem outside.

He volunteered to drive me, but the gas cloud that spilled out of his car when he opened the door felled a passing crow and stained the parking lot.

I politely declined.

At the newspaper, notebook in hand, surgical mask tightly wrapped over my face, I marched into the tobacco gas chamber which was the sad office of Moab's oldest newspaper.

46

CLEM HAD to do most of the work. Gasping and heaving as he did, he was still in better shape than me. Between my cinched arm—stabbed, and my sleep-deprived, drug-addled mind, I was lucky to stay focused on what I wanted and couldn't be tempted by old stories of berry-pie eating contest winners and lost dog notices filling the old *Moab Picayune* pages. Besides, he knew where everything was. He brought me the old issues of the paper I wanted to see, and I put myself in a quiet office overflowing with file boxes. There was a desk in there somewhere, I was assured. Maybe there was, maybe there wasn't. It was easier to just sit on the files. They scrunched under my weight and became a nice form-fitting, collapsing cardboard chair for my final clue gathering.

The newspapers had nothing I didn't already know, but they confirmed what I'd been told, which was what I wanted to check. So far, so good. The real research happened at the computer. My son Randy could make a computer do tricks, find bootleg recordings of the original Gettysburg Address from the soundboard, and find Jimmy Hoffa through his alias pornography subscriptions and credit card hijinks, but there is nothing like a lazy seasoned editor with COPD to make the internet give up its real secrets.

My mask was black with tar and nicotine stains as I peered over his shoulder and followed the money like Deep Throat until we finally, reluctantly, had to make a single phone call to verify the accuracy of a document. I was impressed. Clem checked his data against multiple sources. It was a lost art harkening back to a strong fourth estate and went a long way in explaining why Clem Tucker was a lone editor of a dying newspaper at the edge of the map. Facts were luxuries few media outlets bothered with today. Inference and innuendo were more than enough to sell a dying newspaper.

Clem bragged that he'd only had to make twenty-seven factual corrections in his tenure as the newspaper's only reporter, though he admitted to giving himself total free rein in his editorials when they appeared under no less than five different pseudonyms.

My phone rang. I glanced at my watch. It was eleven thirty. It was Allie.

"Tony, the house is a mess," cried Allie. "There's blood everywhere. When are you due back?"

"I thought you were going to come in and clean last night," I said.

"The key was gone. The one under the white rose bush. It was gone. So I didn't do it."

"Oh, yeah. I took it."

"Well thanks for telling me."

"Sorry," I said. "Don't worry. The blood is mine. I came back last night and got stabbed in the living room. Tell Sophia sorry about the lamp."

"How does anything you just said make me not worry?"

"Uhm," I stuttered. "I'm okay? It's just a flesh wound."

"Did they catch the guy?"

"Not yet," I said. "I'm thinking this afternoon. After lunch? Sophia's got to be hungry and wants to freshen up. Ask her if that's acceptable."

"What?"

"Ask Sophia if this afternoon, after lunch, is a good time to catch Vicky's killer or does she need a little more time to adjust."

"You're kidding, right?"

"I'll be home soon."

"I gotta feed Gandalf. I'll be over afterward."

"Miss you," I said.

There was a pause. This was no accident this time. I meant it, and she knew it.

"Look forward to seeing you again, Tony Flaner," she said. My groin reminded me it was there, and we hung up.

Delayed fatigue hit me like a hammer between the eyes. I knew it was the first of many to come. The next would hurt. The one after that would probably drop me. The one after that promised to put me down for a fortnight. Fifth.

"Shit," I said.

"Sounded like good news to me," said Clem before coughing up unspeakable horror for the next three minutes. During a pause to hork up half his left upper lobe, he added, "Uncirculated. The whole lot. 1916."

"I knew it."

"So how we going to play this?" he wheezed, lighting another cigarette.

"I need a ton of aspirin, a glass of water, and a hammer."

"How big a hammer?"

"Big as you can carry. Time to call Danny."

I swallowed another truck stop capsule, knowing I'd pay dearly for it later. "He should be able to round everyone up."

Clem said he'd meet me at the house later. He probably needed some time in an oxygen tent to get his mojo back. Through Danny, we'd arranged for the festivities to begin at four o'clock. Not everyone could come before then. Some people have jobs apparently.

"Hi, Sophia," I said, walking into the house. "How was jail?"

"Not at all like I'd imagined it. No group showers with Pam Grier or flaming toilet paper roll battles."

"I know. Bummer, right?"

She looked good. After my first stint in jail, I remember looking at myself in the mirror and seeing every minute of my incarceration. Apparently, after her initial shock, she'd settled into a stoic resignation, helped along by constant medical monitoring.

"Are you okay?" I asked. "Medically?"

"Oh, nothing wrong with me but my nerves," she said. "I got the vapors."

"I'll avoid the bathroom. Sorry I didn't visit. I've been busy."

"You couldn't have anyway." She patted my hand and so missed a glorious opportunity to unleash Guilt Buddy's vengeance on me for years to come. "Allie said you're on to something."

"I am. Are you strong enough to operate a metal detector?"

———

We mended the machine with a roll of fifteen-year-old electrical tape Sophia found in a junk drawer. I showed her how it worked and pointed to the spot in the living room. There was a signal, but not great. We went out front and tried the other side of the wall.

"I think something is wrong with it," Sophia said.

She set the machine down and passed me the headphones. After she'd put them on me, she lifted the disk against the wall and the rhythmic beating became a single high-pitched chime I remembered from when I'd found the sacred bicycle chain of the Incas buried at Randy's middle school.

I smiled.

Sophia made coffee.

It was a cold day, and contrary to what I'd originally thought, I would be performing outside where it was cold and drafty. And cold.

At four, cars started pulling up.

I made small talk until everyone arrived. Danny had gone to the extremes of threatening arrest if anyone failed to appear, so we had a full house when Allie finally drove up.

"Shall we go outside?" I said.

No one wanted to, but Danny put his hand on his gun, and everyone followed me to the front yard.

I waved Allie over. I could see Gandalf move to get out of the cab of her car, but she closed the door and told him to stay. She left the window open, which was nice. Why should only the humans freeze?

Assembled were the participants of the auction. T. S. Crew, Owen Weaks from the bank, both looking exceedingly guilty and unhappy. The Ashes, Bill in a thousand-dollar cashmere coat with mink collar, Phil in a down ski parka shedding feathers through a dozen small slashes. Roy Stirps was there, straight off work, still in his uniform. His green Parks coat zipped to the collar and his hands gloved and in his pockets. Tiponi arrived by foot. Where he came from was anyone's guess. He wore several layers of shirts and buckskin under a wool blanket he kept wrapped around his shoulders as tightly as his fingers would let him. The wind was having its way on his sunburned face and his lips which bled freely after he smiled a curt hello.

Skingle, the realtor, was there in a snowsuit and Clem Tucker kept himself warm by the furnace in his lungs. The Moab police were represented by Danny Hinds and Herbert Levis. Levis tried to act like he was in charge without ever actually making eye contact with anyone. He stolidly refused to even look in my direction, which made things awkward as I was in the center of the group.

Danny looked eager and excited. I promised him the capture, and he was very anxious to demonstrate his heretofore unknown competency in front of Judge Shepherd, the woman who'd overseen the auction. She had come after some begging and was visibly unhappy to be there in the yard under the old hanging tree. She cast vengeful glances at Archie Rumbold who sat, leg propped up, in a hospital wheelchair. He'd added a white neck-brace to his medically-themed ensemble since I'd last seen him. It might have just been to keep him warm, but I'd heard a rumor that he'd fallen out of bed the night before and injured himself.

Finally there was Allie, Sophia, and me. We stood in the front yard, spilling off the sidewalk onto the frozen grass behind the rose bushes and under the leafless tree which filtered the wind to allow only the most dedicated gusts to chill the company.

"A random crime is nearly impossible to solve," I began. I paced dramatically in front of the audience. It would have been better with my hands behind my back, but my left arm was still in a sling attached to my chest. I should have had a pipe. A pipe would have been good too. A lost opportunity.

"The thinking goes, that as chance led to the crime, so chance would be needed to catch the criminal." It was a prepared line, one I'd practiced with Sophia in the kitchen. I had another paragraph of prepared remarks, but they evaporated under Judge Shepherd's gaze.

"Line," I said.

"Vicky's death wasn't random," prompted Sophia, rushing ahead half an act.

"Yeah, right. Vicky Racine's murder wasn't random. It was a cold-blooded calculated act by a single individual to force the sale of her property at auction." I waited for a reaction.

They waited for me to get on with it.

"The killer is a patient person, waiting years, but finally forced to act when Rick Racine died, and Sophia Curtis moved in. This caused Vicky to make a will giving everything to her lifelong friend. This was not a bad thing for the killer, because the will said specifically that everything had to be sold. Since the true worth of the property hadn't been discovered yet, the time to strike was now. Every moment of delay could bring to light its hidden value."

"Yeah, we saw this at the courthouse," said T. S. Crew.

"How did the killer know about the will?" asked Bill.

"The killer broke into Archie's office to read it."

"How did he—or she—know to look for it?" said Skingle. "Allegedly?"

"Small town?" said Allie.

"Not that small," I said. "Vicky was private. This town had treated her badly. It had to be somebody close. Close enough to poison her."

Eyes shifted to Sophia, who stared back at each one in turn, forcing their attention back to me.

"I thought she was stabbed," Danny said, wide-eyed. "Wow, good cover-up."

"She was stabbed, you idiot," said Levis.

He was right, but he pissed me off. "She was poisoned too. With gout medicine," I said.

Levis still didn't look at me.

I went on.

"It had to be someone who'd been in her house," I said. "Someone who'd run across her correspondences."

"It's freezing here, Mr. Flaner," said Judge Shepherd. "Why are we outside?"

"It was the property," I said, undeterred. I would have my Agatha Christie moment, dammit. "There is hidden value in the property. Millions of dollars worth."

"But you foiled that by finding out about the water," Bill said. "Sad. Mrs. Racine was killed for nothing."

T. S. Crew glared at him.

"No," I said. "It wasn't the water."

I surveyed the group and picked Phil.

"Phil, can you wield a sledgehammer?"

Clem brought him the hammer, relieved he would not have to do it.

"Phil, smash open that quoin," I said, pointing to the corner of the house.

"What?"

"That square bit of bricking that sticks out of the corner like a block. It's a quoin. Smash it open."

"Why?"

"Just do it. I'm freezing," said Skingle.

"You should wear a blanket instead of white man coat," offered Tiponi, modeling his Indian blanket. "Very warm."

Phil walked over the flowerbed. He glanced at Sophia, then looked at me one more time for confirmation and swung.

"When I was a kid living in this house," I said in between swings. "Rick and I would use these quoins as a ladder. Look how far they stick out. It was easy for kids to climb. Easy for a burglar to use. Practically a staircase."

I raised my voice over the sound of solid red bricks splintering and falling in dull thuds.

"It's all about the quoins," I said, smiling.

The roar of a throaty motorcycle doppled from up the street and then howled into the driveway.

Phil took another swipe, a good hard horizontal one, which sent three bricks skidding into the rose bushes.

"It's hollow. There's something in there," he said.

Everyone looked back to the house.

"I'm going to fuck you up," Benjamin James said, tearing off a black ski mask. All heads swung back the other way.

Herbert Levis stepped aside to let him through, a smile tickling at the corner of his mouth as he finally looked at me.

Danny's hand dropped to his pistol.

Benjamin limped forward, his legs farther apart than normal, his right foot dragging lines in the frozen grass. Though the balaclava might have kept his wounds from freezing solid, tearing the mask off dramatically like he did only ripped the scabs open again. He raised a silver wrench in his duct-taped hand and hobbled forward.

"Officer Levis," said Judge Shepherd in her you're-about-to-go-to-jail voice.

Herbert didn't move.

"Hold it there, mister," said Danny, stepping between him and me. "You're committing assault." He glanced to the judge for verification of his diagnosis, received a nod, and continued. "Drop the weapon and move away."

Benjamin's forehead wrinkled, and then he took another step.

I took a step back.

He glared at me for making this harder than it should be.

"Drop the wrench," Danny said deliberately and carefully, knowing he was under direct scrutiny.

"There's a paint can in here," said Phil, reaching for something in the recess of the quoin.

Everyone turned to the house.

Lieutenant Levis let out a terrible howl and fell to the ground at Roy's feet.

Everyone turned back to the yard.

Levis lay on his side, his chin bleeding under his ear, a spreading spot of urine moistening his pants.

Roy Stirps held a pistol in his hand. Unlike the one I had in the house, this one had bullets. I could see them in the chambers, hollow points staring out of the gun like a sewing circle of malignant cyclopses.

For the record, I checked that he hadn't worn his gun belt to the house. When he came inside, I looked. I did. I made sure, or at least I thought I did, that he was unarmed. Pistol in a pocket. Who'd have thought? I realized too late that I was working on the incorrect assumption that he would go quietly after being so cleverly and dramatically unmasked.

"I thought you used an automatic," I said, confused.

"This one is smaller," he said. "Fits in my pocket."

"Everybody get over there," he said, gesturing us all together under the tree. "Hands up, Danny. Give me that can, Phil."

Phil pulled the can out of the hole while we assembled in a cluster. We passed the pale bucket-brigade style until I got it and walked it forward. It was hard to balance the weight of it with one arm tied to my chest.

"Put the can on the sidewalk," Roy said. "Hands up, everyone."

"Maybe I should come back," said Benjamin. "Buddy, I got nothing to do with this. Just give me one second."

Roy didn't say anything which Benjamin must have taken as permission. He stepped forward.

Keeping my eyes on the gun, I caught a glimpse of the wrench just as its apex came down on my head. Too late. I couldn't avoid it. I braced myself for the blow, taking bets on how high in the Cantu Concussion Scale this hospital visit would rate. My record was two. "But hey," I told myself, "at least he wasn't trying to kill me."

I felt the air burn my face before I heard the shot. The bullet missed me.

Using my newly installed jelly legs, I ducked.

The wrench fell and clattered on the sidewalk.

"Shit! That little turd shot me in the arm!" hollered Benjamin. "Fuck! You going to let that happen? What are you cops for?"

Danny lowered his hands a few inches and drew Roy's aim. His arms returned to their upright and locked position.

"Thanks, I guess," I said to Roy.

He was ten feet in front of us, fifteen feet from the cars. He picked up the can but never took his eyes off the crowd.

"I'm pretty good with this," he said. "My grandfather made damn sure that every Stirps could shoot straight after he couldn't."

"Didn't want another Peaceful Canyon debacle, huh?" I said.

"Exactly."

"He told you about the dimes?" I said.

"Yeah, but by the time I figured out what they were worth, he was dead, and all I had to go on was a brick house."

He backed away slowly, studying each face between each step.

I stood up and dropped my free arm to my side in a beseeching manner.

"Roy, you can't get away," I said.

"I've seen cops in action. I'll get away."

"Yeah, he will," agreed Benjamin. "Cops are stupid."

"Yep, without a doubt," agreed Levis.

"We'll never see him again," echoed Danny.

I slid my hand in my pocket.

"Put 'em up, Tony. I got nothing against you. You were just in the way. I'm sorry about Vicky too, but she was going to die soon anyway."

"Not after Sophia got here," I said. "And stopped your Atophan cocktails."

"Yeah, had to change things up."

"Your pappy teach you ice pick work too?" I said, raising my no longer empty hand.

"Yeah," he said. "Old school."

"Three hundred dollars?" Allie said. "Seriously, Roy? You did all this, spent years of your life stuck in a dead-end town for three hundred dollars in dimes?"

"It's a nice town," said Phil. "Well, maybe not always the town, but the area."

"No, the town's nice too," said T. S. Crew. "We just need an economic boost to make it the Desert Riviera it deserves to be."

"Great history here," added Tiponi. "Many braves shed their blood."

"And blood is what this is all about," I said, silencing the Moab Admiration Society. "Those coins are your blood, right? Isn't that so, Roy?"

"Exactly. The family name is a joke. We've suffered half a century for my grandfather's debacle, but it all pays off."

He was ten feet from his car. I stepped to my right, lining up the angle.

"What are you doing, Tony? Don't do anything stupid."

He backed up two steps and glanced over his shoulder to orient himself. He shot the rear tire of Allie's SUV, effectively pinning the rest of the vehicles in the driveway. His car, I noticed, had been parked on the street. Only the motorcycle could offer chase. Roy put a bullet squarely into its front tire and then turned back to us.

"Ah, man," said Benjamin. He gripped his right wrist against his chest. Blood seeped between his fingers.

Roy stepped over the unconscious Acting Police Chief Lieutenant Herbert Levis and prepared to make a dash for his car.

The line was right.

"You shall not pass!" I raised the whistle to my lips.

Roy followed my hand with his gun and watched me blow. Seeing nothing threatening, hearing nothing at all, he remained calm and didn't shoot me, which was really nice. It surprised me. Still standing, I felt a little ashamed at what happened next, kind of like I'd cheated at cards or something.

After the sick, pregnant pause where Roy could have and probably should have shot me, the air exploded in a howl straight from the Baskerville moors. Everyone jumped. Roy's finger twitched, and the gun went off. Too late.

He never saw it coming. Sensing a mid-air mauling, he turned toward Gandalf, his gun tracking too slowly behind him to be useful.

The dog had sprung through the open window, hit the ground with another leap, and tried to jump over Roy to obey the whistle. The dog was a puppy, the size of a Star Wars Ton-Ton, but still a puppy. He didn't consider obstacles, couldn't stop his momentum, couldn't leap the gunman, and so smashed into him, all three hundred pounds of excited white mammoth dog.

Roy was knocked to the ground. His head thumped on icy concrete. The revolver flew one way, the rusted can the other.

Gandalf ignored the damage he'd done and skidded to an obedient presence right in front of us, almost stopping in time. He missed his mark on the slippery grass and slammed into Skingle, who hit Weaks, who fell into Danny, who took down Bill and Judge Shepherd in turn. The chain finally stopped when Clem stepped aside and let Crew fall into a long-thorned rose bush.

I ran up to Roy and felt his neck for a pulse.

"He's dead," I called to the group.

He rolled over and opened his eyes.

"What?" he said.

"Never mind," I called back.

"There was a yeti," he said. "How was I to know there'd be a yeti?"

"No one could, Roy," I said. "It's like the Spanish Inquisition."

His eyes twitched and couldn't focus. He gasped for breath.

"Did I get away with the loot?"

"Nope," I said.

"Ah shit," he said and closed his eyes.

47

"BET IT WAS VICKY HELPING YOU," Sophia said, "directing you from beyond the grave to solve her murder. Like in *Ghost* with Patrick Swayze."

"Sounds like coincidence," said Allie. "Your mind was just in the zone. It took events for inspiration. If you'd been solving another mystery, you wouldn't have noticed all the coins, but maybe shoes or tire treads if they were relevant."

"Patrick Swayze was so hot in that film," said Sophia. "Wow."

"So there were those quarters in the casino. Two-fifty in quarters worth thousands. Then there was Benjamin's dollar belt buckle, also worth a bunch," I explained. "I remembered Roy saying that the money his grandfather stole was mostly coins and on its way back to the mint. Roy's grandfather didn't mean to rob valuable coins. They weren't valuable then. The mint was recalling them. 1916-D mercury dimes, still in the original rolls. They'd been overlooked in a Colorado bank since issue. Today those dimes are worth about a hundred and forty thousand dollars."

Sophia broke off a corner of a frosted Pop-Tart and sipped some coffee. It wasn't much of a meal.

"Seems stupid," says Allie. "He spent years searching for them. Killed Vicky and tried to kill you too? All for a hundred and forty thousand dollars?"

"You misunderstand," I said. "Each dime is worth a hundred forty-thousand dollars. The whole lot could be worth as much as four hundred twenty million dollars—nearly half a billion bucks."

Sophia spat coffee onto my shirt.

Gandalf barked.

"And you just let them take it all away?" Sophia said.

"It's evidence."

"But all that money…" she said, wiping her mouth.

"What are you worried about? You're going to be wealthy beyond your dreams when the ranch sells."

That calmed her a bit. It had been a big day for her. She'd woken up in jail, and after a treasure hunt, a shooting, and tepid coffee, she had been exonerated and joined the ranks of Moab's millionaires.

As for me, I was crashing. Hard. The last pill hadn't had the same punch as the previous ones. It'd kept me going while I explained to my bewildered guests what had happened. I gave them a quick overview of Roy hunting for his grandfather's hidden treasure in the house as the ambulances strapped Vicky's killer to a board and nursed Benjamin's wrist and Danny's neck. Roy's last bullet had ripped a nice gash in it but hadn't hit anything vital. He'd have a scar and a story and be decorated for heroics. Meanwhile, Herbert Levis hid in the bathroom, waiting for someone to bring him fresh clothes.

I begged Judge Shepherd to let me finish my statement the next day. She agreed since there were no police available to take a statement anyway. She ordered everyone to reconvene at the courthouse tomorrow at two. She wanted to hear the whole story.

Sophia and Allie were not so accommodating and would take their answers immediately. They fed my drug-blazed mind coffee while I told them how I'd figured it out.

"It was all about family," I said. "Family debts and legacy. What does the older generation owe to the younger? What does the younger owe the older? In Roy's case, he felt he was owed the riches his grandfather had stolen and ruined the family name for. The Stirps is remembered as one of the stupidest gangs in the history of crime. It couldn't have been easy living with that."

"All families have black sheep and skeletons," said Sophia.

I thought no further than Danny Poopy-Pants Hinds and the life of Thick Rick Racine to agree.

"Roy would redeem his grandfather and his family by being rich, laughing all the way to the bank. If you asked him, he might not explain it that way. He might have just seen the money and acted, but that's how it fell into place for me."

"How'd you know Roy's grandfather built this house?" Allie asked.

I pulled out a scrapbook and thumbed back the pages until I found one of the houses under construction. The workers were all assembled in a line behind the newlywed couple, part of the scenery. I pointed to Stirps among them.

"I saw that same face in a picture at Roy's house. It was a mugshot in a newspaper article. The papers were having a heyday with him."

"You remembered that little picture to compare? He looks totally forgettable."

"I guess, as Allie said, my mind was in the zone. Once I figured out that Roy had been lying to me, I focused on him, and it all fell together. The books on his shelf about coin collecting plus the extensive research he'd done on his grandfather's crime. I wondered why he'd chosen Moab to settle down. Moab, of all places, still remembers his grandfather's idiocy. It's a tourist attraction, a long-running joke—baddies stealing pennies, burning out their transmission, spending quarters out of a paint can to buy cigarettes, and then having the longest, most ineffective gunfight in history. Moab, for all its distraction, couldn't forget something like that. Even the newcomers, like Archie Rumbold, knew the story and felt sorry for him. But still he stayed. He even passed up promotions that would take him away. He stayed where he was unwelcome. Why?"

Sophia nodded.

"What lie did you catch him in?" asked Allie.

"Oh," I said. "Harvest Gold."

"I don't follow."

"Roy said that he moved into Vicky's as a boarder because his kitchen was being remodeled. When we visited him, it was clear that his kitchen hadn't been renovated since Nixon was in office. He didn't even own the place. He rented. It took me a while to connect it, but it all made sense. He'd lied about why he'd taken a room. The burglaries—all of them, including the two attacks, were done by someone who knew the house and had a key. Once I took the hidden key in the back and was stabbed that night, I knew that the burglar had a key of his own. Well, actually, I just figured that out now. Makes sense though, huh?"

"Very obvious," said Sophia, "in hindsight."

"Okay, well, I figured out he was poisoning Vicky with Atophan. Her medical records showed huge amounts. Toxic levels. Atophan is for gout. Roy told me he had joint trouble when I first met him; he used it as an excuse as to why he hadn't taken a promotion out of town. I saw the pill bottle in his bathroom. He must have been feeding Victoria the drug while he stayed here. When you came, Sophia, with your bacon breakfasts, she cleared up and got better. You really did save her life."

She gave a wan smile and looked away.

"Is that how he knew about the will from when he was here?" said Allie.

"No," said Sophia to the wall. "He must have read her mail when he broke in. She had nothing to do with Rumbold before I got here."

"He knew his grandfather had hidden the dimes in the construction of a house, but he didn't know which one or where. He patiently studied the history and records, becoming a decent local historian in the bargain. Once he found the house, he had to find where in the house the coins were."

"Why'd he hide them to begin with?" asked Allie. "Why in the house?"

I closed my bloodshot eyes against the gathering headache-hangover horror massing in my skull.

"Not sure," I said softly, very softly. "He was probably just dumping them. Mercury dimes were uncommon in the fifties and the papers said to be on the lookout for them. Plus it was just more unnecessary weight. As for the house, he was working here. Another paint can wouldn't be noticed. Better than burying it where gossipy eyes could see. Grandfather Stirps was cleverer than history gives him credit for. He hid coins in the quoins. I like it."

A slab of wet meat pushed my head over. I ducked before Gandalf could open a wound.

"I gotta go to sleep," I said.

"One more question," Allie said. "If you knew the coins were in the bricks and knew it was Roy, why not just go to the police?"

I gave her a look.

"Why invite everybody over here? The Ashe's, Crew, the Judge, all that? Why?"

"I wanted an audience," I said. "Never waste an audience."

———

I was a wreck the next day. Sophia tried to wake me up at one in the afternoon so I could clean up for the judge. She got me into the bathroom by two, but I fell asleep in the tub. I was taking a shower. The hot water ran out while I still had shampoo in my hair and curses in my mouth. I got dressed and fell down the stairs, where Sophia offered to drive.

To everyone's relief, I immediately told the judge that my audience at the house had been there for effect and none were involved in Stirps' evil plans. She dismissed them, promising each a police interview later for the record. Then I fell asleep at the end of the table.

When Clem nudged me awake, it was just him, Danny, Sophia, Judge Shepherd, and a tape recorder. I recounted to them how I'd figured it all out.

"I knew it was about the property, but I was focusing on the wrong one. At least for the murder motive," I began. I mentioned T. S. Crew and Weaks' fraud for the water, but not the Ashe's pot farm. Taking down one Moab town father was enough and I'm pretty liberal as far as legalizing adulthood. I mentioned Tiponi's search for a history he could be proud of and linked it to Roy. They didn't know what I was talking about, so I took a nap while they played that part back.

I pointed them to a website listing rare coins and their values and gave them a ballpark of what Roy was killing for. They were impressed. I was dying from a trucker-pills hangover.

In the end, I signed a statement about the attack at the house and left the "real investigation" to the proper authorities who'd check out my story and get official credit for solving the crime.

"You can't have the coins," said Judge Shepherd. "They're government property. Can't even give you one. But there may be a reward. I'll see if there is and let you know."

"Spiffy," I said, nodding off again.

――――――

It was early in the morning the next day when I woke up on my own. I opened my eyes to the Moab dawn and felt ten again. Until I moved, that is. Then I felt my age and more.

Downstairs, I found Sophia sitting in the easy chair, looking through a photo album.

"*Dawn of the Dead*," she said.

"Arggghhh," I moaned and found coffee and toast in the kitchen.

I joined her in the living room.

The house was cold. The chill seeped through the broken quoin wall in the corner.

"So," I said. "Are you going to Tibet?"

"Depends," she said. "What are you going to do with the house?"

I sipped and munched, pondered and wondered.

"You told me not to lose the house," I said. "It was your only message to me from jail."

"Sorry it wasn't more personal. Did I hurt your feelings?"

She was having me on, but I noticed the feint.

"If I tell you I'm selling the house, what would you say?"

She looked back at the book and turned a page.

"I'd say I'll buy it and live here myself."

"And if I told you I planned to keep it?"

"Nepal bound."

I bit on my second piece of toast. I'd made six. I'd need more.

Sophia turned a page.

"What happened to Lance?" I asked.

"Don't you know?"

"He's dead," I said. "Died years ago."

"Yes."

"How do you know?"

"Vicky told me."

"Tell me," I said.

She took a deep breath and turned the book to face me. It was a wedding picture of Vicky and Lance, the one with my mother, and a wall of white roses.

"Lance came home late. He'd traveled non-stop for weeks, hitching rides and catching buses all the way from South America. It was just a few months before you came."

"'Let all the secrets be known. I am ashamed of none of it. It was all done for love.'" I quoted Vicky's will. "Why'd she kill him."

"She didn't," Sophia said. "He was in a hurry. He took the shortcut behind the house through the weeds and fell down, climbing out of the ditch. Thick heard the noise and thought it was a burglar."

"Oh god," I said.

"He took his .22 and defended the house. He didn't know what he was doing. He didn't think of the consequences. He never did. He probably thought he was shooting a wolf. Or maybe he thought he was scaring off a real burglar. He thought he'd done good."

"He told me about it."

"Vicky found Lance in the backyard, a hole in his forehead. The life gone. She buried him and never said a word. It would have killed Thick to know what he'd done. It would have killed him for sure."

"The white roses in the backyard," I said. "The only white roses on the place."

"Yes. Lance is under there. Not deep. You can't ever pull up that bush. You can't do anything back there."

"Vicky stayed here to guard the grave so Rick would never know."

"You're the only one who calls him that," she said.

"I know."

"Thick didn't mind the name."

"I did," I said.

She took the book back and gazed at the past.

"What do you think now?"

"I think I don't like guns," I said.

Sophia wiped a tear from her cheek.

"It killed her too, you know," she said. "She died that night, part of her. She couldn't mourn her own husband without killing her son. She was the bravest, strongest woman I ever knew. You should be proud to be in her family."

"I was before I knew this. Gotta say it hasn't diminished my respect."

"I'll tell you what," Sophia said. "Let me give you the money to buy the house. I'm rich. I'll never be able to spend it all. You deserve to be paid. You're a detective. It's your trade. You keep the house, and when you think it's time, you bring Lance back up and put him with his family. But not now."

"Are you saying that for Vicky or for you?"

"Both. I'd never get to Nepal if this came out. I'm an accessory of some kind. I've known about this since the day it happened. This town was cruel to Thick and Vicky, and to me. I know it sounds selfish, but Vicky wanted me to be free. I can't be if this comes out. It'd follow me. No one would believe it was Thick or that he'd done it on accident, not after Vicky and I set up house. Not after the rumors. Give me a little time."

"Will you help pay for the brick repair?" I said.

She put the book down, got up, and kissed me on the forehead like Vicky used to. I felt ten years old again, grounded and safe in a scary world, connected and honored. My only worry, the whereabouts of a mean, ungrateful snake called Rattles.

ACKNOWLEDGMENTS

First, huge thanks to all my fans and supporters who encouraged me to keep this series alive.

Apologies to Moab, the place of my imaginings, real and contrived, the dreamscape of childhood memories, friends, first loves, and murder.

Special shout out to Kate Jonez, Chris Loke, Caryn Larrinaga, Terri Baranowski, and Dorothy Diane for their spiritual and material contributions to this work. I was never alone.

Thanks to Patience Bramlett for giving Tony a third chance.

Writers sit in the dark rooms talking to invisible friends. To that end, I'd be remiss if I didn't thank the man himself, Tony Flaner, who just won't shut up.

A LOOK AT BOOK THREE:
IN THE WAKE OF CAPTAIN LORD

Love, betrayal, and a deadly secret swirl through the icy waters of Alaska's Inside Passage...

Tony Flaner's impulsive escape sends him on a thrilling adventure, where he unravels the tangled web surrounding a college crush turned murder suspect. Can he untangle the truth and save her from a life behind bars?

With bullets whizzing past him, Tony must navigate a treacherous Alaskan Cruise Ship teeming with multi-level marketers, comedians, and killers, all on a collision course with chaos.

Get ready for a heart-pounding mix of tourism, murder, and blame that will keep you guessing until the final page. *In the Wake of Captain Lord* will take you on a thrilling ride through a world where trust is as scarce as warmth in the Alaskan wilderness.

Tony Flaner is back, and his newest case is his coldest and most complicated yet.

AVAILABLE SEPTEMBER 2023

ABOUT THE AUTHOR

Johnny Worthen is an award-winning and best-selling author of books and stories. Trained in stand-up comedy, modern literary criticism and cultural studies, he writes upmarket multi-genre fiction, symbolized by his love of tie-dye and good words.

"I wear tie-dye for my friends, but I write what I like to read," he says. "This guarantees me at least one fan and easy dressing in the morning."

Johnny teaches writing at the University of Utah and lives in a house with his wife, sons and assorted cats. There's also a lawn.

www.ingramcontent.com/pod-product-compliance
Lightning Source LLC
Chambersburg PA
CBHW010815250626
47156CB00011B/3081